Aggie's Double Dollies

Aggie's Double Dollies

Family-saga mystery with Aggie Morissey

Izzy Auld

iUniverse, Inc.
Bloomington

Aggie's Double Dollies

iUniverse books may be ordered through booksellers or by contacting:

iUniverse
1663 Liberty Drive
Bloomington, IN 47403
www.iuniverse.com
1-800-Authors (1-800-288-4677)

ISBN: 978-1-4620-2496-4 (sc)
ISBN: 978-1-4620-2497-1 (ebk)

Printed in the United States of America

iUniverse rev. date: 06/15/2011

VICENTE-AULD FAMILY CHART

George Washington and Rose Clark Vicente named their sons after U.S. Presidents, while Raymond Luther and Essie Auld named their daughters after flowers. The Vicente brothers married the Auld sisters, thus producing *double cousins*—Nasty, Aggie, and Lisa (their brothers are not shown on this chart). The just-plain first cousins descended from Teddy Roosevelt Vicente and his sister, Ruby Vicente. Of the older ladies, Nasturtium the First and Hepzibah are still alive, but they play minor roles in the series that mostly features **Aggie, Joan,** and **Nicole**—three generations of lively, mischievous women.

George Washington VICENTE & Rose Clark	Raymond Luther AULD & Annie				
Thomas Jefferson VICENTE	Nasturtium "Nasty I" Auld	Nasty II	Nasty III	Ned Fleetfoot	
Grover Cleveland VICENTE	Violet Auld	Agatha Vicente Morissey & Randy	Joan (Jaquot) Vicente (& Jack Jaquot)	Nicole Jaquot Taylor & Cowboy Billy Taylor	Stevie Taylor
Abraham Lincoln VICENTE	Lily Auld	Lisa Vicente Schwartzkof & Colonel Peter		Beth Schwartzkopf & Brad Gifford	Twins: Brianna Britanny
Teddy Roosevelt VICENTE & Hepzibah	Rudolph VICENTE & Isabelle			Teddi Vicente	
Ruby Vicente	Martha Washington				
	Betsy Ross				

CHAPTER 1

With no hubby and no hair, Aggie didn't want to get out of bed. After losing Randy she found she could sleep twelve-hour nights and still catch an afternoon nap. Or, conversely, suffering from insomnia, she'd catch herself roaming the huge, drafty house that creaked in a frightening manner during the wee hours of the morning, unable to catch any sleep at all.

Awake at last, and barefooted and baldheaded, she proceeded to prowl. She couldn't decide which wig to wear. Her own hair had burnt up, right on top of her head, during a disastrous forest fire.

Then she chided herself. Why wear a wig when she was all alone? She wasn't going anywhere today. Bald, with a mere stubble popping up like new grass after a long winter, Aggie listlessly explored the whole house, all three floors and cellar. Somebody could be lurking beneath the beds or deep in a closet.

She didn't used to feel scared, but that was before the threatening calls!

When the President called, the loud ringing of her land line sent her to shivering. The Caller-ID then alerted her that the call was placed from the White House. Of course it was her Dom. Who else? He worried about her, always had.

She jumped, but not quite out of her skin. Then she giggled. What would Dominic think if he were using the Skype program and could see his good friend standing there, with no hair and no skin. Uh, the latter was stretching a metaphor.

Their conversation was brief, for President Davidson invariably ran against the clock. Dom said, "You okay?"

"Sure," she replied. One definitely did not elaborate on the mundane topic of insomnia with the President of the United States. "How's your daughter?"

"Recovering, but somewhat slowly, it seems. I'm taking her and Julia with me to Zurich next month, to the international summit on economic development. The trip should be good for Jerica. How about you? Planning any trips?" Dom knew she liked to travel. Aggie and her double cousins called it the wanderlust—the call that beckoned so many of them to visit far places. They were actually *double* cousins because their fathers had married sisters, their moms. Three brothers dating three sisters, all through high school, as if there were only two families in town.

"You must be psychic, Dom. Lisa and I leave tomorrow for the British Isles and France. She convinced me that I should get up and get moving. Can't sit here in this big empty house moping all the time."

"Still researching the family history, eh. Who are you looking for now?"

"Um, yes. I lost interest for awhile. We're looking for local color in Wales and the Court of Versailles with this trip. Our great-great-grandmother Rose apparently escaped the French Revolution with her head intact. No gallows for her. We'd like to learn more about the paternal side of the family, the Vicentes." What Aggie didn't say and had no intention of sharing was that she was afraid. The anonymous phone calls threatened to do her bodily harm if she didn't cease and desist (yes, those were the very words) her work on the family history. Now why on earth would she even consider relinquishing their precious project? How the clan's personal history could in any way hurt somebody she could not begin to imagine. So of course she was leaving town.

She wasn't only running toward something—hopefully some juicy gossip to uncover; but she was also fleeing somebody—the owner of the threats!

They broke the connection when the President was called to another among many meetings. He promised to call again soon. It wasn't that Agatha didn't believe him, but she did respect the demands of his office.

"Heck, Steve, I'm sure sorry I broke your bronc," Dom said over the phone to a friend, a rancher and state senator from Wyoming. He loved that ten-inch bronze statue, a gift from Steve. With old friends the President typically unearthed a variety of mild expletives common in the fly-over states, from gol-leee, darn, gee whiz, and pete's sake, to Aggie Morissey's favorite, good grief.

Dom was a down-home kind of guy. Full name, Dominic Alexander Davidson, nickname, DAD, as used in his presidential campaign and spotted on bumper stickers: "DAD of the country," and "DAD is here for YOU." Following Zippergate, the public, hungry to see moral integrity returned to the White House, had literally run to the polls to vote yes, yes, and yes for the North Dakota PK. "Preacher's kid," that is. Tall and slender with craggy features and dark facial and head hair, the President was a younger version of Abraham Lincoln. He wore his mustache and beard for the same reason—to cover a weak chin and jaw line.

Steve Norman, when wearing his traditional uniform of Stetson hat, jeans, western cut shirt, and hand-tooled leather cowboy boots, topped out at nearly seven feet. Though two decades apart, the President and the state senator made a fine-looking pair when standing together. Close in height, similar in build, Dom was dark complected. Steve, with his butterscotch hair, had sandy colored skin. Both men came with faces weathered by the wind, the sun, and the blizzards of the northern climes. The pair had something else in common—Aggie Morissey, the woman who had taken young Dom into her home and heart when he was a gangly guy matriculating at the university. Steve and Aggie were also friends of long standing. She knew the Norman ranching family from way back. So that made them a trio of pals. Preferably on the golf course, or else the dance floor.

Steve laughed into the phone from his seventy-thousand acre spread. "I read you, Mr. President. I've already commissioned a new miniature statue. The sculptor promised me that your exquisite bronze bronc would be finished soon."

"'Dom'. You always called me Dom, Steve. My job changes nothing. You coming back to D.C., soon, Steve? I understand from Julia that she's scheduled another meeting of the National Council on Environmentalism."

Steve chaired the state group and the First Lady chaired the national council. "Yes, I'll be there, uh, Dom. With your bronc. You can count on it."

The President changed the subject. "How's our little lady friend doing? You see Agatha Morissey now and again?"

While Dom was taking a degree in political science, he had spent a summer boarding with the Morisseys. Aggie, though a mere decade older, served as mother hen to the shy, backward, pimply PK. Under her comforting wings Dom came into his own. He grew confident, and clear faced, he ran for and won the position of student body president, he met, wooed, and won the beautiful Julia, of the well-educated, affluent Minnesota Dawson family, and then Dom returned to North Dakota following graduation, where he eventually won his home state's senatorial election the first time out. The rest, as they say, is history.

No, Dom, said, he and Julia would never forget the sweet, compassionate, petite lady from the wealthy pioneer family, the Vicente-Auld clan.

"Haven't seen Aggie lately," Steve said. "Randy and I played golf occasionally. And, of course, I know Agatha's cousin, the secretary of state—Nasturtium the Third, better known as Nasty Three. Everybody out here in Wyoming must know that Famous Frontier Family."

Dom thought Steve made the clan sound like it should be spelled with capital letters. Perhaps so. The Vicente-Auld Clan had a long history, dating back long before Wyoming became a territory, back to the days of the wild frontier, of buffalo and Indians and the railroad people hacking their way across the west.

"When you see her, give Aggie our love. The Davidsons will always respect and care about that little lady. You know she must be suffering, losing her husband so suddenly like that."

Within a few days, Aggie was suffering, all right. But her dead darling wasn't the only problem. She was certain she was being stalked! Or would be sure, if she knew how to spot a tail. Should she tell Cousin Lisa, though?

At that moment Aggie Morissey and another among her double cousins, Lisa Schwartzkopf, were on a train out of London en route for Wales. The express traveled at nearly a hundred-fifty miles an hour, smoothly whooshing into and out of stations, or whizzing past the tiny depots that were not on the fast schedule. The ladies had already "done" London. After no more than eight hours of sleep to accommodate their jet lag, they had launched themselves like diving from the high board into the tourist scene. Opera and a concert, the Tate Museum, Shakespeare's Macbeth, and, yes, the changing of the guard at Buckingham Palace. And shopping, of course. But the "girls" had taken this sort of tour before, in New York City, in Dubrovnik, and, a few years back, Abu

Dhabi. Seasoned travelers, they were less fascinated with tourist spots and more interested in local color, especially in any clan connections they might uncover.

Aggie stared out the window at the very green meadows and equally pristine hedgerows, the occasional grazing cow lifting her head to stare back. "This is silly, Lisa. It's too soon for a widow to be traipsing about abroad. I should be home." What she really meant was that she didn't like the looks of the man across the aisle and two rows behind them.

"Twisting your hanky? Bawling your eyes out? I don't think so."

Lisa ran a hand through short-cropped blond hair. Aggie knew Lisa meant well, but she merely sounded sarcastic. "I simply cannot see you in widow's weeds. In fact, I must tell the truth. I don't much miss my cousin-in-law. Randy Morissey, geologist—hopping round the globe in search of oil and dragging you with him, not for the sights but to play secretary and valet." Aggie scowled. "My dear, I admit Randy was a great dancer, but that's about all I can say for him."

Agatha gasped, a hand with lace-trimmed hanky flying to her bosom. Yes, at five-six, Randy had made an excellent dancing partner for both of them. Aggie and Lisa stood but a scant five feet tall, and a hundred pounds and ninety-nine, respectively. While Lisa's husband, retired Air Force Colonel Peter Schwartzkopf, towered above them at six-four. They all knew Peter preferred dancing with Aggie's granddaughter, Nicole. Nickee, another six-footer, could hold her own with just about anybody, except, of course, her first husband, the cowboy she'd eloped with at the tender age of sixteen, who turned out to be a wife beater.

Now Agatha picked up the gauntlet. She didn't really feel like sparring with Lisa, but putting on her armor and taking out her lance—in other words, taking on the aggressive role—was just about the only way to shut Lisa up. Hold a mirror up to the dainty blonde with the sharp tongue, let her look at herself. Or, as sometimes happened, give her a dose of the same kind of poison she dished out.

"With Randy dead and gone, Lisa, I guess you'll have to resort to dancing with your son-in-law." Brad Gifford, insurance agent, couldn't get his wife to dance. Talk about a switch, usually it was the reverse among husbands and wives.

Lisa bit her lip and dropped her head, looking sheepish. Aggie knew the signs. She was feeling guilty for her cruel words. How could Lisa be so flippant, so lacking in compassion and sympathy? Surely she must recognize in herself a woman who could sound unutterably cruel at a moment's notice.

"Randy was the light of my life," Aggie said.

"Yes, dear, I know. He called you his fence post, because you're so slim and physically fit, while you called him your floor lamp. Not very flattering nicknames."

"He was bright in the head," Aggie said, ducking her face into the handkerchief to blow, quietly, and with dainty little sniff-sniffs. About Randy's death by head-on collision with a truck: "Somebody walked across the room of my heart, and turned off my floor lamp."

"Yes, yes, dear, I know. You keep saying that."

"Well, pardon me. I didn't realize I was boring you to pieces."

Lisa bit her lip again, this time substituting a series of pats to Aggie's knee.

"Tell me something nice about Randy, Lisa."

"Uh, well, you two little athletic people, everybody said the Morisseys looked great together, on dance floor or golf course or tennis court at the country club or on the ski slopes out in the Medicine Bow National Forest."

"Tell me, Lisa. Why did you never ever warm to Randolph?"

Lisa straightened in her seat. With nobody next to them to eavesdrop and the train zooming on across the country side, Lisa said she might as well spell it out. "Because, frankly, my dear, I'm sick of your moping about. There were plenty of things you didn't like about Randy, either. He was a pain in the butt, actually. He snickered openly at females, calling us double cousins "girls" in disdain. My Peter sometimes calls us girls, too, but with affection, as in: 'You girlies going out for sherries at the old saloon?' or 'You girls have fun jogging?'"

Aggie smiled sadly. "You've made your point, though you exaggerate."

"Here's a bigger example, then, Agatha. When President Davidson went out among the people—you recall, Mississippi and Missouri, Wisconsin and Wyoming, following a tour of the coastal metropolises—to collect opinions about whether to go to war in southern Eurasia, your Randy absolutely turned up his nose when he thought the issue was getting help for the Tzikastan women who were being traumatized by the Taliban. But when Morissey the geologist heard that another, larger, issue, was a confrontation over natural resources, especially petroleum, in Afghanistan, and the location of existing versus proposed pipelines, he was all for battle, no matter how bitter. Now, Aggie, do you understand?"

Agatha mused a bit before counterattacking. Except she wasn't talking about Afghanistan now, but others and elsewhere among that series of small *stan-named* countries. "True, Lisa, I can admit the pocketbook is often the bottom line, but fourteen trillion dollars worth of oil and gas riches in the area is nothing to cough over, especially with an emerging energy cartel that included Iran, Hamas, Hezbolah, and Russia, among others. The Caspian, a body of water twice the size of Oklahoma, is a landlocked sea embraced by Russia and a group of former Soviet republics—Azerbaijan, Georgia, Armenia, Kazakhstan, and Turkmenistan."

Aggie continued to muse and remember, part personal and heart-breaking, since she was thinking of her dead hubby, and part public and political. "Think back a few months—it seems like a lifetime ago, since Randy was alive then—the four of us were just glued to the news: you and Peter, me and Randy."

"I recall, dear. We worked hard at our charity fund raisers, to send money to help the poor beleaguered women and children halfway around the world."

The cousins lapsed into silence, as the train sped onward. Agatha pondered that Lisa was only half right, and she said so. She hadn't been mourning Randy so much as thinking about something else altogether. "Sometimes Lisa, you can be as off the mark as if you'd diagnosed measles instead of small pox on your arm."

Lisa looked peeved. "Okay, then, what were you thinking about? Which kind of tomatoes you'll grow this year? I like beefsteak tomatoes, myself, not those little cherry size. But of course you aren't interested in my opinion."

No, Aggie's thoughts were not on Randy, they were much closer in time. They were on the here and now, and moreover her worries were far more urgent than puzzling over which type of tomatoes to grow. But she hadn't decided whether to confess to Lisa now or wait awhile.

Agatha was well aware of Lisa's motivations. To give her credit for being a nice person, she was no doubt truly interested in helping Aggie fill her empty hours. Hence Lisa had enticed her cousin away from home on a quest for genealogy. This was a renewal, a project which had gone on the back burner during Agatha's dreary days and weeks of mourning. Now they were on their way to Wales in search of their maternal grandmother Estelle's origins. They already knew the basics, about both Estelle and her husband, Luther Auld.

The Deightons, Estelle's birth parents, were Welch coal miners who had immigrated to Rock Springs, Wyoming, to look for similar work. Meanwhile the Aulds, from Ireland, had become horse trainers, also in Wyoming. Which was where the Deightons and Aulds got acquainted.

Now the dainty duo from modern-day Wyoming was looking for atmosphere and family stories. Following stops in the British Isles, they were bound next for Paris and the roots of their paternal grandmother, Rose D'Gade.

As they left England to enter Wales, Aggie stared morosely out the window of the speeding bullet-like train. Abruptly she pointed to the depot signs, written no longer in English but in Gaelic. This was just an excuse. She was busy glancing furtively at her tiny compact mirror to stare over her shoulder at the man who both looked and acted sinister.

"Look, there, Lisa," Aggie whispered, still pointing at the signs. "Can you read such gibberish? I know I can't. Let's get out of here." Aggie grabbed her wrap and book and stood up from their seat in the coach class. Next time they would travel first class.

Lisa tugged at her cousin's lavender skirt. "What on earth?"

"Let's return to London. I don't want to be here."

The double cousins were nothing less than impulsive. Lisa shrugged. She agreed they could return to Wales and Ireland any time.

"Where to, then?" Lisa asked. Moving about was easy, for they carried no more than fanny bags and thin vinyl backpacks for luggage. They had left the remainder of their personal belongings back in their London hotel.

Soon they were on the railroad platform awaiting an east-bound train that would be along any minute. Aggie studied the departure-arrival schedules posted on the outside wall of the depot.

"How about hopping off the train at both Bath and Oxford, first?" Aggie suggested. "Then we'll return to London and take off tomorrow early for Paris."

In Bath they shopped the boutiques along Pulteney Bridge over the River Avon, wandered the Roman baths and the Bath Abbey, took a double-decker red tour bus around the Royal Crescent and above the city to get a birds' view from Prior park. Then they rested awhile near the obelisk in Queen Square, where they crunched apples. Later, in the Parade gardens, they nibbled bananas. The fruit substituted for lunch, since Aggie said she didn't want to sit around and Lisa agreed she didn't care for an English boiled dinner while standing at a food bar in a pub. A story that fascinated both of them had it that English ladies of yesteryear believed that bathing was harmful to the health, so they went to salons to be powdered profusely on a regular basis. Unfortunately, the powder contained lead and thus many a fine lady died young of lead poisoning.

"Talk about bad health practices," Lisa said.

"I wonder what our great-great-great grandchildren will find incredibly odd about our health and physical fitness habits."

Lisa said it appeared that Agatha's motive for dashing about was to wear herself completely out so she could sleep without nightmares.

"Without Randy, I admit to having bad dreams. Think about how you'd feel without Peter."

Thus Lisa agreed to tag along, letting Aggie set the pace and their agenda.

Actually, Aggie was racing from one spot to the next because she wanted to lose their tail. If indeed they had one. She was no longer so positive.

Back on the train, they collapsed, and closed their eyes for fifteen minutes of shuteye. Then they changed trains once more. This time for Oxford.

Atop another, red double-decker bus in Oxford, they extracted from their fanny packs small packages containing plastic rain gear, in their usual colors—lavender for Agatha, pink for Lisa. The day was misty and damp.

"Funny," Aggie said at last. "Back home when somebody says Oxford University, we think of a single institution, like UW, not dozens of separate colleges like Christs Church or Rhodes."

"I like sinking into the atmosphere," Lisa said. "Makes me feel like we're reliving Dorothy Sayers' books: walking these streets and the campus along with Peter Wimsey and Harriet Vane."

"Oh, yes, yes. Now we're getting into the mood. I wish we could be time travelers and look at the world through the eyes of our great-great grandmothers and see what they saw."

"Neither Rose nor Essie was from here, dear."

Aggie nodded absentmindedly. She bent to study the Oxford brochure.

Lisa leaned forward and cupped her ear, better to hear the tour guide's spiel. All of the double cousins were hearing impaired, an affliction they inherited from their maternal grandfather, the Irishman and horse trainer, Luther Auld.

Before catching another train back to London, the pair strolled the cobblestone streets of Oxford until they found a pub that appealed. They picked at and actually ate a bit of Shepherd's Pie and sipped warm dark ale, both of which made Lisa curl up her lip with distaste.

It was in the Oxford pub that Aggie again spotted her stalker.

CHAPTER 2

The man who was following Agatha was actually no real threat to her. His name was Allan Greenleaf and he was a retired inspector, formerly with Scotland Yard. He thought Aggie was the cat's meow. He'd like to hold and cuddle the soft, kittenish little lady. The blonde was pretty, too, but the brunette reminded Allan of his sweet wife, bless her heart.

A widower of some two decades, he'd also been celibate and he'd always been shy with women. So to think that he'd approach this small dainty person was out of the question. That he knew how to tail people, usually without getting spotted, came with the job. This time he was careless, though. No reason to hide, except habit. Greenleaf noticed the darling duo on the train, when they'd hastily departed to arrive on the railroad platform in Wales to turn right smack around and head immediately back for England. Very peculiar. Then the way they'd dashed through Bath, the brunette dragging the blonde. Off again, this time for Oxford. Same pattern: dash, dash, dash.

Inspector (retired) Allan Greenleaf was having a great time. Back to his old ruses, spying round corners, hiding behind an open newspaper, keeping his target in view by staring into a plate glass window at the reflection over his shoulder.

When the brunette pulled the blonde into the front door of a department store and then straight through and out the back door, Allan guessed he'd been made. After that he was more careful. Too late, though.

No reason for Aggie to be aware of a tail. Normally she would be trotting blithely on her way. But she had more than one reason to fear strangers. Since Randy's death her house was so quiet. She couldn't return home, even in midday, without checking every room, every closet and even beneath the beds. That she'd turned paranoid, Agatha had little doubt.

And then she got the first fax. The really bad, scary fax!

She thought it was the faxer who was following her, stalking her all over the British Isles. She was right about a potential threat, wrong about his persona and his actual whereabouts.

The real true stalker, not the romantic one playing games, was still back in Wyoming. Plotting his next move.

CHAPTER 3

Before they'd left Wyoming, before she'd conferred with Lisa about their travel plans to the British Isles and the Continent, Aggie heard the fax machine on the credenza behind Randy's desk go ping. Once upon a time that would only have meant incoming petroleum instructions for her husband. Nobody sent faxes to Aggie.

Wrong. This time the fax was for her. Two faxes, one right after the other.

She read the first brief demand: "Quit the family history or be sorry." Another ping, another fax, this one with a more ominous tone, a threat: "Stop or you'll die." Aggie began to shake, as if with palsy. Should she call the police?

No, not enough information. Tell Lisa? Aggie didn't want to spoil their trip. The ladies would meet Lisa's husband Peter in Manhattan after returning from France. That might be a good time to confess. If, that is, she decided to tell Peter too. The threats made Aggie afraid, but they also made her feel like digging in her heels, lifting her chin, displaying her obstinate side. Of course the cousins wouldn't stop working on their family's history! Ridiculous notion!

Curious as a kitten, Aggie wanted for the first time in a long time to actually pursue their quest. Merely lukewarm in the wake of Randy's death. Now she smiled at the memory of Lisa's reaction to her change of emotion. Sudden enthusiasm for the project might be suspect. Agatha decided to tread cautiously.

They left London an hour after they arrived from Oxford. Aggie hailed a cab for Heathrow Airport. Seeing the stalker on the train, and later at Oxford, had sent her running pall-mall and willy-nilly all over the place. Were it not that she was the *grieving widow*, Lisa would think she'd gone completely daft.

Could she keep her mouth shut about the threats? That was the thing. Aggie and Lisa, best friends and soul mates as well as double cousins, told each other everything. To the despair of Randy who, before he'd died, could never understand the women's need to gossip. Lot of baloney, he protested to Agatha whenever the two little ladies gushed with their girlish glee.

Having left London almost as quickly as they had arrived—the second time around, this time from Wales, which they did not see at all—they were off for France. At Orly Airport in Paris, the limousine Lisa had booked awaited them. They checked into their deluxe hotel, the Victoria Palace, and were off again. Amaud, their chauffeur, said he was an Egyptian honeymooning in Paris with his Japanese bride. They were stateside students majoring in international marketing.

New to the city, he was as unfamiliar with Paris as his passengers. Getting trapped in the traffic circle produced effusive apologies from the diffident young man, but Aggie giggled reassuringly. They insisted that Amaud accompany them up the series of elevators to the top of the Eiffel Tower, which he agreed to, during his off time and at their expense, but he demurred at taking a riverboat down the scenic Seine.

Aggie had thought Amaud might be good protection, although she hadn't spotted the same English stalker who'd sent her fleeing from Wales to Bath to Oxford and then right straight back out of London all over again. She still imagined that someone was following them. Everybody with a camera or a pair of binoculars or who merely made eye contact with her she pinpointed as a potential candidate for authoring those hateful faxes. Aggie was a nervous wreck from surveying their surroundings en route, but also from keeping silent, not confiding in Lisa, who would be furious once she learned of Aggie's secret fears.

Lisa and Aggie bought scarves by Hermes and perfume by Chanel but they did not buy dresses. Too short—them, not the gorgeous gowns. The petite ladies at five feet tall were day and night: Lisa, a blonde with pale coloring inherited from their Welsh ancestors, Aggie, a natural brunette (despite her variety of wigs) with a smooth olive complexion passed down from their French-Sicilian forebears. The Nasties, including Wyoming's secretary of state, from the third double-cousin line, were redheads, like the Irish Aulds.

The ladies made the sight-seeing rounds, shopping the boutiques along the Champs Elysees, and visiting the Louvre—where husband Randy had once ridiculed the Mona Lisa, saying it was much too small for all the international hype. Agatha liked the works of the French impressionists—Edgar Degas, Charles Daubigny, Claude Monet,

Renoir, Cezanne, and Mary Cassatt. Lisa preferred the Dutch painters, particularly Rembrandt and van Gogh.

Everywhere they went Aggie peered from beneath half-shut eyelids into the faces of passers-by, those who looked suspicious, those who looked at her. Which meant she glared harshly at the Japanese tourists squinting through their camera lens at her. Anybody lurking or pretending not to lurk could be a stalker.

Lisa said she loved the grand boulevards and narrow cobblestone streets of old central Paris. She reminded Agatha that modern Paris with a population of over twenty-million stretches all round forever. Aggie said she wanted to visit Notre Dame Cathedral, to light a votive candle and say a prayer for both Randy and Nicole—her beloved granddaughter, Nickee.

The pair of ladies breakfasted on café au lait and brioches. They lunched at sidewalk cafes—which Randy claimed he'd hated because they were too crowded and too small. Over dinner at a bistro, Lisa had tournedos with toulonnaise and Aggie a fish dish. She spilled clam sauce on the long puffed sleeve of her purple silk dress.

"Oh, you," Lisa chided cheerfully. Aggie had always been a bit messy, but now she was even more absentminded and impetuous than usual, even for her, all this senseless flitting about. Lisa suggested these *little upsets* were symptoms of her grief. Agatha demurred. Let her cousin think whatever she liked.

Aggie's daughter, Joan, along with a Frenchwoman colleague, had uncovered ages-old family records. Joan's professor friend was researching French literature when she'd discovered and translated the old diary. When she shared her findings with Joan, Aggie's daughter immediately called her mom.

The diary's author, Rose D'Gade, was in fact the double cousins' great-great-great grandmother. Discovering more about Rose was the reason for this trip. At the Court of Versailles their objective was merely atmosphere. Daughter of a powerful clergyman, Rose D'Gade had escaped the French Revolution and the risk of losing her head in the year of 1789. Pregnant by her lover, a commoner by the name of Jacque (no last name), Rose had disgraced her family, who paid her passage to New Orleans in America.

At the impressive Palace of Versailles, the envy of all Europe during the period, the Wyoming cousins visualized the noblemen and clergy rising up against King Louis XVI, the ruler who, it was said, was too lazy to rule. Under threat of bloody battles, Rose D'Gade was lucky to get out with her head intact.

The cousins promised each other they must soon visit New Orleans, where Rose D'Gade had given birth to a son. That boy, Ronald, had grown up to become a river captain, and yes, Aggie agreed—between watching for suspicious characters—they really should retrace Ronald's journeys.

Except that Aggie couldn't imagine when. She should never have agreed to this trip so soon after Randy's death. Everything made her think of him. Even his petty complaints would be welcome, if she just had him back in her arms. Now Aggie wanted only to return to the states and the haven of her own home.

Except that Aggie had purposely left home, on the run from the person who threatened to do her bodily harm if she didn't quit the genealogical search that once had so appealed to both cousins.

Somewhere in all this family history, though, there must be a clue as to why somebody was so desperate for them to quit their quest that he (or she?) would actually send her a death threat. Instead of making her stop, Aggie was even more determined to keep looking. Somewhere within the tangle of ancestors and their descendants' lives must lie the vein of gold. She must not stop mining, no matter how frightened she was.

Someday soon she would tell Lisa what was happening to her.

In Manhattan they met Lisa's husband, Peter. Colonel Schwartzkopf took a shuttle up from Washington, where he was serving as a consultant at the Pentagon. Following cocktails at the Top of the Sixes on Fifth Avenue, the Schwartzkopfs and Aggie checked into their suite at the Waldorf-Astoria. They had often stayed at the Plaza, while it was still a luxury hotel, and also at the Warwick on Central Park South. At the Hilton, too, but they much preferred the old-world elegance of the Waldorf-Astoria.

Aggie and Lisa listened with genuine interest to Peter's accounts of turmoil in Eurasia and the Arab oil countries, and the country's preparations for war, should it come to that. Colonel Schwartzkopf, though, had been against war since Vietnam, and later, the wars in the Gulf and in Iraq, and in Afghanistan and elsewhere. "Not to mention in

Ireland, and between Ireland and England for nigh onto eight-hundred years," Lisa pontificated solemnly.

"But we're still playing Big Brother," Peter said. "A prosperous, Christian nation like ours cannot turn our backs on the plight of the homeless, downtrodden refugees of war-torn nations, particularly the poor mistreated women. We must help stop terrorists, aggressors, and revolutionaries."

"Yes, indeed," said Agatha, giving every indication including body language that she agreed with her cousin-in-law, "But not if this country goes broke in the process. We can't keep giving people and countries hand-outs." Her recent financial losses bore heavily on Aggie's heart. She had no idea how she was going to survive, financially.

Eventually they progressed full circle, back to discussing the French Revolution and their recent interest in and quick visit to Paris. "America had just fought and won its independence from England," Aggie said. "The French people, too, wanted to be free of the bigotry and corruption of a ruler who couldn't rule."

Aggie was glad now that she hadn't shared her awful news with Lisa, who would naturally tell Peter. Both of the Schwartzkopfs would undoubtedly laugh at her. She supposed she was being silly. Seemed ridiculous now, so far from Wyoming and those threats.

No further sign of a stalker in Paris, either. So perhaps she'd only imagined seeing someone tailing her in Wales and England.

Back in Wyoming a few days later, Lisa and Nasty Two cornered Aggie for cocktails. They met at the Cloud Nine Lounge at the airport, a stone's throw from downtown Cheyenne and the capitol complex. Nasty Two, mother of Wyoming's secretary of state, was the family gossip. She'd been pestering Lisa to join in a cupid's plan and to share the scheme with Aggie.

"Nicole finally dumped Cowboy Billy," Nasty Two said of Aggie's six-feet-tall, auburn-haired granddaughter, whose divorce would soon be final.

Aggie, too, was glad of the fact of divorce, but not just in a general sense. For her, it was very personal, though she could never imagine how anybody could manage to beat up on Nicole. All along she had worried herself sick over Nickee's plight, so now she should be gleeful over the divorce. Yet, simultaneously, and especially since Randy's death, Agatha couldn't help but feel sorry for Nickee, who felt sad over her failed marriage and her lost years.

"We've got someone we want Nickee to meet," Nasty Two said, nodding at Lisa, to show that the two of them were thinking with one set of brains.

"Rather too soon, don't you think?" Aggie protested over a tiny sherry.

"Oh, not right away. We're patient," Lisa said, also sipping sherry.

"Speak for yourself, Lisa. Wait too long, some other gal will get him."

"Who?" Aggie asked mildly. "Who do you want Nickee to meet?"

"Senator Steve Norman."

Agatha couldn't help but think of Dom. Steve and the President were good friends. Fixing Steve up with Nickee would bring the whole group full circle—Aggie linked to Dom, Dominic linked to Steve, and Steve hooked up with Nicole.

Wow. Moreover, Steve chaired the state committee that the First Lady chaired on the national level, and the clan's cousin, Nasty Three, worked with Steve—she, as Wyoming's secretary of state, and Steve Norman as a state senator. Yup, all intertwined and mixed up, both professionally and personally. What fun.

CHAPTER 4

The October wind that blew in an early snowstorm from Canada was depressing, Harry Morton muttered. He stared through the bank window at people huddling in heavy coats. He hated for winter to arrive this soon.

Harold the Banker Morton was a pipsqueak. He didn't adjust well to his small stature. Never had, never would. Neither smart nor easy to look at, Harold couldn't pass for a science freak or computer nerd. He was no Bill Gates.

In his youth, the cruel kids and teens let him know he wasn't wanted, neither his company nor his membership in their clubs. Unlike the boys at Denver's Columbine High School, Harry didn't commit mass murder or blow up his school. No, he took revenge in small ways. Slinking around corners, fading into the furniture, he'd eavesdrop, plot how to foil their plans and foul their lives.

Harry didn't torture cats or pull the wings off butterflies. He was more subtle: steal and destroy a homework assignment, a set of car keys, a love note, intercede in love-note passing to compose insulting replies and laugh behind their backs when loving steadies cried, fought, and broke up.

Morton's pranks followed him long into adulthood. From his front-window seat at the bank, he had discovered he could wreak his own style of teensy havoc. He did it with a laser beam on the end of a slender pencil-like gadget. Shine it just so, and he could annoy foe and stranger alike by shooting sharp focused light in their eyes. While pretending to work on paper files in the desk drawer, Harry the Tormentor actually stared out the window, eager to pick his next target. Like Dracula, he could wait for a perfect victim from whom to suck their life blood.

From his banker's chair, Harry Morton scowled at Steve Norman, the tall rancher striding confidently down the street. Harry hated the Normans, always had, from their daddy and uppity mama to the older son, Charley, Harold's schoolyard nemesis. Just thinking about the Norman family made Harry's left cheek muscle twitch.

He saw Charley's younger brother, Steve Norman, toss something in the bed of his metallic green pickup and move on down the street. Harry squinted. Yeah, he could read the dumb bumper sticker: "Don't you buy no ugly pickups." Steve, the mischievous one. Didn't have no respect for his own dead kinfolk.

The muscle stopped twitching as Harry stared at his reflection in the window, the Normans and his desk work forgotten. Harold Morton, in his forties, had a short attention span. He grinned at himself, his image reflected as a slimly suited banker with starched white shirt.

To his finicky suspicious boss, the VP, though, Harold might still be gazing at passers-by through the plate glass window of Cheyenne's First Bank. It felt like sitting in a fish bowl, all his movements open to the public, as if, said the bank's owners, a group of well-heeled Cheyenne businessmen, their bank and their bankers were completely open and honest. Absurd. He hated the arrangement nearly as much as he hated the rich Wyomingites, those who owned the banks and those who owned everything else, like the big Norman family ranch.

With his polished fingernails, Harry smoothed mustache and hair, both darkened with Grecian Formula. He liked his looks, figured his third wife had made a good bargain getting him. Actually he still preferred bedding Wifey Two.

He fished around in the bottom desk drawer. Where was his laser beam when he needed it? He could have been playing games with Mr. Big-Shot Senator Norman. Suddenly sensing a presence, or perhaps the vice president's eyes on him, Harold reluctantly swiveled back around, nearly jumping out of his seat to discover Steve Norman sitting across the desk looking comfortable and arrogant.

Scowling, fumbling with self-importance at the untidy mess of papers on his desk, Harry kept his eyes lowered. He harumphed, coughed, blew his nose in a white starched pocket handkerchief and rubbed at the twitching cheek muscle, all meant to delay for another few moments the inevitable confrontation. He wished his cell phone would chirp or his computer would ping with an e-mail.

Harry wished Norman would move his banking business elsewhere. Why didn't Steve stay put in Albany County, home of his ranch? Then

Harry grinned. Ah, of course, the wrong county gave Morton an out. He needn't serve him at all.

"Sorry, Steven," the bank's loan officer said. "I'm sure your credit's good, but you'll have to see the banker boys over the mountain in your own county."

Steve Norman decided he'd try to read the banker's mind. What a twerp.

Undaunted by Harry's scowl or malicious grin, Steve smiled. He stared at Harold, who dropped his eyes. Harry wore a three-piece charcoal suit with red tie and matching pointy-cornered pocket handkerchief. Steve didn't know why, but Harry Morton had always hated the Normans. Went back to maybe the third grade. Harry and Steve's brother in the same class, some contest or game that Charley had won, something like that.

Big brother Charles had spent a single year living with their mom in Cheyenne. Steve had spent a single year at the one-room country schoolhouse, where his older brother had matriculated for seven of his first eight years. Maybe Normans and Mortons had crossed paths some other way, Steven didn't know. Until Steve learned otherwise, Morton's attitude was Morton's problem.

Casual, as if he were merely requesting a glass of water instead of a few hundred thousand dollars, Steve Norman slouched in the captain's chair in front of Morton's desk. He slouched a lot, too tall to fit most chairs. Didn't mean to be snotty, just get comfortable. Creamy ivory Stetson hat propped on one knee, knees bisecting long, slender, well-muscled legs that ended in scruffy but one-time expensive hand-tooled leather cowboy boots, Steve sat quietly, barely moving. Finally he leaned forward, friendly like.

Harry jerked back, intimidated by both size and confidence but determined not to show it or give in—go after the money Steve wanted from the loan committee, as Norman had proposed a week earlier. Morton didn't offer to let Steve complete the application papers, either.

"Don't want the money for the ranch, Harry."

"Don't call me Harry."

"Money's for opening a Cheyenne business. Saddles and such."

"Why?"

"Why not?"

"Don't you have enough of everything already?" Harry demanded, a full cup of resentment on his saucer. Realizing his attitude was showing along with his twitch, he abruptly changed tactics. "Does Nasty know about this? I'll bet you've already called Nasty."

"Nasty Two or Three? What do the Nasties have to do with it?"

Harry reminded himself that he was a banker, married into one of the best families in the state. He half rose from his chair and puffed out his chest. Bankers from best families didn't have to sit quietly taking pot shots from anybody, so what if Steve was big and handsome? So what if his family had gotten everything they'd ever wanted dumped in their laps? Harry conveniently forgot about the plane crash, the deaths, marital desertions, divorces, or the low-price, no-profit years suffered by the cattle ranchers.

Harry had suffered the slings and arrows of Wyoming's better classes for as long as he could remember. Rejected not only by the most prestigious fraternity on the University of Wyoming campus, he wasn't even rushed by any UW frat houses. None. Earlier, while living in the battered trailer where his father regularly battered his skinny, defeated mother, the kids at school periodically battered Harry with hurtful words. Scrawny, strange, Harold had no smarts. No looks. No friends.

At UW, where Harry got a financial-need scholarship and a part-time job bussing dishes, not even waiting tables, Charles Norman, Steve's older brother, was back under Harry's nose. The big UW Cowboy football captain had starred in Harry's bitter memories since third grade.

Back then Charles, along with the other kids, had ignored Harry and then nearly smothered the smaller boy when Morton lit a match to Charley's hand-made prettily decorated Mother's Day card. Charles hadn't even given Harry the dignity of a fist fight.

Charley had dropped a plastic bag over Harry's head and pushed him, face down, into a filthy mud puddle. He could have died! Well, probably not. The bag was loose. Blubbering, sputtering, snot and tears running down his face, Harry got up to the mockery of the rich kids who were Charley's friends, and went home to his mother, who also ridiculed him. The rest of that school year Charles and his bunch ignored Harry. Worst kind of discrimination, the adult Harold concluded—ignore a guy, like he didn't even exist.

No, Harold had neither forgotten nor forgiven the Normans. People ought to watch out who they ignored and ridiculed. They'd get their just due someday.

What Harold couldn't have known about Charles Norman was how hard he'd worked on that Mother's Day card. The kid was trying to earn his mother's love—a mama who obviously loved her youngest son better, since she took Steve Norman but not Charley to live with her after their parents divorced.

Today, Harold, too was affluent. His fortune hadn't come from his own or his forebears' labor and certainly not from any of their wise investments. His financial status belonged to his wives, first and third. Definitely not to his second wife, bartender Dollie. She was great in the sack, but what good was that to the pocketbook?

Hands splayed flat on the wood-veneer desk allotted to junior-grade loan officers tolerated for the sake of a wife who'd asked for the favor, Harry hissed at Steve, "Nasty Three is my wife! She's Nasturtium the Third, Secretary of State, as you must know. It's the secretary of state who approves charters for new state corporations."

"Not looking at incorporating," Steve said. "But so what?"

"I'd tell Nasty to disprove, that's what."

Steve quietly harumphed, an uncontrollable snort. He knew Nasty Three. She'd as likely arrive at state government decisions based on Harry's input as she'd ask her husband to pound a nail for her. Pound a nail, he'd likely hit his thumb so hard gangrene would set in and Harry'd blame his wife for the loss of his whole hand. The mating of Nasty with Harry was a state-wide mystery. So was the big chip that sat on Harry's shoulder, but who knows another's burden? Who cared?

"Harry, Harry, Harry. What's your problem?"

As if from apoplexy, Harry Morton didn't seem able to speak beyond a loud squeak. More like a series of loud squawks. His cheek muscle tweaked and his left eye blinked. Realizing finally that he was making a scene, Harry looked around the bank past the pint-size fence that marked off his territory. He glanced from beneath carefully plucked eyebrows to see if people were staring. His arm pits felt damp and he worried, suddenly, that his sweat might stink up a storm.

Consumers and business people awaiting their turns to see bankers and loan officers looked over quizzically. From behind his full-size glass wall that partitioned off one of the few private offices, the bank vice president scowled and tugged gently at his dark tie with the narrow gray stripes. Catching Harold's eye, the Veep shook his head, then actually shook his finger at Morton. Harry couldn't believe it, like a principal reprimanding the school yard bully.

Face flushed, Harold Morton got up. Reluctant to face his boss, eager to be shed of Norman. "Gotta go."

"Yeah, me too," Steve mumbled. He wasn't doing any good here.

Harry's colleague, the loan officer at the next desk, sneered when he asked, "What you got against Senator Norman, Harry?"

"That's for me to know and you to find out. And don't call me Harry." He flashed his laser beam in passers-by eyes.

"You back on the school play yard, Harry?"

Down the street, off to the old saloon with the long long bar, Norman shook his head a time or two. Strange fellow, Morton. There were other places Steve could go after money, without getting put through the wringer: Harry's notion of club ritual or initiation before letting go of the purse strings? Peculiar way to do business, turning away banking customers like that. What was a bank, after all, except a money store; a store that made money by charging interest on loans. No loans, less income, so Harry was nothing less than weird. You might say he actually enjoyed biting off his nose to spite his face, a most apt saying to describe Harold Morton's behavior.

Morton had asked Steve why he wanted to open a saddle shop. Seemed obvious—out here in ranching country. Norman might be worth several million, but it was all on paper, tied up in land and cattle. Nowadays many ranchers, men and women alike, had to seek paid employment elsewhere, while still operating their ranches. Steve's proposal to supplement his income, increase cash flow, was to open his own retail outlet as a city entrepreneur.

Steve knew, too, that there was a hidden agenda here, a bottom line that a mature man wasn't likely to talk about. The clue to which was a long history of Norman women. The Norman men seemed cursed, destined to fall for city-bred ladies. Starting with great-grandma, who'd died at age seventeen in her second pregnancy. Then there was grandma. She'd died on the ranch, too—a depressed, bitter, suicidal dried up old woman, which is the way Steve remembered her. Steve's own mom wouldn't stay on the ranch, either. She claimed to like the bright lights and excitement of Cheyenne better.

Why didn't any of the women the Norman men fell for and proposed marriage to ever enjoy the ranch life? Anybody asked him, all those women had had it pretty cushy. Out on the Norman spread, especially, with its comfortable home—not like the old days of outdoor privy, kerosene lamps, pumping and hauling well water to the house. With today's vehicles, pretty easy to get back and forth to town—except during blizzards and other problems, naturally. Not only the condition of their house, but the situation indoors. The Normans employed a cook and housekeeper, their delicate wives didn't have to lift a finger, except tend to their babies, but none of them seemed to care much about children, either. Strange.

Beauty, privacy, fresh cool air, horses, cattle, dogs. He figured there were men who'd kill to own a place like his. Why couldn't he find a woman who'd love the ranch too, and want to make a home with him out there?

Their dad had also built Steve's mom a fine two-story plantation style house in northwest Cheyenne, with the notion of reformulating the family in town, he'd told his two adult sons. That must have been when Mother conceived me, Steve realized. Apparently she had tried ranch life a time or two after that, but soon gave up entirely. She must have tried mothering Charles periodically, too, because Steve's older brother did spend that one year in town with her. Eventually she gave up on Richard, Charles, even Cheyenne. But not on Steve.

She took Steve and moved to Boston, where they lived with her parents. He loved the ranch and the lifestyle, but felt torn between his western and eastern families. As a kid, he was allowed to return to Wyoming for the summers, but it was never enough. Now he was here for good. But it was all he had.

Steve's own wife couldn't stay put, either. After his dad and Charley died and Steve took over the family ranch, he'd wanted his wife and daughters to move out there with him. They'd keep the family home in Cheyenne, he promised her, where they'd live during legislative sessions. Instead, she took their two little girls and returned to Boston, where she and Steve had met while he was completing his law degree at Harvard, thus forcing her husband into repeating his personal history. Wyoming-Boston-Wyoming. Peculiar fate.

"I married what I thought was going to be a lawyer, not some drunken cowboy," the tall willowy blonde said, without preamble and without emotion.

Why, he'd thought, did a cowboy automatically have to be drunk, and didn't Norma Norman know the difference between cowboy and rancher? Too late to correct whatever problems she perceived, Steve shrugged and turned his back. To her, he must have seemed cold, uncaring, shallow and empty.

After completing a law internship with the Gerry Spence office in Jackson and before Steve had had time to join a law firm or open his own, his dad and older brother Charley went down with their Cessna when they hit Sheep Mountain west of Laramie during an unexpected mid-summer fog cover. Now there was only Steve left. Steve and the ranch, and his two little girls. But how long could he count them? Hard to imagine that Norma would acquiesce to all the custody time he wanted.

Waves of pain from these recent disasters washed over Steve like alternating attacks of fever and chills. He shook his head as if to fling away the scabs from wounds that too frequently festered. Now he was forcing himself to make plans for his shaky, uncertain future. Steve wasn't ready yet, but he suspected he soon would want to find another wife. He liked being married, though he could no longer stand the frigid Norma.

So before Steve Norman went looking for another wife, he was going to make sure he had a nice Cheyenne setting awaiting her—a Cheyenne business to ensure himself a purpose in the city along with a city income, and the Norman family's stately city home. Wouldn't it be great to get lucky, though? Maybe he'd find a Wyomingite suited to the Norman men's kind of territory. But Norman men always dreamed that dream. They were born romantics despite the harsh reality of their lives. What was that old saying, oh yeah: *hope springs eternal*.

So how was he to find the Wyoming woman of his dreams? He wasn't going to do the single-bar scene, not his style. Saloons, yes, where ranchers and legislators hung out, but he wouldn't purposely seek out women for a drink or any callous one-night stands. Let it happen, unfold like the magic flying carpet.

In the old saloon with the long long bar, Steve ordered a Coors from Dollie, the bartender. Then he excused himself to pull out his cell phone.

"Going to call your girls back east, Steve?"

"Yup." He stepped to the back of the room for privacy.

Later Dollie fretted in his face over the silent pensive cowboy. "You're awful quiet, Steve. Your girls all right?"

"I'm okay, Dollie. Cindy and Sissy are okay too, they say."

"What you thinking 'bout, then?"

Steve sipped his Coors and grinned. "Thinking 'bout whether to eat steak or fish for supper. When do you get off?"

"Coupla hours."

"Wanna join me?"

Dollie Domenico Morton, Harry Morton's second wife, nearly whooped. Wow, a dinner date with Steve Norman. Wouldn't Harry just die if he knew.

CHAPTER 5

Dollie swabbed the bar top with a gray, food-encrusted rag. Feeling over the hill at thirty, she tossed her thin blond hair over a shoulder. Thinking of her troubles, she mumbled a "Whatta ya have?" to her next customers The elderly tourists shoved their heavy flanks onto the authentic, saddle-topped bar stools and grabbed the saddle horns to swing back and forth like a couple of little kids.

When the husband wondered what "The Equality State" meant, a slogan they'd discovered from reading a travel brochure, Dollie motioned down the bar toward Steve. "Ask him." But neither the couple nor Steve budged until the wife asked about jackalopes.

Steve's eyes brightened, his shoulders straightened, and a grin of pure devilment spread across his face. Unfolding to his full height, he hovered over the couple as they looked up and up. He sat down in a nearby captain's chair.

"Many long years ago," Steve began the farcical tale, "we crossed a jackrabbit—one a those big ole things from down Texas way—with a Wyoming antelope. Took a few years worth a tryin' but pretty soon we got a rare Jackalope. See?" He pointed down the bar to a glass case holding a peculiar looking creature. Stuffed by a local taxidermist, the animal had an antelope head and a rabbit's rear.

Before the couple could refute his seemingly sincere story of state lore, Steve continued with a more truthful tale. "As for Equality State," he said, "We were first in the nation to give women the franchise, the right to vote, back in the 1860s, and then we had the first lady governor. To be honest, though, Texas also elected a woman as governor that same year, in 1924, but we beat 'em by inaugurating our own dear Nellie Tayloe Ross first."

"I recall that story," said the tourist wife. "But didn't she just finish out her husband's term as governor after he died? Something like Sonny Bono's widow did in running for office? Or perhaps it was

Nancy Pelosi." She looked to her husband for confirmation, but he merely shrugged, as if to say, who cared.

Dollie snickered into the ice bin. That's just how Harold Morton would put it. Make out like a woman's part in anything of value was pure-dee accident. But not Steve. Except for the jackalope joke, he'd tell it like it is.

"No ma'am," Steve countered. "Nellie's husband did die in office, like Sonny Bono, that's true. But people, the Wyoming people, already loved and respected the state's First Lady, and Mrs. Ross got the job all for her own sake."

It tickled Dollie how the Boston-raised, Harvard-educated Wyoming rancher who was also a state senator liked to put on the down-home act for strangers. Shucks, no skin off her nose if the coasties had no clear idea what people in the fly-over states were really like. Not that she did, either.

Harold the Lover Morton would be enraged if he learned that his ex-wife had even talked to Steve, let alone agreed to eat supper with him. Get Steve to swing by the bank in his gorgeous metallic green pickup truck, Dollie by his side. Boy howdy, make Harold Morton the banker jealous. Lord luva duck, Dollie didn't know why, but she still loved Harry. She overheard Steve down the bar quote what had become Wyoming's common historical knowledge.

"Nellie Ross said, and I quote, 'I was elected to measure up to a man. Texas Governor Miriam Ferguson was elected to avenge her husband.' Mrs. Ferguson's husband was impeached. She was elected, so they say, as a figurehead, with her husband continuing to make decisions like he was the real governor."

That sounded like Harry, too, Dollie thought. Now he had some scheme he'd been trying to tell her about if he could get her to listen after leaving her to go after Nasty Three. Hah, she could imagine how Harry's scheme would actually pan out. Get his new wife, Nasturtium, to run for governor, was what he'd said. Sure, and Harry would run all over the state as her campaign manager.

What Harold was apt to do, instead, was spread the word that he was the real power behind the chief. Dumb dodo. Didn't her Harry realize that everybody loved Nasty Three but nobody hardly even knew Harold? Those what did know him, didn't think much of him,

Dollie suspected. Harry always talking about state affairs like he knew what was going on. Dollie never did understand much about civics or government, even with all Harry's yakking about it. Yeah, so maybe she was dumb, but she wasn't stupid about people.

Dollie filled a mug for an old bar fly. Then she glanced around the saloon to see if other mid-afternoon drinkers needed service.

Drat! Here came Harry the Huffy.

When Harold Morton saw Steve Norman sitting at the bar, Harry's left cheek muscle started twitching, even though it didn't appear that Steve even noticed Harry's existence. Dollie grinned. She understood her ex-husband's twitch. It meant he was coming on to having a nervous fit. Hah, served him right.

Harold quietly moved into the shadows. He stood behind an old column with the paint peeling off in long strips. Dollie snorted. What was Harry doing, hiding? Trying to outwait Steve? He dumps me, yeah sure, she thought, yet Harry keeps hanging around. Can't keep away from me, can he? Don't want me, but don't want any other guy to get me.

Unaware that his presence and especially his casual invitation to supper had created a whirlwind of turmoil inside the tummy of scrawny Dollie Domenico, Steve sauntered out the door, a quick wave and his parting message: to meet him out at the truckstop at five, right after she got off work.

Whatta letdown. The truckstop. At five o'clock? Some dinner date. She'd hafta go in her soiled tee-shirt and faded blue jeans. Plumb pitiful.

With Steve gone, Harold the self-described Historian, the civilian expert in Wyoming history, told the tourists, "Let me tell you some interesting things."

Dollie sighed. She knew what was coming: all that stuff Harold had drilled into Dollie, all about social classes. She'd never known there was such a thing as social classes. Harold charted the classiest families on a map, from Cheyenne to Jackson Hole, from Cody to Sundance, from Casper and Douglas back south to Cheyenne. All about how Cheyenne got to be high society, high fashion, for the entire state. Before Wyoming was admitted to the Union, U.S. Presidents often appointed men they knew personally to serve as territorial governors. Educated, famous, or courageous Civil War ex-generals of rank and class. These kinds of men married ladies with similar claim to status and culture.

"My, my," said the man tourist, motioning to Dollie to give them a refill. Harold the Histrionic continued with barely a sip of water.

"The society women of yesteryear were accustomed to balls, theatre, opera, and the propriety of social visits," continued Harry the Boring. "Their husbands built lavish homes on what became known as Millionaire's Row and furnished them with period furniture, draperies and carpets, and paintings from the East and from Europe. They hired plenty of servants too. Despite a lot of children, First Ladies made time for charity and committee work along with their social hostessing duties as wives to the governors, whether territory or state."

"My goodness."

"Rose D'Gade—one of my ancestors, as a matter of fact—had some gold, mined from the Centennial Mine. The Centennial Gold Mine and the town that sprung up as a namesake were so named because gold was discovered during the country's preparation for the Centennial Celebrations. Only town in the nation named Centennial, too, by golly. Anyway, this ancestor of mine, Rose, got some of the gold from a gambler who owed her money. So Rose winds up with a lot of gold—bought land back in the 1880s here in what would become downtown Cheyenne. Very expensive real estate now."

Yeah, sure, Dollie thought. Your ancestor, my foot. Why don't you be honest and say Rose D'Gade was your new wife's kin? Why else had Harry married Wyoming's current secretary of state, if not to bask in the shadow of her limelight? Some spot, like Nasty was a Broadway actress, playing center stage.

"Rose also used the money to build one of the nicest mansions this city has ever seen."

"Is it a museum? Open to the public? We'd like to see it."

"No. Another descendant, Aggie Morissey, lives there now. She inherited it. Mrs. Morissey, that is. She's a cousin of our secretary of state."

While you're at it, Harry, Dollie thought, why don't you tell them how you were waiting in the wings to marry Nasty the minute she was elected secretary of state? I'd sure like to hear how you pulled that off myself.

"My wife's the secretary of state," Harold said abruptly.

Hah. Dollie knew that Harry her former Honey would find some way to work that in, showing off about his current wife. Talking about Nasty Three's kinfolk as if they were his own must have made Harry think of his third wife. Ha, that's funny. Dollie giggled. Nasty Three, Harry's third wife, when the "Three" really stood for the secretary of state's position in the line of Nasturtiums who'd descended from Rose and Etienne D'Gade and Essie and Darwin Deighton. (Dollie oughta know, Harry'd told her enough times to make her head spin.) She didn't know what had happened to the famous women's Mormon husbands. Nobody ever heard of them after the little ladies left the wagon train headed for Utah territory and the Great Salt Lake. Maybe they'd been scalped on the way.

"We've got to go find a hotel," the tourists said in unison.

Harold the Ridiculous didn't take the hint. "The decade of splendor in Cheyenne, 1875 to 1885, was known as the Gilded Golden Age. It was a time of social brilliancy, of cultural refinement."

Dollie knew all that too by now, could have quoted Harold the Huffy almost verbatim, just the way Harry told it, and told it, and then told it some more. Why his head was in the clouds over social class she couldn't imagine. Maybe it was nothing more than that he was losing his hair, losing its color. He wanted more of just about everything, and more and more and more.

At last the tourists were given a reprieve. They left. Harry was still all puffed up over getting to tell one of his favorite tales. He mumbled that he really must return to the bank. Where he was an official bank officer.

Instead of leaving immediately, Harold the Has-been scolded Dollie for talking to Steven Norman. Harold reminded his ex-wife that he hated the Normans, and whoever he hated, she must hate, too. But he'd never said why.

"Whassa matter with you?" Dollie responded dully, still thinking about her half-date with the handsome rancher. "Gotta wait on customers, don't I? As for you, Harry, you better remember your job and how angry the vice-president gets if you're late back to work after your break. What did you want to tell me, Harry?"

"I dunno," Harry the Hesitant mumbled. "I forgot." He rushed out the door on the heels of the tourists, who edged back against the outside wall of the saloon, as if to avoid him and more of his bragging.

Had anybody asked Steve what he was thinking this time, he'd probably have paused, pondered, and wondered who'd win the game tomorrow afternoon, Wyoming Cowboys or Air Force. Home football games were mostly scheduled in the afternoons, too cold at night. Sitting under a blazing sun at only forty degrees was okay, but not at twenty degrees whether the sky was star studded or stormy.

His list of errands completed, Steve was returning to his pickup. He barely looked up as he strolled along toward the parking lot, except to nod at a man or tip his hat to a lady who crossed his path.

So he didn't see the old off-white, rust-spotted small Cadillac come careening around the corner. Barely missing Steve as he crossed the intersection, the car weaved this way and that and then crashed smack into the bank window where Harold Morton sat. Leaping a fireplug, Steve sprang to the rescue.

A crowd immediately began to gather but nobody seemed inclined to do anything. Mass paralysis, not fear of involvement, had apparently set in.

Trunk lid loose, Steve reached in to grab the tire iron. Then he worked fast and furiously to pry open the smashed door so he could reach the lone occupant of the baby Cad. He heard no human sound, not even a moan, just water or gas trickling. "Gotta get her outta here. Help me, somebody."

Released at last by Steve's single shout of command, several men and a couple of women rushed to assist. Steve's eyes blurred from sweat as he shoved the iron into the mess of mangled metal to make way for extricating the woman.

He knew immediately that it was a woman. Bright orange dress. Like orange juice. The door popped loose and Steve scooped up the woman wearing orange juice. He held her tight. Then he ran with her. He didn't think to yell for people to get back, the drip might be gasoline. Somebody else thought of that.

Everybody ran, but nothing happened.

Across the street where he'd left his pickup, Steve jerked down the tailgate with a pointy boot toe and hitched himself and his burden into the back of his truck. He should have remembered you're not supposed to move an accident victim. He didn't think about anything, not the appetite appeal of steak versus fish for his dinner and not who would win the football game. Nothing.

Steve just sat there, motionless, staring down at the face. The woman's face with eyes closed, a woman's face with no expression of emotion, pain or joy. Eventually—it could have been a week or two minutes—she opened her eyes. Her big round brown eyes, somber, serious, but with assurance. There were no questions in her eyes or on her lips. Slowly her lips parted: "I know you."

The statement from this stranger did not seem strange at all. He didn't know her either. Yet he did. "Yes."

"Don't spoil it."

He didn't ask what, because he knew what she meant. He didn't ask if she were okay, because that too would be redundant. She could hurt all over but she was still okay. More than okay. So he said, "Steak or fish?"

At last she smiled. "Doesn't matter."

Grinning as big a grin as he'd grinned since his dad and Charley had died in the plane crash, surprise and realization hit Steve like a revelation. "It doesn't matter, does it. Where?"

"Anywhere. That doesn't matter, either. Truckstop's okay."

Inside the First Bank, Harold was buried beneath his desk. The white baby Cad owned by the woman dressed in orange juice hadn't come close to hitting him. He lay there moaning nonetheless. Up came the bank vice president, with Harold's loan officer colleague. They stared down at Harold.

Unnoticed was the laser-beam gadget Harry clutched tightly in his closed fist. Without close scrutiny, it could have passed for an expensive writing pen.

"Oh, get up Harold," said Harry's colleague.

"What on earth's the matter with you?" said the Veep.

CHAPTER 6

"Why did you suggest the truckstop?" Steve Norman asked.

"Just popped out," Nicole Taylor said. "I used to waitress in a couple of truckstops. Down in Fort Worth. And over in Laramie."

Steve wondered if the latter was where he'd seen this gorgeous woman. She looked so familiar.

Before he could get around the truck to open the door for her, she had already jumped out of the pickup. Boy, some big girl. He hadn't noticed when he carried her from her wrecked car to his truck. Must have been operating on a Superman's adrenaline high. "Wait a minute. Come here first."

"What?"

"How tall are you?"

"I don't normally like to say, but seein as how you're a lot taller, I'll admit to six feet. Barefooted."

"I think you can fit under my arm."

"No, I can't."

Silly bantering, beneath the warm glow, behind the warm looks flashing back and forth between them. He liked everything about her, her easy way of talking, walking, smiling, the long, thick, wavy auburn hair and eyebrows to match. Smile as wide as Julia Roberts', nose as straight as Julie Christie's. He even liked the bright orange shirtwaist dress with the brass buttons and said so.

"This thing? Yeah, I do too. Orange isn't supposed to go with red, well, auburn hair, but why not?" She didn't bother to add that it was one of only two dresses she owned, the other a black cotton-jersey thing that she could wad up and toss in the back seat or a corner of her backpack and it'd come out all right. Add a scarf, pair of pearls, create a cocktail dress or formal wear.

Another thing she didn't tell him was why she was wearing a dress. Nicole, like Steve, normally wore faded jeans, shirt, and cowboy boots.

But she'd just come from the capitol and a visit to her cousin, Nasty Three.

The previous summer, her paternal grandfather, Jason Jacquot, had been riding the range on his old horse when he'd spotted a strange-looking rodent, the Preble's Meadow Jumping Mouse, who, along with its habitat, was numbered among the protected species, except, at the time, he was ignorant of all that. Beating the mouse with a twig off a nearby Aspen tree, Jacquot was startled by a pair of short people dressed in jodhpurs and pith helmets who commenced taunting him and screaming at him with "Citizen's arrest, citizen's arrest."

Using stick and rifle, they'd bound and bundled the bewildered old man like a sack of garbage and tossed him face down into the back of their Land Rover to rush him off to the nearest town. In the Douglas police station neither the cops nor the county sheriff knew what to do with Jacquot or the Jodhpurs. So they called the governor, who called the secretary of state, who called Senator Steven Norman.

Nasty Three knew that Senator Norman chaired the state council on environmentalism. Steve in turn called Julia Davidson, the nation's First Lady, who'd told him to stay out of the fracas: "We deal with conservation, not animal rights. Don't get involved, Steve."

Later, Wyoming's secretary of state suggested that Steve get busy with the legislation designed to institute an exemption for agriculturists who might come on to the mouse or its habitat in the course of managing their farms and ranches.

Nicole didn't know the complete story, much less Norman's part in the whole scenario, and his name didn't come up when Nickee visited her cousin. It just seemed appropriate that she wear a dress when seeing the secretary of state.

When Steve thought Nicole looked familiar, he made no connection between the orange dress sitting across from him and the woman who'd attacked him publicly during a teleconference session conducted between Julia Davidson in the White House with a dozen western state councils. The council meeting, as the First Lady said, did not address protected species.

Nicole, eavesdropping outside the teleconference room, had only heard the local members snicker and joke about Jacquot and his jumping mouse. So she'd assumed the meeting had convened to further chastise her grandfather, who had never quite recovered from the confrontation: "Invaders on Jacquot land." and he'd been going downhill ever since. Assuming the worst, Nicole had rushed into the room and, from behind, had rained tight-fisted blows upon the chairman's head, back, and shoulders. She didn't catch his name and she did not see his face.

It would be awhile before either Steve or Nicole made the connection.

On the way into the restaurant, Steve asked Nicole if she liked the food bar at this place.

"Yeah, but I like their country fried steak with smashed potatoes and cream gravy and corn better," she said. "What does it matter? We don't need to impress each other, do we?"

The hostess arrived to seat them. They chose a booth and took menus and pretended to ponder a bit. He looked up, surprised.

"Hey, what's your name?"

"Nicole Taylor. Age twenty-two. How 'bout you?"

"Steven Norman, thirty-four. Hey, notice that? We're two Englishmen, well, English people."

"Not me, my own name's Nicole Estelle Vicente Jacquot. Vicente was my paternal great-great-grandfather, a Sicilian who married a Frenchwoman. On my maternal great-great-grandparents' side, I'm Irish and Welsh, and my dad is another Frenchman. Taylor is Cowboy Bill's name, that's my ex-husband, who could be English, I don't know."

With all that rigmarole, her paternal name, Jacquot, went unnoticed.

Clattering dishes, chattering diners, everything beyond their table and each other went unnoticed. A rose-colored world had enveloped them.

"Oh." Steve thought about the French-Sicilians. "'Vicentes', you said?"

"My great-great-grandfather, George Washington Vicente, from Sicily, married Rose DuBois, a Frenchwoman. The first Rose, Rose D'Gade, escaped France during the Revolution. Her son, Ronald, was born in New Orleans and became a river boat captain. His daughter, another Rose, traveled with him to disembark at a settlement on the Mississippi called Nauvoo. That Rose, Rose D'Gade, traveled by wagon train out here to Wyoming."

"Sounds like a lot of Roses," he said. She was so cute, he just grinned, which produced an equally cute dimple. Their dimples liked each other, too.

"I guess you can tell we believe in naming girls after their mothers, like Nasturtium One, and the Nasties that followed."

"You really know a lot about your family history."

"Thanks to my gam, who's been working on it for ages, towing her first double cousin along to all sorts of wonderful places in the name of 'research' : Paris, Versailles, Belfast, oh I don't know, lotsa places." Nickee sighed. "Enough about me."

He smiled, waited to see what else would happen. Interested more in Nicole than her extended family, gentlemanly courtesy demanded nonetheless that he inquire further. "Gam is for grandmother? What's her name and, what did you say, her *double* cousin?"

"Aggie Morrisey and Lisa for Elizabeth Schwartzkopf."

He jumped back, smiled that great big smile. "I know them both. Played golf with your grandfather, Randolph. And your gam, I believe, is a friend of the President."

She grinned. "That's the one. So, you knew Randy, too. I didn't think it was that small a world. Oh, I know what they say, 'everybody who is anybody in Wyoming knows each other'. It's just that I've been away for the past five years. So I've forgotten, and a lot of people may know my family, but not me. It's your turn. Tell me about you." She sipped coffee that grew cool.

Plenty of time, he said. Yes, she said. Both understood what went unsaid.

Had he noticed her "smashed" potatoes? "My son says that."

"My little girls say that too, Cindy and Sissy, they're four, they live in Boston with their mother." He reeled off all that in a single sentence, as if to get it over with. "What's your son's name and how old is he?"

"He's four, too. Name's Stevie." She blushed at that, as if Steve Norman had fathered Stevie, like maybe she'd met and known and loved Steve long before giving birth to a boy with Cowboy Bill.

She said that Stevie was spending the evening with his third cousin, Ned Fleetfoot, who managed a South Cheyenne Laundromat.

"Ned, Ned. Sure," Steve said after nudging his memory. "He's the son of Nasty Three, from an earlier marriage, right? Wait a minute, you mean the secretary of state? Those Nasties are your cousins?"

Then he remembered (some of, but by no means all of) her background. This was the woman who was married to Bill Taylor. Sure, the rodeo cowboy who'd won big at Cheyenne Frontier Days, the "Daddy of 'em All"—the big annual ten-day rodeo and entertainment extravaganza. Last July, that was. The same time President Dominic Alexander Davidson and his wife Julia were in Wyoming.

Steve tried to fit Nicole into the big family he knew. Couldn't do it, didn't think he'd ever heard of a Nicole Taylor. In-law Bill Taylor, yes, Nickee, no.

Dollie Domenico entered the truckstop through the convenience store near the cash register stations. Where was she supposed to meet Steve? Was he paying for gas, what? She knew he'd beat her here, she'd seen his pickup with the quirky bumper sticker in the parking lot. Might as well make a potty stop and then go look in the restaurant for him.

It was fun to eavesdrop on unsuspecting gossipers from behind closed stall doors. This time, though, Dollie immediately hated the chit-chatters, and the gossip was no fun at all. The players and the topic, both, made her want to cry.

Here's what she overheard:

"Why, Nickee, what in the world are you doing at this place?"

"Having supper with Steve Norman, Nasty," Nicole replied. You recall ever meeting him or his family?"

Nasty Two, slender, petite, the seventy-one-year-old mother of the secretary of state (thus mother-in-law to Banker Harold Morton), and daughter of Nasturtium One, was also Nicole Taylor's double cousin once removed, or was it second cousin removed, Nickee asked herself.

"Oh, of course, Nickee. Steve Norman's a state senator, has a big house in northwest Cheyenne, has another big house on the Norman family ranch southwest of Laramie. His father and big brother, Charley, died in a plane crash a few months ago. Can't believe you have to ask."

Mention that she was filling her gas tank, and with no other gossip from Nicole, Nasty Two appeared eager to leave. From the back, Nasty's bald spot on her crown showed. All the Nasties had lost their hair in their early thirties, but only in the back. Nasty Two's daughter, Nasty

Three, compensated by wearing unusual hats. Lately, it was a straw hat covered in grapes and daisies.

Nicole asked Nasty Two whether Steve could by any chance be the same guy her gamsy had been trying to set her up with. Nasty Two neither confirmed nor denied the suggestion that Aggie was playing cupid. So Nicole demanded to know whose idea this match was, anyhow? It was Nasty Two, the clan's chief gossip, Nickee proposed, who must have planted the seed with the double cousins, including Nicole's gam Aggie, and Cousin Lisa.

Oh well, Nasty One said huffily, her daughter, Nasty Two, didn't care about getting credit, she just wanted to see it happen.

"Well, pardon me." protested Nicole, as Dollie silently sobbed from behind the stall door, still sitting on the toilet with her panties pooled around her ankles.

Their voices fading after the sounds of hand washing and blow drying stopped, the two cousins exited the restroom. Dollie couldn't believe it. Why had Steve asked her out if he was meeting Nicole? From Harry's family chart, Dollie knew who Nickee was, who Nasty Two was, too. Let's see, if Nasty Two was Harry's mother-in-law, did that make her Dollie's mother-in-law once removed?

Nuts, being silly could not save her feelings. Dollie would much prefer heading straight over to their table to dump a pitcher of ice water over their heads, but what's the use? Not her day. When was it ever?

Steve Norman would do as he pleased. And so, apparently, would Nickee.

In a rush to get away, Dollie whirled around and left.

"What do you think caused the accident?" Steve inquired solicitously of Nicole, not having stuck around long enough to get a police report and not wanting to pressure Nicole before he could get her checked at the hospital. Nickee claimed she was fit as a fiddle and was released.

"It was the strangest thing, Steve," she said now, looking pensive. "The sun was in my eyes. Or something bright like the sun. But I thought about it while getting poked on at the hospital. The sun could not have been coming at me from that direction. So the bright light that blinded me must have been a reflection off a car or something. Right?

Yet I couldn't get away from that blinding light, no matter which way I turned." She paused. "Why would the light follow me, Steve?"

"While you were dodging the light, you also dodged about on the street. Didn't see the bank, either."

"Yeah, something like that," Nickee said vaguely, as the waitress served two country fried steaks with smashed potatoes, cream gravy, and corn.

CHAPTER 7

He walked through the house to assure himself he was alone. He smirked and rubbed his hands together. Then he closed himself into the den, locked the door, and turned on the computer. He had thought that his threats to Aggie a couple of weeks earlier would have scared her off the family history by now.

The gossip circulating around town let him know that she was continuing. The guy couldn't tolerate that. He had to stop her.

His first fax threats told her to quit or be sorry. Next, to stop or die. Should he hire somebody to scare the hell out of her, beat her up? He'd like to think of some catchy or menacing phrase that would finally achieve his purpose. Get her to forget it, without his having to go to any more trouble or get serious.

First he composed a detailed letter. Then he worried that too many specifics would give himself away, reveal his identity. Finally he produced two more messages.

Disguising his voice by using a high falsetto, he entered the threats on her answering machine, one at a time, with no more than five minutes between them.

"Quit or be sorry."

"Beware! Stop your history project. Or else."

CHAPTER 8

When Aggie Morrisey awakened, she found herself in hubby Randy's recliner. She must have fallen asleep during the news. What should she do now? Without Randolph, her husband of forty-five years who'd been dead only a few months, she didn't know what to do with herself. News time was cocktail time. She had sworn she wouldn't become some sorry alcoholic widow, so should she drink fruit juice or coffee? How about grapefruit juice in a martini glass?

Aggie wanted to call Lisa. Not during the cocktail hour, though. Lisa and Peter had been planning to play racquetball earlier that afternoon. They could be eating dinner at the club. So, no, she'd better not bother the Schwartzkopfs.

The Vicente brothers, Aggie's father and uncles, were named for U.S. Presidents. The Auld sisters, Aggie's mother and aunts, were flowers: Nasturtium, the first of the Nasties, Lilac, Lisa's mother, Violet, Aggie's mother. Then there was Pansy, who had courted a Vicente brother but hadn't married him. And Pansy's twin, Petunia, who had died as a child. Finally, there came Camellia and Daisy Auld.

Aggie and Lisa thought they had uncovered evidence of another Auld flower sister, but as yet there was no real proof. This sister, if she'd existed, could be anywhere, or she might be dead. This story was shrouded in mystery.

The Vicente-DuBois and the Auld-Deighton couples, each with ten children apiece, had produced a lot of other cousins not accounted for among the three exclusive *double cousin* lines. The just-plain-first cousins and their descendants often claimed discrimination from the very special doubles. Lisa said she didn't care, the "just-plains" were exactly that—completely plain.

The three Nasties were as petite and cute as Aggie and Lisa. Put these five women in a car and they disappeared. They all liked big cars, dating from back in the sixties, when huge station wagons were popular. Whoever was driving could only see by peeking through the steering wheel, all of the passengers slipping down below vision. Peculiar sight—"empty" car putzing along, and then all four doors opening and five Vicente-Auld girls popping out.

A widow, Nasty One at ninety-two was likely to be anywhere doing any type of *Wanderlust* thing: on African safari, on an exhibition to explore the South Pole, taking flying, or King Fu lessons. Guess long enough, somebody might hit the mark. Because, more recently, she had been down in San Miguel de Allende, Mexico, studying Beginning Spanish for the third time.

Thanks to Luther Auld, all of the double cousins, if not the just-plain cousins, were hearing impaired. Only the Nasties were going bald, however. That trait, too, came from their maternal grandfather, Luther Auld.

Nasty Three, secretary of state, now age fifty-two, had married an Arapaho the first time. Together, they had produced the dark-complected, dark-haired, Ned Fleetfoot. Ned, now thirty-two, hadn't married or produced anybody.

Nobody knew for sure what had happened to Ned's father, Nasty Three's first husband, beyond the fact that supposedly he'd died on the sidewalk. Neither Nasty Three nor her son was talking. Nor could the family imagine what had come over Nasty to have married Harold the Mutt Morton.

Aggie thought about all these people, wondering who among them could be threatening her. She couldn't imagine a single one as the culprit. If she were to call Lisa, she could use the excuse that she was ready to cave in again, namely, let Lisa book some new destinations among their upcoming travels.

Recently Lisa had resumed the pressure. She wanted Aggie to get out of her widow weeds and her widow doldrums, and leave town again.

"Despite our crazy trip to the British Isles and France?" Aggie said. "I can't believe you're willing to travel with your discombobulated cousin again."

"We still have lots of places on our list to check for the family history," Lisa begged. "If you're not ready for Sicily yet, couldn't we go to New Orleans?"

Aggie didn't mind Lisa's pestering. It was nice to know she was loved.

Just then her land line phone rang. No matter who it was, human contact was a relief, and therefore an exciting part of any day.

"Agatha, dear, guess who I saw with Nickee." exclaimed Nasty Two.

"What? Who?"

"Steve Norman! Isn't that terrific? He's the guy we wanted her to meet. You remember, we talked about it the first time back before Randy died. Am I right, or am I right?"

"You're right, dear. Thanks for telling me."

Nasty Two invited Aggie to the club for dinner that night, with a quick, "I know it's short notice, but if you don't have anything better to do . . . ?"

Admit it, Aggie told herself, you don't have anything to do, better or worse. She agreed. Clutching her full-length leather coat from the closet and pulling it close against the evening cold, Aggie left the house without checking the answering machine.

As predicted, they found Lisa and Peter at the club. The evening passed swiftly. She could hardly swallow the tiny bites of her filet mignon, but so what? It was company that counted. Aggie had a lovely time with the Schwartzkopfs and Nasty Two. Double cousins were indeed special.

Late that night Aggie pressed the button that brought into the sanctity of her home the two horrible messages left for her. She gasped and sank into Randy's comfortable old leather chair, custom-made to fit his small size.

She really ought to tell somebody. She closed her eyes and trembled. Then she fell asleep, until three o'clock when she awakened stiff and cold. It was then she prowled round the house, checking doors, windows, closets, and even peeking beneath the beds. Being alone was so dreadful. And so was this ridiculous habit. She must break herself of it. Of course nobody lurked behind closed doors or in the old armoire left to her by Great-great-grandmother Rose.

The following afternoon Aggie joined the Schwartzkopfs to travel to Laramie for the big football game, Wyoming Cowboys versus Air Force. She was so frightened, she felt like the last leaf of autumn fluttering alone to the ground.

If she shared her fears and the news of the telephone threats with Lisa, Lisa would tell Peter, and Peter might scoff. If Lisa had also received notice to quit or be sorry, let her speak first. Aggie kept silent, wondering who to tell.

She thought first of her granddaughter, but what an awful burden to lay upon the young woman's shoulders, so recently buried beneath her own traumas. Nickee, though, was strong. And capable. Also, she was not close to her mother, Joan. And Aggie and Joan were not exactly confidantes, either. Yes, Aggie would tell Nicole. Her granddaughter was no longer tied to that no-good bum, Billy, meaning Nickee would have nobody close to gossip with about her gam. If Nicole could survive all that she'd faced—a bruising, hateful husband, poverty and uncertainty—to come through the tunnel of her dark despair seemingly unscathed, perhaps she could understand what her gam was feeling. Nickee might have some good ideas about what to do—like, tell the police? Or the Clan?

Thinking of Cowboy Bill Taylor, Aggie wondered if Nicole's ex-husband could be making these threats from prison. It was the Morisseys, after all, who had testified against their grandson-in-law, effectively throwing him in the pen and tossing away the key. Billy had forged Randy's signature on six-thousand dollars worth of checks from the Morisseys' bank accounts. Question: was Bill smart enough to use the family history as his excuse for threatening her? A cover, a blanket of fog behind which to hide his real true identity?

CHAPTER 9

Big Jack gulped from a thick mug of strong, hot coffee and shoved a big bite of biscuit around in his gravy. "I wanted to see you, Nicole, before you left for Missouri. Where's Stevie? He going with you?"

"He'll stay with Beth and go to preschool with her twins," said Nickee.

Before leaving with Steve for the football game in Laramie, Nicole had agreed to meet her father, Jacque Jacquot, otherwise known as Big Jack. He was in town on business. The two could have passed as clones save for gender and hair length. Both had auburn hair, both dressed as they usually did, in Levi's, cowboy shirts and boots, hats, and denim jackets, with worn silver buckles. And both of them generally towered over the heads of their companions.

"I can't wait for you to meet him, dad," she said, meaning Steve Norman, who was even taller than her father and grandfather, the ranchers who also owned a sale barn, or, as they preferred to call it, a livestock auction market.

Big Jack smiled but looked sad. "Cowboy Billy wasn't good enough for my daughter, but then I'm not sure anybody is. Okay, girl, I know you want to tell me all about him, this Steven."

Nicole hadn't mentioned Norman's last name. If she had, Big Jack would immediately have made the connection. Steve Norman—fellow rancher, state senator, artist, also the chair of the state's environmentalism council. The man whose back Nickee had pummeled when she was so furious over her grandfather's "citizen's arrest". Had Nicole correctly identified Senator Norman, would the big rancher be admitted to her heart? Not bloody likely.

"I don't know a lot about him, yet," she said, nibbling at an English muffin and sipping orange juice. She didn't have much appetite.

"Looks like you're in love already, girl. You only met him yesterday?"

Her big brown eyes popped open. "You can tell just by looking? How do you do that?"

"You aren't interested in eating. And you glow."

She actually blushed and dropped her eyes. "Well, we'll see. I don't want to rush into something."

"Like you did before, you mean," Big Jack stated flatly.

"Yeah, something like that."

He ate heartily. She toyed with her food and fumbled for words.

"What I wanted to see you about, Nickee, you know there's a place for you with us when you finish your auctioneer training. You know that, right?"

"Oh good, that's a relief. I need some way to make a living."

She didn't tell her daddy that she'd already sat for auction training. Except that was a couple years earlier and she hadn't told anybody but her gam and Lisa and they'd kept mum. Without ever using her auctioning skills, they had grown rusty. Now she needed a refresher course. As far as her dad and any other family members knew, this was her first time around. She might feel stupid about the whole thing, but look at cousin Nasty One, three times enrolled in Spanish One and still she couldn't understand or use the language effectively. The language of auctioning would return to her with a brush-up course, Nickee felt sure.

"Yes, you'll be needing to support yourself and Stevie, what with Billy in prison. But earning a living can take most of your time and energy for decades. It's nice to find something you enjoy."

She laughed, a nervous little chortle. "You would have to remind me about Bill. I can't help but be relieved, can I? With him behind bars, we're safe now. Besides, if you think Cowboy Billy was much of a support, financially I mean, you're mistaken. He rarely won at rodeos, he was absolutely not that good. Living the rodeo life was fun, I'll admit that. Traveling all over, even after Stevie came along, even living in that sorry trailer we pulled around, all that was fun. When he wasn't drinking, gambling, angry, or mean to us, that is. Subtract all that and Billy was fun. Most of the time we acted like the kids we were when we ran off from your ranch to elope."

"Young Stevie's about ready for school, though."

"Yes. Preschool this year, kindergarten next year." She sighed.

"You don't much like the idea of growing up, do you, Nickee?"

"Not if it means settling down, staying in one place."

"Maybe you won't have to."

"What's that supposed to mean, dad?"

"Maybe, instead of working full time with your Granddad Jacquot and me, you can freelance."

Her eyes lighting up, she smiled. "Really? You think that's possible? Boy howdy," she said, sounding like her Granddad Jacquot. "I'll check it out back at the school." She had enrolled in the Missouri Auction School again. The brief but intensive training program was scheduled to begin the following week.

Early Saturday morning he arose, tiptoed downstairs to the basement playroom and another computer. He composed a quick fax. This message read, "Stop the History or Die."

Next question, when to transmit it. He didn't want Aggie to get it before she left for the game. He figured she would surely go. Everybody who was anybody in this state would be there. He, too, was going to the U and would leave early. He wanted his threat to be waiting for Agatha when she returned home.

In the last half-hour before departure he came up with a toothache as excuse to leave the house. He would use the coin-operated fax machine out at Laramie County Community College. Nobody would question his appearance there, a quiet Saturday notwithstanding. With his commitment to the college he could certainly come and go without question. The fax written and transmitted, he could participate in the afternoon festivities with none the wiser. His actions would surely spoil Aggie Morrisey's weekend when she got home to find his fax.

CHAPTER 10

When the University of Wyoming was established in Laramie in 1887, Wyoming Governor John W. Hoyt—with his First Lady, Elizabeth, with her Ph.D., who became a professor of philosophy and logic—left the capitol to assume the presidency of UW. Henceforth, there was always a close relationship between state governor and state university president. The state had no other university, just the one, plus seven community colleges. Thus UW belonged to everybody.

"And if you don't believe that, you haven't seen the highways and byways of Wyoming during UW football and basketball seasons," Steve liked to tell tourists. "Wyomingites regularly call the governor or the UW president to advise on government or education. Every issue, every thing, belongs to every citizen, and many take an active role in making state-wide decisions on matters small or large, and telling the state's leaders what to do. It's government of the people, by the people, and for the people, just the way the American government was designed to be.

"All roads lead to Rome, or in this case to the University's stadium and arenas, including the big rodeo arena," Steve would say, adding that vehicles line the roads, tailgate parties proliferate, and numerous Laramie households have stay-over company or parties. For awhile, from the 1940s to the late 1970s, there was a special train that ran from Cheyenne to Laramie, full of government, business, ranching, and other socially significant folk all flocking to the game.

"They called it the 'Treagle' Train, for *The Tribune* and *The Eagle,* Cheyenne's morning and evening papers—before they merged. These two newspapers sponsored the train, until they dropped the scheme in the late seventies. Too much conflict. It used to be a guy thing, until the gals came along and wanted in on the fun."

This year the tradition had been resurrected, as a special publicity stunt. On the train this year was the full entourage of state governor with a range of staff members, including the state school superintendent, the treasurer, the auditor, and the secretary of state, Nasturtium Three, with her husband Harold Morton, the banker, in his element to be a part of Team One.

Arranging for a picnic lunch together were the Schwartzkopfs in their RV—Peter and Lisa with double cousin Aggie Morissey, the Schwartzkopfs' daughter Beth with her husband Brad and their twins, Brianna and Brittany in the Giffords' car, and Steve and Nicole, with Stevie and double-cousin Ned Fleetfoot in Steve's green pickup. Stevie sat in a belted junior seat behind his mommy. Ned, too, sat in the back seat of the big, fancy truck.

North of the football arena on Willet Drive sits the larger than lifesize statue of Fanning a Twister—Steamboat, by sculptor Peter M. Fillerup, otherwise referred to as the Wyoming Cowboy. The statue reportedly symbolizes "The ruggedness, resourcefulness, and independent spirit of Wyoming People," or so the plaque reads. It also appears as a logo on everything officially Wyoming, or even quasi-official, from the state's license plates to tee-shirts and souvenir cups.

It was this statue that was the model for the small bronc that Steve Norman had had especially commissioned for Dominic Alexander Davidson, the bronze bronc the President had broken and that Steve was replacing. When Dom had lived with Aggie during his college days, he'd admired her bronze. Now he wanted his own back. And he wanted to see Aggie and Steve again.

North of the big bronc statue and across the street stands the UW Art Museum and American Heritage Center in the Centennial Complex, the seventeen-million-dollar facility built from gifts to the U from Eleanor Chatterton Kennedy and Joe and Arlene Watt. A giant charcoal colored cone, this building was nicknamed simply the tepee and, besides the research center within the cone shape, the art gallery to the back includes nine separate galleries containing over seven thousand paintings, sculptures, works on paper, photographs and crafts.

The tepee and the bucking bronc statue face each other. Behind the bronc and a row of tall evergreen trees, the grassy slope continues. During football games, before and during, the perimeter is filled with open-air tents offering everything from fast food and souvenirs to tee shirts, balloons, and pennants. Pickups, RVs, SUVs, mini vans, and cars park in the area along Willet Avenue that runs along the north side of the end-zone bleachers and the scoreboard. Here's where the tailgate parties spring up like over-night mushrooms and fans swarm and buzz like hornets beat out of their homes. In a state where it seemed that everybody knows everybody, the bantering and name calling flows back and forth like a brook out of bounds during flood season.

Nicole bubbled over with excitement at introducing Steve and her gam to each other. When she did, Aggie worked hard at keeping a straight face, since this was exactly the match that the girl-double-cousins, namely herself and Nasty Two and Lisa, had been plotting. The three "girls" could hardly keep from giggling. Aggie winked and poked Lisa and Nasty as reminder of the trio's silent pact. Too early in this tentative romance for the double cousins to tell the young couple about their cupid game, which hadn't mattered after all, since the young people had met out of coincidence and all on their own. So much for playing cupid.

Steve reminded Nicole that he'd played golf with her maternal Grandfather Randolph and also that he had already met Aggie, Lisa, and Peter. Nasty Two, smirking, stepped up to be introduced. Nickee wondered what was the matter with her gam and Lisa and Nasty. They were acting like little kids with a secret.

Gentle hugs quickly replaced handshakes. Everyone talked at once, gabbling and babbling, motioning and interrupting.

The kiddies, Stevie and the Gifford twins, Brianna and Brittany, tumbled out of their vehicles to run and stumble on short fat legs to join each other. Accustomed to the way of kids, Ned Fleetfoot, Nasty Three's son, asked if they would like to visit a bathroom as the first item of business on their agenda.

"Adenga, what's that, cousin Ned?"

"What kinda bidness we going to have, cousin Ned?" squealed the BBs, grabbing and holding on for dear life to Ned's hands.

"Really, Mom, Lisa, why do the girls allow their children to speak like that?" demanded Joan, Professor Joan Vicente, who'd taken her mother's family name (Joan's Sicilian grandfather's) after separating from Big Jack Jacquot.

"Oh dear, here's the Grammar Cop, already," Nicole said of her mother to tiny blond cousin, Beth Gifford. Beth giggled while her husband Brad frowned.

Steve and Nicole returned to the pickup truck to get coolers of iced beer and soda pop, napkins, rolls, and a relish tray. The others also dispersed to unload their contributions. Lisa had volunteered to ramrod the affair to ensure that everything they needed arrived. She might have been labeled Cheyenne's leading social matron, so it was no surprise that she took over. The family let her.

Out of the Schwartzkopfs' RV refrigerator, Aggie hauled her green salad in a wooden bowl big enough to hold the head of John the Baptist. Peter got his lemon loaf cake. Brad, the five-feet-six insurance agent (and perfect dance partner to the shorties), set up the charcoal grill and laid out hamburger patties and hotdogs. Steve and Nicole—touching and patting and grinning at each other—arranged folding chairs, and Beth sorted accoutrements of catsup, mustard, chips and dips. Steve's pickup tailgate served as serving table.

Aggie touched her daughter's arm. "Joan, we have less than ten minutes before Nasty Three and her husband are likely to show up."

"Mother, Mother, how can you do that?"

"Do what?"

"Speak like that. It's 'fewer' minutes, not less. And don't overuse 'up'."

"Good grief, how can you tell?"

"Tell what?"

"When to use 'fewer' compared to 'less'?"

Joan breathed deeply, unaware that she stood in the middle of all the commotion without volunteering her help. "'Fewer' is used with measureable objects, 'less' with bunches or groups of things: 'This glass has fewer ounces of water than that one has, that glass has less water than this one has."

Traffic flowed around Joan as she continued to pontificate. "'Up' this and 'up' that. It's perfectly dreadful the way people throw around prepositions these days, especially when they insist on tacking them on the end of phrases and sentences." Now that Nicole had divorced the man Joan hated, and her daughter still resisted her mom's suggestion that she enroll at the University, Joan's frustrations had returned to what the family called petty issues.

"I'm not following you, dear," Aggie mumbled.

"All right, I shall illustrate. Are you listening, Mother? Here are some examples of inappropriate if not incorrect grammar using prepositions like 'up.' Type UP a letter. We never did type up, we typed down a page. And everybody wants to know where people are at. They get in trouble by overusing the apostrophe. Ask 'Where is he?' not 'Where's he AT?' Do you comprehend what I'm saying?"

With no more than a quick nod, Aggie turned away from Joan to speak to Lisa. "How about a river boat cruise? We could fly to New Orleans and take a boat up to St. Louis. Then rent a car and drive to Nauvoo."

"Love it," Lisa said, adding in an aside to Nasty that she guessed Agatha meant to get away from Joan. "What do you think, Peter? Want to come?"

Peter Schwartzkopf, retired Air Force Colonel, turned to stare at his wife. He might not always tune in to their gossip but, as he told his son-in-law, Brad, he did appreciate the double cousins' spirit, their energy and verve. They made people feel good with their bubbly natures, their goofy projects, their joy.

"No thanks," he said, shrugging his big, hulk-like shoulders. "But you girls go ahead. Have fun. Bring back some good stories and a lot of photos to share with the rest of us." They might be well into middle age, but he still called them girlies, even when he got a roll of the eyes from any of the three double cousins.

Their plates filled with mostly salads, Lisa and Aggie moved their plastic lawn chairs away from the others. "To plan our trip," Lisa told her husband, loudly enough so that others (especially Joan) could hear and understand their self-inflicted isolation, which obviously excluded everybody else.

"I'm so excited about our trip, Aggie. When shall we leave?"

"The sooner the better. Nicole is heading for the Missouri Auction School tomorrow. Can you be ready to go then, too? I brought all the brochures and phone numbers."

Aggie was pleased that Lisa had pinpointed the desire to make a fast get-away as due to Joan. Mother and daughter did not always see eye to eye, and Joan could fret so. Just as well for Lisa to hold this notion in her head. Aggie didn't want to reveal the real cause: same as last time, when they'd hopped the pond for Europe. Now it was down the river to New Orleans, or vice versa. Better to keep Lisa in the dark about reality. The little blonde would lose her buttons if she knew the truth. Probably demand they cancel the trip and engage the police, something awful like that. Agatha wasn't ready to relinquish control. She wanted to solve her own problems, just not yet. Run away for now, think big later. Like what on earth to do about identifying her stalker, the anonymous voice on phone and fax.

They accessed the Internet on Lisa's laptop computer, sometimes following up with their cell phones to make reservations for planes, hotels, river boat, and rental car. They booked reservations after choosing a few discounted bargains, and paid by credit card. True Vicentes, they enjoyed traveling. They kept their passports updated, their bags half-packed, and could leave for anywhere at almost a moment's notice. Nicole and the Nasties were the same way, but not Beth nor Ned. They were nesters.

Aggie looked around for Nicole. Telling Nickee about her trip should dispel some of her granddaughter's worries when Aggie shared the bad news about the fax and phone threats. By being out of state, she'd be out of danger, no?

Donning matching brown felt cowboy hats and re-knotting gold scarves around their necks, the family and Steve prepared for the brown and gold Cowboy football game. Brown and gold wool lap robes and brown leather gloves were other essentials for a climate that, although sunny and bright now, could turn dark and cold a half-hour later.

The three couples—Steve and Nicole, the older Schwartzkopfs, and the younger Giffords—plus the singles—Ned, Joan and her mother, Aggie—finished lunch and cleaned up. Not Joan, though. Planting herself in the middle of the group, she lectured them on educational, psychological, and communications theories: Maslow's hierarchy of human needs when commingled with transactional analysis and whole-brain thinking. While Joan held her audience captive, the Nasties appeared.

Ned and his mother, Nasty Three, greeted each other. Quiet acknowledgment of the comfortable relationship they shared, undemonstrative, because Ned didn't like Harry and Harry disdained Ned.

Nasturtium Two also wore a cowboy hat. She needed it, she said, to cover her balding crown. She'd shoved it down hard on her forehead to keep it from blowing off. Nasturtium Three wore a straw hat with a bunch of daisies pinned on the brim.

Nasty Three also wore Harold Morton.

"She wears him like an albatross? Or a corsage?" Lisa muttered to Aggie.

When Harold spotted Steve Norman with Nicole, who was now Harry's second cousin by marriage, his cheek began to twitch. Then his left eye.

Aggie whispered to Lisa, "Wonder if he's Harold the Banker today or Harry the good ole boy?" The three-piece pinstripe banker's suit with three corners of a red handkerchief poking out of his jacket pocket should have been a clue.

"Wait and see," said Lisa around her giggles. "Don't say anything until we know what roles we're supposed to take."

Aggie peered from beneath half-shut lids at her family. Looking at her kin as if they were strangers, she felt like Sherlock. She needed a special magnifying glass, some kind of new invention that would allow her to look into their hearts. Surely none of her loved ones would be devastated by the uncovering of family secrets. So destroyed that murder was an option? Under what unturned rock lay someone's personal scandal?

CHAPTER 11

Nasty Three, with her new groom, Harry, apologized for missing the picnic. She said they had lunched aboard the train with the governor and cohorts, including Lionel Falstaff.

"And his grotesquely ugly wife, Lucy," Harry added.

Nasty Three and Nasty Two clutched a hat apiece against the breeze. Harold's image required a hat, too, he confessed, pontifically. Not a cowboy hat, of course, because he'd sooner be caught dead, and certainly not a baseball hat, either. He sported a brown felt fedora with brim, right out of the fifties.

Steve and Brad pulled the lawn chairs into a circle and the family made ready for a good gossip—if Joan didn't correct their grammar. They reminisced about UW Cowboy football games out of the past, talking of wins and losses.

"Remember when we all went to Tucson for the Copper Bowl?" Lisa said.

"All of us at that resort, the El Conquistador, for luncheon with the cowboys, the UW administration and board of trustees, and Coach Roach," Nasty Two recalled.

"Even though the Cowboys lost," Beth finished.

Left out, Harry fumed to himself, yet his facial expressions spoke of his disgust, loud and clear. Excluded, because he hadn't as yet been part of the family when the family had made that Tucson trip, Harry the Reject fumed and scowled. In-laws didn't count, he concluded. Married into one of the best families in the state and still he was left out? That figured.

"So, Madam Secretary of State," Steve said, at some point. "What's the news from the capitol?" The state legislature would not reconvene until the following January, and Steve as a senator was not required to be around much in the interim. Everybody looked to Nasty Three, ready to be informed.

"Environmentalism and economic development, the two biggest issues."

Harold plastered his face with a look both sincere and deeply serious. Scowling, he put his finger to his chin like The Thinker. He wanted to shower his in-laws with the benefit of his vast experience and knowledge. "Expect conflict," he stated in a stentorian voice, shaking his finger at the bunch.

Nobody even looked at Harold the Thinker. Except Joan. She told him that Stentor was a Greek herald in the Trojan war. "In the Iliad it was said he had the voice of fifty men."

Harold said huh? Ned said yeah, I heard that. Brad looked confused, and nobody else said or looked anything. Nicole wasn't listening, she patted Steve.

Since most of Luther Auld's descendants had inherited his hearing impairment, someone familiar with the family could not be sure whether a clan member truly hadn't heard, was ignoring others, or was simply ill-informed.

Nasty Three continued as if never interrupted. Perhaps she was already accustomed to her new husband or had quickly joined the clan with their newly acquired habit of ignoring Harry's utterances. "Tourism is now one of the biggest income-generating industries in the state—after mining, petroleum, and agriculture. Also, the state council and the county economic development committees are hard at work, with new businesses coming into the state—in Casper, Lander, Rock Springs, and down here in our southeast corner of Cheyenne and Laramie."

"What?" said Lisa. "Huh?" said Beth. "Eh?" said Aggie.

Steve winked at Nicole and took her hand to hold.

"The job market is therefore looking good." The secretary of state paused to look meaningfully at Senator Norman, state chair of the council on environmentalism. "More people are interested in your efforts, too, Steve."

Nicole perked up, eager to listen to anything involving Steve. In her junior year in high school, she'd served on the student council, when a major project that year was saving natural resources.

Agatha's family and the Normans were all conservationists. In a state like Wyoming, that is so high and arid, where water is so precious, protecting the land, water, and air are natural as breathing. When it came to animal rights—wild creatures, compared to domestic animals used to make a living—there were second thoughts. Elk and deer break down fences and let the stock out. Elk, deer, and antelope often kill new trees, too, eating the tasty bark before tender shoots get a start. Thus the clan supported the protection of wild animals, but only to a point, that being where the wild and the domestic animals clashed, or competed for the use of the same natural resources. Human needs, too, deserved preservation, thus read the Family Doctrine.

"A happy balance," Nasty Three said. "Surely it's possible, if we work together and people can resist going to extremes."

Nicole thought about the animal rights people, specifically the jodhpur-clad, pith-helmeted pair in the Land Rover who had invaded her grandfather's land to arrest him when he'd destroyed the habitat of the Preble's Meadow Jumping Mouse. That was going to extremes. Conservation, yes, jumping mice, no. It didn't occur to her to wonder about Steve Norman's theory on rodents.

Everybody dispersed for the game, except Ned, who didn't care for football. He typically volunteered to baby sit, although the three children were getting a bit old for coddling. Still, they enjoyed Cousin Ned's treats. They went first to the UW art gallery and then for ice cream cones, before their naps in the Schwartzkopfs' RV.

Meanwhile, among the grownups, Harry clung to Nasty Three's arm, trying to keep up to his fast-paced new bride and her family, trying to think of something important to say. He saw Joan trailing behind them, but ignored her.

At halftime, after the Casper Troopers, a nationally renowned drill team, had provided the feature entertainment that everybody agreed was well worth waiting for, Aggie signaled Nickee to join her. En route to the Ladies—after looking over her shoulder to ensure that nobody they knew was within hearing distance—Aggie told Nicole about the threatening messages left on her answering machine.

"Sounds like somebody wants you to quit working on the family history." Nicole hugged her gam and made fretting murmurs. "Have you told Lisa? What's she think?"

"Lisa and I are leaving tomorrow, just like you. If I'm out of town, nobody can get to me." Agatha swore Nicole to secrecy and her granddaughter promised. But not before suggesting that her gam should call the police. "They'd laugh at me," Aggie said.

When Steve came striding past, Nicole reached for him. "Wait up. Where've you been?"

"Calling my twin daughters in Boston."

"Being around the BB twins and Stevie make you lonesome for Cindy and Sissy?" Nicole hugged him.

He grinned but not sheepishly. "I call them every day."

"Wow, that's a very good-daddy thing to do."

"Shall we leave the game early?" Steve suggested. "Looks like UW is beating the socks off Air Force." Nicole had agreed to join him at his ranch, southwest of Laramie, since she would be leaving the state the next day.

By the time the couple had reached the fifty-yard line, half-time events were over, people were gobbling snacks, and family members were stirring around, standing up, sitting down, calling to one another. Steve overheard Nasty's hushed tones and Harry's high-pitched, squeaky voice. Senator Norman tuned in, for no other reason than he had caught his own name spoken by somebody.

"What's the matter with you, Harry? What have you got against Steve Norman?" Nasty Three, the new bride, demanded. "You ignore the senator when he's right in front of you or you get away from him like he'll contaminate you."

"That's for me to know and you to find out."

Exasperated: "That's what I'm trying to do, Harold, find out."

"You don't understand," he mumbled.

Wearily: "Try me. Some day will you just try to make me understand you?" The secretary of state turned away. She walked off with her mother.

Steve sat down, thinking about that. He was right, then. The scene Harry had made in the bank the day before wasn't merely his imagination. Harold Morton actually hated him: Steve Norman, the rancher? Norman, the senator? or Steve, Charley's little brother?

For the first time in a long time Steve thought about the plane crash that had taken his dad and brother. Maybe it was no accident.

Could there have been sabotage? The FAA had gathered up the plane's pieces and parts to analyze and, hopefully, to determine the cause of the crash, if any existed beyond the obvious: running out of gas or losing control of their Cessna in the dense fog.

Steve didn't know why Harry's attitude or hate game made him recall the accident. What was it with Harold Morton?

And what caused him to think of sabotage?

Which brought Steve full circle. Now his thoughts switched to Tom Rotter, his dad's longtime enemy. Had Rotter finally made good on his recurrent threats to get even with Steve's dad?

CHAPTER 12

Tom Rotter went into Laramie to attend his church's conference, a two-day affair, with business sandwiched between prayer meeting and Bible studies. His well-worn black suit, shiny in the bottom, was relieved only by a starched white shirt. He wore a black string tie, black leather shoes, a scrappy old black felt hat, and he carried a big black leather-covered Bible.

Cheyenne bartender Dollie Domenico was no football fan. She didn't know anybody who was, except Senator Steve Norman. If she had, she wouldn't have spent the money on a University game. She would much rather go to the southeastern regional conference of her church. Which is what she decided to do, at the last minute. She caught a ride from her trailer park in Cheyenne to Laramie with a church member. She wore shiny black patent leather shoes with black bows to match the string tie at the neck of her white blouse. She grabbed a black shawl and headscarf and tucked her Bible under her arm.

Timid, she held back at the door. There were a lot more people attending than she'd expected. Retreating, she bumped into an old man, sweat-worn felt hat atop his head, hair poking out from under the rim, and from out of his ears, and from inside his nose.

He grabbed her by the arm and snarled in her face, "What you waiting for? In the House of the Lord, God waits for no man."

"I ain't no man," she said. Ick, he had bad breath and crooked teeth. Dollie drew back, appalled. "Who are you, and what do you want with me?" Her shyness disappeared with her revulsion.

"Tom Rotter's the name," he smirked, like she should know without asking. "Rotter Ranch?" Pause, no recognition. "Out west of town, up next to Sheep Mountain? Near where Dick and Charles Norman crashed."

What was he talking about?

"Tom Rotter, Rotter Ranch. Don't tell me you never heard a me. Somebody ought t'tell you."

#######

Half time was over and both teams were back on the field. The band played and everybody on the Wyoming side cheered the home team. Surely the Cowboys would win. Steve told Aggie he was taking Nickee and her son to see the ranch. They would probably spend the weekend.

Aggie said, "Did she tell you she's leaving town tomorrow?"

Arms akimbo, Nicole stood up in front of them. "How's that grab you, Cowboy?" she said to Steve. After five years of marriage to the possessive Bill Taylor, Nicole expected Norman to protest.

"But, uh, we just met," he said.

"I know, but months ago I booked into a ten-day training school. Back in Missouri. I'm taking the noon plane out of Laramie."

"Okay, I'll get you to the airport in time. What about Stevie?"

"He'll stay with the Giffords."

Looked like that was the end of that, Nicole mused, comparing Steve to her first husband. Steve Norman, the gentleman? Granted, they hadn't known each other long, they'd certainly made no commitment to one another. It was just a feeling she had. That they belonged together. (But not every minute.)

Except that Aggie had the last word. "The thing about the Vicentes and Aulds and many descendants, Steve—a lot of us have the wanderlust. If you expect to get along with the Vicente-Aulds, you've got to be willing to see them leave you all the time. Travel is our middle name."

Back in Cheyenne that evening, Nasty Two called all the cousins, even the just-plain cousins. She had some hot gossip to pass along: the budding love affair between Steve Norman and Nicole, plus the complicated plane-boat-car trip that Aggie and Lisa were taking. As usual, gossip turned to rumors.

News flew swiftly, from one family member to another, to adults and children, blood kin and in-laws, double and just-plain first cousins. And, in some cases, to outsiders.

CHAPTER 13

Stevie said he couldn't wait to reach Steve's ranch and go exploring. Like his mom, he was as much at home on the range as the antelope that roamed the wide open spaces. Steve said he was eager to show off his place while it was still light. He stopped the truck to unlock the gate, Nicole and Stevie popping out too.

What's that thing?" Stevie asked, pointing at the apparatus on the gatepost.

"Video camera with two-way audio. Visitors push that button," Steve pointed, lifting the boy up to try it. "At my home, in the cowhands' bunkhouse, and in the foreman's house, speakers turn on automatically. Anybody on my ranch who responds can talk and also see who's out here. Can't be too careful, cattle rustling's still a problem, junkies after funds to feed their habit."

"Hey, that's neat." said Stevie. "Anybody looking at me now?"

"Probably. Say something, anything."

"Hi there, sonny," came the reply in a low gruff voice.

"That's Joe Joplin, ranch foreman," Steve said, sticking his own face in front of the camera. "Sorry to bother you, Joe. Just demonstrating the equipment to my friend here. So, how're things?"

"Gotta cow we're having trouble with. Could be a breech birth. Ornery, that's what she is, getting herself bred so late in the season."

Steve said he'd hurry along, but Joe assured him there was no rush. "Be prepared, though. You could be up all night with her."

Turning away, Steve apologized to his guests.

"No problem with us, is there, Stevie?" said Nicole.

"Oh boy, can I stay up late too?"

"'May I'," she corrected her son.

Norman took his time traversing the fenced-in, locked-in terrain of the three-and-a-half miles between gate and home place. They did stop once, at the creek. He pronounced it "crick".

Much of the Norman ranch consisted of lightly rolling land with scrub grass and prairie chickens, antelope, rabbits, red fox, porcupine, coyote, ferret, a few snakes, and lots of insects. Birds, bees, butterflies, blue cranes, grasshoppers in summer, sage hens.

"Ever seen a sage hen?" Norman asked. "Sage hen is so dumb, you can walk right up to him and hit him with a stick."

"Why would you want to do that?" Stevie asked. He didn't wait for an answer because he'd already pulled off his sneakers and socks to stick his feet in the cold water. Autumn was often like this in the high country—fling an early blizzard at you one day and three days later tempt you to wade in the crick. Nicole didn't stop her son. She knew he was hungry as a bear after hibernation to get back to nature. She didn't blame him, she couldn't wait to get on a horse. Maybe not this time. The light was waning, the evening with Steve inviting.

Aboard the pickup again, they came over a rise, and suddenly the big Norman house loomed before them. Nicole caught her breath but said nothing. Constructed of logs and fieldstone, with a long deep porch like a veranda, the house made her think of the Jacquot spread. She was pleased to note wicker rockers and a porch swing. Indoors, the great room stretched across the front of the house, facing a floor-to-ceiling fieldstone fireplace. Braided rugs were scattered about the wide-planked flooring, deep leather couches, chairs, and ottomans, with oak coffee and end tables completing the comfortable scene, along with Arapaho Indian rugs and artifacts and original oil paintings on the walls.

While Stevie ran around, upstairs and down, Nicole stepped closer to study the paintings. Half or more of them were signed by Steve Norman himself. Above the fireplace was his masterpiece, Buster the Bronc.

She could with honesty praise his works. "I don't know what I like, but I know art," she said, purposely revising the quotation. She got a hug for her efforts to amuse.

"Your home reminds me of something, but I can't think what."

"The house in that classic TV series, *Bonanza?*"

She snapped finger and thumb. "Right. I've seen reruns."

"Don't ask if we modeled the house after theirs," he said. "Could be the reverse, though. Great-granddad built this place back in the twenties."

The kitchen was small. Nobody was there, and no delicious odors emanated to assure them that dinner awaited.

Nicole might have raised an eyebrow but she didn't. Instead, she proposed, "The real kitchen, the big place, is out back?"

Steve confirmed her educated guess with a nod, leading the way to say hello to the cook, who did double-duty, feeding both the ranch hands and the ranch family. Since their womenfolk had all disappeared, the Normen men ate whatever everybody else did, with no special requirements except for special occasions, like tonight was supposed to have been. In Cook's big kitchen, the aroma they might have expected in the house greeted them, making Nicole's eyes water in delicious anticipation.

Paul Hardy, the cook, was just taking their dinner out of the oven. He said they could eat whenever they were ready. Paul described the rolled beef stuffed with fresh spinach and seasoned with cream cheese, tongue, white wine, and a variety of herbs and spices.

"Sounds great," Steve said. "After cocktails we'll serve ourselves, so you can get back to the cowpokes."

"Maybe you'll want to check on your pregnant cow first," Nicole suggested.

Big Steve excused himself. First, though, he directed her to the upstairs rooms where she and Stevie could freshen themselves after the long dusty afternoon.

It was then that the first tiny doubt nudged her mental membranes. The bronc painting had done it. It had been stolen, she recalled, without remembering the details. Back when she'd only just returned to the state with her husband, Bill Taylor. After five years on the road. The cops—or was it her own gam?—had found and retrieved the painting during the visit of President Davidson.

For all their talking and sharing so far, Nicole had not thought to describe to Steve her life with her dad's family—at their livestock auction market or on their ranch. Perhaps she assumed that he would recognize in her a native Wyomingite, a woman as acclimated to the land as the sage hen or porcupine. Inside her head Nicole was smiling, thinking that ex-husband Billy had called her prickly as a porcupine, but that was near the end of their marriage when he claimed she'd begun to fuss too much at him. Cousin Beth said Nicole was zippy as a hummingbird, zooming around from spot to spot.

Early the next morning, Nickee's eyes popped open. Already, she knew she liked this guy. He was a wonderful lover, knew all the right buttons to pet and punch (wow!). The funny things they'd talked about so far. Steve had at last fallen asleep. She'd watched him awhile before catching a few winks of her own. She knew she needed rest, she ached all over from the wreck of her car smashing into the bank, for no reason except a bright light shining in her eyes to distract her. Too excited to sleep, now. Feeling so warm and wonderful with this man. Even this soon, and corny as it might sound, it felt like they were made for each other.

About each other they now knew that his favorite color was purple, hers blue, he wanted his eggs fried over easy, she liked them scrambled. He preferred jazz, she liked country western, they were both conservationists and found Wyoming politics, tourism, and economics fascinating. Already it seemed he was a soul mate.

Strange that they hadn't talked about their former marriages or shared preferences for important things like city versus rural living. She had yet to discover whether he liked to travel. That was important to her. Since she'd told him she was leaving tomorrow, he hadn't mentioned that either.

CHAPTER 14

Dollie Domenico didn't think it was fair. She didn't have anybody, and barely a pot to pee in, and she had to pay full fees to park her trailer, and there Nicole Taylor was, from a great big, mostly wealthy family, getting to park her little trashy trailer for free. Just because the trailer park owner loved rodeos and thought Nicole's ex-husband Cowboy Bill was hot stuff, performing at rodeos all over—even Calgary, Canada, and here in Cheyenne at Frontier Days. Never mind that he was in prison or, as Nicole said, was "a guest of the state."

Just because Dollie lived in a trailer didn't make her trailer trash, like Harold the Big Shot called her. If anybody was trailer trash, it was Nicole, her with her tiny banged-up trashy trailer down at the trashy end of the trailer park.

Dollie gripped her Bible to her chest like it could save her, when she knew she was already saved, as of yesterday at the Bible Conference in Laramie. She couldn't afford to keep running back and forth between the two towns, and the good Lord knew she didn't have the money to blow on a motel. Her pastor had said that the Laramie church folks would put them up over night. But by the time she'd stood in line—and missed the free juice and muffins—to go to the bathroom and then stood in another line for another hour—and missed the prayer and testimony meeting—to register for a room, the free rooms were gone.

She had witnessed, though. Got down on her knees and wailed her pleas to the Lord to beg his forgiveness for her sins. The preacher patted the top of her head and then anointed her with some messy oil stuff—which ruined her carefully washed and coifed hairdo—and told her to arise in the Joy of the Light and said she was saved. She was a new-born babe now and her wickedness had been wiped from her.

So that was that. She could stop worrying, store the feelings of guilt, as if in some old trunk. Dollie stashed the Bible on the top shelf and went to inspect her sweet premises.

She loved her little home, mostly because it was all hers. As an incentive to accept the breakup of her marriage to Harry without squawking or causing him a lot of trouble, he said, he "gave" her this wonderful home. Dollie put quotation marks around the word, *gave*, whenever she said it, because in truth the bank had repossessed the trailer and then, via various paper shuffling and computer switching, none of which she understood, Harold had "come by the mobile home with not a single cent out of pocket."

A redwood deck with pots of artificial geraniums standing along the railing top invited guests to enter a tiny room—a mud room in summer, an air pocket in winter to protect the main facility from the cold winds of Wyoming's super frosty blizzards. Once inside the foyer, turning right took you to the master bedroom and bath, turning left into what was for Dollie a spacious twelve by twelve feet living room, open to the dining area. Dollie kept the adjoining kitchen as spick and span as a surgical operating theatre.

Beyond the kitchen was another bathroom and a guest bedroom, home to her two cats, Frigid and Rigid. A neutered female, Frigid would have nothing to do with guy cats. When yawning, Rigid stretched out long and lean, rigid as a corpse with rigor mortis. Frigid was ginger striped, Rigid was black as night, or black as death, depending on whether Dollie was mad at him.

Yes, Dollie loved her home, and no, she wasn't trailer trash. Yes, she was happy to be saved, no, she'd said "No thanks" to Tom Rotter's suggestion that they get better acquainted. Why in the world would she want to get to know some old goat with bad breath and hair sticking out of his nose, even if he did go to church?

CHAPTER 15

Lisa and her husband dropped Aggie at her front door. Peter wanted to escort Aggie inside, but she said she'd be fine.

Why was he so solicitous? Aggie wondered. Had Nicole told Beth, and Beth told her mother, Lisa, and Lisa told Peter about the threats? No, surely not. Then she remembered. Peter had been this chivalrous ever since Randy died.

Before undressing, putting away her things, doing anything at all, Aggie checked her answering machine for disturbing calls. She supposed she ought to sign up for voice mail, but Randy had resisted. He wanted a machine he could operate, a machine with a tape. That, he understood. Now that he was gone, she could do as she pleased. Oh, well, some day she would get around to switching over. Not now, though, too many other things to think about. Like bad people.

She checked her mail for warning letters, and finally breathed a sigh of peace, as if holding her breath under six feet of water.

Passing the closed door to Randy's study, she thought of something else: the fax. Oh, God, no. But, yes, there it was, another threat!

Back she plunged into the deep waters of heart-stopping turmoil. With no other thought save to escape, Aggie ran to the front closet, snatched her purse and perpetually half-packed bag, and dashed straight back out of the house.

Now what?

It wasn't quite dark yet. She probably looked silly. She ran next door, where she asked the neighbors to let her use their phone, making up a crippled lie about locking herself out and needing a cab, and losing her cell phone besides.

While she waited for the cab, she ran back indoors to search frantically for her cell phone. In desperation she used the land line phone to call herself, and then listened carefully for the pretty little bird song she had downloaded as her ring tone. Finally, she heard it, but barely, chirping away from inside the closet. When she'd snatched up her wheelie the mobile phone must have fallen from a pocket. Whew, not too late, now she was armed again.

When the taxi arrived, Aggie's quick thoughts bounced from one side of the court to the other. She couldn't stay with Nicole, Nickee and Stevie were with Steve Norman. Yet Nickee was the only one Aggie had told about the warnings and her fears.

Lisa would want to know everything if Aggie went there. So would Lisa's daughter, Beth, and her husband, Brad.

Feeling desperate again, and swiping wee droplets of perspiration from her forehead, she set her mind to running down the list of kinfolk. Ned Fleetfoot would be surprised, but at least he wouldn't question her or gossip to the others. Nasty Two certainly would. And Aggie really couldn't see herself spending the night in the same house with Harold the Nut Morton, even if Nasty Three was a favorite cousin. Any other cousins were just-plain as opposed to double cousins and if Lisa heard about it, and she certainly would, she and Beth would have a fit.

Aggie told the cab driver to take her to Little America, Cheyenne's finest, a convention and resort facility. No, somebody she knew might see her. "Make it the Holiday Inn," she said.

The cabby kept right on traveling down Interstate 25. "Makes me no never mind," he said.

"Wait, wait," she called from the back seat. "Take the exit at Central and go downtown to the Ranchers Hotel."

A cocktail in the lounge, dinner in the old dining room where the new chef turned out some tasty dishes, and she'd get a good night's rest. Nobody would think of looking for her there. No, maybe she should order room service. Safer to stay in her room.

Oh dear, what if Lisa called her at home and got no answer? The Schwartzkopfs wouldn't know what to think. She couldn't call Lisa from the hotel. Their Caller-ID service would reveal a phone number that was not her own.

All right, then, she would just have to wait until morning. Then she could call Lisa from the airport. Arrive early and call early and tell Lisa to hurry so they could have a cocktail in the Cloud Nine Lounge before departure. Meanwhile, she'd totally forgotten she'd found her cell phone and could have simplified her life considerably if she'd had the good sense to use that little thing.

CHAPTER 16

Going first class, which they invariably did, meant they could usually get last-minute reservations, whether for plane, hotel, or other accommodations. Awaiting Lisa in the airport lounge, Aggie sipped a Virgin Mary. Unconsciously she stirred the mild drink with its stick of celery so fast the drink splashed over.

She could hear Lisa now, scolding like she did when they were kids making mud pies. Aggie was the quick, messy one, while Lisa was slower, more organized, and definitely more tidy.

Lisa would want to know where her widowed cousin had gone last night and why. Aggie supposed she would eventually give in and explain. Then Lisa would understand why she hadn't got an answer if she'd called. Aggie couldn't imagine that Lisa wouldn't have called, she always did. She had already questioned Aggie's sudden desire to leave town, especially after resisting all of Lisa's efforts since the European trip to travel again. Lisa would also ask why Aggie had left half her stuff at home. They could shop in New Orleans, Aggie would say, before embarking on the steamship cruise up the Mississippi River.

Naturally the first thing Lisa did was berate Agatha. "I do wish you'd remember to turn your cell phone on. I called it and your land line, both. No answer. Good grief, Aggie, you live all alone, now. You must let us check up on you on a regular basis."

Nevertheless, Lisa greeted Aggie with a hug. Then she sat down on the banquette beside her cousin and ordered a Bloody Mary. Out came her airline-ticket packet, along with a small leather-bound notebook and gold pen. She peered at her notations. "I'm glad we got a suite at the Monteleone, Aggie. I love the French Quarter," Lisa said. "So, what kind of detective work have you got on our agenda?"

Aggie looked bewildered until she remembered their reason for traveling—researching the family history. Lisa was right. They'd begun to feel like private investigators, with all the digging necessary to search for their lost forebears.

"Nothing in particular," Aggie mumbled. "We'll keep on the lookout for family stories, perhaps."

On the commuter plane from Cheyenne to Denver International Airport, they didn't talk much. Agatha was too tired, though she didn't explain why she'd hardly gotten more than a couple of hours of sleep. Insomnia was a bitch. At DIA they had just enough time to race along A Terminal to the subway and then down the long B Terminal to Gate 55, where passengers were already boarding. On the next, bigger plane, they napped or read digital novels from their twin Kindles.

Lisa looked for their chauffeur to identify himself and escort them to the limo she had reserved. Soon they headed for their hotel on Royal Street, where they spent a mere few moments unpacking.

"You know what they say about New Orleans," Lisa said. 'We'll soar with the eagles in the daytime, and hoot with the owls at night'. What shall we do?"

"Shop."

"For what?"

"Clothes." Aggie stood beside her open suitcase, the tears running over and dribbling down her cheeks.

"Oh, poor baby." Immediately solicitous, Lisa rushed to hug, pat, and pet, simultaneously. "I remember, now. The last time you were here, Randy was with you. You miss him a lot, I'll bet."

Was that what was wrong with her? Agatha had supposed she felt all jittery because of the threats. Had Randy been with her, he would have ridiculed her fears, but he would protect her, nonetheless. He'd know what to do. Whatever it was, he'd do it, and they would both be laughing by now.

Of course. It was merely a cruel prankster, taking advantage of the poor little widow. Perhaps that was all this was. Similar to getting obscene phone calls from a stranger, a psychopath who had chosen her name and number at random from the phone book. She must get an unlisted number. The idea that the threats that had scared her half to death were somebody's idea of a joke was still incredible, but no longer incredulous. It really was absurd to think anybody could be serious. To date she and Lisa had not uncovered one single thing that could possibly hurt anybody in the family.

Ridiculous business. So Aggie told all, laughing nervously while unfolding and refolding the few items of clothing she'd brought along.

Lisa was naturally upset. She patted and petted Agatha again. "When we return home, perhaps you should move in with us for awhile. Until whoever it is decides to stop tormenting you."

"I'll think about it," Aggie said, pondering what that would mean: relinquishing her privacy, allowing a prankster to drive her from her beautiful home. "We don't have to decide now, anyhow. We're here to have fun."

Each of them had visited New Orleans several times, usually with their husbands. Mardi gras was fun. Mardi, Tuesday, gras, fat, fat Tuesday, the literal French meaning, or Shrove Tuesday—the day before the beginning of Lent.

She and her husband had once visited America's version of Paris for a petroleum industry conference, Randy leaving her free to shop and browse while he was attending meetings. Some of her favorite haunts centered around Bourbon, Royal, and Decatur Streets, the St. Louis Cathedral, and Jackson Square—the hub of many historical homes. She supposed she was a typical tourist, for she liked the French Quarter with its mix of antique stores, souvenir shops, clubs, even the voodoo vendors.

Aggie (but not Randy) could stand for hours watching the artists. She (but hardly her husband) enjoyed hovering on the fringe, observing artists and gays in Faubourg Marigny Distrct, a neighborhood that reminded her of New York's East Village. She (alone) appreciated the African and Asian art, Degas' impressionist works, and Faberge's jeweled masterpieces at the New Orleans Museum of Art, in the striking beaux-arts temple. At last she found some things beyond petroleum to entice her husband's interest. Together they visited the Zoo and Aquarium, and strolled leisurely through one of the above-ground cemeteries

"That's because New Orleans sits below sea level," Randy lectured her.

She usually awaited Randy's return from the convention center at the end of Canal Street by sinking into a warm bubble bath and catching a nap. Another few times they had rendezvoused for cocktails at the top of the World Trade Center, in the revolving lounge with its terrific views of the city, the Mississippi River, and the river traffic of barges and ships coming in from the Gulf. Randy took her to visit the petroleum exhibit, courtesy of five oil companies, which extolled the benefits of oil rigs to the sea. Which was before the BP oil spill.

Now the cousins compared favorite Creole, Cajun, and fish dishes. Lisa recommended jambalaya, gumbo, or muffulettas. Aggie countered with stuffed eggplant and oysters on the half shell.

"Or we could order croustade de barbet." Then she played Randy's role, lecturing her cousin. "That's a fish mixture in a pastry shell. Or how about Doulet du Duc—chicken in a creamed mushroom sauce."

"I know what's in those dishes, Lisa."

"Sorry. Guess I sound like 'Professor' Joan."

Aggie shrugged. Her mind was on Randy, perhaps that's how Joan had gotten so stuffy, she was emulating her dad. "How about this, then," Aggie said. "Gratin de langouste with lobster, and escargot, and a souffle for dessert."

By now they were giggling, Aggie bending over at the waist as if to vomit. "I'm full, and nearly sick just from recounting all the possibilities."

The double cousins, with Professor Joan's help, had already discovered that their French ancestor, Rose D'Gade, had lived in the city—not far from where they were staying at the Monteleone—at Jackson Square, in one of the grand old homes that still stood in antique splendor, with their wrought-iron railings like lace on a string of dowagers. From the diary Joan's colleague translated for them, they discovered that Rose had taken room and board from a family, in return for housekeeping and an au pair assignment. She had borne Ronald out of wedlock and raised him quietly in the even then bawdy town.

"Apparently she was never reunited with her lover, who might have wound up in French Canada," Lisa said.

"Or maybe he migrated to Wyoming for the hunting and trapping."

Rose D'Gade had recorded for posterity a bit of news about her grown son. Not much, perhaps what she wrote was all she knew. Ronald had gone to work on the river and eventually was promoted to steamship captain.

Ronald's daughter, Rose, named for her grandmother, was born on board her father's boat. To whom, they didn't know. Some anonymous woman? a performer or wife, who had died or run off? They didn't know.

Ronald raised his daughter awhile but then she, this second Rose, was passed off to the DuMauriers, a St. Louis family who'd converted to Mormonism. By 1842 the Mormons were settling Nauvoo, a frontier town up north on the Mississippi River—a swampy, mosquito infested area just north of Mark Twain's Hannibal on the river separating Missouri from Illinois.

For the subsequent story, the cousins had switched to young Rose's journal. This document they had uncovered after going through a whole lot of trouble and putting their new-found detective skills to work.

Thus they knew that Ronald's Rose fell in love with Etienne, the DuMauriers' son. The newlyweds, eager for a life of their own, decided to spend their honeymoon on the riverboat, en route from St. Louis to Nauvoo where they planned to settle. The older DuMauriers decided to go, too.

"So much for a 'life of their own'," Lisa said dryly.

The double cousins were destined to relive their ancestor's trek, which would culminate in the now small village of Nauvoo, famous as much these days for grapes as for the vanished Mormons.

"What do you want to do now?" Lisa asked, from her bed at the Monteleone. They had already decided Aggie could borrow Lisa's clothes. No need to shop for them. Instead, they would purchase souvenirs, bobbles, voodoo artifacts, anything that took their fancy.

"I brought you a poncho shawl," Lisa said.

Aggie knew it was one of many crocheted by Isabelle Vicente, the typically silent wife of Cousin Rudolph. Not a double cousin, Rudolph was easily distinguishable from Randolph Morissey because of just-plain-first-cousin status plus Rudolph's bulbous red nose. And his hell-fire-and-damnation preaching.

Solemn Rudolph had married somber Isabelle. She rocked and crocheted. Rudolph's one-hundred-and-four-year-old mother, Hepzibah, rocked and knitted; one long scarf, until it reached twenty-six feet. Then Isabelle, who lived with her mother-in-law, would be directed to unravel the wool so old Hepzibah could start knitting anew. The two women often sat silent, side by side, in their rockers, or in the parlor on the horsehair settee, or, in summers, on the front porch in wicker chairs.

"First, before anything else," Aggie said, "I want to light a votive candle at the Cathedral and say a prayer for Randy."

They plotted their schedule, deciding to save Brennans for brunch on the morrow. Tonight they would enjoy a Creole dinner at Antoine's, followed by dropping in at Pat O'Brien's for a Hurricane, and, after that, jazz at Preservation Hall. Both ladies were enthralled with New Orleans jazz, a style developed between 1900 and 1925 and characterized by collective improvisation on simple harmonies by a front line of clarinet, trumpet, and trombone.

"If we're up to it by then, we can club hop, and then wind up at Cafe du Monde for beignets," Lisa said, clapping her hands like a school girl.

Over dinner they reviewed the detective skills they had developed while learning how to conduct ancestral searches. First they attended a few meetings of the Cheyenne and Laramie genealogical associations, to listen to lectures, question members, and paw with the rest of them through old books with tiny dim print. Some useful things to use, they'd discovered, were cemetery and church membership rolls, obituaries in newspaper morgues, city directories, and public records available at city halls and county courthouses citing births and deaths, real estate deals and other financial transactions. For current data, it was recommended that they use utility companies, credit bureaus, and various other public records to identify and access motor vehicles, names and addresses, and revealing ID and personal traits for identification purposes. To date they had used some but not all of these sources.

The Mormon or Latter Day Saint Church's vast store of genealogical data was also helpful and so were the LDS personnel who assisted and offered them advice. The double cousins discovered family members among the ranks of saints, particularly those who had traveled by covered wagon and push cart en route from Nauvoo, Illinois, to Salt Lake City, Utah. The ladies already knew that some of their kin did not make that whole, grueling, two-year journey. Instead, a selected few of them had helped settle the frontier that eventually became Wyoming Territory.

The little ladies discovered that it could often be difficult to access records, not without some kind of authorization. "Hey, I know," Lisa suggested. "We could get our PI licenses."

"What? Become real-life private investigators? Good grief."

At Pat O'Brien's bar, they ordered a huge Hurricane, whose recipe commingled rum with fruit juices. They split it by ordering two straws, while sitting on the patio in the cool of the after-midnight evening, where ultra-violet heaters hidden in the trees warmed them. Lisa suggested they go over the mostly as yet unwritten family history.

With Joan's help, however, they had already developed several meaningful appendices to use as quick resources, for example: Appendix A was the family chart, B—current address list, C—old photos, which Aggie had color-copied or computer scanned and laminated for preservation, D—the reproduction of significant diary and letter pages, and E—national and world history events to tie family happenings into the larger setting. Section F was devoted to maps and property or local sketches—including photos and drawings from yellowing newspapers taken from the LDS in Salt Lake City and also from the Reorganized Latter Day Saints archives in the Headquarters Auditorium of the Community of Christ in Independence, Missouri.

Aggie's daughter, Joan, had expected them to be thorough. Groaning, Aggie complained to Lisa that they might as well have signed up for a master's degree covering historical research methodology under *The Professor's* direction.

Rather than all the that tedious digging through old records, many of which attempts had proved futile, which meant back-tracking and starting over, and getting bogged down with it all, what The Girls much preferred was live-action research. By that they meant re-enacting their family's personal history. Pretending they were creating a documentary for the History Channel, something like that, Lisa said lamely. "It's like playing dolls, acting out, that sort of game."

Before they could get started on their quest-within-a-quest, Lisa glanced around the patio of Pat O'Brien's tavern. She spotted a man staring at them. He probably thought they were two pretty ladies, she mused aloud, though so quietly Agatha barely heard every other word. Lisa glanced away and said nothing more.

When Aggie spied the same man, however, she was so startled she jerked, and knocked over the big glass of their Hurricane. Lisa looked appalled.

Aggie leaned forward, while ducking her head into cousin-in-law Isabelle's crocheted shawl, like Zorro peering out from beneath his cape. "Psst, Lisa, do you see that guy looking at us from over there?"

"I already suggested he probably thinks we're cute." Lisa giggled.

"Get real. Lisa, am I paranoid or what?"

"Not paranoid. I saw him, too. Let's get out of here."

Later, at Cafe Monde, at two o'clock in the morning over beignets, Aggie daintily licked the fresh powdered sugar from her fingertips. "Mmm, these warm pastries are so delicious."

Lisa suggested they review what they knew about Rose DuMaurier; rather, Rose d'Gade—the one back in France. "She surely came from literate people."

"I agree. She wrote all those tear-soaked personal diary pages."

"What exactly do you propose we do in Nauvoo, Aggie?"

"Do the tourist bit, I suppose. Soak up atmosphere. I'd like to pretend that you and I are Rose and Essie. That it's the mid-1800s."

"Oh? And I suppose you get to be Rose? And I'm Essie?"

Aggie looked the soul of innocence. "I'm dark like Rose. You're blonde like Essie. Makes sense, doesn't it?"

They had also retrieved journals from Essie, another forebear.

Suddenly Aggie spotted what appeared to be the same man staring at her from across the semi-outdoor room. She poked Lisa. "Be careful, drop a hanky or something, but look behind you. Isn't that the guy we saw at O'Brien's?"

Leaving their pastries unfinished, the duo casually got up and left the cafe. "Is he looking, is he following us?" Lisa whispered.

"I don't know, I'm too frightened to look."

They tried to find a cab, to no avail.

Lisa peered over her shoulder. Then she whispered in a voice that came out like a mouse squeaking: "He's coming, he's coming! What shall we do?"

"Quick," said Aggie, clutching her cousin's arm and pulling her along. "Let's push ourselves into the tail-end of this crowd of conventioneers. It'll look like we're with them, not just two women, all alone and vulnerable."

They edged themselves into the middle of the noisy, happy group with the name tags on their lapels. Association members probably didn't even know each other and they might think nothing of having two more party goers joining them.

It worked. Soon they were back in their suite, fast asleep.

CHAPTER 17

Exhausted from their previous night's excitement—all that fast traipsing around, eating, and adventuring—both women slept late. Last night Aggie had worn her own clothes. Today she chose from Lisa's plentiful assortment a two-piece light-weight dress in vanilla voile, with gold-link necklace and matching bracelet. Aggie continued to wear her gold wedding and engagement rings. She might never remove them, dead husband or not.

Lisa's makeup, a task that seemed to take forever to achieve, as usual was flawless. She wore a pale orange and beige dress of pleated cotton jersey, with a skirt that swirled at the slightest turn or twist.

Under the "complexion as season" theory, Lisa was a *summer*, Aggie a *winter*. Lisa had taught her cousin to make appropriate selections, surrounding herself even in her home with deep, vibrant, passionate colors—purple, crimson, navy or royal blue, and bright yellow. Aggie preferred lavenders and purples. Now she had to make do with substitutes from Lisa's stock.

At Brennan's they were escorted to a window seat overlooking the garden. White linens, sparkling spot-free crystal, and delicate china graced the table along with a vase of fresh pink carnations and roses. "Roses." Lisa exclaimed. "For Grandma Rose and all our other Rose ancestors."

Eggs Sardou, Caesar salad, Bananas Foster, and Mimosas to drink renewed their energy and their determination to lock away last night's fears like a bride closeting her wedding dress. Presumably, the gown nor their fright would require resurrection.

"We think we're such hot-shot detectives," Lisa said over coffee, a gourmet blend with an aroma of hazelnut. "Why can't we identify the culprit?"

"Culprit? The man we imagined was following us last night, or the author of scare tactics at home?" It was then that Aggie described her fears in Wales and England. "I'm sure I spotted the same man following us in both countries, but not in Paris. Which is why I dashed from place to place. To lose him."

"You could have told me sooner," Lisa said, on a pout.

"Sorry."

"What if it's the same person?" Lisa glanced furtively around the restaurant, as if the offender might be lurking behind a potted palm. "This guy that both of us spotted here and the one in the British Isles?"

"So far from home? Unbelievable."

"Forget that, then." Lisa said lightly. So what if Aggie discarded Lisa's idea as if they were dirty bath water. The double cousins often brainstormed this way, no matter the issue. Utter aloud an idea and it no longer belonged to you. It went into the common pool like a rock tossed into a pond. You hoped the circles generating outward would produce pure bubbles of wisdom before they dissolved on the shore.

"I think you had a good plan last night," said Aggie. "We should review our notes, chart the kin on paper . . . ."

"I thought we did that, already. Isn't Appendix A the family chart?"

Aggie disagreed: "Not really. Appendix A just lists who begat whom and when, who married and divorced whom and where."

"You're proposing that we handwrite an actual chart. I know," Lisa said. "We could use butcher paper or poster boards, tack them around the room . . . ."

Aggie brightened, getting excited, agreeing this time. "Just like police detectives trying to catch a serial killer. Besides charting kin on posters, we could make notes on . . . ."

"Three-by-five-inch cards," they completed the sentence in unison, laughing at how their minds worked, often like two halves of the same apple.

"If we were two or three decades younger, like Joan; or even Nicole and Beth," said Aggie, "we'd be creating our charts and notes on the computer."

"We can still convert, Agatha. But first, let's use paper and cards."

While the waiter refilled their coffee cups, they spoke innocuously of Wyoming versus Louisiana weather. They seldom used an umbrella in the high-plains country.

"Sounds like we're not going to do much reviewing until we get home," Lisa said after the waiter left.

"We can buy the cards and pens, and brainstorm. Record notes as they occur and save them to sort and label later."

Each paid her own bill, using plastic. Agatha knew she was spending too much money, but Lisa would have questioned her cousin if Aggie had suggested economizing. She didn't want Lisa to worry at any change of habits or what such abrupt modifications would imply.

Her relatives seemed to think that Randy had left her as affluent as the Morriseys had always appeared to be. Aggie wasn't. There was a half-million dollar insurance policy on Randy's life, so at least she had that, and the insurance company had paid off without argument, thank God. Agatha had immediately invested it, but otherwise she hadn't touched a dime. It might not be hers to spend. What if she weren't entitled? What if Randy had committed suicide? She'd been living on money in her private savings account, but that fund was nearly depleted.

Agatha shuddered. Absurd. Randy had no reason to kill himself. She was imagining things again. Her grief was making her crazy.

#######

This time neither woman noticed anybody staring at them. Which was only because the stalker was extremely careful. In Wyoming, the man paying the stalker insisted that if he was going to take the job, he had to get on it immediately. Not next month or whenever Mrs. Morissey returned home. Now!

Okay. Charge the bugger a bundle. That's what the stalker concluded.

#######

They were walking to Canal Street, where they could catch the Charles Avenue streetcar. Their afternoon sightseeing plans would take them through the Garden District. En route, they would pass the campuses of Tulane and Loyola Universities, heading for some walking exercise in Audubon Park.

On the busy sidewalk, Aggie felt someone pressing against her. She thought nothing of it, the streets were as crowded as if they were in Manhattan. Just as they were about to cross at the intersection, where they stopped for a huge heavily loaded semi-trailer truck to lumber by, she felt a push, a hard shove. She felt herself falling forward, directly into the path of the vehicle.

Suddenly her weak ankle gave way, so instead of tumbling beneath the truck's wheels, she crumpled into a heap on the curbstone. Aggie shook all over. She wasn't quick-thinking enough to immediately try to identify her assailant.

By the time she did, he (or she?) had vanished into the crowd.

Lisa bent over her cousin. "Oh, Agatha, dear, what happened?"

"This very unsteady ankle of mine. I think I've sprained it."

"Oh dear, dear heart. We must get you to a hospital."

"Don't be silly. Just get a cab so we can go home."

They called everywhere home—any hotel, motel, or house where kinfolk might have invited them. "Lay their hats down ten minutes," Peter Schwartzkopf said, "And they'll turn it into a home with no more than the contents of their handbags. They're like little birds. They make nests."

Lisa's insistence prevailed. Whipping out her cell phone, she punched the single button to alert an emergency dispatcher, and an ambulance pulled up shortly.

Lisa crawled into the back of the ambulance with Aggie, and soon the vehicle wailed its way down the street, weaving to pass clumps of tourists, shoppers, and local residents. "Safe, at last," said Lisa.

"Speak for yourself. I'm hurting, here."

"Well, yes, of course. But they'll fix you up pronto in the ER and then we'll be on our way."

It wasn't that fast nor half as easy. Between a shot of pain killer and pills to take thereafter, Agatha was in and out of semi-consciousness and only half lucid. She agreed to Lisa's suggestion of calling a taxi and returning to their hotel from the hospital under their own steam, but not until the ER doctor on duty had reluctantly agreed to release her. Aggie's ankle was swathed in a sports bandage.

"Thank God it's not broken," said Lisa, no doubt straining to comfort.

"A sprain is nothing to sneeze at," said Aggie, quoting her nurse.

At last they were safe inside the Monteleone Hotel and the security of their suite. "Whew, we made it," Lisa said, collapsing on the deep sofa.

Agatha made no reply. Pulling up the comforter without even bothering to try getting out of her clothes, she was already sinking into the black abyss of pain and drugs. Her last thought was that their stalker was real, and he had connected.

CHAPTER 18

Aggie was putting this entire expensive trip on credit cards. To pay the bill, she knew she'd have to sell something, like the beautiful mink coat Randy had bought for her last year. What was he thinking about, when there was no promise he could pay for it on his pension? Aggie was stymied. Where had all her money gone? The investments she had inherited from Grandma Rose, and that Agatha had assumed Randy was managing effectively. Had he speculated on a bundle of risky stocks? Withdrawn huge funds by forging her signature to buy real estate? Surely he had never gambled away her funds on a Ponzi scheme, or, heaven forbid, in casinos. He'd had ample opportunities, of course—Monte Carlo, Paris, Reno, Atlantic City.

Never mind, she'd deal with all these money issues later. Perhaps she would try to sell a painting, or the Etruscan vase Randy had liked so much.

To make their vacation as special as Lisa expected it to be, Aggie reminded herself to try to relax and stop worrying about so many things. Like the big beefy man who could be lurking anywhere, down in the lobby or, even now, awaiting their arrival on the steamship. Yes, she and Lisa had carefully studied him at the odd moments they agreed he was no doubt stalking them. And yes, he was somewhat bulky, if not outright obese. But then, wasn't everybody? Three out of four, or four out of five Americans? Some horrible figure like that.

"Oh, Agatha, I can't wait," Lisa said, while re-binding her cousin's ankle in preparation for departure. "I'm so happy you agreed to our booking the very best suite on the Mississippi Queen."

"No other choice," Aggie said dryly. "Not at such short notice."

They had opted out of brunch at Brennan's, given Agatha's condition. After spending an entire day resting in their suite, they were headed now for their riverboat adventure. Room service was adequate, and with the help of pain killers, Aggie hadn't even thought of what they now referred to as her stalker. No doubt safe indoors, but of course this wasn't the type of trip they'd planned. How could they get into the proper mood for their "live" research project, if they didn't get a move on? Get up and get out there. Get with it.

Lisa read from the colorful travel brochure describing their luxurious riverboat: "'Four sumptuous meals every day.' Can you imagine?"

"When we get home we'll have to get back into our AquaRobics class, and walk five miles a day. No, wait, not on this ankle."

"Ride our bikes," Lisa revised. "I know, I know, even if we gain three or four pounds, it'll be worth it, won't it?"

No sign of the brawny man, although Aggie looked every which way from her wheelchair as they passed through the lobby and out to the limo Lisa had ordered. Now that they had left their suite, she again felt vulnerable. Express checkout let them bypass the front desk, where the rental people would retrieve her chair. Whisked along through traffic and out to the boat dock, Aggie used her compact mirror to watch the cars following and passing them. Lisa didn't notice or, if she had, was probably pleased that for once her cousin was paying attention to repairing her makeup. Lisa was nothing less than perfection personified when it came to personal appearance.

Their triple-A cabin on the promenade deck was a veranda suite. Private bath with a private veranda overlooking the river. There were four decks below them and one above, the latter a sun deck. Down one floor was the observation deck with its grand saloon, library, gallery, gift shop, dining room and the upper paddlewheel lounge.

Agatha was prepared to take the elevator down there for meals. Let Lisa explore the rest of the boat by herself. If the evil man was aboard, he surely wouldn't attack her. Aggie didn't realize it but subconsciously she was putting two and two together—at home the threats came to Aggie only, not to Agatha **plus** Lisa. In one's wildest imaginings, there couldn't be two men after Randy's widow. Had to be all of a piece. Which could only mean one thing—the man sending her threats in Wyoming and the man stalking them in New Orleans was the same guy, and therefore he had followed her all this way.

Their suite contained comfy twin beds, ample drawer and closet space, the sofa and armchairs, occasional tables and lamps, also a lovely bathroom. The decor was superb, blue and orange print on print, with drapes, sheers, and wall-to-wall carpet. One deck below the pilot house, their picture windows gave them a steamboat captain's view of southern America. They would pass lovely old antebellum mansions, towns, and villages that had seen Civil War battles.

She suggested that Lisa explore the rest of the boat by herself. Aggie was determined to put aside her fears, to concentrate on the river life—all the boats and barges coming and going, along with the fishing folk. "Let's try to imagine Ronald, our ancestor," she said. "I want to see things through his eyes."

"You're the one with the imagination, dear. I see only what's here."

Aggie shooed Lisa away to settle herself on the sofa. Unlike their journal, Ronald's sojourn passage had preceded the war between the states. As if to better imagine what their riverboat captain had seen, Aggie squinted her eyes into slits while gazing out the window.

What did Rose DMaurier's son Ronald see, what did he stew about? Were there river pirates in those days? Thugs or con men aboard the boat? Did some passengers sometimes fall overboard, if so, did they get safely rescued? Aggie imagined skimpily dressed showgirls and gamblers, card games, shootouts and saloon brawls. Perhaps this vision was warped, came from too much television. But what was his young daughter, Rose, doing all this time?

After gulping another couple of pain pills, Agatha let herself fall asleep.

Bustling into the cabin later, her arms laden with packages, Lisa bubbled over with news about the boat. "Met some nice people, Aggie. We're booked at the same dinner table with them. Arise, dear, I've got another wheelchair ready for you down on the observation deck. You haven't even opened your book."

Aggie set aside the library book she'd brought—*The Vertical Smile*, by one of her favorite authors, Richard Condon, now dead. "I kept falling asleep."

The ladies chose two beautiful gowns from Lisa's closet to wear at dinner. Bathed, coiffed, they set out for a lovely evening.

# # # # # # #

From the Monteleone Hotel lobby, the broad-shouldered burly man with the bushy eyebrows telephoned Cheyenne to contact the guy paying the bill. "Look, guy, there's a problem."

"So, fix it."

"Not that easy. I missed her the first time. I shoved her hard, she was supposed to land in the path of an on-coming truck. Instead, she fell, but not in front of the dadgummed truck. Sprained an ankle, perhaps. Now they've booked passage on a riverboat, moving along upriver."

"Try again. Get on the same boat. Take care of her there, like maybe shove her overboard."

"Think so? She's not on an ocean cruise. Just a river."

"So, it's the Mississippi, a broad river with swift current."

"I'll try."

"Do better than that. I'm paying you enough."

The hired hit man got more instructions. He was directed to avoid using his cell phone, and to forget land lines coming in at the paymaster's work or home place as well. "Call from a public phone, preferably a booth out in the open where nobody can overhear you. Give me the number and I'll return your call."

Jeez, sounded like this was an international terrorist operation, not a simple target of some little bitty middle-aged old biddy.

CHAPTER 19

Nicole's heart beat wildly, like she imagined she would feel if cornered by a big brown bear. She couldn't decide whether she was excited or frightened. Maybe both. How did she know whether she could still learn, remember, and be able to pass the tough paper and performance exams?

She had enrolled in a few university classes once when she'd left Billy—and temporarily left her senses, capitulating to her mom's demands. But she didn't stick it out long enough to even sit for mid-term exams before Bill convinced her to come back to him. Otherwise she hadn't been to school since skipping out of her senior year to elope with Bill Taylor, a dropout already determined to become a professional rodeo cowboy. Poor guy, he never did make it big.

At the MCI Airport—M, for Missouri—Nicole joined a group awaiting a shuttle to travel the twenty-nine miles north to St. Joseph, where she would attend the century-old Missouri Auction School. She would spend the next ten days living in a dormitory. From reading the registration literature, and listening to the tapes the school forwarded to her ahead of time, she knew that over twenty certified instructors would teach them how to chant, sell, and run their own auction firms. She remembered much of this spiel from her first experience.

The first time through the course Nicole had supposed she knew a lot already from shadowing her dad and granddad around their livestock auction market. Perched atop a wood rail fence, like a magpie quietly choosing some cow's back on which to nibble, Nicole had been practicing chants like an auctioneer since she was "knee-high to a grasshopper," as Granddad Jacquot liked to say. So she wasn't as afraid of the afternoon small-group performance sessions as a complete novice might be. Still, she recalled how hard, how demanding they were. You couldn't let down your guard one minute. So much to remember.

So she already understood that there was a lot more to it than one might think. Some auctioneers were generalists, like their medical doctor in general family practice. Some auctioneers were specialists, like professors and other doctors and lawyers. Auctioneers offered for sale by auction everything from antiques, art, autos, and collectibles, to household goods, precious jewels, livestock, machinery, real estate, business liquidations, and more. Some people worked freelance, getting a mere few jobs per year, rather like a hobby. Others ran big businesses, employing lots of people to do lots of things, from the physical work of managing inventory, whether cows and goats or cars and trucks, to the office jobs of operating computers, handling money, and doing the accounting.

Her dad proposed that she join the Jacquots as the third-generation member, become an eventual partner. Nicole perceived a problem with that. Their sale barn was off in Douglas, a good one-hundred-fifty miles from Cheyenne, and about the same distance from Laramie if she took the cut-off over the mountains. That was too far away from Steve Norman!

Or, as her dad suggested over breakfast, she could start a business. As her own boss, she could generalize, advertising and hopping all over Wyoming. Branch out elsewhere, too. Sell anything anybody typically sold at auction.

Like her gam and Lisa, Nicole slept on the plane between Laramie and the Denver International Airport, and also between DIA and the Kansas City, Missouri's International Airport. Even in her restless dreams, Nicole held Steve close. She could see Steve and Stevie and herself together for years to come. On the Norman ranch, in Cheyenne, with family and friends, and during their very own intimate time together, just the two of them. She loved his home, his ranch, his cattle and horses. Question: did she love him enough for a lifetime? She had already made one great big whopper of a mistake in the marriage department. Could she trust herself to make a smart decision the second time around?

On his ranch over the weekend, with Stevie asleep in Norman's guest room, and the cook, Paul, sitting up to watch the little boy, she had donned sheepskin-lined denim jacket, gloves, and her cowboy hat to go search for Steve and his pregnant cow.

"Better take my pickup," Paul had said, handing Nicole the keys. "It's a fur piece over to the big barn and corral, where they've likely taken her."

A full moon and the bright photo-voltaic yard lights helped light her way along the one-lane dirt road that led from the big house to the working end of the home place. By the time Nicole arrived, the calf was born. With a breech birth, Steve had donned long rubber gloves to assist the cow with birthing the calf. Cute little thing, still damp, wobbling around on shaky legs. Mama cow was already bonding with her babe, anxious to be shed of humans so she could get busy with her mothering.

An arm thrown comfortably around her, Steve drew Nicole against the inviting warmth of his body. He admitted he couldn't believe she had come to see what was happening. Never once had his first wife left the house to join him, to discover what his work was all about. Steve came right out and confessed he was imagining them together for years to come. Nickee tingled all over. Imagine, a man being that up-front with his feelings. When she asked him what visions he was seeing, Norman stared off into the star-studded night. He said he saw Nickee at his side, the two of them ranching, loving, parenting Stevie and his own two children, Cindy and Sissy. In his pickup they would drive all three kids over to Tie Siding—population, a whole seven humans—where the Boulder Ridge Road met Highway 287, to catch the school bus into Laramie. Later in the afternoons he and Nicole would repeat the trip to get the kids.

"Sounds like a lot of trouble," she said. She couldn't help grinning.

"Fun, though, just the two of us, until all three kids hop off the bus."

Nicole noticed how Steve conveniently forgot that Cindy and Sissy did not live with him year round. They might someday, though, he said, if Norma Norman grew tired of the parenting burden.

"She used to complain bitterly about how much time and trouble motherhood was, how it took away from her own "real" life."

"How awful."

At the Laramie Airport, Nickee noticed that Steve almost cried when she and Stevie gathered up their things, ready for departure. Nickee on the plane, Stevie with Beth and husband Brad Gifford and the BBs—Brianna and Brittany. Again she pondered how he would adjust to her flying off here and there, if and when they got around to committing themselves to being a real family.

But maybe he'd be more sure of her by then. First things first: he had to win her hand, and she had to win his. On the plane she mused over his plan to open a store featuring saddles and gear, western clothing and accessories in either Cheyenne or Laramie, perhaps both.

Nicole didn't know it, of course, but while she flew east to Missouri, Steve was driving back to the ranch in his pickup, his head awhirl with plans and notions. Like, would Nickee, if she agreed to be his wife, prefer a town store and a town home over ranch living, or just the reverse? Meantime, what would happen as a result of her auctioneer training? Strange goal for a woman. Oops, was he being protective and chivalrous or male chauvinist?

Equally important, to his dream of making a family with Nicole, would Norma Norman agree to relinquish custody of his little girls? Probably not. But he could petition the court for double time, maybe all of every summer, and every holiday as well. Norma merely wanted to punish him, he felt certain, by insisting she should keep them with her most of the time. She didn't care worth a twit, not a snap of her fingers for the welfare of Cindy and Sissy, nor for the concept of Motherhood. As usual, she enjoyed digging in her heels and making life miserable for him. All because she'd wanted a Boston lawyer for a husband, not a Wyoming rancher. He'd put together the puzzle of what made Norma tick piece by piece, watching, listening, trying to figure her out and whether he could respond and still keep his own soul intact. You didn't just throw yourself away, not completely, in order to keep a mate happy. At least he didn't believe so.

# # # # # # #

When Nasty Two's rumors got around to him by Friday night, through the local pipeline consisting of a half-dozen second and third cousins, the guy stomped around his basement computer room. What to do now. No Agatha in town to get his phone, fax, and letter threats. She'd escaped!

There was no time to waste. The rumors he'd heard, and there was no reason to disbelieve them, reported the near completion of a half-dozen appendices to the family history.

So what if she hadn't yet written any actual chapters? When Aggie stopped running around and sat down in quiet contemplation to analyze her notes, he'd be in big trouble. The pieces were right there, awaiting her ability to put the puzzle together. If she died or was otherwise incapacitated, some other family member could retrieve her files and resume this massive project.

He had to get Aggie out of the picture, put somebody on her trail, and be snappy about it. Then he had to destroy all her data. Obviously, it would do no good to set her house on fire, burn the place and all her records to the ground. No doubt the woman was smart enough to have used a flash drive or memory stick to back up her files and store them somewhere safe. However, he had never imagined Agatha's cousin, Lisa, as the recipient of the stored files. Although a bright enough butterfly on the cork board of social hostessing, she was a big cipher in office management. Which was why he had never included Peter's wife in the equation.

Get rid of Agatha, destroy her records permanently. That was the plan.

CHAPTER 20

Nicole survived the first day of classes. She met her roommates and the other women in the program and the dozen or so of mixed gender in her small group. She'd taken her meals in the cafeteria, and was on her way to party when her cell phone vibrated against her hip in the pocket of her blue jeans. At home or away, she wore her standard western attire. The mid-west auction school was hardly the venue for her bright orange shirtwaist dress, nor her black jersey dress designed for playing dressup. Besides, lots of people dressed like she did.

"Hi, Nickee," Steve said in her ear, his voice deep and sexy. She thought she might crumple up and fall in a heap from heart palpitations. Absolutely astounding how just hearing him speak those two simple little words could turn her into a bowl of mush.

"I was just thinking of you," she said. Nickee couldn't help smiling, her lips splitting nearly from ear to ear. "Where are you and what are you doing?"

"Thinking about you, of course. Got some things to take care of and then I thought I'd fly back to Boston. See my girls while you're gone. Also, I'll go to D.C. to visit with Dominic and Julia . . . ."

"The President? Wow."

He chuckled. "Yeah, we're old friends."

Nicole couldn't help making comparisons: her former life in the Taylors' tiny trailer on the dusty trail with third-rate rodeo cowboy Billy, and now dating a man who was friend to the U.S. President? Some change! Of course her gam and the President were also on speaking terms. But that was somehow quite different. Gam was older.

"I'm taking the Davidsons a present—a bronze statue of the Wyoming cowboy on a bronc." Then Steve asked about the auction school and how she was doing, and got an earful of replies. "Made any new friends, yet?" he asked then.

"Sure. There are one-hundred-sixty-seven men enrolled and just thirteen women. Pretty good odds," she replied, teasing him. "A bunch of us are getting ready to go down to K.C. to party."

Steve Norman felt himself wanting to chide her, suggest she get some sleep. What he really feared was an alienation of affections. She was so beautiful, so friendly, any guy would want to go after her. They'd had so little time together, he wasn't sure she felt like they were "a couple," "an item," like he did.

Steve listened attentively as she chattered about the instructors, the classes, and her fellow students. He couldn't help comparing her to Norma Norman, but then ordered himself to quit it. There was no comparison at all, that would be like juggling—not apples and oranges, more like lemons and strawberries, the sour with the sweet. Nickee consistently came out way ahead in the Dear Love department. He hoped with all his heart it would ever be true.

"In our afternoon session," she continued with her little story, "there's this young skinny guy from down South. He introduced himself as: 'Ah'm LE-roy. Ah'm a raid-neck from Alabama.' Of course it took him ages to get that out.

"Oh, Steve, the instructors are so good—all professional auctioneers, some own their companies, a couple are lawyers, several are part-time college instructors, one's from Christies. They lecture about an hour, each, and if they don't perform for us right off, the whole student body starts calling out at the end—'demonstrate, demonstrate!' So this one lean lanky guy with string tie, boots, and cowboy hat auctions for us to beat the band, hopping all over the stage, pretending he's getting bids from the audience. Says he's been in the business twenty years, and every single day, seven days a week, all those years, he's practiced. Warms up with the chants, from two to four hours per day. I don't know if I could ever be that diligent or expect to get that good."

"Sure, you will," Steve said, when he could finally get a word into the slot machine of her rattle, clatter conversation. When she resumed, after his reassurances that he'd help her practice—prompt, play auction bidder, whatever she needed—he hit the jackpot.

She whispered, "I love you, Steven J. Norman."

Before he could reply in kind, which would sound pretty lame now, she changed the subject. "Hey, what's the 'J' stand for?"

He laughed. "Nothing exceptional. John, just plain John."

"Nothing is plain about you, Big Bwana."

She was off again, back to her auction school. "This is probably the only night we can go out and have fun. They expect us to practice three to four hours a night. Beginning Wednesday we'll also be attending several auctions in the area, all kinds: estate sales, vehicles, livestock, equipment, et cetera. By next week we'll intern, actually do the selling ourselves, with live auction bidders. Like we're real auctioneers. Oh, Steve, it's so exciting. I'm already starting to feel like a professional."

Steve wanted to say he would stop over in Missouri en route from Boston and D.C. to Wyoming, but bit his tongue and kept still. This was her time, her scene. Nicole might not welcome him into this new world she'd discovered. Too soon for him to intrude. Leave her to get acquainted with herself in this new role.

By the end of her training, when she'd passed all the tests—he saw no reason why a smart gal like Nicole wouldn't—she might be glad to see him. To resume their relationship.

"Talk to you later," he said. This time he added, albeit a bit hesitantly, "I love you, too, little darlin'."

Too late. She'd already closed the connection.

CHAPTER 21

Harold the Lover knocked on the door of Dollie's trailer. Staring at his reflection in the window of the door, he straightened his tie, patted his hair, and smoothed his mustache. He figured Dollie would be eager to see him again.

When she at last opened the door, it was not the sweet welcome Harry expected. She was huffy.

"Took you long enough to come by again. What's up?"

Offended, he puffed out his chest and pushed her aside to walk into the dim interior. He frowned at spotting the cats, kicked ginger-striped Frigid out of the way, and got a screech of angry protest. Had Harold attacked Rigid, the big black male cat would likely have hissed, leaped on him, and given the animal hater a good scratching. Harry had learned his lesson early on, now he knew better than to take out his futile frustrations in that direction.

Without a word Harold walked through the mobile home, smirking at how clever he'd been in getting it. Manipulating assets in an old blind lady's account was a snap. So far, so good. Looked like he'd gotten away with the swindle. To be safe, he'd put the title in Dollie's name, but nevertheless it was his, not hers.

He made a fast survey of every room. "Looks like you're keeping the place neat."

"What'd you expect, Harry? I'm no tramp."

"Don't call me Harry. No tramp, eh? Prove it."

"What do you mean?" Dollie cowered against the wall in the hall as he swept past her to take the only good chair in the living room, a recliner he said he was buying for himself. He expected her to reserve it for him without question.

"Come sit down," he said, patting his knee. "Here, where you belong."

She told herself she was too stupid for words, a sucker for a kind word and the promise of a little loving. Did Harold the Important mean it? Was he going to let her back into his life if she did what he commanded her to do? Not bloody likely. Nevertheless, she succumbed to her body's demands and sank onto his lap.

CHAPTER 22

The day following Nicole's departure, Steve mounted his palomino to search for a lost calf, the one he'd helped deliver Saturday night. A new mother cow often hides her newborn calf, away from the herd, out of humans' way. What that did, Norman figured, was to complete the bonding process and somehow, through "cow communication," alert her youngun to the rules of the land, of survival and obedience.

The trouble was, mama had to eat. After hiding the calf, usually in some remote spot, she would depart. She expected the tiny newborn to stay put, come hell or high wind, while she went off to graze. Sometimes she'd forget all about her new baby. Like human mothers, not all mama cows have the maternal instinct. If she refused to nurse her (or him), rejected the calf totally, the poor orphan was likely to die. Unless another cow adopted him (or her).

That was the lawyer in Norman the Rancher: legal talk, specificity.

With several thousand head grazing on his spread, there were a lot of mother-calf combinations to track. However, most of his cows were bred in spring and summer to ensure that calving took place in late winter-early spring. Outsiders sometimes suggested that calving ought to be timed for late spring-early summer. No, not on the high plains, Steve told them. It was okay to drop a calf in the snow, they could handle the cold. Give birth when the days bring a mixture of snow-thaw-rain-freeze, and the poor little critters are in for it. "Their hides get wet and freeze. They're at risk of pneumonia and death."

As Joe Joplin, ranch foreman, put it, this mama was an ornery cow. She had somehow found herself a boyfriend at the wrong time of year, three consecutive years this same cow had done the same thing. Drop a calf in autumn and it could hardly gain sufficient growth before the hard winter hit.

Steve felt like the Good Shepherd, worried about this single lost calf when ninety-nine others were okay. This was what he hired cowpokes for, among other things, to room his seventy-thousand acres to check on animals, search for and round up lost ones, and bring back to the home corral the sick and injured ones. Then there were all the other chores—fixing fences, nursing animals, branding and tending, and repairing equipment. And, by the by, tending to themselves.

Not to mention the hours and days they wasted herding and corralling some other rancher's stock. Take a wild steer, it might take up to four or five days to gently and quietly herd the frightened, frenzied critter into the cattle truck and haul it off to the sale barn, where the brand inspector was expected to identify and notify the animal's owner. After that, settling up expenses for feed and gasoline, but not wages for Steve's cowhands, was the business of neighbors, who generally stayed on good terms, helping each other. But not necessarily, and not always. Not if there was a long-playing feud over some darn thing, possibly from way back in the past. Like cranky old Tom, the geezer with the nose and ear hair.

# # # # # # #

This day, but not until he'd located the cow-calf pair, Steve Norman headed to Cheyenne and the capitol to attend a legislative subcommittee meeting of the state legislature.

Passing the secretary of state's office, he ran into Harold Morton, Nasty Three's husband, the *banker extraordinaire*, which was the label Steve glued to the weird fellow. Not because of Harry's reputable or memorable banking services, rather for his extraordinarily peculiar behavior.

"What the . . . . What are you doing here?" Morton demanded. "Come to tattle, haven't you."

"What in the world are you talking about?"

Upon arriving in town from his Albany County ranch, Steve had stopped by the trailer park to check on Nicole's trailer, and also for the purpose of locating and FedExing a pair of worn sneakers, plus her old cowboy boots to her.

"These new ones are killing me," she'd said over the phone.

Outside Nickee's trashy trailer, Harold the Suspicious saw Steve's green pickup going by Dollie's place while she was snuggling in Harry's lap. He figured the hateful rancher-senator was spying on him and would tell his new wife that he was still besotted with Dollie. Which he was, but that was his secret. Both of those damn Norman brothers. Always out to get Harold. He knew it was Steve, couldn't mistake the ownership of that pickup, not with its dumb bumper sticker, "Don't you buy no ugly pickups."

"You can't fool me," said Harold now. "I know what you're trying to do." Huffy Harold pushed rudely by Norman and ran—literally ran—down the corridor.

Steve stood there scratching his head, oblivious to the cause of Harry's turmoil. "That man's a sight," he murmured aloud.

"What, what? You talking to me?"

Startled, Norman looked down at a man a foot or more shorter. "Sorry, Lionel. I was merely talking to myself."

Lionel Falstaff, from the governor's office, scowled and stepped into the elevator, neither accepting nor refusing the Senator's apology. Five-feet-five with red hair, Falstaff had come into his position via political favors—doing enough of the right things for the right people to get him on staff. It was merely a pacifier stuck in his mouth to shut up his shrill and repetitive demands that they owed him.

Lionel had repeatedly told his wife, Lucy, that he'd won a hard-earned election. It was easy to fool her, she neither read nor listened to the news.

At home, Lionel's tall, acne-scarred wife with the crooked teeth ordered him to take her out to eat. "I don't feel like cooking," Lucy said. "I thought when you got this job, we'd be going out a lot. To glamorous parties. All those people currying favors from you should be inviting us everywhere. Instead, we have no social life at all. Just like always. What's the matter with you? What are you doing wrong?"

He felt like telling her to go look in the mirror, That's what's was wrong, his wife's appearance and lack of manners and proper vocabulary. "Lay off, Lucy. Our time will come."

"Never mind that. You're always making promises. I don't know why you don't want to go to the country club," she whined. "You are retired Air Force. So let's at least go to the officers club out at the air base ever once in awhile."

Falstaff figured they might as well. Anything to squelch her whining. New officers coming and going all the time. Maybe they wouldn't run into anybody he knew. Lucy was right. His government position didn't mean squat. People treated him no differently now than when he was a plain civilian.

Falstaff was not popular. Any excuse, any untoward behavior, would be reason enough for the power brokers to get rid of him. The secretary of state could have told him that. Nasty Three thought he surely knew. Like a gnat, Falstaff was worth no more bother than a quick swat in his general direction, then quickly forget him. She was no gossip, anyhow. So why would she have thought to tell the family anything about Lionel Falstaff? Meantime, he didn't appear to be doing much around the capitol, neither helpful nor harmful. People who don't bother to do their jobs and who don't make themselves useful in some way or another either get ignored, and thus passed over, or else kicked out on the street. Lionel was as determined to avoid the latter fate as he was to fall in the lion's den.

Wrong. Or at any rate, Nasty's assessment didn't go far enough. Lionel Falstaff was searching for a cause, some issue or event he could spearhead to rile the populace and get press notice. He had big dreams, more than enough to fill his whole head. Call them daydreams. Not for him the business of merely coasting through his work days, he expected his shenanigans to pay off in rewards, praise and raises, and preferably promotions to a position of importance. He puffed up at the very thought of the power jobs over his head and mostly out of his reach.

Finally a purpose dawned like the sunrise. Though not an original idea, since anything Falstaff thought was no more than a carbon copy of something else. Why not reopen the issue of Preble's Meadow Jumping Mouse, he mused. He bet there were a lot more animal rights people in this state than ranchers any more. Surely he could find them anywhere, people who would stand behind him and against the ranchers. Ranchers like big, tall, handsome, powerful Norman.

Or ranchers like Jason Jacquot, that sale barn auctioneer and rancher up Douglas way. Jacquot had beat a mouse to death and destroyed its habitat. Hadn't got much news notice at the time, but maybe the event wasn't handled right. With Lionel's promotions and protests, the murder of a rodent numbered among the protected species ought to rile some of the youngsters over on the UW campus. Maybe Falstaff himself could help promote a demonstration. Then he'd alert the press. Watch things escalate from there. After all, didn't the whole Egyptian revolution begin with a single Facebook page written by some college kid? Well, a youngster of indeterminate age, at any rate. Surely Falstaff could beat that.

Feeling better about himself and his chances of making a splash in the media, getting noticed, getting in with the In crowd, Lionel easily acquiesced to his wife's surly and shrill demands that he take her to dinner out at Warren Air Force Base. She didn't know anything about the base, so Lionel told her.

When Francis Emroy Warren had arrived in Wyoming following service in the Civil War, he had a mere fifty cents in his pocket. First he clerked in a furniture store. Later, with his Baptist wife, Helen Maria Smith, the couple had organized the Warren Livestock Company, and Warren eventually became one of the largest stock raisers in the entire western territories.

Cheyenne's mayor in 1885, Warren was appointed by President Grover Cleveland as territorial governor, a term he held for two years before getting elected as Wyoming's first state governor, following seven territorial governors. Wyoming received statehood as the nation's forty-fourth state in 1890.

Warren was only in office forty-five days, in 1889-1890, but then he was elected to the U.S Senate, representing Wyoming. He got a fort named for him, though, which became an Army Air Corps base during World War II and then it was renamed Warren Air Force Base. Lionel told Lucy the base history, but she didn't care. He almost liked to torment her, though he called it "teaching her."

Leaving the capitol, Norman thought about visiting another bank to look for financial backing for his store. Steve didn't know why he didn't just wait and let things unfold. See what Nicole wanted to do, if indeed she'd consent to marriage. It should be fun planning the store together.

Conversely, there was something about the idea that made him want to surprise her. If she were bent on this auctioneer nonsense, she'd probably want to operate out of Cheyenne, not off some ranch. If he were to get things going in her absence, he'd better get started. First thing: go find some money to finance operations. Forget about Morton. He was some kinda nut.

Steve also had some fast rounds to make while Nicole was out of town. Dominic Alexander Davidson had called with an alert. The President wanted his special personal advisors to convene at the White House. Another perilous issue with China was erupting. Steve would also present his gift of the newly commissioned bronze bronc statue to Dom and Julia during a private dinner.

Then Steve would hop a shuttle for Boston, visit Cindy and Sissy, his precious little twin daughters. On his way back out to Wyoming, however, he was serious about stopping over in Missouri to see Nickee, the new light of his life.

Wait a minute. Steve stopped suddenly, in the middle of the sidewalk, smack dab in front of the old saloon with the long, long bar, Dollie Domenico's place of business.

Dollie spotted Steve, of course. And nearly drooled. If she couldn't have Harry, why not Steve? Man, that would be terrific.

Oblivious to the commotion Steve had caused to erupt in the flat chest of skinny Dollie, he was busy asking himself the big question. Did he mean it? Was he this serious about Nicole? Marriage, was that what he was thinking?

Yessiree Bob!

A big grin split Steve's face. When he resumed, his step was lighter, quicker, it could have passed for a dance step.

Dollie didn't know that. She wanted to believe that he had noticed her, and this happy stance was the impact she had made upon her new dream man. Dollie Domenico's heart went thump thump thump, nigh on to bursting from her chest.

CHAPTER 23

When Steve Norman went into the old downtown saloon with the long long bar, complete with the antique silver dollars under the scarred glass top, and the saddles for stool covers, he found Dollie, at the moment a pouting bartender.

"What's up, Doll, you having a bad day?"

"You should know. And don't call me Doll."

Steve mused that Dollie sounded like Harold, the Strange, Morton. "Okay, but don't pull that old saying on me."

"What saying?"

"You know the phrase: 'If you don't know, I'm not going to tell you'," he said. "Come on, give. Aren't we still friends? Tell me about it."

He was too cute to resist. "Yeah, sure." Dollie dabbed her eyes with her apron tail. "You really don't remember? You invited me to supper Friday and then when I got to the truckstop, you were already there—with Nicole Taylor! Cowboy Bill's wife."

"Ex-wife," Steve corrected Dollie. "So that's it." He reached across the bar top to pat her hand, which she quickly withdrew.

"Don't you recall?" he said solicitously. "Or didn't you see the wreck?"

"You mean Harry's bank window getting smashed in?"

Dollie bit her lip. Dollie Domenico had been working at the time, a half-block away. How was she supposed to know about it, unless Harold had told her. But Harry kept reminding her that nobody should discover their "continuing relationship," as he called it. He was a married man, he said huffily. Married to a very visible lady, well-known throughout the state. And so was he, now. "Visible," he meant.

Yeah, in a pig's eye. Who cared about Harold Morton? Nobody but her, Dollie figured, for once hitting the bull's eye with her surmise.

Meanwhile, Steve was prattling on about Nicole. It was she who was in the wreck, he said. "I pulled her out, then followed the ambulance to the hospital. Took her to eat afterwards. In all that commotion, I forgot about meeting you. It wasn't a date, anyway, was it? I thought it was just supper between friends."

Humph, Dollie thought, feeling a big pout coming on. So that's all it was s'posed to be? Boo hoo. She couldn't bare it. "So you say," Dollie muttered, trying not to sound all whiney. Harold hated that, so Steve probably did, too. Men! What did they want from a woman, anyhow?

"Please accept my apology." Steve hemmed and muttered a bit before continuing. "How about dinner tonight? I'm leaving tomorrow for the East—Boston, to see my girls, among other stopovers."

He didn't name drop or add that he would dine at the White House. If he had, she might have been too surprised to believe him, or too intimidated by his connections to pursue her attraction for the big handsome rancher.

"I'll meet you at your house and we'll go to the Hitching Post. That okay?"

Choking back her tears, while brightening, Dollie nodded. She told him where she lived and how to get there.

"I know that trailer park. Nicole lives there too."

Just when she was feeling better, he had to go and spoil it all again. If he knew where Miss Fancy Pants lived, it must be because he'd been there.

Steve pulled his cell phone out of his pocket, stepped aside, and called his girls and their mother. Norma didn't let him talk to Cindy or Sissy, so he gave his ex-wife his estimated time of arrival. Then he heard the girls in the background and insisted on his rights. He had part-time custody, he cared.

Back at the bar, Steve told Dollie Domenico that his twins were excited that their daddy was coming. From the gleam in his eyes and the big grin, the little girls weren't the only ones eager about his trip. He acted like a little boy awaiting Santa Claus. Dollie loved watching him play daddy.

Next, Steve described Nicole's puzzlement over the strange light in her eyes that had caused her to crash into the bank. "It seemed to be following her, she said. Isn't that peculiar? You ever see anything like that around this neighborhood?"

Dollie blanched, gasped, and, making excuses that she had to visit the ladies room, ran away from the man she would most like to find in her bed. She knew exactly what Steve was talking about. Damn that Harry. Obviously he'd been at it again, playing his childish game with the laser. Yes, he'd told her, laughing his head off. Harry was a nut. But he was still hers, even if he did claim marriage to the secretary of state.

In Dollie's absence, Steve shrugged, feeling a sense of déjà vu. First, Harry Morton, now Dollie Domenico. Were they starting to sound alike or was it his imagination? First Dollie pouts, then she blossoms like a spring tulip, then she nearly faints and dashes away. And Harry? Last time Steve had seen the banker was in the capitol, where Morton had accused Steve of spying and tattling. About what? Who cared? Some peculiar people in this town, Steve figured.

He had better things to do than try to figure out the likes of them. Steve had to go after some money for his store before leaving town.

# # # # # # #

Lionel Falstaff cornered the secretary of state in her office to get the latest economic and corporation info, he told her. Falstaff could have accessed the Internet or eavesdropped on other government officials at the Cloud Nine lounge or airport cafe. What he was really after were juicy news-breaking tidbits so he could scoop the political cronies who regularly ignored him, or disdained him as a know-nothing.

If the Falstaffs were ever to make it socially in this town, never mind politically in the state, like winning the next election, he had to get in good with the good old boys who ran things. Falstaff figured that by campaigning for some of those snotty rich fellas—and a few gals—around the state, on his own time and with his own money, they'd be bound to welcome him into their inner circle. Amend that: gang, that's what they were, the hardcore know-it-alls who were in the know about every little thing, big things too it seemed, even before the really big important things even happened. Lionel Falstaff had campaigned especially hard on Nasty's behalf. He'd stuck to her like sticky tape, engendering Lucy's ire at his long absences, all designed to win Nasty's confidence. And most important of all, her allegiance. So that when he was ready to make his move, she'd be right there on the front row rooting for him. And persuading her big powerful brothers to come up with a big hefty pot of campaign dough.

Harold Morton was busily doing the same thing, only Harry had somehow managed to go a lot further: he'd up and married the wheeler-dealer, the secretary of state herself! Falstaff was still working on Nasty Three, though. If he couldn't get into her bed—he wasn't the least bit interested in that angle—he still oughta be able to find a niche for himself within her inner circle. Somewhere, doing something important.

What Lionel wouldn't give to be a part of it all. Lucy was right. His new position in the capitol should have opened the doors to acceptance. How did they do it? All those power brokers that ran the state, never mind the nation. How had Nasty Three done it? Of course she was born to the Purple, that helped.

Did it really make that much difference what one's spouse was like? Lucy certainly wasn't socially acceptable. Yet look at Nasty's husband. Morton the Mutt was no jewel, for all his tailor-made clothes.

Why had Nasturtium Three married such a misfit?

Ahah, Lionel had an idea. If he could dig around, uncover some dirt on the secretary of state, like overturning a rock to let the bugs out, he might find the solution to the state-wide mystery of their marriage. What if Morton was holding something over Nasty's head? Maybe he'd blackmailed her into the marriage? When (not if) Falstaff knew that, he'd have the key to some blackmail of his own.

What Lionel really wanted, beyond acceptance and invitations to parties so Lucy would stop her yammering, was authority. Power.

#######

Out in his rough-hewn log cabin on the ranch that snuggled against Sheep Mountain west of Laramie, Tom Rotter reached up to the shelf and took down his family's ancient black leather Bible. He sat in his mother's old rocking chair, pulled a warm afghan, also his mother's, over knobby knees, and settled back to sip coffee and contemplate.

Eyes weak these days, Tom reached for the magnifying glass. Even his reading glasses weren't much use and he let them slide down on his nose. The Bible on his lap, he didn't search for comforting or enlightening scriptures. Rotter didn't need either.

In the old days people used the family Bible to document important events: marriages, births, deaths; but few if any divorces, though. A lot of folk died young: accidents often took the men, while sickness, childbirth and disease did in their women and children.

The men on the Rotter side had each gone through several wives that way. The women in his mother's line had lost their husbands from trees falling on them, since they were timberers. Or else they'd bought the farm in gunfights and barroom brawls.

Unable to see clearly any more, even wth aids, Rotter set the Bible on his knees. He flipped open the book to the many pages where he'd made of the Bible a personal diary. He had long since committed the best stuff to memory. Tom stroked the words lovingly, as though they could love him back.

What would happen to the Bible when he was gone? Tom suspected he was not long for this world. Never once had he seen a doctor or been inside a hospital. Too late to start now. Never seen a lawyer, neither, nor made a Will. He had two heirs, maybe three, but he wasn't sure that anybody save one should inherit.

Better make a Will, to be sure. Leave it in the Bible.

#######

Harold the Restless worried about how long his marriage to Nasturtium Three would last. She didn't appreciate him like she should have. After all he'd done for her on the campaign trail, she paid no attention to his needs. Of course she didn't know, so she couldn't appreciate that he'd trashed his one true love like old rubbish for Nasty.

The secretary of state never asked his advice, not for the little nor the big things, neither for the personal nor the political. She said nothing when people ridiculed and humiliated him right in her presence. Why didn't she brag on him?

She didn't use his name, insisted she was a Vicente. Okay, but she'd been Mrs. Fleetfoot before she married Morton. What was wrong with his name? She wanted no obvious association with him, was that it?

Harry had to do something about the situation before he went batty. She made him crazy. Why had he married her anyway?

Oh, yes. Prodding his unreliable memory, like poking a failing fire, Morton remembered. He wanted recognition, acceptance among Wyoming's top social and economic class. And, he wanted money.

Nasty kept the purse, pulled tight the strings. What a cheapskate. She wouldn't even pay his golf fees or buy his clothes. Ms. Vicente owned her house, paid the utilities and insurance policies, kept their cars maintained, bought the groceries. He begged for a new Lincoln and a personal allowance.

"No way," said Nasturtium the Third. "What do you do with your banker's salary, little man?"

Degrading, driving around in last year's Cadillac. Wearing clothes off the rack. Why wouldn't she finance a trip to London, let him get an English tailor, attend operas and concerts, museums and art galleries? At least then he'd have something worthwhile to brag about. Dollie would flip.

At the bank Harry put away his miniature laser. He could no longer risk playing his little game with pedestrians and drivers. Not after Nicole Taylor had broken the bank window, nearly crushing him. Harold the Self-Centered cared not one iota that she'd totaled her car, nearly killing herself.

# # # # # # #

Aggie daydreamed about her granddaughter and the rancher. She wanted so badly for Nickee and Steve to get together. Nicole's marriage to Cowboy Billy was such a sorry tale. Nickee was a good mother, though, albeit she had birthed Babie Stevie at age seventeen. Stevie's sunny disposition and good manners testified to Nickee's diligence at motherhood.

"Now where's your head, Agatha? Back in the past again?"

"No, out home in Wyoming. There are so many people in this family to worry about. I was centered on Nickee and whether she'd make a marriage with Steve. If they ever get around to it. And there's Nasty to fret over, too. Lisa, what was Cousin Nasty Three thinking of to marry that little squirt?" With just that tiny descriptive adjective, she thought longingly of her dead and gone Randy. Agatha suddenly teared up, great droplets spilling over and running down her cheeks. "Now Lisa, don't look like that, all smug-like. You know that Randy was nothing at all like Morton the Mutt. I'm thinking I despise Nasty's new husband."

Lisa frankly admitted then that she'd hoped this trip, with its emphasis on family history, would help fill Agatha's time and heart. Between focusing on the past and fretting over their Wyoming family, there'd surely be less space in her head for grieving. As if to distract Cousin Aggie from falling down the black hole of sorrow, Lisa quickly probed: "What about Nasty Three? Why are you so worried about her?"

"Haven't you noticed, lately, Lisa? Nasty avoids us. She refuses to accept luncheon invitations, doesn't return our calls. Can't even make eye contact when we're with her in person. I think she's made a miserable marriage and has finally realized it and won't admit it. Not even to herself."

"She could divorce Morton, if the marriage has really gone sour. She owns everything, anyway. No assets to divide."

"Oh, Lisa. Surely there's more to marriage than assets."

Lisa appeared thoughtful. "Come to think of it, Wyoming is a community property state, and Nasty's the secretary of state, with a degree in economics. Surely she knew enough to protect herself by making Harry sign a pre-nup."

Appalled that Nasty might have forgotten, Aggie's face crinkled up in horror. "Surely she did."

"Agatha, tell me something. You never used to be such a worry wart. Oh, sure, you worried about your daughter—Joan wandering around the country from coast to coast, getting all those university degrees. And you fretted whenever Nickee was out of your sight—off with her mother or up with the Jacquots in Douglas, and certainly during her five years of following Billy on the rodeo circuit. But otherwise, you seemed pretty happy-go-lucky. When you and Randy were hopping about the globe on his search for oil, did you stew about people back at home?"

"No, of course not. I was too preoccupied with Randy and our life together. His death has left a great vacuum, dear. But I suppose I'll recover, given time. The thing is, will Nasty recover from Harry? Lisa, once a woman is alone after living in tandem, as one of two bookends, you start seeing things differently. You feel vulnerable, unprotected, insecure, and often frightened. Even if I hadn't been threatened, I'm certain I'd feel this way, Lisa. As for Nasty Three, she has Harry, now. But is that the best thing for her? If she does get out of this marriage, will he retaliate? He worries me, Lisa. He may be small, but he's feisty, I think. I worry about Nasty."

"But why worry about Nickee, too?"

"You remember what you and Nasty Two both said. That Steve Norman is probably the most desirable eligible bachelor around. Since Norma Norman left him and the divorce became final, there's bound to be a whole bevy of beautiful women fluttering like butterflies around him. Tantalizing, flirting, getting his attention. He's human, after all. Hard to resist loving glances and personal attention."

"Ah, I get it, why you're stewing. They barely meet, Nickee and Steve—with no thanks to the three of us double cousins, despite our scheming—but it looks like they're a matched set anyway. But instead of sticking around to cement their relationship, Nickee takes off for Missouri, leaving Steve at the mercy of all these twittering, hovering butterflies you imagine are circling."

Aggie grinned. "Put like that, Lisa, you make both scenarios sound silly. Nicole and certainly Nasty Three are grown women. They can surely manage on their own in the absence of their loving grandmother and double cousins." Aggie promised to relax. "And now it's time for us to sink our teeth into the past of our personal and family history."

"You got it, hon."

How little did they know.

CHAPTER 24

Lisa awakened to discover Aggie on the floor. "What are you doing, Agatha?" Rubbing her eyes into wakefulness, Lisa answered her own question by looking. Then she tumbled onto the floor beside her cousin. Still in their pajamas, both women launched their exercise program of leg lifts and sit-ups.

"I ate too much last night," said Aggie. "All those delicious dishes and drinks in the lounge, followed by that midnight snack. I feel all logy."

"Me, too. Wish we could swim," Lisa said, between huffs and puffs. Both ladies were expert swimmers. Swimming was one of their favorite ways of keeping fit, along with tennis and golf at the club, and skiing in the winter.

Aggie imagined she would have to forego some of these sports, if she must soon take a job to supplement her funds. When would she have time for them, or where would she get the money? She might have to drop her club membership. Horrors. That would be like dropping out of school, leaving all your friends. She felt depressed at all the necessary adjustments. Widowhood, humph. She'd rather have lost an arm than her precious sweetheart.

Better to think of something else, before Lisa noticed her cousin was in a funk. "Think we could withstand the Mississippi current if we fell overboard?"

Lisa stopped exercising to sit up and scowl. "What's the matter with you, dear? Are you frightened again?"

Aggie had too many burdens to bear, all alone. So she told her lifelong chum about the New Orleans accident. "No accident, kiddo. I was pushed hard. Deliberately."

"You should have told me," Lisa scolded. "We should have called the police. Sure, I was worried about somebody following us in New Orleans, but I didn't suppose it was serious. Just a man on the make. But Agatha, you're talking murder! Really, dear, we should have gotten the police into this."

"No way. I had no proof. And by the time I righted myself to look around, he was gone, anyhow."

Lisa asked whether Aggie had spotted the harasser on the boat anywhere thus far. "Harasser, hell. We really are talking about attempted murder, here. I just don't understand you, not for one minute."

Aggie said no, she hadn't seen him, and yes, she was definitely looking. "Very diligently, I might add."

After their showers, they looked through Lisa's closet. "Sorry I ruined your vanilla voile dress," Aggie said. "It was ripped beyond repair."

"No problem. Plenty more where that came from."

On the early November cruise they needed warm clothing. They chose wool slacks and vests, Aggie a purple turtleneck sweater, Lisa a pink one. Aggie switched from her red wig to the platinum one. Then they left the suite looking almost like twins: same size and weight, same short-cropped hair—Lisa's blond, Aggie's, silvery. "Let's relax and have fun, that's my advice," said Lisa.

Their cruise was billed as a romantic "Steamboatin' Vacation." They were charmed by the heritage, history, and hospitality. The boat docked periodically. With Lisa pushing Aggie's wheelchair, they could stroll along with their fellow travelers to gawk at and appreciate the opulence that graced some of the Southern plantations they spied through the trees. Besides, their river boat made periodic stops for guest tours. In St. Francisville they saw 1800's homes—including Rosedown Plantation—whose hostesses wore period costumes. Baton Rouge, Natchez, Vicksburg, and Memphis were other ports of call.

"Fur traders, cotton kings, and lumber barons made fortunes," said their guide, who was called a Riverlorian. "It was the days before income taxes, so these wealthy people got to keep their riches, many of whom spent it on building gracious mansions and estates."

"Just think," Lisa whispered. "Our great-great-something Grandfather Deighton was into lumbering. He, too, must have been quite wealthy."

"And great-great-grandfather Jacque trapped and traded furs."

"I can't see what you mean about our reliving the scenes of our ancestors, though. Can you visualize Ronald aboard this boat, or his small daughter, Rose?"

"Perhaps if we walk around the deck with the cold spray in our faces."

"That might help. But I doubt it. I wish they would come more alive for us. But, you know, Agatha, I never was much into pretend games. You'll have to daydream for both of us."

"Maybe when we get to Nauvoo. The preservation of old buildings might spark your imagination."

From their promenade deck, they looked over the balcony railing into the paddlewheel lounge with its sparkling crystal chandelier, watched and listened to the pianist at the grand piano and to the strolling banjo players. Lisa exclaimed over the lovely gowns and jewels worn by the ladies. Aggie admired the graceful staircases, the paintings, and the drapes and furnishings that made of the Mississippi Queen a floating palace.

"Surely this is a far more elegant setting than the river boat our Ronald captained," Lisa said.

"Perhaps not. Europeans, especially the French, have always appreciated beauty and luxury. What they didn't have back then were the appliances and facilities that make our lives both convenient and hygienic."

The next few days they went easy on the food, limiting themselves to salads and fruits in lieu of heavy entrees with rich cream sauces. With no sign of the bulky bad guy, they relaxed a bit, met new friends, saw many new sights, and slept the deep sleep of innocent babes rocked gently on the river. "Like Moses in the bulrushes," Lisa whispered, before falling fast asleep one night.

Aggie's ankle was getting better. By the time they reached Nauvoo she should be able to get along without renting another wheelchair. From Nauvoo on the Mississippi River, the pair planned to travel across Missouri to visit Aggie's granddaughter in St. Joseph.

"I wonder how Nicole's getting along," Agatha fretted.

"Maybe she's met another man," Lisa teased.

"What? Oh dear, what if she does? Imagine her falling for somebody from New York or Mississippi. She'll move away again and we'll seldom see her."

"Stop that, Agatha. I was only joking."

#######

Nicole couldn't believe how hard she had fallen for Steve Norman. Wreck a car, get knocked out, then rescued. Open her eyes to her knight in shining cowboy clothes, and she was hooked.

"Fell for him like a ton of manure," Big Jack had said on Saturday over breakfast, shaking his head and smiling. "Like with Cowboy Billy all over again. When a young heifer gets in heat, there's no keeping her away from the bull."

"Oh daddy, really. 'Manure,' 'heifer in heat.' Can't you think about anything except in livestock terms?"

"It's my life, babe. Could be yours, too."

"We'll see."

Nicole called Big Jack from Missouri to tell him how she was doing as an auction student. "I miss Steve, though, dad. It's going to be a long fortnight."

"My stars, you've only known him a few days."

"How long did you and mom know each other before you married?"

"Touche. You got me there. Three days."

"See?"

"Marriage. You already thinking of tying the knot?"

"Sure. What else? He hasn't asked me yet, but I know he will."

"Confident, aren't you?

"We both are, in each other. In this business called love."

"Speaking of business, I guess this means you won't be moving to Douglas to come into the partnership with your granddad and me."

"Nope, 'fraid not." Nicole shared some auction school experiences before cutting the connection. She concluded she might make a pretty good auctioneer.

CHAPTER 25

Senator Norman escorted Dollie Domenico to Little America—a complex of gasoline station, hotel rooms, swimming pool, restaurant, lounge, and a dozen meeting and conference rooms, including one gracious ballroom. The skinny bartender couldn't believe it, an actual dinner date with Steve Norman to the gorgeous resort hotel. The original owner had planted two-thousand evergreen trees, which matured and graced the rolling hills around the golf course.

Dollie got herself all dolled up and now she wore her hair in a jumble piled-high with floppy locks dribbling down in front of each ear. She wore a tight Kelly-green dress made of Spandex that came with a very short skirt hiking up her rear end and a very low scooped neckline showing plenty of cleavage. A parrot clinging to a cheap chain around her neck matched the small parrots nibbling on her ear lobes. Four-inch, spiked-heel shoes with her dirty toes poking out and calloused heels showing in back completed her ensemble. No hose, darn it, her last pair had laddered, and her toenail polish was chipped. Well, it couldn't be helped. She'd done the best she could.

"Aren't you cold?" Steve asked.

If he'd been truly solicitous, he would have noticed she wore no wrap before they left her pretty little trailer, which she'd rushed around making tidy, which gave her no time to shower after her shift at the saloon. She made do by spraying cologne to cover any odors and now walked around in a halo of scent.

One nice thing he did—Steve drove right up to the front door to let her out before parking his pickup. Which meant there she was, standing all alone, wondering what to do. Dollie twisted a ringlet of floppy hair drooping from the beehive atop her head, and cocked one hip to the side. She wondered whether to sit on one of the big leather couches in the lounge-lobby-waiting room, whatever it was. Better wait, Steve might miss her, leave without looking very seriously.

Men in suits with name tags passed her and leered. She blushed at the messages they conveyed. At the saloon, her own bailiwick, she knew how to handle guys. Here, she wasn't so sure.

Must be some kind of convention going on. She knew from Harry that Little America was a popular watering hole, like when the Legislature was in session. Representatives, senators, lobbyists with all sorts of interests to promote. The Legislature wasn't in session now, though. Must be something else happening.

Looming before Dollie was a smartly suited, scowling man. "You'll have to leave, miss," he said. "We don't allow hookers to prowl our halls."

She blushed more deeply. With her pale skin, Dollie's face looked like a thermometer—blood rushing in, draining away.

Before she could protest, Steve arrived to rescue her. Unaware of her humiliating predicament, he took Dollie's arm. He smiled at the assistant manager, who he greeted by name, and they passed on into the dining room.

She had wondered what in the world they would talk about, but she needn't have stewed. Dollie barely had him to herself. Everybody seemed to know Norman, and he, them. People stopped by their table or waved from across the room. Ranchers, lawyers, prominent citizens, she imagined. Tourists wouldn't know Senator Norman from a fence post.

Dollie spent her time nibbling on dry bread sticks and glancing from beneath her sagging hank of hair at the other couples. The men, like those in the lobby, mostly wore suits, business suits, a few fine western suits. But no jeans, no sweatshirts. The women were more interesting. They wore demure little suits, very plain dresses with little jackets, tiny pearl necklaces or fine gold chains. Nobody, not a single lady, bared her shoulders, showed off her breasts, or wore short skirts. Oh dear, she'd dressed all wrong. When would she ever learn? No wonder her Harry insulted, criticized, ridiculed, and humiliated her.

"Will you look at that?" From the lobby just outside the restaurant, Nasty Two nudged her mama, who had arrived in town without notice from Tahiti, where she had gone to hunt exotic birds and flowers.

"What, who?" the ninety-one-year-old said in a loud voice, for Nasturtium the First, like many in the family, was hearing-impaired.

"Steve Norman with that little snip of a bartender, Dollie Something. Would you look the way she's dressed! Half-dressed, I mean."

"So?"

"I thought, we all thought—meaning, the clan—that he and our Nicole were out to make themselves into an item. Now look at the senator. You can't trust a man two inches, that's what I always say."

"How you young people talk," Nasty One said to her seventy-one-year-old daughter. "'Item.' What's that supposed to mean?"

"Couple, then."

"What? Speak up. I can't hear you."

"Yes, mama," said Nasty Two, tugging on an arm. "Let's get out of here before they see us."

"But I wanted to eat in the dining room here."

"We can go to the hotel downtown. The dining room's great there."

"Right. We should have gone there in the first place."

Nasty Two couldn't wait to get home and call everybody. Boy, would Nicole be mad when she heard.

When the cat's away, the mouse will play.

# # # # # # #

In St. Louis Aggie was getting excited. Her ankle was improving and they were getting closer to Nauvoo and the source of their quest. Like searching all your life for, and finally discovering the mouth of the Nile.

Disembarking from the Mississippi Queen, the dainty duo rented a car. Before leaving the city, they went downtown to lunch near the river in the restored section of old St. Louis, near the golden arch, symbol of the mid-western city. "Lisa, I'm beginning to get a sense of our great-great grandmothers."

"How can you, amidst all this modern stuff of today?"

"Don't you feel it, too? Riverboat Captain Ronald must have laid over here, along with his wee daughter. St. Louis is where he turned over the care of Rose to the d'Gade family. It must have torn his heart out to leave little Rose. I wonder why? Was he ill?"

"He must have kept journals as part of the captain's job, but nothing personal that got passed on. And what of young Rose? How awful to be parted from the only parent she'd ever known. I hope the d'Gades were good to her. I hope they treated her like one of their own."

"Oh, Lisa, I hope so too. From her diaries, though, I wouldn't think so."

"Let's do get on our way. Maybe, like you, I'll be able to imagine her life better once we reach Nauvoo. From great-great-grandmother Essie's journals, that's where the two of them—Essie and Rose—met and became fast friends."

# # # # # # #

Also in St. Louis, a mere block away from the cousins, Burly Boy called the guy in Cheyenne. This time they went through all the rigmarole of public phone-to-home phone to give the man with the bucks the phone number, and then he had to stand out there in a poorly lighted neighborhood lined with tenements and trash blowing down the street in the cold wind, awaiting the call-back.

"What took you so bloody long?" he demanded of the paymaster.

"Calm down. I had to make my excuses to the wife and get outta there to go find a safe phone. And you know what? There aren't hardly no public phones any more. Like hunting for a needle in a haystack."

"Whatever. Like I'm in Belfast and you're in Bosnia and we're plotting to overthrow the Irish government, assassinate Britain's Prime Minister, or go spy on Yugoslavia. Well, it's too bloody cold to go through all these shenanigans every time."

"All right, a'ready. Next time find a warm place. And buy yourself a handful of cell phones. Use one, toss it in the garbage. Meanwhile, I'm ready for your report. Past-ready, in fact. Did you do the dirty deed?"

"Nope."

"What? Wassa matter with you? Why do you think I'm paying you all this money?"

"Haven't seen a nickle yet."

"You will when you've earned it and not a minute sooner. Quit stalling. What's the problem?"

"Got passage on the wrong steamship. I was on the Delta Queen, while they was on the Mississippi Queen."

"What? You blasted imbecile."

"Keep your pants on, I'm headed for Nauvoo."

CHAPTER 26

1842

Rose and Essie greeted each other at the public well, where they went every day to get drinking water. Several women and older children were ahead of them. That was all right, gave them time to visit.

"Did you hear Brother Brigham Young's sermon, yesterday?" Essie asked, as she lifted her long gingham skirt out of the muddy path. They sat on a crude wooden bench near the well, the women's gossip hub.

"Yes. He's quite compelling. In my opinion, however, he's not as good a speaker as the Prophet," sixteen-year-old Rose replied, lifting her skirts to join her new friend on the bench.

"Joseph Smith is so, I don't know—exciting, I guess it is," said Essie.

"'Charismatic,' I think that's the word," Rose replied.

The Nauvoo settler wives sat patiently, like two robins waiting for a worm. The city was growing so rapidly. New converts were arriving every day, some from as far away as the South Sea Islands, others from England. Both distant places were where both their husbands along with a number of other Mormon missionaries had journeyed to preach the Gospel.

"I told Etienne I didn't want him to leave," Rose said. "Guess what he said: 'My good wife, ye must gird up your loins with strength'."

"You know what the French Emperor, Napoleon Bonaparte, said: 'Women have two weapons—cosmetics and tears.' Perhaps you've used tears too often."

Rose countered with another complaint. "Etienne turned a deaf ear to me, dear Essie. He left me to attend another priesthood meeting."

"Or worse, they go on a two-year-long foreign mission, instead of a two-hour prayer and business session." Essie's husband, Darwin Deighton, had left Nauvoo and his tiny wife about the same time as Etienne d'Gade had departed.

Both women were petite, Rose, a smooth-faced, olive-complected brunette, her coloring, she said, having come from her French ancestry. While Essie was a peaches-and-cream blonde, a gift from her Welsh heritage. Rose's Eteinne was tall for the times and so was Essie's Darwin. Both couples, or so the little wives whispered, hoped to produce tall boys and wee lassies.

"What did Etienne's mother say?" Essie asked.

"She, too, quotes from the scriptures. She doesn't like me," bleated Rose. "Not since I married her favorite son. I've heard her complain that I'm not big enough to bear children, or to serve and care for Etienne."

"I'd stay away from your mother-in-law, iffen I were you." Essie was a lusty lass. She missed Darwin in the marriage bed. Wedded to the Mormon missionary in body as well as spirit, neither the young woman nor her husband discussed the physical side of their marriage. "Joined at the hip," Essie called their marital bliss. But only inside her head, to speak aloud would be unseemly. What worried Essie in Darwin's absence was the lust she felt now for some of the brethren left behind, especially their prophet and president, Joseph Smith, and also Brigham Young, who was the head of the Quorum of Twelve Apostles.

Both church leaders were tall and handsome, powerful and charismatic. Essie sighed. But she was no more likely to reveal these sinful longings to her friend than she was to stand on her head in front of the two men she lusted for.

By contrast, Rose d'Gade dreaded coupling. What a nuisance. Etienne hopped onto and off of her in such a hurry, the elders might have been awaiting one of his dull, boring sermons. A born romantic, innocent Rose didn't know what she had expected from love. Cuddles and kisses, surely, like the stolen ones they'd shared on the d'Gades' front porch during their courting days. Even those precious moments were ruined by Mama d'Gade, however, who had caught them more than once.

"Don't be dirty, don't be filthy." Dawin's mother had screamed at the young couple. Later Etienne's mama muttered to Rose that it was a wife's duty. "You must give in to a man's carnal demands. But don't expect to enjoy it."

Mother d'Gade was right. Rose didn't like it one bit. Way too messy.

To each other the young women shared their personal—not their intimate—feelings, such as their qualms about the thriving Mormon community. By the close of the first two years of settlement, Nauvoo was already a big, raw, unfinished town—twice the size of Chicago—and growing like a mushroom.

Two years ahead of Rose in local citizenship, Essie Deighton had witnessed a scene of rigorous pioneering, from the first folk pitching tents to their clearing of the swampy land, the planting of their gardens and crops, and on to the more civilized scene of erecting cabins and permanent homes of brick and frame. Those first inhabitants had suffered a-plenty, for the settlement was founded in a low, swampy area at a bend in the Mississippi River, where mosquitoes and dampness plagued them eternally, until the freezing winter descended on them.

Essie was learning midwifery skills. She'd assisted the neighbor ladies in giving birth, and proposed to do the same for Rose. Her delicate friend blushed.

With so many new arrivals, the bustling city was no longer getting only the better educated and more affluent immigrants. Rose and Etienne had discovered the consequences of their leaders allowing just anybody to settle inside the city limits when they had two of their three chickens stolen. The couple was devastated and dreadfully angry over this great loss, but soon Etienne had good news, information he'd been privy to at Joseph and Emma Hale Smith's house.

"Some bad people get in here, now and then," he told his new wife, "But the honest, plain dealing church members don't suit the chicanery of the thieves, which the latter soon discover. I'm told the departure of the criminal element is often a good chance to buy their houses and lots pretty cheaply. They need the money from selling out in order to pack up and to leave."

Which was how Rose and Etienne d'Gade got their own wee cabin.

"I wish my husband would join the new Nauvoo Militia and maintain a lengthy stay in town for awhile to help protect us," Essie said.

At last it was their turn at the well. They half-filled their wooden buckets, two apiece, and hoisted them on each end of long, sturdy sticks they wore as shoulder boards. Full buckets were too heavy for them and were apt to spill from the sloshing about. One half-full bucket wasn't enough, two buckets balanced the load. Together they set off down the path, their buckets swinging gently, sloshing slightly, their worn high-top shoes squishing in the mud.

"Do you believe the rumors that the Prophet will run for the United States Presidency?" Rose asked. New to love, new to The Church, new to Nauvoo, Rose needed a host of instructions about all sorts of things, both big and small.

"It's not only a reality but also a necessity," said Essie, four years older than her new friend and ten years ahead in Mormon membership. "We've got to stand for our convictions. We always have been courageous. We don't go along with slavery, like people in southern Illinois and southern Missouri. Rumors among the Gentiles favoring slavery has it that the Mormons are operating an underground passage for run-away slaves, helping them escape to Canada . . . ."

"Are we, Essie? The LDS, I mean?"

"Well, of course. Meanwhile, the Whigs and Democrats are vying for our votes. Makes one think we would be extremely popular, not the reverse. Brother Smith hasn't been able to get redress from the U.S. Congress for all the wrongs committed on us. Rose, I'm sure you've heard how we were attacked wherever we went—back in Ohio, out here at Haun's Mill and Far West, in Missouri. Escaping across the Mississippi River, we discovered the wee village of Commerce, which we renamed Nauvoo, which is Hebrew, for 'beautiful city'."

Rose remembered what Etienne had said about their prophet's fruitless journey back east. First, though, Brother Smith had initiated petitionery correspondence with President Martin Van Buren and other political figures of the day. After spending eight weeks on the trail, traveling by two-horse carriage to Washington, D.C., Smith was told by Van Buren: 'Gentlemen, your cause is just, but I'll do nothing for you. If I did, I would lose the vote of Missouri.'"

"I wish you'd tell me something about the persecution," pleaded Rose. "I'm new to all this. I feel like a Johnny-come-lately. What happened to the Latter Day Saints before you came to Nauvoo, and why?"

"From Palmyra, New York, the Saints moved to Ohio in 1831 and to Missouri in 1838. I had married a third cousin, so I was a Deighton and stayed a Deighton. We Deightons left Minnesota—where my father and his brothers and cousins were timberers—and every single one of us were baptized into The Church. We've been Latter Day Saints since our conversion, when we left everything to join the LDS in Ohio. That was ten years ago."

They interrupted themselves frequently to speak to friends, wave to neighbors, and to watch the brethren working on the huge limestone temple. A community effort, women supplied the workers with the food they cooked, and the socks and mittens they knitted. The Nauvoo House, another public building under construction, was intended as a hotel, as the Prophet Joseph and his wife, Emma Hale Smith, were wearing themselves plumb out with hosting so many round-the-clock visitors in their home until the newcomers could find shacks to rent or build nice houses of their own.

Once past the busiest part of town, Essie continued. "Mobs rose up against us everywhere we went, Rose. They called themselves vigilantes, some of whom purported themselves to be members of a local militia. Oh, my dear, it was just awful, because they sometimes tarred and feathered our men folk and ravaged the young maidens. Many's the time I hid behind the privy to avoid discovery."

By that time they had reached Essie's little house, of which she was so proud. "Please come in," she invited warmly.

Rose happily agreed. From a side pocket she pulled out a packet of tea. "I have tea, if you have the cups."

Essie dipped water from one of her buckets into a pot and set it on the potbelly stove. Her dwelling measured thirteen feet, with whitewashed rough-hewn walls. Because the room was rather small, during the day she pushed the bed on its side against the wall. Her table was just three feet, she had but two chairs, plus a rocker. "For when the babies come." Essie had arranged her few dishes on a shelf. She and Darwin hung their few clothes, the ones they weren't wearing on any given day, on wooden wall pegs.

Settled over tea, Essie sipped and purred. "Hmmm, this tastes so good. However, dear Rose, you know we aren't supposed to drink tea, coffee or liquor, don't you?"

"Whyever not?"

"The 'Word of Wisdom,' Section 86 in the Doctrine and Covenants, admonishes the Saints to avoid strong drink . . ."

"Liquor I can understand. Tea and coffee, too?"

"Yes. Although I don't know why, except as a matter of expediency."

They sipped and giggled. "Oooh, aren't we wicked?" Essie whispered. "Shh, I won't tell if you don't."

"Expediency? Please explain, Essie."

"The 'Word of Wisdom' came as a revelation while the Saints were in Ohio in 1833. When we were building the temple at Kirtland, everybody helped, exactly as we're doing here in Nauvoo. The women contributed our gold rings and jewels, broke up all our fine china, and cut our hair. The temple walls glittered with all the precious gems we sacrificed. Our hair helped to hold together the materials that went into the external walls."

Amazed, Rose sat silent a few moments. At last she returned to their earlier topic, urging Essie to continue. She was interested in the tarring and feathering, she said, though of course it must be a sorry tale.

"Yes, indeed, my dear. Raiders also stole or burned our possessions."

"How terrible."

"Yes, it was. Once, when our men sent out a white flag, they were fired upon and quickly retreated. To no avail. The mob entered our houses on the pretext of searching for arms. This unlicensed band of thieves kocked down our sheds, tipped over haystacks, tore up the floors of buildings, grabbed anything that struck their fancy, and burned the rest. In their brutal lust, members of this band violated the chastity of young wives and virgins, whose protectors were powerless to prevent the hellish disgrace." The young women sat in silent contemplation.

Both Rose and Essie spoke intelligently and precisely, for they were well-educated for the times. As children, Rose and her future husband, Etienne, had private tutors. Essie Deighton, whose family had converted to Mormonism when the group settled in Kirtland, had received her education through The Church.

Rose noticed a pile of books sitting on the floor. "Where did you get these, Essie?" Rose picked them up and stared at them, one by one: Lockes' Essay on Human Understanding, Thomas Dick's Philosophy of a Future State, Mosheim's Church History, and books by and about Shakespeare and the French Emperor, Napoleon Bonapart.

"From the library. Everybody's reading and talking about them. You must read them too, then we'll have even more to discuss.

You're French, is that right? Try Napoleon's biography. Joseph Smith is determined that we should have the best education possible. The University of Nauvoo was established in 1841. Besides the band, we have also organized choirs, an orchestra, and a debate group called the Nauvoo Lyceum. That's why I said you should read these books. We'll be debating them soon during Lyceum meetings."

"What else do you do for enjoyment?" Rose was lonely without Etienne. They had been married so short a time before he'd departed.

"People write letters, such as to an absent husband and to family members and friends we left back home," Essie said. "Departing missionaries serve as postal carriers, as do those who return from the field. When news reaches Nauvoo that an elder has arrived from laboring in the same mission area as a loved one, the latter's family is anxious until they have a long-awaited letter in hand, telling them their father and husband is safe."

"Yes, I write some letters, too, but only to Etienne. I have nobody else. The d'Gades, who raised me, are here already. My father, a riverboat captain, died last winter of the influenza. I don't want to sit home alone every night writing letters. What else?"

Essie got up to fetch the teapot that whistled loudly from atop the stove. She refilled their cups.

Just then Essie's neighbor, Ann Pitchforth, stopped by. The ladies poured and drank more tea. Following introductions, Ann set forth with more instructions for newcomer Rose. "Meat is cheap, four cents a pound, eggs, same price, fowls twenty-five cents. Meat is cheap but vegetables are high. Rents are very high owing to the increasing value of the land. You should be glad, Rose, that you and Etienne were able to get a place. I intend to save money to buy a house and lot. By paying $100 down, I can secure a house and one acre and leave the remainder to be paid at $50 a year until free and clear.

"You'll love it here," Ann said in conclusion.

"Yes, I'm sure you young married women will," Etienne's mother said from the doorway. The tall, skinny, nosy woman, who habitually looked severely and critically down her nose at her daughter-in-law, took the two steps from door to table to peek into their cups. "Ahah! I thought so. You girls are drinking tea. Shame, shame on you all."

Rose blushed and jumped from her chair. She spilled the last of her precious tea, a drink she would have to forego henceforward, she realized with sinking heart. Besides the Latter Day Saints elders making it verboten, this was the last little packet she had brought with her from St. Louis.

However, she would soon be thrust into the community where she would experience many good times among her neighbors, particularly the young grass widows—those ladies, like herself, who were left alone to cope on their own while their equally young and innocent husbands went off to preach the gospel to the heathen in far-off lands.

As Rose would discover over the next two years, the Nauvoo community was socially active, and very soon Rose and Essie were caught up in the social whirl, in the company of each other or with their husbands, during the short sojourns when the latter were in town. As Essie had described, there was swimming in summer, sleighing in winter, corn husking parties, quilting bees, wood-cutting bees, barn and house raisings with lots of food and dancing afterwards, and rides in the Prophet's buggy. Oh yes, there were many good times, though Rose didn't count the couplings with her husband among them. That part of marriage was her duty—God's command.

Etienne's father instructed the young couples in local economics. "The economy of Nauvoo is different from that of other flourishing western towns," he said. "It's not a center for marketing, manufacture, transportation, or government, although some of these activities take place. Instead, it is primarily a religious center. Consequently, the business of trading and improving land, important in any rapid-growth center, takes on greater importance. In lieu of other goods and services, land and buildings are the town's chief products, and trading them is the most lucrative business." He then cautioned the young people to live frugally, save their money, and get into the buying-and-selling business themselves.

"The original idea was that the rich were to purchase 'inheritances,' which are then supposed to be divided among all, according to need. In reality, there are far more of the poor to claim inheritances than saints of means willing to provide them." Pausing for breath, Rose's father-in-law sipped tepid water. "I can tell you right now, Etienne, I for one am not buying property, only to turn it over to the poor. In the words of Marie Antoinette, 'Let them eat cake!'"

The months and years passed. The husbands returned and left again, repeatedly. Rose gritted her teeth in the marriage bed, while Essie moaned with passion in hers. Their church leaders continually admonished the congregation to avoid strong drink, including tea and coffee.

Essie used her big porcelain coffeepot to heat water for various purposes and Rose planted flowers in her lovely china teapot. Purportedly, the Nauvoo House was the only hotel in America at that time which did not serve hard liquor.

Meanwhile, their Illinois neighbors feared the growing strength of the Mormon Militia. To the Mormons, they were taking the defensive, preparing to defend themselves, if once more attacked. To outsiders, so the rumors circulated, the LDS were aggressors preparing to take the offensive.

Once again, the Saints would be persecuted. Yet again, they would be driven from their homes and community.

CHAPTER 27

In Washington, the Wyoming Senator and the President of the United States greeted each other effusively, not only with hugs but also with strong handclasps and pokes to the arms and slaps to the back. Dominic Alexander Davidson, son of a North Dakota clergyman and former chum and rodeo teammate of Charles Norman, Steve's older brother, welcomed Steve in the Oval Office before they retired to the First Couple's private quarters in the West Wing.

Senator Norman, like other patriotic Americans and foreign tourists, had taken the grand tour years earlier. He had seen the red and green rooms that flank the blue room, all three of them facing the south portico. The blue room was also oval, like the Oval Office a floor above. Also oval is the diplomatic reception room on the first floor, which is flanked on one side by the map room and on the other by the china room. Behind the vermeil room is the library. Out on the beautiful grounds and in addition to the rose garden, there are many historical trees: an American elm planted by John Quincy Adams, and a magnolia planted by Andrew Jackson. The White House grounds are maintained in the classical tradition according to standards established in 1935 by landscape architects. Brightening the indoors are many floral arrangements taken from these gardens. Lining the corridors are also portraits of former Presidents and First Ladies.

To Julia Davidson, Steve said, "You and your image will go down in history on these walls. How does that make you feel?"

"Inspired to 'live a good life', Steve," she replied quietly.

Later Norman watched the First Lady pour cinnamon herbal tea from an elegant Wedgwood china teapot. Tall, slender, elegant Julia wore her hair in a chignon with wisps slipping away from the front to curl over her dainty shell-like ears. She wore an undecorated, straight-line, burnt umber dress cut on the bias. A single strand of tiny seed pearls and her diamond-studded wedding band were her only adornments.

The President joined them, looking like a young Abe Lincoln with his craggy face, dark hair, mustache, and beard. He sprawled his long frame comfortably in his chocolate colored favorite chair, which Julia had given him. The chair and its matching ottoman had been custom designed to fit Dom's physical specifications by a Cheyenne leather upholsterer two decades earlier.

Dom grinned like a seven-year-old temporarily released from the prison called school for a short recess. Had he suggested they play catch, Steve wouldn't have been surprised. Norman had had plenty of exposure to the President's serious side, his passion for politics and power, his compassion for the "real" people out in the "hinterlands, the outback," as he called middle America, including his own and Steve's states. So many issues to worry about. On the domestic side, the economy and social problems, crime and drugs, the seniors and the youth, immigration and education. And always the issue of money, controlling it, budgeting it in a manner that would forego the raising of taxes. He took seriously, too, his role in international leadership, the necessity of dealing with the greedy, power-hungry dictators bent on inflicting their subjects and their neighbors with horror stories that, though on a much smaller scale, were reminiscent of the horrible Holocaust of the forties with the Nazis in Germany.

So many things, Dom told Steve, are beyond the President's control, from the Federal Reserve to the postal service, this union and that one, to all the special interest groups lobbying and protesting for this or that, often one in conflict with another. Take environmentalism and animal rights versus the rights of private landowners, public corporations, and independent operators. "Yes, Steve, it's a delicate balancing act all around."

Familiar with the pair, Steve knew that both Dom and Julia had a finely honed sense of humor. "What does that grin of yours imply, Mr. President?"

"'Dom'. For heaven sakes, cut the formality while we're alone. Where's my present? That's what I want to know."

"Hah. I figured you'd remember." Steve fished out of his briefcase a small, beautifully wrapped box about ten by twelve inches in size.

Julia got up from the flowered chintz sofa to join the men and echo Dom's ahh with her own oooh. The specially rendered bronze statuette of the Wyoming bronc was beautiful, superb.

"Steve," Julia said, after giving the statue a place of honor on the mantelpiece beneath a softly lit spotlight. "What happened in Wyoming over that incident with the protected specie rodent? I forget its name."

"'Preble's Meadow Jumping Mouse'. We're working on a bill even as we speak to introduce when the Wyoming Legislature reconvenes. To make an exemption for ranchers who manage to disturb the mouse or its habitat in the course of operating their ranch businesses."

"Yes, but what about that old man who was arrested for doing just that?"

"He wasn't arrested. Given a warning and released, apparently. I wasn't witness to the episode. The secretary of state of Wyoming called me, that's all."

With no further news or interest in that topic, Dom introduced a new one. A history buff, the President began making comparisons: between the sophistication of today's media-weary public figures and the naiveté of yesteryears' officials. "Take Martin Van Buren, for example." Then, before completing that thought, Dominic detoured by way of introduction. "Steve, you know Agatha Morissey, the woman who took me under her wing throughout my University of Wyoming years?"

Norman grinned, thinking to share with his powerful friends his new love and the coincidence of her grandmother being the President's friend. No, not yet, the developing affair was too fragile as yet, like transplanting a tiny tomato plant from hothouse to outdoor garden and hoping it would flourish. Steve wasn't sure their love would survive the imposed separations and numerous other traumas he predicted lay along their future road, for no other reason than perhaps he was superstitious after what had happened to so many of the Norman men with their wives. So Steve merely mumbled that yes, he knew the newly widowed Agatha Morissey, but not well.

"I talked to Aggie last night. She and her double cousin, Lisa, are still researching the family history, which they appear to have renewed after a hiatus of grief in honor of Randolph Morissey. At this very moment, our daring duo are following the trail of their long gone great-great grandmothers to Nauvoo, Illinois, where the Mormons lost their prophet and president, Joseph Smith, to assassination at the hands of a mob. Anyhow, my point, Steve, is that Smith went to Washington to seek redress for the wrongs committed on the Mormons and was told by then President Martin Van Buren that 'No, I can't help you, to do so would lose me the vote of the Missourians, who favor slavery. And you Mormons don't.' Can you imagine that, Steve? Nowadays, no politician in his right mind would admit such a truth—that the keen desire for the vote of one group should alienate him with another group. To do so would be to commit political suicide. To admit that the vote was more important than the affairs of a battered people? No sir. Van Buren should have rushed out to Nauvoo and told the Mormons that . . . ."

"'I feel your pain'," Steve finished for the President. The trio laughed.

Since this particular discussion could lead from the "daring duo," as Dom called the little double cousins, to far more serious discussions, like the after-effects of Hurricane Katrina, the British Petroleum oil spill in the Gulf, the tragedy of Nine-Eleven, and the more recent bombing of Seattle, it was literally an unspoken pact among them to cease and desist this detour of their discussion.

"Keep it light, that's the ticket," muttered Dom at Julia and Steve.

The Davidsons asked where Steve was off to next. In Washington a day and a half by then, he mentioned having already met with the stockgrowers association; also, he'd talked to the Secretary of Agriculture. In Japan, Singapore, and in some European countries, American beef had recently taken on a poor image, too many corporate establishments using steroids and supplemental feed filled with additives. The Normans, like a lot of independent ranchers, used natural methods and feed grown by organic means. Issues of concern included how to get into the international market, sell their cattle to the prickly foreigners, and fight the low prices they were getting from the big meat processors in America. These were all questions Steve and his fellow western stockgrowers were raising in Washington and elsewhere.

"Now I'm off to Boston to see my twins."

"Oh, those darling little girls. I know you must miss them terribly," Julia said, rising along with the President to escort the Wyoming Senator to the door.

In Boston Steve Norman approached the Back Bay brownstone off Commonwealth Avenue with some trepidation. He always did. Here was where he'd romanced Norma, here was where he'd asked her father for her hand. Old-fashioned, of course, but then Steve was an old-fashioned, romantic kind of guy. Another point of similarity—Norma's family home was much like the one Steve grew up in, while living with his Boston-bred mother and her family.

Flashing before his eyes like a fast movie promo were scenes from his youth with his mother and her parents; the latter, stern, cold people, who nevertheless loved him. In their way. Steve flicked off the remote in his mind. Yes, his mother's parents must have cared for him. They had financed his law degree at Harvard, though not the bachelor's, which he took out in Wyoming.

Richard Norman had helped his son get scholarships for Steve's first degree. Living on the ranch with big brother Charley and their dad at the time, Steve commuted into Laramie, home of the University of Wyoming. His father thought Steve should study agriculture, Steve compromised with Ag-Economics. Before taking two more degrees, the last one at the famous old university.

Founded in 1636, Harvard is the oldest college in America. It has graduated more future U.S. presidents, and has the largest university library. Steve recalled the law college and its courtroom, which looks much like the U.S. Senate chamber. Participating in mock trials in that old impressive facility made it easy to envision oneself in state or national senate chambers or serving one's country in the Congress.

Steve pondered upon the easily recognizable Boston accent, as distinguishable as an Australian's, made famous by President John F. Kennedy, if not before. Norma Norman had it, too. Steve grinned now. Aloud, he mimicked his ex-wife: "Please pawk the caw in the Hawvad Yawd."

In Cambridge, Norman took each little girl by the hand to sit on the steps of Widener Library on the Harvard campus, across the Charles River from Boston. Norma had bundled her children like sore toes in winter clothing. They ate ice cream. In Cambridge they also visited Longfellow House, home of the poet and before that, home to George Washington.

Steve told his girls, "I have a friend out in Wyoming whose great-great-grandfather was named George Washington."

"Really?" said Sissy, who had no idea who they were talking about.

"Oh, don't be silly, father," said the more precocious Cindy. "At preschool we learned he was the Father of our Country. He lived over two centuries ago."

"I remember now," Sissy butted in. "He cut down a cherry tree."

Steve told them about Nicole, his friend. "Her great-great-grandfather was named for the American President, just like you two are named for my great aunts. That way, famous or family names get preserved."

"What's reep-served mean, daddy?"

Norman had a feeling Sissy wanted his attention. The little blonde didn't care what they talked about or what unfamiliar words meant. He hugged her close and answered her anyhow. "It means 'to save' or to take good care of something, if not forever, then for a long, long time. Like I'd like to take care of you two."

"You can't, father," Cindy said matter-of-factly. "We belong to mother."

The honesty and directness of children. They could cut him to the bone.

"Did you ever hear of the story, Little Women?"

"Of course, father," Cindy said. "Boston's our home. Mother has already told us that Louisa Mae Alcott lived near here."

Shot down in flames before he'd flown them back home to Wyoming. What next?

Back in Boston they tumbled out of his Hertz rental car to explore. Bean Town. Boston Tea Party. Lot of historical significance hereabouts. He thought of local lore he needn't share with such little girls, although Cindy might have surprised him with her knowledge and perspicacity. Boston: seaport, center for electronics and medicine, strong national influence on American education and letters, the largest state capital building in all fifty states sitting atop Beacon Hill, hub of commerce and industry, home of many colleges and universities.

Home to his babies.

That cold, blustery afternoon in November they strolled a few blocks along the Freedom Trail, but not the whole three miles. The twins' daddy pointed to buildings and famous landmarks: Paul Revere's house, the Old North Church, and the cemetery behind a wrought-iron fence. "People are just dying to get in there," he said with an attempt at humor that fell flat.

"I'm cold, father," said Cindy, minutes older than her echo, Sissy, who said, "Me, too, Daddy."

They sniffed and munched popcorn while watching a video of Disney's 101 Dalmations in his hotel suite at the Marriott. They nibbled Mrs. Fields' chocolate chip cookies and chocolate-covered strawberries that he'd bought from shops in Copley Square Shopping Galleries, which adjoined the hotel by covered pedestrian walkway so they didn't have to go outdoors again.

"I'm sick to my tummy," Cindy said.

"Me, too," chorused Sissy.

Steve canceled the room service order for hotdogs. Now what? What did you do with two four-year-olds in a big city? His repertoire exhausted, Steve wished with all his heart that his two little blond angels were back on the ranch with him. His cook would know how to feed them properly.

He ordered a bottle of Pepto-Bismol and Cheerio's cereal for the girls and a Kansas City cut steak with baked potato and salad for himself. Then he recommended baths before room service arrived.

"Too sick, daddy," Cindy moaned, childlike, rolling around on the bed.

"Me, too," said Sissy, before spewing vomit in his face. He'd been leaning over them to offer comfort.

Steve gagged at the stench. He rushed to the bathroom to wet some towels. He splashed cold water on his face and hurried back to his daughters' bedside. Egad, what would Norma say?

To his amazement, when he returned the girls the next day, their mother resisted her typical fussing. She merely laughed, and sent the twins to their room. In the pleasantest of moods, Norma invited Steve to stay for tea. She actually posed questions about Wyoming and the welfare of his livestock.

Norma Norman wore fine tweeds, pearls, and low-heeled dress shoes with sheer hose. Both makeup and nail polish were muted, pale pink. If you didn't know she'd done her face, you might think she didn't need to. Her thick auburn hair piled high on her head recalled to mind Dollie Domenic's attempt at dressing up. So different, though. How was that? Steve briefly pondered.

"Are you going out?" he asked.

"No, just having tea with you." She smiled. "I should have told you how sorry I was that you lost your dad and brother."

"Why should you be sorry, you didn't kill them," he muttered.

"Oh, you. Big macho-man, can't express your emotions," she said calmly, a soft smile tempering her derision. "Did you ever discover the cause of their plane crash?"

"The Federal Aviation Authority looked over the parts of the plane they recovered. Pretty perfunctory analysis, probably."

After that first glance or two, Steve looked away. He didn't want to rest his eyes on the face and body he'd once loved so much. He glanced around the old room with its massive mahogany—at the antique furniture and the horsehair sofa nobody in his right mind would sit on, at the thick, dark purple, velvet drapes drawn to keep out the light in the dim room lit only by wall sconces holding weak bulbs behind dusty shades. In here it felt like a mausoleum filled with the dead.

How could anybody live here? What were these people and this place doing to his two bright sunny little sweethearts? How he wanted them with him, at home on the ranch.

"The FAA in Wyoming must be a small, disorganized operation. Like everything else out in that corny, backwoods place."

"Could be." He ignored the urge to defend his beloved state. "Norma, I've been thinking. Let me take the girls home with me. They could stay through Christmas. They'd have a lot of fun. I'd look after them . . . ."

"Sure, you would let them eat junk. Freeze to death. Catch pneumonia. Fall off a horse." Letting the girls go was obviously too absurd for her to contemplate. "You didn't answer my question. What did the FAA find?"

"Empty gas tank. Gas tank punctured. Small hole, like from an ice pick. Probably happened when they crashed. Freak accident, I guess. Due to the thick fog that rolled in suddenly that day."

Norman rose abruptly, leaving his tea cooling in the delicate Wedgwood china cup. Mrs. Norman, ever the gracious hostess, rose too. A hand on his arm, she escorted him to the door.

Then she reached up to touch his face, softly, tentatively, sending shivers of better times, old loving memories, down his spine.

"I could come out, though, Steve. For a little while, I mean. A short visit to bring the girls for awhile."

Fires of joy shooting from his eyes, Steve couldn't resist. He hugged her. Quickly backing off, restraining himself, he let go. Her touch might have been a hot coal on his bare flesh. "Please do, Norma. Any time."

#######

Aggie and Lisa left St. Louis in their Avis rental car to travel north on Missouri Highway 61. They passed through small villages, observing fields at rest for the winter. Lisa said the haystacks were formed to look like giant golden loaves of bread fresh from the oven.

They stopped at Mark Twain's Hannibal, where they toured his landmarks, including his boyhood home, restored to its 1800's appearance, and the Mark Twain Museum featuring original Norman Rockwell paintings. After collecting brochures and pamphlet guides, they bought Mark Twain books so they could read Huckleberry Finn and Tom Sawyer to their grandchildren.

Back in Mark Twain's day, Nauvoo and the Latter Day Saints were given—or they gave themselves and their city—a variety of nicknames: the Mormons, the Saints, the new Jerusalem, Zion, the Kingdom on the River.

The ladies carried with them the journals and diaries written so many years ago by their ancestors. Lisa as always had packed everything that occurred. "Except the kitchen sink," she tittered.

As Aggie and Lisa drew close to Nauvoo, Agatha said it seemed to her as if the spirits of Rose and Essie rode with them. "What would they think of all our modern-day conveniences?" she wondered. "Cars, planes, space ships, electricity and phones, television and radio."

Gliding smoothly along over the countryside, they laughed and shouted, trying to outdo each other:

"Big changes in communications and transportation . . . ."

"Medicine and science, oceanography . . . ."

"Banking, stock markets, international finance . . .'"

"Computers, satellites, the Internet, of course, and robotics in manufacturing . . ."

"Agriculture, defense, e-mails and seeing each other with the Skype program, digital cameras and producing our own slide shows and videos."

"Office technology, household appliances, credit cards and bar scanners."

"Yes, yes, microwave oven and dishwasher, washer and dryer, blender . . ."

"Refrigerator, electric stove. Best of all, the PILL."

The next morning they visited the jail in Carthage, where Joseph Smith and his brother Hyrum had been left unprotected by then Governor Ford, who had promised to disband the mob. Instead, the Illinois governor had chickened out, left town, thereby allowing the brothers to be assassinated by the mob of vicious vigilantes surrounding the small local jail.

"Oh, those poor people," said Aggie, touching what she thought were their blood stains on the walls and floor of the old jail. Lisa didn't know whether her cousin meant the Smith brothers or all the saints left without their beloved leader, the charismatic man they had called prophet.

They left Carthage to press on for historic Nauvoo.

"'Alienation of members within the church works two ways'," Aggie read to Lisa from Rose's journal, while the two ladies paused in the Nauvoo House to rest Aggie's ankle. "'Sometimes an individual member displeases the group and is cast out. And sometimes the group or the leadership displeases an individual or a whole family so much that they withdraw'."

Said Aggie further: "Rose wrote that she shared these rumors with Etienne, who at the time was home for awhile. Listen, Lisa, to how Rose describes his scoffing: 'That's trivial news, wife. Something you heard at the well. It's nothing but a storm in a washbowl.'"

"I don't think I care much for Etienne," Lisa said.

"Nor I, but he too is kin—our great-great-grandfather."

"And his St. Louis parents are our great-great-greats."

Lisa read from Essie's journal: "Political differences, including the slavery issue, also erupted, until the cry arose to eliminate the Mormons, every man, woman, and child, and to lay Nauvoo in ashes.'" Lisa leaned back and sighed. She glanced out the window at the quiet little village that Nauvoo is today.

That night in their motel room, Lisa wondered at the reaction of the Mormons to losing their leader. "I'm too tired to think, but I'd like to find some sort of closure before leaving for St. Joseph and Nickee."

Raising herself from the two-pillow stack behind her head, Aggie glanced knowingly at Lisa. "What you really want to know is what happened to Rose and Essie. Tomorrow while you drive, I'll read from their diaries. Meanwhile, do you care for a cup of tea?" She reached over to pour from the thermos.

Soon Lisa fell asleep. With eyes closed, sleep failed to come to Aggie. Her heart touched, her mind was gripped by the story of the Mormons. She wanted so badly to center on the feelings and thoughts of Rose and Essie.

From the warmth of his room in a sleazy hotel near the riverfront and the gold arch that tells visitors they're in St. Louis, Burly Boy placed another long distance call. There was the usual wait while the guy found a pay phone.

Sniffing, sneezing, the beefy-bodied, bushy-eyebrowed man could imagine his client running about like a house afire, thinking of an excuse for leaving home suddenly, something his wife would believe, while he availed himself of one of several cell phones he would later toss away. As for Burly Boy, he was too sick to go shopping, so he'd put off buying his own stock of cell phones.

Bundling himself into overcoat, wool scarf, fur hat, leather gloves, galoshes . . . . sneezing, snuffing, wiping his runny nose on the sleeve of his coat.

Finally. Before speaking, the hit man coughed into the phone.

"That you?" the caller whispered.

"'Course it's me. Who'd you think? Why are you whispering?"

"Snowing here, car wouldn't start. Came back indoors. Wife's in the other room, so be quick. Good news, right?"

"Wrong."

"Why the devil not?"

"I caught a cold."

"So?"

"So, I'm still in St. Louis. Ordered hot tea, hot chicken soup, picked up cough drops, cough medicine, nose spray and aspirin from the . . ."

"For cryin' out loud, I don't care about all that. I'm in a hurry. Gotta get off the phone before the wife gets suspicious."

"Yeah, well, I'm just tryin' to tell you why I haven't got myself up to Nauvoo yet."

"Forget it."

"What?"

"The contract, whatever you call it. I'll do it myself after the ladies return."

"Hey, I've got expenses, man. You shoulda saw what it cost to fly, rent cars, especially the riverboat fare."

"Alright, already. Come home, and I'll pay you. Expenses only, though."

"Awh, whatta you mean, man? I can catch up with them in St. Joseph, that's where they're going after Nauvoo. I eavesdropped in New Orleans. Gimme one more chance, okay?"

"Okay, okay."

Burly Boy was spending money from his last heist—robbing a Cheyenne mansion and nearly getting caught. Posing as a bum in south Cheyenne and living in a cold, trashy trailer was not his idea of the good life. If this job didn't pay off, he'd have to go back to breaking and entering, his typical means of making a living.

Wait a minute. The guy said he'd do it himself? Hah, Burly Boy figured that would be a cold day in hell. Doing the job personally was way too risky for the inexperienced civilian. The guy sure wouldn't want to incriminate or besmirch hisself.

CHAPTER 28

1844-1848

Rose miscarried with her first baby. Out of the country on another mission, Etienne was not available to comfort or assist his wife. Essie doctored her friend, whispering soothing words in Rose's ear.

"There'll be more, dear." Essie had lost her first child, too. To pneumonia from the hard, cold winter in her drafty little house.

"What will happen to us, Essie?" Rose moaned. Everyone in Nauvoo was privy to the dissension in the LDS leadership.

"I said to Darwin, 'It's plain as the nose on one's face that our leaders cannot have Christian love while vying for power.' He agreed with me. Darwin studied the situation and concluded that they are cutting off their noses to revenge their faces.'"

With people taking sides and bickering among themselves, it was difficult to know whom to trust. At the well again, Rose whispered, "Whatever happens, let's stick together. Promise?"

They vowed that their friendship should endure, forever and ever.

"Above all else?" Rose needed reassurance. She was so afraid their husbands would take them in opposite directions if, or perhaps when, their beloved community and church should disband. Rose was unaware that she put Nauvoo before their religion. Her little home, her nest, was her first priority, Essie the second. Etienne, too, had he been around long enough for Rose to get used to him.

Unable or unwilling to share her most intimate problems with her friend and certainly not with her mother-in-law, young Rose continued to submit to the physical side of marriage. She prayed long and hard that she could perform her wifely duty without grimacing.

"What God has joined together . . . ," Rose recalled from Scripture and her marriage vows. Surely, the marriage act was God's will. Her husband, when at home, pursued his desire for coupling. Yet even Etienne appeared to take little pleasure from their frantic joining. His mother was right, he once told Rose. It was a dirty business, something to do quickly, like discarding their garbage.

Meanwhile, Essie flourished like a blossoming lily with Darwin's every return to Nauvoo. She banished from her mind, like exiling the city's thieves, her lustful daydreams of hopping into Brigham Young's bed. The only real problem with sex—she got pregnant every time Darwin came home. Essie wanted children, of course she did. But not a dozen. If only she could discover how to prevent conception, make of it a matter of choice. In both time and number. To date, however, Essie had either miscarried or borne a single dead baby.

"Can't put too much faith in a house and possessions, Rose. We've lost them before," Essie said now. "Who says it won't happen again?"

"The Prophet promised, Essie."

'Yes, but look what is happening. Governor Ford promised us protection from the mob, to promptly turn his back on us. Even as we speak, the Prophet and his brother, Hyrum, sit rotting over in the Carthage jail."

Following an appeal to the Illinois Governor, the Nauvoo Legion quickly called out nearly four thousand men to guard their families and homes. In Carthage, Governor Ford took command of the mob to muster them into service for the state. Then he ordered Joseph Smith to disband the Legion in Nauvoo.

The Smiths returned to Nauvoo to comply with the order, the brothers assuming they were in safe hands when they rejoined Ford in Carthage. Then the Governor made a big mistake. He introduced them to the mob as *General* Joseph and *General* Hyrum. Angered anew, the men refused to disband. Upon learning that the two Nauvoo generals had been examined, bailed out, and were to appear later in Circuit Court, the mob mutinied. With this complication, the brothers were again jailed, supposedly for their own protection.

The Illinois Governer traveled to Nauvoo to address the citizens, leaving a mere handful of guards at the Carthage jail. In the Governor's absence and any clearcut control in Carthage, the mob murdered the Smith brothers in cold blood.

Early on June 28, a doctor left Carthage with the bodies of Joseph and Hyrum Smith, accompanied by their brother, Samuel, and a guard of eight soldiers. As the solemn procession approached Nauvoo, sorrowing saints filed out of the city to meet them. For more than a mile beyond the temple, the dusty road was lined with the bereaved saints.

In that year of 1844, Rose turned eighteen, Essie twenty-two. They had already aged well beyond their years.

Clinging to each other, their tears streaming down their cheeks, Rose and Essie were among the crowds lining the street when the Brothers Smith were returned to Nauvoo. More than ten thousand people filed through the room that June to say their goodbyes before the burial, including Rose d'Gade and Essie Deighton.

Meanwhile, as it was later reported, the mob's leaders gathered the chips from the Carthage courtyard, chips stained with the blood of the martyrs, and sent them from one to another as tokens of triumph. An unidentified source reported further that by boom of cannon, clang of bells, and the toots of whistles of steamboats and mills, the news of the Prophet's assassination spread.

Throughout Illinois, Iowa, and Missouri there was great rejoicing.

In Nauvoo a strict police was maintained for several days, although the Nauvoo Legion was unarmed at the time. They guarded incoming roads and avenues, lest their persecutors come to town in a rage of discrimination that would see them plunder, pillage, rape, and murder, just as a long string of others, before them, had done so many times in the past. The government, that was supposed to protect people and allow them the freedom to worship as they please, had again let them down.

Engaged in bitter debate about what the saints should do, Etienne d'Gade and Darwin Deighton barely listened to the pleas of their wives to take them somewhere safe. One group left Nauvoo for Michigan to reorganize under similar though somewhat different doctrinal dogma. Darwin suggested that he and Essie should go, too. She demurred.

Another loosely connected group chose to travel back east, return to New York, still another to Ohio. Darwin believed both of these destinations also had merit. Essie again disagreed. She didn't know what she wanted, but she thought she would know it when she saw it. As yet none of Etienne's proposals sounded or felt quite right.

"I hope I have scotched both of those notions," Essie told Rose, when they met secretly at the Deighton's small house.

Rose's mother-in-law had taken to following Rose wherever she went, reporting to her son, Etienne, what his wife was doing. It was too eerie for Rose, she didn't understand the why or how of any of it. Etienne's mother had apparently never forgiven Rose for drinking tea. Or perhaps for marrying her son in the first place. He was the apple of her eye.

Only half listening, while sneaking peeks out the two wee windows, Rose asked her friend, "'Scotched,' What does that mean?"

"To inflict such hurt upon, as to render harmless for the time', *Macbeth*, Act 2. Rose, Rose, I thought you were going to commit to memory some of Shakespeare's words. How can we discuss his writings, and make comparisons with the scriptures, if you refuse to read and memorize?"

Tossing her head, Rose protested. "No point now, Essie. Our whole world is falling apart, and you want us to memorize?"

A number of saints chose to temporarily disband, and to scatter, for safety, for the purpose of awaiting the Prophet's young son to reach his majority. They prayed diligently, and they sincerely believed that young Joseph Smith the Third was called to eventual leadership, that he would reorganize them a few years hence, when he grew to be a man, and when it was safer to reconvene.

Etienne brought every new idea home to Rose.

"Please, husband mine," she pleaded. "Don't separate me from Essie."

"I'm not sure you care a fiddlestick about the church," Etienne accused his wife. "You're more interested in your house and your friend." Etienne stormed out of their little home to rejoin the debates, while Rose stood in the middle of the room. She was flabbergasted. She thought he understood her priorities.

"Where are you two going, Essie?" Rose demanded of her friend that very afternoon.

"Why, we'll follow Brigham Young, of course. As head of the Quorum of Twelve Apostles, he's the natural one to succeed Brother Smith. Darwin agrees with me." At last Essie had identified the man she could follow.

Etienne, too, came to trust in Brother Young's leadership. He left a note on the eating table for Rose, telling her of his decision and ending with this statement: "We must turne the leafe, take out a new lesson."

Rose stomped her little foot and said aloud for nobody but herself and their dog, Winter, to hear: "But I don't want to turn a leaf."

She had named the dog for that dismal winter just past. He was her only company while Etienne was absent, out beyond the pale in the missionary field.

She had supposed that Etienne's parents would join their wagon train, but she was wrong. Disillusioned about the command to turn over their hard-earned properties to the church, and then getting caught and severely chastised over a much lesser infraction at last proved to be the final straw. They left for St. Louis, without even saying goodbye to the girl who had been like a daughter to them, before she was wife to their son.

"Rose got away with drinking tea, why not I?" The senior Mrs. d'Gade fretted with dismay at being parted from her son, but she did not complain aloud.

Rose couldn't believe those remaining would actually set off to travel with Brigham Young across all that unsettled, unknown territory, where they had heard that wild Indians and great herds of buffalo roamed. "Oh, Essie, I'm so frightened. Our husbands will be scalped, we'll be kidnapped and forced to live with some far-away Indian tribe. Never see white people again. Torn from each other."

"Oh, pooh. Where's your sense of adventure?"

# # # # # # #

In 1846, two years after their Prophet's death, the young d'Gades and Deightons, two young couples among many, young and old, set out to join the wagon train headed West.

"What will we eat? How will we live?" Rose wailed.

Impatient, Etienne tramped off, leaving his wife to confer with the other women. Rose fretted over Essie, who was with child again. Praise the Lord, Rose said to herself, that she herself had not conceived. Easily nauseated when expecting, Rose couldn't imagine jolting along in a wagon if she were.

What they would pack and what they would eat soon became clear. They needed equipment and tools to get them across the vast land, they needed equipment and tools to use when they arrived: pick and shovel, hoe and rake, ax and long heavy iron bars to use for levers, tools to repair the wagons and wheels en route, seeds for planting. Canvas tarpaulins and tents. Wooden, iron-rimmed barrels to hang outside the wagon to hold water, flour, meal, cured bacon, salt pork, dried beans, and more. With his musket and gun powder, Etienne would shoot rabbits and wild game; with his fishing pole, he'd catch fish.

To Rose, the absolute basics included medical supplies, spinning wheel and churn, her rocker, pots and pans, dishes and utensils, bedding and clothing, and rags for when she had a little visitor. They again had three chickens, which they hoped to keep for the production of eggs. A cow tied to the back of the wagon and trailing along behind would provide milk and butter. But you didn't get milk from a cow unless she'd been with child, so yes, they had a calf, too.

That was the plan. Two teams of oxen pulled the heavy Conestoga wagon, one of the best, thanks to the young d'Gades' decision to follow his father's advice to trade in land and houses, plus their careful scrimping and saving. Essie and Darwin were not so fortunate, their wagon was much smaller.

"Doesn't matter, dear heart," Essie said to Rose, who worried that her friend would suffer envy and jealousy. They had seen enough of such devastating emotions, the sheer caterwauling, among the church leadership to last a lifetime.

On the trail the women would wear the same things they always wore, not counting their Sunday best: long print dresses, aprons, shawls or capes, and bonnets. Essie loved the bonnets Rose had made for both of them. The latest fashion, the front was held up by a long wooden spoon, turn the double-sided material over and tie it around your waist, and it became an apron with the spoon in a center pocket. Voila! One item did double duty. They each had several.

One of the first challenges the group faced was getting across the ice-choked river. It took time to stop and build the rafts to carry their wagons, their possessions, themselves, and their animals. The women, and all but the younger children, walked more than they rode. The rutted trail out of Nauvoo and into Iowa quickly turned to deep mud, the women's long skirts getting damp and muddy halfway to their waists. Wagon wheels bogged down.

With so many handicaps, and the need to stop frequently, they made only two to five miles per day. It soon became obvious that only a few hardy souls could or should venture onward. The remaining pioneers settled in for the long hard winter, planting crops and vegetables, and building crude shelters. And so it went, slowly but finally, all across southern Iowa: Montrose, Garden Grove, Mount Pisgah, and on toward Council Bluffs. Wherever they went they left graves, for there was much sickness and dying.

Rose cried easily, but Etienne showed her no sympathy. He sat with straight spine, and straighter eyes on the trail ahead, as he snapped the whip and urged the oxen ever onward.

As they walked along the trail, Essie said to Rose: "The French writer, Stendhal, wrote that 'women are always eagerly on the lookout for any emotion.' Seems that describes you these days."

"Oh, Essie. Everything makes me cry."

"You must be with child again."

"Oh no! I have prayed to stave off another conception until we reach Salt Lake, and this awful ordeal is over." Both Rose and Essie had conceived somewhere along the trail. Both young women heaved and vomited, until there was nothing left to come up but bitter yellow bile. They lost weight until they were gaunt, with no fat and little flesh clinging to their stubborn bones.

Riding the swaying, bumping wagons made them ill, like a seasickness, yet walking was very tiring. Nevertheless, as Essie had predicted, both women continued to prevail. Rose birthed a son, and later buried him, somewhere past Council Bluffs, past Cutler's Park. Somewhere. Essie's baby boy died shortly thereafter. So much to endure, so much pain—so many wounds to the soul.

On and on they traveled, across the wide, treeless plains, where the tall grasses swayed in the wind, past buffalo herds so huge they stretched beyond their vision, past bands of wild-looking Indians—some friendly, some not. Curious small children sometimes wandered off, most to be found, some, not. Lost forever, some to Indians, who knew? They had to move on. On and on.

"Whatever happens, Rose, I aim to hang on by my eyelashes."

"Oh yes," agreed Rose. "Let's vow here and now to keep the spark of life, even while staving off disaster."

Not all was dismal. At night they often danced, which was acceptable. But Brigham commanded that they cease with their playing of cards and their lusty hoaring. Singing was acceptable, so they took great advantage and sang long and loud at their evening gatherings. They also raised their voices in worship and Hosannas.

They helped each other. They worked together.

The women made stews and cooked them in huge iron pots, their handles hanging from tripods over the open fires. Rose and Essie made grease cakes, called *candidates*, a favorite dish of their beloved former President and Prophet, Joseph Smith. Other women produced cornbread in iron Dutch ovens over the hot coals, turning the bread as needed until it was cooked through and golden.

The women met in a circle, facing outward, their long full skirts held wide to form a privacy barrier for the women inside taking care of their elimination needs. They delivered each other's babies, and sobbed over their deaths. Dozens of deaths, buckets of tears.

Rose spotted Darwin Deighton gazing lustfully at the young virgins. So that's it, Rose muttered to herself. Essie's husband had a wandering eye. Should she tell her friend? No, hurting Essie was not to be borne. She probably already knew. That's what she must have meant when she said her husband was both strange and silly.

In the end, it didn't really make any difference, it didn't matter a wit.

Out scavenging for game, Darwin Deighton met his death by scalping at the hands of a wild band of Indians, thus bringing to pass Rose's dire prediction. Essie was alone. But by then she was an expert horsewoman and wagon driver, a midwife and medical practitioner. "I'll make it," she said firmly.

"The Lord is testing us," Etienne told his wife sternly. "We must be strong." He spoke no words of sympathy for the loss of Darwin, nor of all the dead children who had gone before.

The number of wagons had dwindled by the time the group reached Fort Laramie. Countless people had died or turned back. It was mid-summer, nearly two years after they had left Nauvoo.

At the fort, a delegation of brethren came to talk to Essie, who replied, "Please, Gentlemen, you must speak by the card. I fear I do not take your hidden meaning."

When Essie shared this news with her friend, Rose requested a translation.

"Shakespeare used that phrase in *Hamlet*, Act V, scene 1, Rose. The clown takes everything Hamlet says literally, so he decides to be precise, not subtle. I wanted the elders to do the same and not make mere suggestions."

"Did they?"

"They most certainly did. Oh Rose, I don't know what to do." exclaimed Essie. "There are too many single and widow women needing support. I'm supposed to marry old Brother Witherspoon."

"But he already has a wife."

"Exactly." Standing arms akimbo behind the d'Gade wagon, Essie peered furtively around the canvas. "I'm not going to do it," she whispered. "Sorry dear, but when the wagons leave tomorrow, I'm staying right here."

Had the elders assigned Essie to a good-looking virile man, perhaps Brigham Young, Essie might have been tempted. Not a bad mate, that one. She was still drawn to power and ambition.

Essie knew she would miss the coupling. "Oh Darwin," she moaned, alone at night and clutching his pillow in her arms. "Why did you desert me?"

What Essie wouldn't miss were all those unwanted pregnancies. Was she finished with men? She hoped not. She mustn't let herself think about it now, though. Too much to do, her present worries multiplying like rabbits—along with the Mormon's multiple marriages.

"Oh, no, you can't leave us, Essie," Rose said. "I'll miss you so."

However, Rose understood her friend's fears, even if Etienne didn't.

"We must obey the elders. It's God's will," Etienne stated without equivocation.

Rose still cried easily. Only now she had good reason. The friends said tearful goodbyes.

"I'll never forget you." Rose sobbed.

Essie's midwifery skills could prove useful at Fort Laramie, she was sure. She could also cook, clean, and shoot like a man. If they didn't want her, she proposed to hook up with any wagons heading back East. "Some people are finally getting some sense in their heads and are returning to civilization. I know, I know, Rose. I was eager to embark on this adventure. But experience has long since changed my thinking. Don't worry about me, Rose. I'll be all right."

# # # # # # #

Farther along the trail the remaining Mormon travelers organized a ferry on the Platte River, and here Rose would give birth again, naming her daughter Rosie. Essie, but not Rose, would marry one more time. Rose had only little Rosie and no more children. Essie would also birth a daughter, naming the baby after her mother, Estelle. Then Essie's second husband, who had no other wives save her, would die in a barroom brawl, a shoot-out, a quarrel over a two-dollar poker bet.

Many years and many tears would pass before the two dear friends would meet again. By then, however, so many things would have happened to each little lady that they would be quite different people in many ways. In other familiar ways, they would always be young brides together, each recognizing in the other something of herself.

CHAPTER 29

"I don't think you should do that," Nasty One said to Nasty two from the latter's stately brick home on Pershing Avenue. "It's not nice."

"Come now, mama. Protests from the Master Gossip? Who was my role model? Who taught me, eh?" Nasty Two was set on blabbing both fact and fiction around town. She would mix the two skillfully to make of the recipe a tantalizing stew. She wore an old blue plaid bathrobe and fluffy bunny slippers with powder blue whiskers.

Her mama was decked out in Khaki jodhpurs and matching safari jacket, its many pockets stuffed with survival essentials, from toothbrush and matches to miniature flashlight and folded plastic rain parka. The latter in bright sky blue, of course. Nasty One must be planning to take off again, her daughter suggested.

"Those days are long past, daughter. Unfounded rumors can cause pain. I should know, I'm the one who gathered and distributed the dirt in the old days."

Intrigued, Nasty Two lay down the phone before commencing to place the first of her series of calls. "You're keeping family secrets? What? Tell me."

"Never mind, child," the ninetyish mama said to her seventyish daughter.

"Better they go to the grave with me than leak them to you. You'd tear up this family in a New York Minute."

Ahah, her mama wasn't out of touch at all. A "New York Minute," indeed.

When the oldest living member of the Vicente-Auld family said she needed a cuppa, she meant her favorite herbal tea. Nasturtium knew a bit about herbs, which she'd learned from her mother who'd learned from Essie and also Nasty's mother-in-law, who'd learned from Grandma Rose, who was student to Walking Mule, her Arapaho friend. In summer and fall, Nasty One roamed the county, especially the foothills, looking for selected plants, carefully digging them herself to protect the roots. Some of her favorites were Te de Cota, an Indian tea, evening primrose for cough medicine, and grindelia for bronchitis.

This time she drank Mormon Tea, named for Jack Mormon, not for the family's religious forebears. Nasty liked it as a beverage to substitute for coffee. It once had a reputation as a treatment for the "French Disease," she said, a euphemism for syphilis.

That was strange, Nasty Two mused, because her double cousin, Aggie, had discovered reference to this usage in Essie's journal. Why would great-great-grandma Essie have been interested in that? Supposedly Jack Mormon introduced the herb. He was credited with claiming that the tea was standard fare in the waiting rooms of such "houses" as Katie's Place, in Elko, Nevada.

After drinking the Indian tea, Nasturtium said she wanted a little snooze. Leaning back in the rocking chair that Estelle Auld had used to rock her ten babies, Nasty One dozed. Soon she was snoring loudly.

Nasty Two left the room. She took her cell phone.

"Guess who I saw dining with Steve Norman at the Hitching Post?" she said, trying her best to tantalize the first recipient of the many calls she would make that evening. The last person on her list was Nicole.

Before closing the connection, Nasty Two dropped her bombshell. "What puzzles me, Nickee, is why you took up with Senator Norman in the first place. After all, just a few months ago, back when your Grandfather Jacquot was molested and charged for destroying a Preble's Meadow Jumping Mouse and its habitat, you were the one who beat up on the chairman of the state's environmental council. Right on TV. With the First Lady watching you from the White House."

Never mind that their coupling had been her idea in the first place, Nasty Two couldn't resist poking the hornet's nest. Life among the family had been all too calm lately. The inveterate gossip craved some excitement, if only man-made.

With Nicole's gasp and demand for more information, Nasty chortled and paused only long enough to let her first news sink in before plunging into deeper waters. "How does that work, Cuz? First you beat up on Senator Norman. To get his attention, perhaps? And then you bed him?" Another gasp, another quick pause. And then Nasty jumped the river she had let burst over the dam to launch her second big topic. Pursuing a good story was her forte, like building a raft out of sticks to forge the rapids.

"And now it looks like your handsome busy-body rancher has taken up with a sleazy bartender in your absence. He had a date with Dollie Domenico. She lives in the same trailer park as you do, tends bar at the downtown saloon. So, my girlee, what do you think of your Senator now?"

In St. Joseph, Nicole set aside her phone to stare out the window at the dark night. Listening to Cousin Nasty Two made Nickee so upset she could barely study her class notes. Several lectures apiece from a total of twenty-one instructors on more than a dozen topics over ten days. Tough going if her mind were perfectly clear. It wasn't.

There ought to be some explanation for why Steve would have a dinner date with the tacky bartender. But for the life of her, Nicole couldn't think of one beyond the obvious. And then she returned to Cousin Nasty's first news.

Why hadn't Steve said anything about the Preble's Meadow Jumping Mouse? Although Nicole hadn't seen his face and didn't catch his name when she beat up on the state environmentalism council's chair, surely Steve must have recognized her, the very moment he rescued her when she'd wrecked her car. He should have recalled it was she who'd beat him up. Surely it wasn't every day that a tall redhead knocked the stuffing out of him, and on closed-circuit television, to boot, with connections to the White House and a dozen other western councils.

Was she naïve, innocent, foolish, or what? Her dream-come-true was turning into a nightmare. And here she'd supposed Steve Norman was a man she could trust. After discovering her first husband's secret life, she had been wary of all men. Well, not her own menfolk—Granddad Jacquot, and her dad, Big Jack. With Steve she had only begun to relax. Hah, she'd been right about men the first time. Who among them was worthy of her love, her hopes and dreams?

Because as head of the state's environmental committee, didn't that make Steve Norman the chief protector of that damn mouse? The one that was the cause of all her granddad's troubles—getting arrested, going to jail, that big fat fine, all of which resulted in the dear old man's half-losing his marbles? Yup, her dream guy was the bad guy, no question about it.

Moreover, an image of Dollie Domenico also popped into Nickee's head. She vaguely recalled the skinny dishwater blonde coming and going in the trailer park where they both lived. Was she after Steve, or the reverse? Perhaps Nickee had merely interrupted something, and the minute she left town he had resumed their lusty affair. Cousin Nasty Two had gone into great detail in describing their dinner date—the romantic music, wine and candlelight, steaks with baked potatoes, Steve wearing an expensive western suit and new boots, and Dollie, too.

"All decked out," Nasty had cackled. "You should have seen her, Nickee. Tight, and I do mean tight, green dress up to her buns, and the neckline? Half-way down to her naval."

Heart pounding with pain, Nicole muttered, what on earth? Then Nasty proposed that Dollie was a prostitute. Next, that theirs was a long-standing affair.

"Why the senator would want to take her to a public place, I can't imagine," Nasty Two had cackled in closing.

In addition to the written exam, Nicole, like the others, must orally demonstrate her refreshened auctioning skills. Leaving the exam notes for awhile, she joined some of her new friends in the dormitory lounge, where they practiced and prompted each other. That night she hardly slept. How could she sit for exams or be expected to perform when she felt like dying?

Oh, if only her gam were here. Nicole wanted to cry on Aggie's shoulder.

CHAPTER 30

Back in Keokuk, Iowa, the double cousins drove west on Missouri 136 to Interstate 35, south to Cameron, Missouri, and west again into St. Joseph. En route, Lisa and Aggie recalled what was for them a rugged travel experience. Back before the stalker had entered Aggie's life, before her precious Randy had died. It was the summer of the Mormons' Sesquicentennial—one hundred and fifty years since that first wagon train left Nanvoo for the Great Salt Lake and the new home of their church. That was the train of covered wagons that took two years to get there. For Aggie and Lisa it was not supposed to be a religious experience. It was a reenactment, imagining the troubles and travails the cousins had read about in the diaries and journals of their great-great grandmothers, as they crossed what is today America's heartland of Iowa cornbelt and the great plains of Nebraska's corn and wheat into the state of Wyoming. Reenactment travelers could sign on for the whole trip, equipping themselves with covered wagon or pushcart and the same necessities those first Mormons, including Rose and Essie, had packed. Or the modern-day travelers could walk along a few hours or a few days. Horses, not oxen, pulled the authentic-looking wagons, including a long one with benches to be used as a bus for the elderly, handicapped, or temporarily fatigued.

Nasturtium One rode the latter, as she insisted on being a part of the months' long celebration. Lisa and Aggie had alternated between riding the bus with Nasty One and walking the dusty trail. Hay and water-tank wagons for the animals and Porta-potties in more wagons, for the people, brought up the rear.

The cousins ate what their ancestors ate, they slept under the sky on tarpaulins like Rose and Essie had slept, they stared at the same stars. What Nasturtium, Lisa and Aggie could not feel was the sheer terror of the unknown, uncharted land, the roar of a buffalo herd bearing down on them, the shrieks and howls of Indians wearing war paint circling their wagons. They did experience the cold of Wyoming's high-country nights, the smell of sage brush, the howl of coyotes. They shared the camaraderie of cooking out, walking along, singing and praying together with others, and the small personal trauma of keeping up and keeping on.

But that Mormon reenactment experience was years ago. And now they were on the trail of where their great-great-grandmothers' trek west had begun.

Arriving in St. Joseph in late morning, Agatha and Lisa checked into the Drury Hotel and ate lunch at the Golden Grill cafe down the street. Aggie ordered Nicole's favorite meal of country fried steak, "smashed" potatoes, and corn.

"Lot of calories, there."

"Right. Healing burns a lot of calories, ten-thousand a day."

"Silly. That's after a wound, major surgery like having my gall bladder removed."

Both laughed. Years ago they had vowed to avoid that old-age rut of talking about aches, pains, and operations. Still another thirty years in the future, they wondered whether they could maintain their vigilance in regard to good health. In the grill they were eavesdropping. "Lot of old and elderly people, a few seniors like us." Hah, they hadn't even hit the magic fifty-five yet, the age at which some restaurants and hotels allowed the senior discount of ten percent.

"St. Joseph is an old town," Lisa read from the brochure she'd chosen off the cashier's counter. "There's a riverboat with casino on the Missouri River. Are you up for that? Or shall we explore the city first? Or call Nicole?"

"She's probably studying for her exams tomorrow. Let's do the town. Save the casino for tomorrow night. Perhaps Nickee will join us." They already knew that St. Joseph was famous for the Pony Express. So that's where they started, visiting the museum and again collecting brochures. They giggled at the recruitment poster, made famous from yesteryear.

"WANTED. Young skinny wiry fellows not over eighteen. Must be expert riders willing to risk death daily. Orphans preferred. WAGES. $25 per week. Apply Central Overland Express, Alta Building, Montgomery Street."

"Look at that," Lisa said. "'Orphans wanted'. If that doesn't make it clear they'll be facing death-defying experiences, I don't know what is. The Pony Express didn't last long. But the system sure was famous."

They shared information. The Pony Express had carried mail for a mere eighteen months between St. Joseph and Sacramento, a two-thousand mile trip covered in ten days. It ceased operation with the completion of the transcontinental telegraph lines along the railroad right-of-way in 1861. Although Samuel Morse had invented what came to be called Morse Code in 1838, it took another quarter of a century to be able to use it in sending and receiving transcontinental telegraphs. One needed telegraph poles and thousands and thousands of miles of telegraph lines. Yet it was another news source, another way to get and distribute information.

"Just think, Lisa. When grandmothers Rose and Essie passed through near this part of the world, there was neither railroad nor telegraph."

"And just think, Aggie. Today we simply take those poles and lines for granted. It never occurs to us how many men were employed installing them, how much blood, sweat, and tears, and all those jobs created by a new industry."

That night Steve called Nicole from Boston. "I thought, if you're amenable, I might lay over at MCI, grab a rental car and come up to St. Joe," he said, oblivious of Nicole's cool greeting. "We can celebrate your achievements. Do you get a diploma, a graduation certificate, or what?"

He stopped himself. He was beginning to prattle. Norma Norman's suggestion that she might visit him was discombobulating. Thrilled to get his girls out to Wyoming, he didn't know what he felt about his wife—uh, ex-wife—coming along. What about those emotions rushing through him when he was with her? Not love, couldn't be that. Something, though. Made him feel guilty now, with his new love on the phone. He shouldn't be thinking about his ex-wife.

"I don't think so, Steve."

"What? Sorry, I wasn't listening . . ."

He wasn't listening? Great. Nicole fumed silently. Probably thinking about Dollie Domenico. Or he could be planning how he could champion that damn hopping mouse, while her beloved Grandfather Jacquot wasted away, a shell of the man he'd once been, before the jodhpur-clad mouse defenders burst onto his land. The people she hated were strangers bent on taking away his freedom, his independent operation of land that had been in the Jacquot family for generations.

Nicole's mind hopped around so much it could have been the jumping mouse, itself. Next, she was furious over Dollie. Nickee hadn't thought of the barmaid with the stringy hair as much competition, until now. One never knew.

"'Don't come, Steve'. That's what I said."

He couldn't hide his alarm. "Why not? What's the matter with my little darlin?"

"Don't call me that. Obviously I'm not little. And I'm not yours." Nicole slammed down the phone.

Bewildered, Steve went to the United Airline counter at Boston's Logan Airport to change his flight, direct to DIA and home.

#######

Nicole passed her tests, though barely. Without Steve to share her accomplishment, there was no joy. Overnight she had decided to keep her mouth shut. She absolutely couldn't share her troubles with her gam and resort to crying on the shoulder of that tender-hearted little lady.

Forget it. Forget Steve Norman. He was history and she didn't want to hear her gam making excuses for him.

Nicole quietly celebrated her achievements with Aggie and Cousin Lisa, trying to contribute to the conversation, or at any rate to appear interested. They ate chicken quesadillas, fajitas, and salads at Applebee's.

Aggie said she and Lisa planned to drive north into and out of a corner of Iowa, and on west to Ashland, Nebraska. "We've heard there's a grave out there that we should see. One of our ancestors—yours, too, Nickee. Want to join us? The first baby that Rose lost and buried somewhere along the trail would be—uh, what? Help me, Lisa."

Lisa counted on her fingers. "If Rose and Essie are great-great-grandmothers to us, then they are great-great-great-great grandmothers to Nickee, but only three greats back from my daughter Beth, Nicole."

"Oh," said Aggie. "So that makes Rose's baby boy three greats back from Nickee, also."

Nicole laughed and shook her head. Hard for a young twentyish woman to think about all those people who had lived and died so long ago. But she supposed she might be interested someday. She planned to preserve her copy of the family history for some future time, when she did care, if and when her gam and Lisa ever finished the durn thing. Seemed like they'd been researching the family history next to forever already.

Meanwhile, Nicole wasn't going to let them see her bawling her eyes out over Steve while her gam was tiptoeing down the historical trail where all those great-greats had walked. She would think of something else to tell Aggie.

Nicole begged her excuses. "I'm eager to get home to Stevie," she said. "Gotta embark on my career, too. We're dead broke."

Hugs and goodbyes. And then they parted.

Nicole's gam was bubbly from their familial and historical searches, yet she asked Lisa for her best guesstimate as to why Nicole hadn't mentioned her new beau. "I suppose she'll talk about Steve Norman when she's ready."

What Aggie thought she had seen in Nicole's cloudy eyes was fatigue. Sorrow hadn't occurred to her.

The next day Nicole flew home via DIA, again taking the small commuter plane to Cheyenne. Big Jack had picked up his grandson Stevie from the Giffords. Two of the three most important men in her life stood waiting for her.

"Changed your mind about stopping over with us, I see," Grandpa Jacquot said, when they appeared on his ranch doorstep out of Douglas. "You look beat, Nickee."

His back bent with fatigue and loss of hope for the future of ranching and his own land in particular, Jason Jacquot perked up a bit with hugs and smiles, touches and giggles from Nicole and Stevie. He well recalled how his granddaughter had met the rodeo cowboy, Billy Taylor, her ex-husband now incarcerated at the state prison. Right here on the Jacquot ranch, it was, where Bill was breaking horses and she was only sixteen, a high school senior. She didn't quite graduate. They eloped instead. Though her mom had made sure the school board provided a certificate of completion. Professor Joan wasn't about to abide the notion of a school dropout in the family.

"We'll talk tomorrow," said Big Jack to his darling granddaughter. "I want to take you and the youngun around the place. How about if I let you auction? How's that sound?"

"Scary, Dad." Nicole tried to smile, act appreciative. She wondered if she was deceiving them.

CHAPTER 31

In Ashland, Nebraska, the cousins discovered a memorial rather than a gravesite. The first gas station attendant they approached knew exactly what they were talking about. They didn't find what they sought, though. Aggie and Lisa were so disappointed. Interested, but disappointed.

The Belnap family had erected a monument to their lost ancestor, three-year-old John McBride Belnap, who had died of the cholera. He was the second child and son of Gilbert and Adeline Knight Belnap. The boy's mother and grandmother both had contracted the ailment but lived. Young Gilbert didn't. The memorial, it was noted, had been erected during the Mormons' 1997 Sesquicentennial.

"We could do that," Lisa said, seeking to assuage Aggie's disappointment. "The inscription on this monument says the child was buried in an unmarked grave. Rose's and Essie's children's graves are probably unmarked too. Aggie? Agatha, talk to me. Would you like to do that? Put up a memorial for our family's long-lost children?"

Aggie turned away, too sad to talk. Where were their graves?

They believed that Rose's and Essie's baby boys might have been buried somewhere in the region. "Winter Quarters," supposedly near present-day Omaha, didn't mean much to the modern-day double cousins. Rose hadn't provided any clues in her journals, probably because she didn't know anything about their location at the time. Aggie didn't know where to go from here. The cousins had the diaries, but they couldn't be sure about the exact burial place, either. Old names lost, new towns built.

Another truckstop meal, of BLTs and salads, and they were back on Interstate 80 heading west, into Lincoln, the Nebraska capital and home of the state university. They didn't stop, but continued on west.

"Sky looks ominous, Aggie. I'm going to pull over at York to purchase some cold-weather gear."

They filled the rental-car trunk with the necessities, comparing their purchase plan with their great-great grandparents' packing list. The cousins' list read: first-aid kit (which favorably compared with the d'Gades' and Deightons'), tire chains (that didn't), shovel (yes), snow brush and de-icer (no), blankets (yes) dehydrated foods (no), flares, flashlight, and booster cables (of course not).

At Ogallala, Nebraska, Lisa's prediction came to pass as if she were a meteorologist broadcasting the weather news. A blizzard blew in from the west.

"Never mind chains and all those emergency items. Let's stop, Agatha."

They holed up at a Comfort Inn to await the storm's passing. They got the last double room. Other travelers had the same idea. With I-80 closed now, dozens, perhaps hundreds, of big semi-trailer trucks lined the roadsides and parking lots of every available motel, restaurant and truckstop.

With the wind howling outside, the windows rattling, icy cold air seeping in around the windows, the ladies huddled under warm covers in their beds.

"Let's review our notes, Lisa," Aggie said from her propped-up position. "We mustn't get complacent, I mean about forgetting or ridiculing the guy who stalked us in New Orleans. I don't want to take our apparent safety for granted. He could be lurking anywhere. If so, why? What on earth is it that we're missing in the family history that makes it so critical for somebody to keep hidden?"

"I can't imagine what. We've followed Rose and Essie clear across mid-America into the Old West. We haven't turned up any real dirt about anybody."

"Perhaps we should be looking at our family's more recent past."

# # # # # # #

Down the hall in the same motel, Burly Boy huddled and snored between his blankets. He didn't call Cheyenne until days later, just before departing the motel to get back on the road. He was too sick and fussy feeling. He didn't handle a cold well, despite all the over-the-counter remedies he had accumulated.

#######

The storm was so bad, the blowing snow drifted into great high heaps. The motel guests all over town—and everybody else—couldn't get out, they were trapped indoors. Aggie and Lisa couldn't get to the restaurant two doors down, or to the convenience store right next door. One-hundred-dollar fines were in effect for any non-emergency appearances on the streets. Almost everybody stayed put. Those who didn't—like police officers and fire fighters—were out to help those who, heedless to the warnings, had ventured outdoors. The snow had drifted completely over some buildings, piling itself into fifteen-feet-high igloos in some places, while blowing completely clear or to no more than an inch deep elsewhere.

The motel manager, a kindly gray-haired woman wearing granny glasses and warm wool clothing of slacks, vest, and turtleneck sweater, cooked for the entire motel clientele.

"Agatha, do you suppose she keeps the freezer full of food in the winter for just such emergencies?"

"Hush. Dig in before it's gone."

Biscuits and gravy for breakfast, the menus for other meals included great pots of chili, barbecued beef, potato salad, Cole slaw, the big urn repeatedly refilled with fresh-brewed coffee, and great hunks of homemade bread. The motel guests also emptied the snack, drink, and emergency-necessity machines.

Phone lines were down, too, and both little ladies had inadvertently left their cell phones in the car, which they could not get to. With the air filled with blowing snow, few if anybody's cell phones were getting a signal. The ladies both checked before giving up to hunker beneath the covers. So nobody at home or away knew they were stranded in a blizzard, but safe, nonetheless. It was naturally a mystery why neither one had called anybody.

Peter Schwartzkopf kept tuning to the weather channel, so he knew what Lisa and Aggie must be facing. He wasn't especially worried—not too much—about his wife and her cousin. Descendants of hardy pioneers, they had grown up under winter's most severe conditions, those to be found in the mountains and high plains, and they knew how to cope. Lisa would take the proper precautions. He nevertheless longed to hear from her.

Aggie talked about her granddaughter and Steve Norman, and then about her own friendship with President Davidson. She shared stories with Lisa of her informal visits to the White House and of the formal state dinners with foreign dignitaries to which the President and First Lady had sent Agatha invitations.

Lisa pulled the quilt up tight beneath her chin. "I suppose there's a protocol officer to advise you about the different cultures. The military does."

"Did I ever tell you about the time the President introduced me as the 'grandmother of the country'?" Lisa shook her head, looking amazed. "I was seated to the left of Dom in the state dining room—with Julia at the opposite end of the long beautifully decorated table—and he stood to toast me. 'If I'm 'DAD' of the country, then I'd like you to meet the grandmother. She's been like a mother to me. I never knew my own mother, who died when I was an infant.' Then he briefly described the summers living with me between his college years at the university. Everybody stood and drank to 'Aggie, Grandmother of the Country'."

"Good grief, how embarrassing. From now on, if any of those present ever run into you again, they'll be semi-certain you're older than dirt."

Aggie looked surprised. "I was more thrilled than embarrassed. Speaking of exciting, did I ever tell you Dom suggested that I go undercover with the CIA?"

"You're kidding. You're putting me on."

Aggie sat up in bed, pulling a towel around her head. Even the room was drafty and she felt a sneeze coming on. "No, Lisa, really. If I'd accepted, I would not be allowed to tell you, or even Randy, and that would be unthinkable. We never kept secrets from one another . . ." (Then she thought a moment, Randy had hidden something horrible from her in the last months of his life but what it was she had yet to discover.) Amending herself, she said, "I certainly told him everything. Besides, Dom said I'd be sent first to Langley for weeks of intensive training. Now that would be pretty hard to hide from Randy. We've hardly ever been separated and only then due to his work, not my interests. No, Lisa, the whole idea was unthinkable."

"But why you? I don't understand."

"No, of course not. Who would? But this was early in Dom's administration and he was no doubt feeling his way through the treacherous waters of foreign affairs and international espionage. I believe you and Peter were in Texas or perhaps Turkey at the time. Randy and I had already been to Turkmenistan once and were en route for a second assignment when we stopped in D.C. at the President's invitation. Randy didn't attend the dinner, though. Hmm, I wonder if Dom would have introduced my husband as 'grandfather of the country'? No, not bloody likely, because Randy had pretty much ignored Davidson as a young boarder, saying I was a silly compassionate woman to have taken him in."

"Aggie, for heaven sakes, get back to the story. You working for the CIA."

"Yes, of course. Just recalling the time that all this happened. Before you and Peter left Cheyenne, remember we were all involved in raising funds for the beleaguered women of Afghanistan under the Taliban regime. You and the Nasties and Joan and I were frantically writing letters, sending telegrams and e-mails and faxes to the White House, the Pentagon, the United Nations, and raising all that money.

"Dominic knew, of course, how impassioned we all were. My having lived temporarily in neighboring Turkmenistan and by then was headed back there again, led the President to believe I could keep in touch, go places where others couldn't, gather information and report my impressions. That's what he said."

"Agatha, I swear, you are one nutty woman. How could you even contemplate such a thing?" Lisa paused to reach for her warm socks and pull them on beneath the blankets. "On the other hand, maybe you should have considered the proposal. Think about the skills you would have learned from the CIA training at Langley. Why, with that experience, we'd have no trouble at all spotting your stalker and slipping away from his spying, if that's what he's doing. We'd sneak up behind him and disable him. Chop-chop, karate chop to the neck, gouge his eyes, stomp his instep, kick him in the balls with our high-heeled pointy-toed cowboy boots . . . ."

"Lisa! For heaven sakes. Where'd this vicious streak come from? Anyway, when was the last time either of us wore cowboy boots?"

"I mean it. You should have taken the CIA assignment."

"Silly. Can you imagine me traipsing around those Eurasian countries searching for spies or international secrets and espionage?"

Lisa laughed. "Why not? You've had plenty of adventures in your life, alone and with Randy. You'd be a natural. Who would ever suspect a five-feet short, wig-wearing 'grandmother of the U.S. of A'? Frankly, though, I'm jealous. If Dom ever recommends you again, you've got to include me. We're a pair of bookends, we go together. Or was he kidding?"

"I thought so at first, but turned out he was dead serious. He wanted me to informally infiltrate and check out the Taliban, on behalf of those poor women."

"And on behalf of oil," Lisa added dryly, in reference to Agatha's geologist husband. "The bottom line is often economics."

"Well, sure. That, too. After all, we have to fuel our cars, planes and ships, heat our homes, and run our manufacturing equipment, don't we?" Aggie got out of bed to take a potty break, returning quickly to crawl back beneath the covers. "Now you've got me thinking, luv. About our investigative skills. May I propose another project for us? Let's see if we can get to the bottom of Nasty Three's marriage."

Lisa looked puzzled. "She married a jerk, that's the answer. What's Harry the Hun got on the secretary of state, is that what you mean? Like, maybe he blackmailed her into marriage? Oh, Agatha, all this talk of the CIA and spies and stalkers has gone to your head. You suspect nefarious plots everywhere."

Aggie fought the notion that she be offended. After all, she should be used to her cousin's insulting banter by now. Just like Randy. The two people she'd loved the most had often hurt her, but Aggie typically glossed over their hurtful words, telling herself, in the words of her dead husband, that she was too sensitive. "Could be. Never mind. Are you with me?"

Lisa sighed, nodded, and made her own trek to the bathroom.

When Aggie had no more to say on that subject, Lisa switched back to Nickee. "You like the idea of her and Steve together, I know. After all, this is the match we three double cousins had begun plotting ever since their divorce proceedings went on the docket. The fact that they met accidentally without any of us intervening is beside the point. They met, they seem to have fallen hard for each other, and things are moving right along. So what's to fret about?"

"We haven't been truthful with Nickee, Lisa. She doesn't know we planned to play cupid and she doesn't know who Steve is. 'Her worst enemy,' she called him only last summer."

"Because he chairs the state environmental council? But what's that got to do with Nickee's Granddad Jacquot and that hopping mouse?"

"Preble's Meadow Jumping Mouse. Nothing. But Nickee doesn't know that. She thinks the council chair—whose name she wasn't told and whose face she didn't see—was responsible for setting those animal rights pair people out to haul in Jason Jacquot."

"Ooh, what'll she do when she finds out?"

"That's what I'm worried about."

# # # # # # #

Burly Boy didn't appear at any of the motel meals. So he didn't know his prey was within a few yards of him in their room down the hall. He stayed in bed, nursing his cold with whiskey. And sacked out, half-sleeping, mostly snoring. He felt sick as a junkyard dog.

# # # # # # #

Finally it was over. Out came the snow plows. Their hostess, the motel manager, was first on the list to get the motel parking lot cleared.

"I called for the bulldozers early, when I first noticed the sky turning dark," she said, grinning at her own ingenuity. The tip jar was filled to the brim with folded bills from her patrons' grateful acknowledgment of her kindly services and delicious food.

Back on the highway, the next challenge came from ground blizzards. Snow was piled into drifts in the fields and filling the burrow ditches along the sides of the four-lane highway. The women were familiar with this sort of scary bad scene—wind blowing at thirty-forty-fifty miles an hour picks up the piled and drifted snow, to hurl it across the roads to freeze. Result—icy highways, blowing snow when none is falling, almost total blindness, black ice. White sky blends with white air covering white ground. Patches of roadway that looks innocent, but isn't, as colorless ice covers the road to threaten the naïve traveler.

"Can't see a blinkin thing." Lisa exclaimed.

"Then pull in again. No need to rush about endangering ourselves."

They stopped at a roadside café, its weathered old walls leaning to starboard, the establishment filled with others waylaid by the aftermath of the storm. Welcomed by steaming mugs of hot coffee, they continued to wait out the ground storm.

The whole business abated at length. The wind died, the sun came out, their world turned sunny, the snow glistened. Pretty.

"Oh, look there, Aggie," Lisa exclaimed, braking but not too hard lest the car slip on black ice, to go thundering headfirst down the hill next to the barrow ditch. She pointed behind them into the ditch, then stopped to back the car up to get a better look at the overturned vehicle.

"Somebody's inside." Aggie yelled.

While Lisa called for help on her cell phone, now completely operable, Aggie threw both crocheted ponchos over her shoulders that were already layered in tight-fitting cotton and wool garments, tied a scarf tight around her head, and pulled on leather gloves. Both women wore warm heavy boots, the type of winter gear regularly advertised in L. L. Bean catalogues, but invariably available in their home town wrangler shops. As always, Lisa had thought to pack all but the kitchen sink.

Aggie ran and stumbled in the deep snow to get to the overturned car. Through the snow crusted over with snow and ice, she could see a man hanging upside down by his seatbelt.

"Are you hurt?" she hollered through the tightly closed car window. He managed to roll it down an inch. She told him her companion had called for help on her phone. Then Agatha stood by, helplessly wringing her hands and offering soothing comfort.

Soon a Nebraska highway patrol car pulled over, and two officers helped the disabled man out of his car. They blustered, and Aggie stood by, watching.

"Can't thank you enough," the burly stranger with the bushy eyebrows mumbled in Aggie's direction. He made no eye contact, just stared at the snow. He'd recognized her, of course.

But she had no idea why he looked vaguely familiar. The only time she'd seen him was in New Orleans, but she didn't get a good look then. And this stranger meant nothing to her.

CHAPTER 32

1848-1850

"I just can't go on." Rose d'Gade screamed at Etienne. Her husband drove the oxen while she walked. "I ache something awful."

"So, hop in the back."

She tried and fell, hanging on for dear life, afraid her long skirt would get caught and pull her beneath the big heavy wheels. That had happened to a couple of small girls. Killed one, broke the other's back and she died shortly, in terrible misery.

At last Rose let go of the back of the wagon to throw herself to the side of the trail. She yelled to those who followed that she was all right. She needed a bit of rest, she said, before resuming.

The Mormons had built a ferry across the Platte River. Like crocodiles in a swamp, the covered wagons, livestock, and people slowly and laboriously crossed the turbulent waters. Bringing up the rear, Rose caught up to the wagons in time for the long wait. She decided to find a resting place. The young wife, pregnant once again, thought her back would break from the terrible pains.

Again stopping off, and somewhat distant from the crowd and the ferry, Rose found a dugout cut into the rise of earth not far from the river's edge. The circle of rocks in front of the small man-made cave suggested that Indians, early trappers, perhaps some lone mountain man had made of this spot a temporary home. Like a beetle she crawled into the cool cavern out of the summer heat to rest. Soon her eyes grew as heavy as her bulging belly. She fell fast asleep.

When Rose awakened, her thighs and legs were soaked. At first she thought she'd wet herself. Oh no, her water must have broken. It was nigh time for birthing!

Stumbling back along the river to the crossing, she noticed a peculiar quiet. In the distance she spotted the dust of her wagon train disappearing along the trail without her. Whatever was she to do? She'd never catch them, not in her condition.

A lone wagon was turning around to face east. "Wait, wait." she called, tripping through the sand and over the rocks to get within shouting distance.

A family of southerners said they were turning back. They did not offer to take Rose with them nor did they appear concerned at her dirty face and rumpled clothes. Everyone looked like that.

A young black woman about Rose's age and size peeked from the wagon interior to ask if Rose were ill.

"Get back in there, girl, and shut your mouth." yelled another woman, no doubt the wife of the man whipping the horses. She told Rose they were leaving the church, going home. "Taking this sassy slave with us."

Rose thought quickly. Her only possession of value was the beautiful gold necklace around her neck and tucked carefully out of sight beneath the high neck of her cheap calico dress. Hidden, so as not to offend her somber husband, who believed that jewelry was an abomination before the Lord.

Her father had given it to her when they'd parted at St. Louis, when he'd passed her off to the d'Gade family. "It was my mother's, child. Mother Rose brought it with her from the Court of Versailles when she fled the French Revolution," the riverboat captain had said. "I promised her I would pass it on to my daughter, if ever I had one. Now's the time if ever there was one. Using this lovely necklace, you can remember her always, though the two of you never met."

With shaking hands, Rose now unclasped the precious link with her past. Thrusting the necklace with its gold glittering in the sunlight at the southerners, Rose tried to avoid pleading. Let it be a straightforward business transaction.

"Here. I'll buy the girl from you."

When they hesitated, looking suspiciously at her offering, Rose abruptly grew calm, straightened her posture, stuck out her chin, looked them straight in the eyes and in a strong firm voice proclaimed, "It's from Paris, genuine gold. Worth a small fortune."

The woman looked covetously at the lovely necklace. "Oh, please," she begged her husband, who grudgingly agreed. "I could sell it, I guess," he said. "We sure need the money."

All the while, the slender young slave looked on with awe. What would happen to her now? She was thrilled at the prospect of getting shed of her taciturn master and his mean, shrill-voiced wife. Willie would miss the master's daughter, but the white girl had eloped before the family's conversion to Mormonism. Miss the master? Not bloody likely! He had raped Willie more than once. Before that, she'd been sexually abused by a couple of the Negro field hands. She understood what men were after. She'd vowed that when her young mistress left the family, that the first chance she got, she'd use it to escape. Was this the opportunity she had prayed and dreamed of?

The young slave felt so alone, so frightened. Willie grabbed a coat, some quilts and foodstuffs and her grip from the wagon, and jumped out of the back. She would never again see her own family, anyway. They was left behind in Virginia when she was sold as a youth to the Louisiana plantation family.

"Hurry," Rose said to Willie, without further preamble. "Bring your things and come with me. We've no time to waste."

Back along the trail the sounds of humans had vanished, leaving the young women with the music of the land: bird song, rabbits, and other small creatures scurrying about to explore the underbrush along the river bank, and the breeze blowing through the few stunted trees.

"I found a sort of cave," Rose said, pointing ahead.

"A dugout. My, my," said Willie, getting her voice back from where it had sunk to the bottom of her stomach in fear and disgust. "What would my young mistress and best friend think about this? She would likely say, 'Willie, you've gone a button-hole lower'. That's from Love's Labor's Lost, Act V, scene two."

Rose groaned, but not from physical pain. "Another fan of Shakespeare, I see. You and my own best friend, Essie, would get along just fine and dandy."

"*My* best friend, the mistress, taught me to read and write. We read Shakespeare and the Bible together." Willie had skin with a texture that looked like silken velvet, the color of milk chocolate. Slender of waist and thighs, her limbs looked strong. She would need the latter.

"What's your name?"

"Willamena, 'Willie,' for short. No last name, though."

"Then you must choose whatever name you wish." Rose was about to tell Willie that she was free. But she held back. What if the girl ran off? First, Rose needed help with the birthing. Tell her afterwards.

No, that wasn't honest, "You're free, Willamena. You may go anywhere, do anything you please."

Willie was flabbergasted. She and her family had always dreamed of freedom, sometimes it seemed they talked of nothing else. They frequently plotted their escape—they would seek passage along the underground, head for Canada. And here, without asking, she was to be set free? To do what? Go where? From this wilderness back to civilization must be thousands of miles. Returning to slave country made no sense. Willie made a sudden decision. "Thank you, ma'am. But I'll stay with you, for now. Where are your people?"

"Gone off and left me, looks like. My husband will no doubt return when he realizes I'm not with any of our friends at the back of the wagon train. Never mind that. What's important now is to get this baby born." Rose patted her bulging belly. Suddenly she moaned and fell to the ground in a heap. "I hope you're a midwife."

'No, ma'am, I sure don't know nothin bout that."

"Oh no! (Gasp, gasp.) "Don't call me ma'am. My name is Rose." She didn't bother with a last name either.

From her apron pocket, Rose drew a crumpled paper with nearly illegible writing. "My friend, Essie, who dropped out of the caravan back aways, wrote these instructions for me. She knows midwifery."

Together they deciphered the note between Rose's pains, which by now were coming harder and closer together. They ripped Rose's petticoats into squares to use for diapers and swaddling clothes and to mop up the blood and birthing goo.

Willie made a fire the Indian way, by rubbing two sticks together—which took a very long time—and drew water from the river that she carried in her felt hat. "Not much water left after leakage, but it's something." She gave Rose a few sips and saved the remainder for the duties she had assumed for herself.

Soon a squalling baby girl was laid on Rose's no longer bulging stomach. With immediate great love, Rose stroked Rosie, her namesake. Later she put the child to her bosom, wondering how long she could produce milk if they didn't find some way to get food.

Although mid-summer, the nights were cold in that high country. "Cold enough to freeze the nuts off David's marble statue," Willie said in jest meanwhile observing with careful eye for Rose's reaction.

"Willamena." Rose said in protest, nevertheless recognizing her friend's allusion to Michelangelo's sculpture in Florence, Italy.

Willamena had cheese, potatoes, beans, and seeds in her grip. In her rush to get away from the southerners, she'd been smart enough to grab a knife. She knew that out here in the wilderness they would need a survival weapon.

While Rose tended the baby and regained her strength, Willie explored. A wounded rabbit was too slow for the fleet-footed Willie, who caught, skinned and cooked it She fashioned a crude vessel from a rock smoothed inside by wind and rain to resemble a bowl, something better than her hat for carting water. Good, too, for mixing things, if they ever had anything to mix.

Days passed. Etienne nor anyone else ever returned for Rose. Eventually they grew tired of waiting and watching.

Just when the women began to wonder, aloud and with great seriousness and fear, how long it would take them to starve to death, a lone Indian appeared on the horizon riding his horse bareback. He was equipped with bow and a beaded buckskin quiver of arrows. Willie doused the fire, saving a few red coals for later.

"Hush, Rosie," Rose murmured to the fussy baby. The women hunkered in the back of their cave, silently praying the Indian would not find them. One of their greatest fears had been of capture. They had heard so many horror stories of what had happened to women kidnapped by Indians. Down in Texas country, a white woman without a nose was recovered. The Apaches had burned it with hot coals every day until there was nothing left but a great gaping hole. Two grown sisters captured by the Comanches had had their tongues cut out. They were no more than wild, vicious savages themselves when found.

Baby noises, skittering creatures, perhaps the glowing coals, something attracted the Indian's attention. Maybe the cave was his.

He rode up, dismounted, and walking gingerly on beaded moccasined feet, stuck his head in the cave entrance and raised a hand in greeting "I speak English, learned it from trappers and missionaries," he said. "I mean you no harm. Please don't be afraid."

He said his name was Walking Mule, changed to Strange One. An Arapaho, he'd been sent away. "'Exiled', I believe you call it."

Mule, as they nicknamed him, didn't say why he was alone or why these things had happened to him, and they didn't ask. It was enough that he posed no threat. He was tall, well muscled, strong and manly looking. His tawny skin looked more golden than red. He had high cheekbones, deep-set black eyes, and long black hair. More handsome than the stereotypical idea of the red man.

Thanks to Mule and his skills, the trio with Baby Rosie survived the autumn and winter. Mule and Willie dug down from the top of the dugout to produce a hole, from which the smoke from the winter fires could escape and fresh air could enter. Thus their winter home was now constructed in the style of an Indian tipi.

Rose shrank from approaching anybody from the unending stream of immigrants who passed. If Mormon, they might suggest that the women join them for the continued trek to the Salt Lake valley. She wasn't sure she even believed the Mormon doctrine any more, if ever she had. Besides, Rose was no longer interested in a husband who couldn't be bothered to come searching for her. If the wagons were headed elsewhere, they were more likely men without women. Could be thieves, scalawags, or lustful males.

Rose was probably correct, for about that time gold was discovered near Sutter's Mill in California and the great rush of would-be gold miners was on. From their hideout near what would soon become Fort Caspar, the temporary settlers cared for Rosie, sought, prepared food, watched and waited.

Mule used his bow and arrows to kill prairie hens and rabbits and the occasional buffalo. He taught the women how to skin the big hairy animal and how to use every possible part of it to survive. He fashioned crude tools from buffalo bone. They wore and slept on buffalo hides. The women learned how to make moccasins and warm leggings. They cooked and ate the meat of buffalo and other animals. They caught, cooked, and ate fish. They ate roots and berries, carefully selected by Walking Mule, who knew how to recognize the poisonous ones. They bathed and washed their few clothes in the river. For elimination needs, they dug holes and covered them with sand, much as a kitten would do.

In the Indian tradition, Mule gathered herbs and showed the ladies how to use them. The seeds of the burdock plant, he said, were good for the elderly or anybody suffering from troubled joints. From the loose red dirt and gray clay in the area, Mule collected what he called gayfeather. He chopped and boiled the root for what seemed a half-hour, providing a liquid to be used as cough syrup. He burned the same root for incense and said it was to be inhaled for headache. The cachana, Mule told Rose, should be carried or displayed to ward off witches' spells. She should display the mal de ojo, or evil eye, to protect her infant.

From a small wagon train, Mule stole a straggling cow in the dead of night, so they had milk and butter. They planted Willie's seeds in the spring, choosing a sheltered spot near the bend of the river, though behind rocks and out of sight of the trail. Summer and fall brought the welcome harvest of produce, corn, and wheat. Now they had something to mix in their stone bowl. They ground corn to make meal and wheat to make flour. They made bread and baked it in Mule's adobe oven.

Occasionally a band of Indians passed, some in war paint, others not. To play safe, for all their sakes, they banked the fire, pacified Rosie at Rose's breast, and hid themselves well.

At night around the fire they told stories. Willamena shared tales of slavery, those remembered and those passed down from her parents and grandparents. Rose mused over the stories of her single life, on the riverboat with her father. Next, from life in the French court at Versailles, also passed down. Mule's stories came from Indian lore, and the yarns of battle, and his life among the tribe, who lived as nomads.

He spoke of Arapaho beliefs. "We pray often, using pipes. The smoke, steam, and our songs convey our prayers to the Creator. It is the responsibility of elderly people to maintain good relations with the Creator. We have elaborate ceremonies and make offerings to the Creator, expressed as gifts to the elderly, gifts of food, tobacco, and sometimes a bit of animal or human flesh.

"The goal of the Arapaho is to work toward seeing that cosmic, natural, and social forces operate harmoniously. We believe that supernatural power, and the life force itself, emanated from the Creator—the 'Great Mystery Above.' The Creator infused this power into other things: the forces of nature, animals, some minerals. The Arapaho appeals to these supernatural beings for help and the rewards of health and happiness. We believe that wish-thoughts might come true, so people refrain from talking about illness.

"The 'Hills of Life' are the four seasons and the movement of the sun. We humans also live through four seasons: childhood, youth, adulthood, and old age."

The women learned that the Arapaho and the Cheyenne warred with the Crow and Shoshoni. The Oglala and Brule Sioux had joined the Arapaho and Cheyenne in driving the Crow into the Big Horns and the Shoshoni to the west, "To the land where water runs both ways," he said.

"Meaning the Continental Divide," clarified Willie.

Mule at last revealed the origin of his Strange One label and his exile. His sexual preference was already perfectly clear to the women. Although he liked women as friends and sisters, he wasn't interested in them in the usual male way. He was as good as they were at tending Rosie, at cooking and making moccasins.

"I don't care," Willie said. "I like him."

"Without Mule, we'd have died many a moon ago," Rose agreed, as she danced in the moonlight.

The following autumn a small group of Arapaho, clutching spears and hatchets, came howling and hooting over the far mountain. Mule went out to meet them, telling the women to shush. Spies must have reported Mule's presence, for they clubbed him to death. They didn't like the Strange One. They wouldn't let him live, even as an exile.

The women mourned, couching their grief in the ceremonies for the dead that Mule had described. Digging his grave was difficult in the hard earth. They took turns, resting often, using buffalo bones and other among Mule's tools. They missed him sorely, for his companionship, his protection, and especially for the survival skills he had taught them. But life must go on. They would remember and honor him by staying alive, as he had planned for them to do without him.

At night around the dying embers of their fire, they maintained the routines that had become so familiar. They retold Walking Mule's tales and they recounted the names and uses of herbs. The ritual was both therapeutic and practical. They did it for remembrance but also they had no idea how long they would have to live like savages and therefore they must remember all that he had taught them in order to survive.

Eventually the women spotted an immigrant family trailing a wagon train headed for California and the gold rush. The two young women begged passage.

"We can take you as far as Fort Bridger, but you'll have to walk," said the man. "The baby can ride, though," amended the woman.

At the already famous Independence Rock, a great huge rock stretching more than a block long, which was also wide and high, they added their names to those who had gone before. To do this, they used sharp rocks to carefully scratch each letter of each of their names deep into the surface of the rock. They estimated there must be thousands of folk who had already put their mark on the rock. Rose could not find Etienne's name and wondered idly what might have happened to him.

After awhile they arrived at and crossed South Pass, which was no more than a small settlement of shacks; miners making ready to become miners in Wyoming Territory. Just before the first snow fell they reached Fort Bridger.

Rose wrote to Essie in care of Fort Laramie, but didn't know if the letter ever reached her friend. There was no reply. Rose repeatedly asked pioneers coming from the east if they'd met Essie, but nobody said they'd heard of a Mrs. Deighton.

Rose continued to write regularly in her journal. No telling who might read it, or when. Somehow it seemed important to record her personal history as she lived it. Meanwhile, Willie quoted passages from Shakespeare and the Bible. She reminded Rose they mustn't forget their learning, Willie said. She was a good companion to Rose, who, if she closed her eyes during Willie's melodious quotations, could almost believe that Essie was still with her. At night, in the dark silence, a few tears sometimes slipped from beneath Rose's eyelashes. She missed her best friend in all the world, but nobody else. Not her husband, nor his parents. As for her father, she remembered little about the river captain.

CHAPTER 33

<u>1850-1890</u>

Fort Laramie, Fort Bridger, and other forts like them along the now famous frontier trails, were not originally established as army forts, but as trading posts. Pioneers on the Oregon, Overland, and Mormon trails needed to re-supply, eat, rest, and seek safety. For there were many thieves, thugs, wild animals, and natives to fear. Before the pioneers, the trappers used the posts. During the period that Essie Deighton made her home at Fort Laramie, the structures grew from one to two dozen, with officers' quarters, cavalry barracks, a store, a saloon, the guardhouse, and the laundry.

Fort Laramie, on the eastern side of what would become Wyoming Territory, was a famous way station for hundreds of thousands of immigrants and gold seekers, as a stagecoach and a Pony Express station, and, as a military fort. Many peaceful Indians were invited to live there and they set up their tipis in the center parade grounds. Essie would use the red man's spelling of tepee. She noticed how the smoke wafted from the tops of the tipis. She especially enjoyed the aroma of roasting buffalo meat from their open fires.

Misunderstandings soon erupted between the races as more immigrants arrived every week. White people often felt threatened by the Indians, but Essie wondered if the fear was perhaps mutual. The Indian tribes included Arapaho, Cheyenne, Crow, Flathead, Pawnee, Shoshone, Sioux, and a few Utes. Soon the conflicts turned to fights, which quickly erupted into fiery confrontations. Following the battles came the wars, with many deaths on both sides. By then the federal government stepped in to switch the forts to military outposts.

Essie did much of the laundry and cooking. She loathed such hard labor, but bit her tongue. She could bear it yet awhile, until something better came along. Some of the men thought she should get into whoring.

Instead, she married Elroy, no-last-name. He wouldn't tell, so they used hers, and she and her little girl, Estelle, went right on being Deightons. In those days a lot of outlaws roamed the country. You didn't ask a man where he was from, where he was going, or his last name if he didn't want to give it.

At last, though, Essie had a man in her bed. Without hoaring or whoring. Another word people spelled however seemed right to them, Essie observed.

Shortly after their quick wedding, standing up before a traveling preacher, Elroy was shot in a barroom brawl. He protested that his two-dollar poker bet went to a cheater. His opponent disagreed.

Essie buried her second and last husband.

"I'm in the dumps," she wrote to Rose. Since she didn't know where to send her letter, she copied the message into her journal. "I don't recall the source or the whole quotation, but Sir Thomas More in 1534 said 'Some of our poore familye bee fallen in such dumpes.'" What she could have added, but didn't write, was that she needed a mate to satiate her, and to still her urgent sexual urges.

Essie used all the skills she had ever acquired, and then some. As a midwife, she delivered babies. As a cook, she developed some new recipes the soldiers liked. As a shooter, she helped defend the fort when every hand was needed. Which happened frequently, whenever the majority of able-bodied men were out on patrol, negotiating with Indians, or off killing buffalo for food.

Fort Laramie sat on the eastern side of the Rocky Mountains. The land was more amenable to farming than elsewhere in the region. Essie planted a garden, then some corn and wheat. She liked working in the soil, made her feel productive. Keep busy, she told herself, forget the burning of my loins.

Unknown to Rose, because her friend couldn't tell her, Essie at last resorted to whoring. Might as well get paid for doing what I like, she mused. Unlike Rose, Essie was not plagued with guilt over her "sinful desires." Had she even thought of it, she would have beat off the notion as pure annoyance, pesky as a mosquito.

A wagon full of prostitutes, headed for Oregon country, stopped at Fort Laramie for a few days. From them, Essie learned about the female anatomy and what caused conception. Hah, she should have known. It was not due, simply, to God's decision to send babies at all kinds of willy-nilly inconvenient times, after all. It was a matter of science, biology, Essie concluded. Then she felt stupid, for she was familiar with animals. They only mated when the female was in heat, so naturally they got bred. She must remember, then, not to couple when she was ovulating. If she did, or wasn't certain about the timing, there were preventative measures she could take.

"Why don't all women know these things?" Essie demanded of a wealthy man passing through on his way to California.

"Rich women often do," came the cynical reply. "Plus a few whores."

Tired of laundering and cooking, she was ready for action. Along with Jane, a soldier's widow, Essie took squatter's rights in acquiring a sod hovel about three miles from the outpost. There she established one of the first hog ranches in the area. Houses of ill repute came by the name, some said, because they were invariably filthy and so were the whores. They often wore faded and torn uniforms cast off by the soldiers, who were also at the bottom of the totem pole of whore-house customers. Essie aimed to change these practices and her reputation.

Thereafter, and using her limited medical knowledge, she kept herself and her girls healthy, and her establishment as clean and pretty as a bouquet of fresh flowers. Her daughter, Estelle, resided there too, after all. The other prostitutes Essie gathered about herself were ordered to live by her standards, though there was much grumbling.

Soon Essie had a whole stable full of women. Healthier, cleaner than most, they got better clients, which meant they could get away with charging more money. Essie was careful to squirrel away her portion of silver and gold, and she told nobody where she hid her secret cache.

In the mid-1850s, Essie at last located her old friend. A bedroom client said that Rose and her daughter lived at Fort Bridger. Essie wrote immediately, and in due course she eventually heard from her dearest friend in all the world.

Unable to travel between the far flung forts, they settled for long, lovely, informative missives and, on Essie's end, complicated and obscure quotations.

Essie continued to practice frugality and with her savings, which she called a stake, just as men did, she bought a few hundred acres of some of the better cropland. She planted, harvested and sold wheat, and with those profits bought cattle. She had long ceased her role as a prostitute, and was now a madam.

Which didn't mean she never bedded a man. She did. Her choices, though—of man, circumstances, and timing. Essie would sooner do without food than go without sex. As for romance, she was too old, too cynical for all that rubbish. Leave the rosy daydreams to the younger ladies.

During the Civil War their clientele dropped away, as the soldiers left the region to go serve in the Union Army against the separatists.

By the 1870s Essie could afford a foreman to ramrod her ranch. She, along with her passel of ladies of the night, moved to Cheyenne. Essie was going big time. In the bustling little city, Essie found more men to gather to her bosom. Discretely, of course.

# # # # # # #

Fort Bridger, in the western corner of the territory, was built in the usual manner for forts in those days. Pickets formed the outside walls, with a timber gate that could be closed against attacks from Indians and other marauders. Lodging consisted of apartments for the officers with wives, plus there were offices, a store and a saloon. All of these structures were built against the outer walls, leaving a hollow square in the center of the fort.

Fort Bridger in the 1850s was developing a colorful history. Rumors passed on to Brigham Young out at Salt Lake described Jim Bridger as a tall and powerful man who was busily provisioning the Indians with powder and lead and specific instructions to go after the Mormons.

Armed with weapons and arrest affidavits, the sheriff and his posse of one-hundred-fifty men arrived to arrest Bridger. They planned to capture his ammunition and destroy his liquor.

James Bridger, with the help of friends, hid himself.

The posse drank his liquor and staggered around.

Their goal of getting rid of Bridger thus thwarted, the Latter Day Saint leaders decided to buy the last outpost along the trail before reaching Mormon country. They paid $8,000 for the Fort Bridger property, only to discover that it could never be theirs. There was no clear title.

Once more Bridger hid himself, again from the angry Mormons themselves. This time he hid in a tree, with his wife providing sustenance.

Rose would have shared all these stories with Essie, but at the time they were still lost to one another. Rose giggled alone, for she wouldn't dream of sharing with Willie what a lusty lass her friend, Essie, was. Essie would likely get all hot and bothered, go goofy, over handsome Jim Bridger. With his frontier-style sense of humor, Bridger seemed to have no trouble at all in attracting women and getting wives—one at a time, however. The first one, a white Mormon woman, bore him James and John. With his Flathead wife, they begat Josephine, Felix, and another John. With a Ute woman, who died in childbirth, Jim got Virginia. And with wife number four, a Shoshone, they begat Mary, Elizabeth and William. Nine children by last count.

The white Mormon woman didn't die, however. She ran off to Salt Lake.

At Fort Bridger, Rose and Willamena settled in, taking jobs as laundress and cook, while sharing with each other their visions of independence and security. They believed that some day, "When our ship comes in," Willie quoted, they would travel everywhere, and do everything.

Unlike her friend, Essie, pretty delicate Rose was not tempted by the lustful overtures of men. Rough, unshaved, stinking of stale sweat and liquor, most of these men repulsed her. She wasn't interested in marriage, and certainly not in coupling, nor in further parenting. One child, her precious Rosie, was sufficient, thank you. Rose remembered all too well how she had vomited the whole nine months of each previous pregnancy. Nor did she believe her small frame was well suited for birthing.

Willie agreed. At the dugout, before Walking Mule had arrived out of the blue as their savior, the black woman had thought she was going to lose both Rose and the baby to the birthing. She didn't want to risk losing her savior again.

As for Willie, no man of any color appealed. Memories of the violent rapes from her white master, and the Negro field hands, besides, had put her off men for life. She, too, had conceived, although she was never once tempted to tell her lovely, gracious, naïve friend, Rose. Willie was carrying a black child when the master's rough rape caused her to miscarry. A little girl. Rose's Rosie compensated, for Willie was part mother, part aunty to the growing child. Life, although difficult, was good for the trio. That either woman's bed was empty of a caring man's comforting love did not seem to matter. They had each other, as good and loyal friends. Let other women look for lovers.

Willamena didn't have much success interesting Rose in memorizing and quoting Shakespeare, but Rose succeeded in interesting Willie in business. "See, it's like this," Rose commenced one day.

"There are just two main principles to remember and practice. One: buy low, add value, sell high. The second: never ever touch the principal."

Clarifying, Rose quoted Mr. d'Gade, her husband's father, choosing familiar examples from their experiences in Nauvoo. 'Buy property when the price or value is low, improve it, sell it at a higher price. Income, minus expenses, equals profit. Live frugally, so you can invest the profits in something else . . .'"

"Wait a minute, the profit now becomes the 'principal'?"

"Right, we'll invest, which goes beyond saving. Money in a coffee can isn't going to grow, earn interest. Money in a bank doesn't earn much interest. But buying stock or shares in somebody else's business, along with our own, is risky, but can pay back good returns. We'll spend or live on the interest, but keep the major part, the principal, for further investments. We'll make money work for us, instead of the reverse. That's how we'll make it."

The two women got their start with fur trading. The great rendezvous of Indians, fur trappers, and fur company representatives was a place of exchange. One such periodic but temporary outdoor market or rendezvous was near Fort Bridger. Firms like the Great American Fur Company hired employees to trap and collect furs. The company also bought beaver pelts from independent trappers and middlemen. Furs of all kinds were popular at the time in both Europe and back East. The market was excellent. Fur coats, hats, and muffs, and fur-trimmed garments were all the rage.

To Essie, Rose wrote that she and Willie—who by then had given herself the last name of Jackson—were making and saving their money. Soon they hoped to get into a more stable kind of business. Rose described her dreams. She shared news from her region, particularly about the French, with whom she felt the affinity of national origin.

"More so than with the British and many Americans," Rose wrote to her friend, "the French readily adopt Indian customs, take Indian wives, and learn Indian languages. Essie, dear, I'm proud of my French heritage and of the Frenchmen I've met."

Rose discovered—to her own and Willie's amazement—something she could quote for her learned friend, Essie. "Said Washington Irving, about frontier life: 'The French Canadians were ever ready to come to a halt, make a fire, put on the great pot, smoke, gossip, and sing by the hour.' Edward Rose, a guide, is one-half white, one-fourth Cherokee, and one-fourth Negro. Mixed children are common here, as frontiersmen intermarry with whatever women they meet."

With the gold strike near South Pass, a city sprung up there over night. Rose and Willie, with Rosie protesting (by then she was old enough to have fallen in love with a stage coach driver), got in on the ground floor of a hotel.

The hotel, a two-story frame building, contained only a dozen wee rooms, each one only big enough for a single sagging iron-bedstead bed with washstand and chamber pot. One window per room. Not a boarding house, the foyer with register counter was no bigger than two of the guest bedrooms.

Mrs. d'Gade and Miss Jackson—their names of preference—immediately set about scrubbing every possible surface with a stiff brush. "It's come to this, then," Rose wrote to Essie. "Willie isn't too happy about all this manual labor, either."

"I was a ladies' maid, not a scullery drudge," Willamena said. She grinned, though, because this experience was different. They were in charge.

Rose was soon able to buy the hotel, not just manage it. Willie in turn, with Rose's financial backing, opened a general merchandise store.

Rose hated using paying rooms for herself and Rosie, so the pair moved into the back room with Willie behind her store. Rosie pouted but Rose put her to work, so young Rosie quickly shut up. She would bide her time. Rosie wrote to her sweetheart, who was still stationed at Fort Bridger: "This is such an awful place. No chance to wear silk, lace, and ribbons, or dance to lively music like we did at the Fort."

Meanwhile, Rose and Willamena kept a sharp eye on economics and values and made ready to take advantage of every possible business opportunity. They sold their South Pass properties before the bottom dropped out. Then they moved back down to the southern part of the region again, this time to the dusty and bustling little town of Rock Springs. They continued to build and to buy more businesses.

While they lived frugally, Rosie complained loudly and with great anger. She threatened to go way beyond rebellion, she meant to revolt.

The two decades of the 1860s and 1870s brought boom times to the region that would officially become Wyoming Territory (carved out of wide open land), with its own territorial governor, capital city, prison, and university. Gold, coal, and copper were discovered and big business and innocent individuals went into these mining businesses. Two 1862 federal acts helped the pioneer women and the region: the Homestead Act and the Railroad Act. The Union Pacific Railroad would lay 540 miles of track, from Omaha to Ogden, Utah, coming through the region in 1868. This meant 2,400 ties per mile, each tie weighing 300 pounds. "Tie hackers" cut and hacked ties from the trees in Medicine Bow National Forest, for which they were paid 35 cents to 60 cents per tie in boom times, compared to just 7 cents later. An estimated six-thousand men, including many Chinese, imported from China, were employed by the UPRR.

Rose saw opportunities all along the UP railroad line. The trio continued to live in a hovel, saving every cent they could for re-investment. Soon they owned shares in all manner of other people's businesses. Rock Springs was built smack over the coal mines. One day Willie came home from her new store to find Rose and Rosie huddling on a carpet tacked securely by its edges—nothing more of the house remained. It had fallen into a big hole from a coal mine cave-in. Willie and their neighbors helped save Rose and Rosie from atop their "magic carpet" that continued to cling for dear life to the edges of the hole, while magically sustaining both Rose and dear Rosie.

Charles Blocker, a pilgrim on the Oregon Trail in 1836 and a companion of James Bridger in 1865, drove a stagecoach between Fort Laramie and Fort Bridger in 1865. His young life had so far been full of much exciting adventure, including a couple of months spent in the service of the Pony Express, which was in operation a mere eighteen months, yet would go down in history round the world.

Rose and Essie planned to take the stage to see one another, but their plan failed. Both of them cried bitter tears. Rose, too, bawled her eyes out, for Charles was her sweetheart and she longed to be with him always.

Blocker was a buffalo hunter for the Union Pacific Railroad in 1868. Rosie met and fell in love with the sturdy man who was born in Sweden the very same year that she was born at what was now called Fort Caspar.

With Rosie threatening to elope, and Rose unable to sanction their union, Mama Rose took Rosie to Europe to enroll her in a Swiss finishing school.

Here Rosie met and married Frenchman Francois Dubois. So much for her undying love for Charles Blocker. Rose smirked, as she and Willie traveled to Paris—by train and steamship—for the wedding. The ladies, decked out in the latest fashions, were no embarrassment to the now uppity French woman, Mrs. Rose Dubois. She and Francois lived with his parents, in a lovely old mansion on the River Seine.

On a return trip to Wyoming Territory, the young couple left their own wee daughter, another Rose, with Grandma Rose. Rosie was eager to show off to her husband some of the wild parts of her home territory, like the Teton Mountains, named by the French, and the hot springs that in 1872 was named Yellowstone, designated by President Teddy Roosevelt as the first national park in the nation.

The wealthy young couple drove a beautiful surrey with a fringe on top. It was pulled by two handsome horses.

They never returned.

From Paris, Francoise wrote that his wife had died in a buggy accident, and he couldn't face her mother. He had returned straight home to France.

Devastated, totally, Rose and Willie spent many days, tears, and dollars on Pinkerton private investigators in a futile effort to locate Rosie's grave.

"Again I am mourning the loss of a loved one," Rose wrote to Essie. "And once again my child is buried I know not where." She repeated her great sorrow for the private eyes of her personal diary.

#######

At last the two long-lost, best friends arranged to meet. Rose and Willamena would take the train from Rock Springs to Cheyenne.

187

Essie now had a fine home on Millionaire's Row. She would not share with her friend how she had been ostracized by Cheyenne society. Word of how she had made her fortune had been passed around, from lady to lady along the social circuit of the capitol city.

Instead, Essie's letters—designed to prepare Rose and Willie for what to expect—reported that they were arriving at a good time in the city's history. Essie wrote: "Perhaps you can get by without quoting Shakespeare, dear heart, but you must realize that nowadays Cheyenne is the Territory's center of social brilliancy and cultural and philosophical literacy."

Essie conveniently forgot to mention such things as Vigilante Committees, the lynching of outlaws, public hangings in the streets, train robberies, or how road agents had attacked her stage coach while she (and some of her "ladies") were en route to Deadwood (to establish another saloon, dance hall, and house of ill repute) and stole all her (and their) money and jewelry.

Rose and Willie were not dumbbells. The ladies had been reading newspapers since their inception in 1868: *The Sweetwater Mines* in South Pass City, *The Cheyenne Leader*, and *The Laramie Sentinel*. About prostitutes they were privy to scant information. It never occurred to Rose that her educated, Shakespeare-quoting best friend in all the world had been a whore and a madam.

Rose and Willie were greeted with great enthusiasm. Both Rose and Essie cried—for all the lost years, and to be reunited once more. Willie fit right in. More perceptive and worldly wise (at least about men's sexual nature), she soon understood Essie's past. Willie agreed with Essie that Rose needn't be told.

From train passengers traveling east from California and Salt Lake City who stopped in Cheyenne, Rose learned that Etienne d'Gade was alive and well. "A prosperous, pompous, big-bellied banker and husband of seven wives," was how he was described.

"Good heavens." was all Rose could think to say.

"With whom," one fellow said proudly, as if the accomplishment were his own. "Mr. d'Gade has already begat fifty-six children and one-hundred-thirteen grandchildren. So far."

"Good heavens," the beautiful and gracious lady, Rose, said once again.

"I wonder, Willie, am I still counted among his seven wives?"

"Better put in your claim," Willie responded, a twinkle in her eye. She liked to tease Rose, who was sometimes so gullible, so readily teaseable. "He dies, you could inherit a Salt Lake City bank. As his first and most important wife."

Rose looked disgusted until realizing the joke. "Silly."

Essie and Rose were now aged sixty-one and fifty-seven in that year of 1883 when the first telephone and the first electric lights for the territory were installed at the Inter Ocean Hotel. Here was where Willamena, Rose, and grandbaby Rose took up residence. They had sold their holdings in the western part of the territory and intended to make Cheyenne their home.

Raising young Rose in the city would be a joy. Grandma Rose hoped the child would someday make a good marriage and have many fine children.

Essie's Estelle discovered romance with logger Johnny Deighton, a distant cousin from Minnesota. He and young Estelle operated the by now vast ranch holdings of her mother.

Life might have seemed perfect for Rose and Essie. At last. Except that young Estelle, Johnny, and Rose's beloved friend, Essie, all died at a railroad crossing in their nice new buggy a week after the reunion with Rose, leaving baby Estelle and Essie's fortune to Grandma Rose.

Another thing—besides the first source of Essie's fortune—that neither Essie nor Estelle had got around to telling Ros—was that Essie had gone to jail for distributing birth control information to women, church-going Christian wives.

Essie whispered her secrets to none save her diary. With her death, Willie volunteered to sort and save Essie's effects and to give away or destroy the undesirable. Rose was distraught with grief. To have found her dearest friend in all the world, only to have her snatched away by the jaws of death was too much to bear.

Thus it was to Willamena Jackson, not to Rose, that Essie's diary came. Willie thought to turn it over to Rose later, when she was feeling better. Then Willie forgot it. When finally she opened and read Essie's personal account, Willie smirked. Essie wasn't the Mormon saint Rose made her out to be.

Willie didn't know exactly what it was she felt about Essie. Jealousy or envy, perhaps. Here Willie had stuck by Rose's side for decades. Yet it was Essie who continued to hold that special place in Rose's heart. Willie could have shattered all that by sharing the diary. Yet she held back. Why? To protect her friend? Perhaps she was merely vainglorious in choosing to clasp to her own bosom Essie's secrets.

Whatever it was, Willie let her motivations lie dormant. She didn't quite understand them herself. Rose and Essie's descendants would be hard put to decipher them many generations hence. Willamena Jackson packed Essie's diaries in a box to secret at the bottom of her attic trunk. Not until the Great Depression, when Willie died, were Essie's books recovered.

# # # # # # #

Nasturtium the First retrieved and read her great-grandmother Essie's journals and then rewrapped them in what was then called tinfoil. Later, she encased both Essie's and Rose's diaries in plastic.

Finally, during the first decade of the new millennium, the twenty-first century, these precious old records would be passed down to Aggie Morissey to use in reconstructing the family history.

But not all of them. Nasty One held back a single book.

CHAPTER 34

Steve couldn't understand what was happening with Nicole. Why had she gone straight to Douglas from St. Joseph, without calling him? Granted, she was close to her father and granddad, but was that any reason to throw ice water in his face? First, she tells me not to come to the school, now she skips out.

Aggie didn't have a clue. He met her for lunch at the Wrangler Hotel in downtown Cheyenne. "Call Nasty Two," said Agatha. "She'll know, if anybody does." Nicole's gam explained that her double cousin was the family hub. "Nasty collects and dishes out the dirt like a garbage man who owns the city dump. She's got a vested interest."

"How's that?"

"Her mother, Nasturtium One, used to do it—spread around the manure like the cowpokes you assign to clean your corrals. Nowadays, Nasty One keeps mum, like she's got secrets she won't share with the rest of us. Drives her daughter nuts. So Nasty Two tries to outdo her mama. Ask Nasty Two."

Nasty Two kept mum too. By the time Steve located and cornered her, she was having second thoughts. The last thing she wanted to do was admit to her part in promoting Nickee's cold-fish scenario.

So Steve still didn't know that Nasty had spotted him at the Little America resort having dinner with Dollie Domenico. Had he known, it wouldn't have occurred to the straightforward-thinking man that his intentions had been misinterpreted and then passed on to Nickee. As for the connection between his new sweet love and Jacquot, the victim of the hopping rodent episode, Steve was also totally clueless.

"Nicole refuses to talk to you," Big Jack ultimately told Steve after he'd called a half-dozen times.

To Steve there was no information in that answer. He left his ranch and postponed working on his Cheyenne store plans to jump in his metallic green pickup and head north across the Wheatland cutoff, past the Sybille Wildlife Refuse, across the mountains, past Wheatland on Interstate 25 and on north to Douglas, home of the Wyoming State Fair and the Jacquots' sale barn.

Steve might get to watch Nicole in action as an auctioneer. After checking into the Holiday Inn, Norman went to find the livestock auction market; otherwise known around the state and on into western Nebraska as a sale barn.

# # # # # # #

Harold the Horrible kicked the cat. The big aggressive male, Rigid, snarled and jumped on Harry's chest, and scratched his neck.

"Yowl." they howled in unison.

"So," Harry said, after insisting that Dollie use a disinfectant wash and Iodine on his teeny scratches. "I hear you and Steve Norman are an item. What do you have to say for yourself?" He smacked her hard on the bottom as Dollie turned away from him to sort through a tidy First-Aid kit looking for Band-Aids.

"Ow! That hurt."

"You deserve it, right? Oughta give you a proper spanking."

"You and who else, little man." She could always get to him by referring to his diminutive size. "You've got Nasty Three, why shouldn't I have somebody?"

Dollie wasn't about to tell her Harry that her "dinner date" with Senator Norman was not a real date, just his apology for standing her up for what he'd figured was no more'n a casual supper. A big juicy steak was the rancher's way of saying "I'm sorry," which wasn't likely from the big macho man.

Harry was too tired and too weak from his ordeal with the cat to abuse Dollie any more physically. Psychological warfare worked better anyway. "Why'd you quit taking flight lessons over at Laramie?"

"What's the point? Mr. Norman and Charley already crashed. Months ago, it was."

Morton reached out to smack her again. She dodged, too quick for his feeble attempt at punishing her. "I told you, how many times?" Harry repeated irritably. "You needed an excuse to be hanging around those little planes. You stop showing up the minute the Normans die, somebody could get suspicious, like the FAA."

"Oh, don't be silly," Dollie replied, leaving the room for the back bedroom to look after her cats.

Like talking to a three-year-old, she fumed. Couldn't get through to Harry that she was through doing his dirty work. She'd been saved, her sins forgiven.

####### #

In Cheyenne in the Rudolph Vicente residence, Isabelle and her one-hundred-four-year-old mother-in-law, Hepzibah Vicente, crocheted and knitted without talking. Nobody in the family had heard either of them speak recently. Isabelle's husband Rudolph—he of the bulbous red nose—was gallivanting off somewhere, looking for another church, one whose membership would allow him to lead them away from the jaws of hell and down the path to eternal salvation.

At home in their solarium—a glassed-in, solar-heated room containing eighty-seven of Hepzibah's plants that she demanded Isabelle water assiduously—they crocheted and knitted. Isabelle crocheted poncho shawls that she distributed among female members of the clan while Hepzibah knitted a continuous wool scarf, now twenty-six feet long.

"Hmph," Hepzibah said, while unraveling the long scarf and nodding at Isabelle, which meant the latter should save the yarn for Hepzibah begin anew another day.

Hepzibah was a beanpole of a thing, reminding her son Rudolph of Jack and the Beanstalk. His mama still had all her hair, though, unlike the string of Nasties Rudolph called cousins (but couldn't call double cousins). Rudolph's father was Theodore Roosevelt Vicente, once engaged to Pansy Auld, who'd gone off and married James Madison Vicente instead of Teddy. Made for enemies within the family for many years. Until all the "presidents" died. Rudolph still carried a bushel full of chips around on his shoulder over that betrayal, but nobody except his wife and mama knew, and they weren't absolutely certain.

Thirteen years his senior, Hepzibah had nevertheless outlived Teddy Vicente by a dozen years. Rudolph, short like his dad, not bean-polish like his mama, had to look up to her.

Rudolph's own wife, Isabelle, hated her name because her brothers had used it to name a cow and then razzed their sister with, "Here, bossy, here bossy."

That's when Isabelle, medium tall but skinny, stopped speaking the first time. She ignored her brothers first, and later Rudolph, neither to bid her husband adieu when he left, nor a hello-glad-to see-you when he returned.

At home alone, the two women's talk ranged from "Pass the salt" and "Time to call it a night," to long silences peppered with loquaciousness. Now Isabelle said, "When are you going to tell Agatha what you know, mama? She'll never know the whole story about the family's history without your input. For that matter, when are you going to tell me? You've always said I was too young to know."

"You still are," Hepzibah sqawked angrily, pushing herself out of the chair to leave the room.

# # # # # # #

"Sit down, daughter," Big Jack commanded Nicole. He pointed at an antique chair pulled up at the wooden kitchen table covered with oilcloth. He poured two mugs of strong, black coffee from his granddad's old blue and white granite pot.

"There was a time when you told your daddy everything. Then you took up with Bill Taylor and you stopped talkin'. I can understand that. Affairs of the heart are a private matter between two people. But when you stopped talkin' to your granddad Jacquot and me, look where it got you! Stuck for five years as a wife to one worthless critter."

She didn't argue. Nicole knew he was right. Besides, he loved her so much, and he wanted only to help and protect her. "Yes, daddy," she mumbled.

"Talk to me, Daughter. Tell me what's happening between you and this Norman fella. Not two weeks ago, you thought he was the best thing since the tractor. You anticipated him popping the big question any minute."

"Two weeks ago I had no idea he was our worst enemy! Yours and granddad's too, dad. It was Steve Norman who set up granddady as a target for arrest by the animal-rights representatives.

CHAPTER 35

At the sale barns throughout the ranching region that fall, cattle trucks and trailers with their bawling animals lined the roads, the roadway cafe parking lots, and the highways leading into Douglas and Torrington in Wyoming, south at Fort Collins, Colorado, and east in Nebraska waiting for their turn to offload and, later, to reload with new purchases. Up for sale by auction were cows, calves, bulls, steers—castrated bulls—and heifers—cows under two years old, and a few sheep.

By late November, the string of trucks had dwindled to a small trickle of late shippers. Steve had sold all the Norman livestock he would ship this season. Now was a good time for Nickee to practice auctioning. Wouldn't matter if she were slow, fumbled, or made mistakes. Not too many people around to notice.

In the sales arena at the Jacquot Livestock Auction Market, five-gallon coffee cans with sandy bottoms were lined up on the ends of benches. Tobacco-chewing, tobacco-juice-spitting folk used them. During any auction, you could hear the occasional spittooee-plop, spittooee-plop and smell the fragrances of hot coffee, hot dogs, tobacco and, over all, the pervasive odor of manure. Animals pushing through the staging arena, although not hurt, are frightened. Frightened animals, like terrified humans, empty their bladders and bowels.

Arranged in amphitheater style, indoors—inside the arena, that is, which was inside the wooden structure—the wooden benches rose around three sides of the room like small bleachers at a Little League softball game. The fourth side was given over to the performance and business area. To the right and left of this raised semi-enclosed stage and counter were two doors, one for animals to enter, the other for them to leave. Cowpoke employees prodded and guided passage of the livestock down below so buyers could see what they were buying.

In the stage-counter area, high above the manure-and-sawdust strewn dirt floor, sat Nicole, microphone clutched in her sweaty palms. Big Jack, behind her, stood ready to rescue his one and only daughter should she do more than falter. He wouldn't resume control unless she requested it. He'd promised.

Clerk and cashier rounded out the management team. The clerk kept records by computer; the cashier, armed with another computer, entered financial data. The buy-and-sell transactions were immediately transmitted electronically to the information boards facing the audience. If the auctioneers talked too fast, and they usually did, for people to understand what was happening, they had simply to glance at the records reported on the boards. No matter where you sat in the arena, you could see them.

Ready for auctioning, the team was dressed in smart-looking western gear complete with beige or gray felt cowboy hats with string ties and silver buckles.

Just then Nickee's cell phone buzzed and Nicole picked up. She didn't talk much. It was time she listened to reason, said her gam in her ear. Big Jack paced nervously, while Nicole's facial expressions changed with a range of emotion, first, anger, next, annoyance and impatience, finally, surprise and confusion.

Nickee closed the connection with her gam and, with a shaky smile that was nevertheless bright enough to light up a coal bin at midnight, she turned back to the crowd and grabbed the microphone.

Sitting behind a group of gossiping ranchers, Steve slunk down on the unpadded, straight-backed bench in the shadow of his selected corner and waited for the show to begin. He figured he was more nervous than "a cat in a room full of rocking chairs," to quote Tennessee Ernie Ford. It felt so personal he almost thought it was himself getting ready to take front stage and center. Well, it would be a drama, Nicole Jacquot Taylor's solo performance.

She cleared her throat, ready to commence. Having taken a seat next to his daughter, Big Jack grasped his own mike. He introduced himself and Nickee and then turned the program over to her.

She did just fine. Rattling away up there, while the cattle came and went, while the buyers casually lifted their auction-registration cards or silently nodded their heads to indicate a bid, she didn't miss a beat.

Nicole recognized each one in turn, alerting the clerk and the audience when a sale was made. "Here's a fine lot of Herefords, with several cow-calf pairs," she barked. "Who'll give me a bid?"

The animals sold by the pound at, say, sixty-to-eighty cents per. With the low cattle prices currently prevailing, she was proud when she got a dollar.

"One-dollah-bid-n-now-who'll-gimme-ten, one-dollah-bid-n-now-ten-now-ten (nodding her head), one dollah-bid-n-now-ten-now-tenwillya-gimmee-fifteen, willyagimme-fifteen . . ." On it went until she'd reached closure with a "Sold! A dollah-twenny-a-pound to the gentleman in the rear." Soon all the livestock had changed hands.

Big Jack didn't have to substitute once. She'd done it!

Last to leave the arena, Steve stepped out from the shadows. Nicole gasped. With barely a breath, she motioned with both hands for him to join her.

A big smile spread across his face. With long strides he reached her side.

They threw their arms around each other. He couldn't hold her tight enough.

"Oh, Steve, you came! I can't believe you came to see my debut."

"Wouldn't miss it. You were terrific."

"You really think so? You're not just saying that?"

"I really and truly mean it."

As if the cold of Siberia had melted between them, Nicole took Steve by the arm to introduce him to Big Jack.

"This is the guy you've been talking about night and day? This is the guy you wouldn't even speak to?" Big Jack grinned at his daughter, reminding her with a look that this was the guy she wanted to see on the FBI's "Ten-Most-Wanted" list.

In an aside to her dad, Nicole whispered. "That call I took before we started? It was my gam. She's back in Cheyenne from her trip. I called her last night. She promised to scope out the situation with Steve. She did so, and reported back to me. Turns out Steve came up smelling like coffee and bacon, pops." She gave Big Jack the thumbs-up sign. "Tell you more, later."

Staring into Steve's warm, loving eyes, Nicole couldn't help thinking: I must have been out of my mind to give up on this guy.

Whatever happened, we can work it out, Steve hoped, inside his head. To date he was still totally ignorant about what he could have done to offend.

"Let's go home for supper," she said.

"Okay," Steve replied.

"Where are you staying?" the big sale-barn owner asked.

"That'll never do," Big Jack replied when he heard about Steve Norman's accommodations at the Holiday Inn. "It's a nice place, indoor pool and all. The Rotary Club I belong to meets there. Ain't home though."

"No, of course it won't do," said Nicole, still clinging to Steve's arm. "You must stay with us on the ranch. Stevie's there, he'll be tickled to see you."

Ranch? Why had Steve supposed they lived in town? Of course they would have a ranch. Nickee had been raised, at least part of the time, on a ranch? Did that mean she liked the country life?

Looked like a Norman man had finally found her at last—an honest to God Wyoming ranch woman to call his wife!

# # # # # # #

By talking with Nasty Three, Aggie had gotten the full picture on the hopping rodent and Steve's involvement. Yes, the Preble's Meadow Jumping Mouse was on the list of protected species. First, the secretary of state had described another confrontation, over in Albany County, where a heated exchange took place between a county commissioner and the vice president of the Stockgrowers' Association. The result was an agreement that the governor's office would assist ranchers from surrounding counties so they could continue working in areas of threatened species' habitats.

"Aggie, even as we speak," Nasty Three said, "Steve is on the committee to draft exclusion legislation. The stock growers said the hopping mouse is one of their biggest heartburns."

The legislation would exclude ranchers and farmers from penalties when they came upon the mouse or its home and inadvertently destroyed either. Aggie had wanted to know what all the uproar was about, so Nasty told her.

The mouse was listed as threatened under the Endangered Species Act by the U.S. Fish and Wildlife Service. "The specie is native to southeastern Wyoming and is recognized as an 'andicator specie'—meaning, its health is indicative of the health of the surrounding ecosystem. Protecting it and its habitat could wind up allowing us to protect other plants and animals. But the ESA ruling could also change where and how ranchers do their business by limiting grazing and irrigation. Thus the exemption that should be going up before the state legislature shortly for approval."

Agatha pondered Nasty's explanation a few moments before inviting additional input. The secretary of state complied, as was her wont.

"Aggie, Steve didn't have a single thing to do with those ESA representatives who attacked Jason Jacquot. Senator Norman wasn't there. He didn't know anything about it. You could have knocked him over with an aspen leaf when Nicole attacked him in front of the First Lady."

Nasty referred to the close-circuit television session of the western state environmental councils, with Steve chairing for Wyoming. Julia Davidson often appeared on the program along with Steven and members of a half-dozen other western state committees. Why Nickee had run into the room to attack him from behind, beating on his back and neck and shouting insults, Steve hadn't understood at the time. And, like Nicole, he hadn't made the connection. Neither of them had seen the other's face and he didn't realize that the woman who pounded him was the same beautiful lady he'd fallen so hard for.

# # # # # # #

On the phone with the guy, Bushy Eyebrows declared, "I'm back in town."

"I can't imagine what trouble you got into this time."

"Whadda ya mean?"

"Aggie Morrisey is also back in town. She went to see her cousin, Nasty Three, the secretary of state."

"I know who Nasty Three is. Don't we all."

"What's that supposed to mean?" The guy was distracted, scared, lest he'd given himself away. "Never mind. What happened to you this time?"

"Got caught inna ground blizzard. Skidded, turned over, got dumped upside down inna snow drift."

"How'd that happen? Wasn't 1-80 closed?"

"Yeah, but I took off too soon. I'd forgotten how bad one a them ground blizzards gets. Snow blowing across the road, freezing, man. My car slipping and sliding. Couldn't see a damn thing."

"Don't swear at me. I'm a religious man, you know."

"Yeah, sure. Some religion, lets you go around offing folk."

"I'm not 'offing' anybody. Anyway, you're supposed to be doing the job, not me. Now get this straight, old buddy, the word isn't 'offing,' it's incapacitate. If you know how."

"I ain't your buddy. I'm your hit man."

The voice on the other end screeched. "Not 'hit'! Incapacitate! Incapacitate, you imbecile."

"Wait a minute. Incapacitate, how? How far, how much? I thought you said 'kill!'"

"Did not."

"Did too."

"No, I didn't."

"Sure you did. Backin' out, now, are ya? Well, you still owe me."

"Yeah, yeah. I'll pay you when the job's done."

Burly Boy got off the phone, more confused than before. The guy never did answer the question.

Ahh, I got it, Burly Boy concluded. He don't wanna say the word "kill" or admit to his self what he wants to happen to happen. Well, I got no qualms. I'll go ahead and do it. Then get my money and get outta this cold icebox town.

#######

Had Aggie been a clairvoyant, she would have shuddered and gone sleepless with nightmares. She would have understood Lisa's sudden streak of viciousness when talking about the potential threat.

Her cousin had explained her attitude back in Ogallala during the blizzard: "I'm sick of feeling helpless, Agatha. Powerless, out of control, with you hounded, attacked in broad daylight on a busy New Orleans street. Don't try to tell me this trip was an impulse born of diligence to the family history. Nasty One already gave you Rose and

Essie's journals. We didn't learn one more new thing on our travels that would help with the project, much less help either of us to identify your stalker and the author of all those faxes and phone calls. Agatha, you were running away, that's all. Our whole trip was pointless. Admit it."

"Perhaps."

"Didn't help, though, did it? He moved from threatening to stalking. See? That's why I wish you'd been trained by the CIA to handle your own personal protection. Pow, right in the kisser."

Aggie laughed in spite of herself. What Lisa hadn't added, bless her heart, was that her wig-wearing cousin wasn't always this shook up. Back in Vermont, where she'd lost most of her hair in the forest fire, she had identified the killer among them. When Cowboy Billy Taylor was abusing her granddaughter, she had taken care of him, too. When President Davidson and his family were in trouble, she had come to Dom's aid. Granted, Aggie didn't think of those acts as courageous. She had sort of stumbled into them.

What was the matter with her now, then? Could her indecision, her fears, her vacillating between taking the threats seriously only to turn right around and think they were mere pranks, mean that she was losing her mind? Aggie could readily imagine that grief over the loss of a loved one was too devastating to articulate. She had read where people get actually, physically ill. What she hadn't figured on was losing her mental faculties, or her courage.

All because her Randy had died? And she didn't know how or why?

CHAPTER 36

After leaving the Jacquot ranch, Nicole and her son stopped at Beth's house. Stevie immediately ran off to play with Brianna and Brittany, next door neighbors to their grandparents, Lisa and Peter Schwartzkopf. Both houses, with identical walk-out basements and floor plans, looked like three-story structures from the back. There were guest suites in both houses, but the Gifford basement also housed play and craft rooms for the little girls, nicknamed the BB twins.

Tiny Beth, like her petite mother, Lisa, had excellent decorating taste. At the Giffords, mini-blinds with blouson valances dressed the windows. Nickee called these ruffles "poof puffs." The country kitchen's warm golden oak was separated from the large, airy eating room by an oak counter. Along the side with the built-in desk was the communication center that came with house-wide intercom for voice and music. Beth's kitchen desk also held telephones for personal and business use, and each came with its own voice mail. Like most families, husband and wife carried their separate cell phones on their persons.

Near the children in the playroom, Beth's sewing and crafts filled many happy hours. Here was where she had designed most of their room decorations.

Pouring tea from a chipped china vintage-1842 teapot handed down through the generations to Beth from Essie Deighton, the petite, blond, home-loving Beth demanded to hear all about everything. "You must have so much news," she said. "You haven't told me about the school yet, and here you're a professional auctioneer already."

"Hardly," Nickee said. "I'd like to try several general-household sales next. Good practice. Before I branch out."

"Doing what? You mean you don't plan to go into business with your Jacquot menfolk?"

"No. Because boy howdee, have I got ideas. Then, too, there's Steve."

"Oooh, tell me about Steve. I thought you were mad at him."

"No, not any more." Nicole grinned.

Just then Beth's mother, Lisa, popped in the kitchen door. After sharing a few anecdotes from her and Aggie's travel experiences, such as the man they had discovered hanging upside down in his car during a ground blizzard, Lisa asked Nicole about her first auction, and, almost in the same breath, about her romance with Norman.

Which was when Lisa heard, for the first time, about Nicole's temporarily shattered romance. When Lisa moaned her dismay, Nickee quickly revived her by saying they'd made up.

Beth oohed, and Lisa ahhhed.

"Nickee," Beth said later. "Let's go downtown and get a look at this bartender." Lisa's clone squealed. Beth sounded and looked just like her mama. Clapping her little hands, Beth jumped up and down, insisting that Nicole comply with her demands. Turning to Lisa: "Wanna come, mom?"

Lisa said she was too exhausted. "Hard to keep up with your gam, Nickee, even with that bad ankle." Beth's mother did agree, however, to look after the trio of rambunctious children while the younger women went out to snoop, spy, and snicker. "And report back to me," added Lisa. "That's the price of my babysitting."

Downtown in the dim old saloon with the long long bar and the six saddle-topped barstools, the girls, so different in looks, and also in temperament, sat at a back table in the shadows. "You order, Beth. Dollie doesn't know you."

"You think she'll recognize you?"

"We live in the same trailer park," Nicole said. "Steve explained to me how he came to take Dollie to Little America that night for dinner. Before the two of us met, Steve was in here and had casually invited Dollie to join him for supper at the truckstop. That was when I crashed into the bank a few minutes later. Steve rescued me and followed me to the hospital. We went to the truckstop to eat. Meanwhile, Dollie showed up and apparently saw us together. That's what she told him, anyhow. To apologize for his thoughtlessness for standing her up, he made an appointment to buy her a proper dinner. Yes, Beth, I'm sure Dollie Domenico would recognize me. She must hate my guts."

Crowded with happy-hour patrons, it took awhile to get service in the downtown saloon with the long long bar. Their server, a pimply faced youth, said he was enrolled at the local community college—L-Triple-C, for short. They were pleased to have Benji wait on them, for that meant they wouldn't have to face service from the skinny, flat-chested, lanky-haired bartender. Through the noisy mob of happy-hour drinkers, the young women could observe Dollie's fast, efficient movements preparing drinks behind the bar.

"People seem to like her," Beth said, noting the good-natured ribbing Dollie got from women and men alike. Banter back and forth, between patrons and Dollie and between Dollie and the servers, confirmed Beth's judgment.

"Look at her appearance, though. What a sight."

Beth, who was as careful with her clothing selections and makeup applications as her mother, exclaimed, "Heavens to Betsy! If anybody were ever in need of a make-over, Dollie Domenico is a prime candidate." Beth Gifford's choice of expletives came from earlier generations. Like Rose and Essie, though, the girls were mostly unaware of their heritage, subtle though it often appeared.

Although neither of the young cousins was aware, Beth and her mom, Lisa, took after Rose d'Gade in their dainty and ladylike demeanors, behaviors, and habits, but not in their appearance, for that came from Essie. Conversely, Nicole and her gam took after Essie Deighton in some of their determined but happy-go-lucky personalities. But they, in turn, looked like Rose. Talk about mixing genes, Aggie and Lisa agreed, when they were comparing past and present kin.

"Hah." Nicole said. "In the unlikely event that you and Dollie should get together, Nickee, how do you propose to get her to sit still long enough or even to get her to agree to your cosmetic tomfoolery?"

"A free make-over? Are you kidding? Anybody would die for the full treatment." Beth could not imagine passing up an opportunity like that. "Poor thing. If I were you, Nickee, I wouldn't worry one single second that Dollie Domenico was ever a serious contender for Steve's affections. No competition for you at all from that quarter."

CHAPTER 37

Lionel and Lucy Falstaff ate dinner at the country club. When his wife had prevailed upon him once again, he gave in to keep the peace. Dressed in a gauzy see-through thing with wrinkled satin slip and undergarments, her hair pulled up and back in what was supposed to pass for a chignon but was falling lopsidedly down one side of her head, Lucy walked proudly into the dining room.

Lucy then demanded a bottle of expensive Dom Perignon. "Coming to the club is a special occasion. Indulge me."

The waiter brought Baccarat wine glasses to the table in a silver wine cooler filled with ice. Mrs. Falstaff, proud to be the wife of the Lieutenant Governor (which is the office she thought her husband held), sighed and purred—like a hungry tiger, not a wee kitten—"Heaven can wait."

Spotting Nasty Three across the room, Lucy pointed a crooked finger, bent with the gnarly knobs of early-age arthritis. "Look, look! Over there. The secretary of state with her wimpy husband. Nasty's wearing that stupid straw hat with the daisies. Tell me, Lionel, Why does she do that?"

"Hush," Lionel snarled in a stage whisper, grabbing his wife's offending finger and nearly snapping the fragile bone. "Nasty Three wears a hat to cover the bald spot on the back of her head."

"Ouch! What's the matter with you?"

"What's the matter with you? People will hear you, see you pointing."

"So what? Everybody I've overheard at the beauty shop wonders whether she was out of her mind marrying that twerp. Tell me. Why did she marry Harold Morton, Morgan, whatever? You must have heard something. What good is that job of yours, if you can't bring home some juicy gossip?" Lucy smirked behind the elegant glass she held.

"What good is it? What good? Pays the bills, don't it? Got you a nice house, okay? What good, you say. You must be dumber'n a barnyard sow."

"Sows ain't so dumb. Pigs're smart."

"Quiet! People are staring." What he didn't tell her was that he'd had to bribe Harold Morton for a guest pass. The Falstaffs couldn't afford the country club. Harry wasn't interested, not until Lionel said he'd tell Nasty Three on Harry. Harold Morton didn't love her, he just wanted to bask in her glory.

Harold gave in. So that's how the Falstaff's got a guest pass.

Harold the Hypersensitive poked the secretary of state with an elbow to her ribs. "Over there, Nasty. Your governor's staff member and his peculiar-looking wife are staring at us."

"Your cheek is twitching again, Harry," his wife said. "The governor is not mine and neither is his administrative assistant. Who cares? Like everybody else in this state, they're probably wondering why I married you."

"Don't call me Harry. Why did you?"

"Better ask, why did you marry me?" Sipping from a glass of Chardonnay, Nasty Three looked knowingly into her husband's eyes. "My mama called me tonight, Harry. She was downtown at the saloon this afternoon. Mama said she caught you holding hands with your ex-wife. I thought you gave up Dollie Domenico when you married me. Apparently not."

With great dignity, the short, wide secretary of state straightened her straw hat, clutched her purse, and stood to leave.

Alarmed, Morton the Maniacal clutched his wife's arm. "Where are you going? You haven't touched your salad and your baked chicken will be served any minute. Sit down! People are staring."

"Who cares?" she repeated. Nasturium the Third, Secretary of State of the great state of Wyoming, left the room.

In fact, just about everybody did notice. Smiling, some of the city's pushers and shovers wanted to applaud. Or stand up and cheer. Harry's left eye began twitching.

CHAPTER 38

Out on his ranch west of Laramie, Tom Rotter thought about calling Dollie Domenico. He wanted to warn her so badly he broke into a smelly sweat. What was wrong with that youngun's head?

When Dollie had married Harold Morton, then a bank teller, Rotter figured she'd be okay. Surely she would quit the Cheyenne bar and stay home. Have babies and bake cookies, cook and clean, like a woman oughta. Rotter could stop worrying about her. He was dadgum tired of spending his life worrying over her.

Her new husband wasn't much, however. Tom called him Morton the Miserable. Short little guy, wispy hair turning gray early, cheek muscle and left eye twitching whenever he got nervous, which could be most all the time. Rotter knew. He'd spied on the new husband through the bank window from the sidewalk or as the occasional walk-in customer. He was checking up on Morton, not on money.

Tom discovered that Morton's marriage to Dollie was his second time around. The first wife, a wealthy but spindly, plain, little mouse of a thing, had died in a home accident. Trying to move a freezer down to the basement. That's what came out in the inquest. Dumb thing to try doing all by your lonesome. The appliance had slipped, and crushed the poor little thing. If the inquest findings could be believed.

Crushed her to death, although from time to time Tom Rotter wondered about that. At the inquest, Harold Morton, the so-called bereaved husband, claimed he'd been at the downtown saloon all afternoon. Dollie Domenico backed him up, said she'd served Morton several mugs of draft beer, one right after the other. If so, Tom figured, it would be a first. Morton didn't drink.

Why did Dollie lie for Morton, give Harold an alibi, if it wasn't true? What was in it for her? When she up and married Morton, Tom thought he knew. Wasn't certain, of course, how could he be? So then Harold ups and marries Dollie, who stays on at the saloon.

Turn around twice, Morton quits Dollie. Rotter had breathed relief, all over again, finally. Good riddance to no-good rubbish. Nothing particularly wrong with him, Rotter supposed, just nuthin' specially good.

Next thing Tom knows, Morton marries the secretary of state. When Nasty's Arapaho husband had died, or disappeared, whatever, she'd returned from the reservation to promptly immerse herself in Cheyenne and Wyoming society.

Her family of uncles and cousins were influential in each of their Wyoming communities. Along with the family's life-long political cronies, they'd convinced Nasty Three to run for secretary of state, with their financial and political backing.

Shortly after celebrating her election, Nasturtium Vicente Fleetfoot ups and marries Morton. Why? Made no sense to Tom.

On his last trip to Cheyenne to spy on Harold—a teller until his marriage to Nasty Three got him promoted—Rotter had followed Harry to Dollie's saloon. Tom saw them exchange angry words. Then Morton trailed Dollie to her trailer, with Rotter trailing Morton. Tom slunk down low in his old blue Ford pickup. He saw Morton glance around furtively before using his own key to get in the trailer.

What was the pair up to?

Now he badly wanted to warn Dollie. Poor little abandoned foster child, Dollie Domenico. She didn't have a chance against a master planner like Harold. That's how Rotter thought of the sneaky Morton. He could be wrong, a'course, but he doubted it.

Tom's latest label for Dollie's weasel husband—"Morton the Manipulator."

CHAPTER 39

Steve Norman proposed, and Nicole accepted. Immediately, just like that. Without thought for her "career," or where they would live or how they would manage their individual and quite different personalities, interests, and life goals. Steve loved Stevie and already Stevie called the big man daddy. They were a trio, a family. No question that they belonged together.

"Yes, gam, it's true," Nicole told Aggie the night after they returned to Cheyenne. "It was love at first sight for both of us."

When reminded of their squabble over the bartender and Aggie's suggestion that maybe they should wait awhile, get to know one another better, Nicole said, "What's to know? We plan a Christmas wedding. Something small and quiet."

"Sure. With this big family?" Aggie was skeptical.

"Anyhow, a month should be a long enough engagement. We feel like we've already known each other forever. Remember, gam, this is the guy you wanted me to meet. You already guessed we'd be right for each other. Why should you be surprised?"

First there was Thanksgiving and the gathering of the clan. Aggie and Lisa were happily formulating food and decorating plans, and making family assignments for the dinner.

Upon his marriage to Aggie, Randolph Morrisey had moved into the house owned by her parents, Grover Cleveland and Violet Auld Vicente, who'd got it from Grover's parents, Rose and G.W. It was Rose's house, built by her grandmother, Essie, and passed on to Rose d'Gade.

Delighted with the old place on what had once been called Millionaires' Row, Aggie and Randy had also inherited a house full of repairs, and demands for remodeling, and maintenance. "Who cares?" Randy said gleefully. Handy with hammer and saw, the cries of the old house demanding a rebirth was excuse for him to buy every kind of carpentry tool and construction equipment he saw advertised.

With sorrow, Aggie surveyed all his stuff now piled up. Down here the basement floor was a rough-and-wrinkled mess, with one big room housing a complaining old oil furnace. Other dinky rooms and crawl spaces completed the lower level. When Nickee had stopped overnight with the Morisseys as a child, she'd loved to explore, and had playacted that she inhabited many a peculiar and fanciful world. "Pretend mode," her gam called the child's pastimes.

Comprising the third floor were four bedrooms, a kitchenette, and a living room—that Agatha had recently adopted as her private hideaway. In the bathroom the squeaky, protesting plumbing trickled water at the rate of one small teacup per half-hour, not much use for bathing, but for hand rinsing it sufficed.

The second floor housed another bathroom and four more bedrooms, plus the master bedroom and its luxuriant bath. In the room Agatha had shared with Randy all those years, the cozy padded love bench piled with colorful pillows in lavender and purple and surrounded by bay windows with hanging plants was ideal for dreaming away the hours, watching birds in the big trees outside, or reading a good book.

The main floor with screened wrap-around veranda and central foyer introducing the graceful curved staircase welcomed the family to their ancestral home. Back in the 1880s, the front room was called a parlor. Next it was named a living room. Now, Agatha supposed, it should be renamed again, to "great room." Also on the ground floor was a solar-heated sunroom, Randy's den, the dining room, and a weird, small room with a huge stone fireplace. "What could Grandma Rose have used this room for?" the double cousins wondered. Or perhaps it was Grandma Essie's personal nook.

The modern but nevertheless countrified kitchen sat at the back of the house along with a sunny utility room large enough to house a party. A powder room, done in lavender, completed the house tour. Aggie adored every square inch. She wondered whether she should fix it up better, see about listing it on the historical schedule. There might even be money to be made, should she give tours. Naw, too much bother, not to mention expense.

The cleaning woman, who had been a live-in while Randy was alive, became a weekly, and then a semi-monthly. Agatha simply could not afford her.

"How will you manage this big house without me?" Clara asked her employer-slash-friend. "You must be too tired to tango."

Mrs. Morrisey shrugged, sniffed, said she would explain some day. Clara hinted that she didn't understand why Aggie was attempting to watch every penny. When the housekeeper offered to come every day during Thanksgiving week, for free, out of friendship and because she'd die if she missed all the rigmarole, Aggie gratefully agreed.

The two worked in tandem to give the house a thorough cleaning. Aggie and Clara then made German apple pies, pumpkin pies, bread and buns, and cranberry "smush"—Stevie's name for his gamsy's dish made with crushed cranberries, crushed pineapple, whipped cream, pecans and sugar.

Peter and Lisa were doing the turkey, dressing, Irish potatoes and gravy. Nasty Two, a ham, and Nasty Three, a roast beef. The girls, Nickee and Beth, were making salads and vegetables, and the silent Hepzibah and Isabelle, their special sweet potato pie. Ned Fleetfoot always brought his macaroni-and-cheese dish with the secret ingredients that made it unique. The professor would no doubt show up with something peculiar. Last year Joan had brought a Sicilian recipe with sausage, pasta, several cheeses, eggplant, garlic, and tomatoes.

"Imagine," Nickee had whispered to Beth at the time. "Sicilian pasta for Thanksgiving. I'll bet you a bright new penny she conned a student into fixing it."

"Wonder what pet peeve the 'Grammar Cop' will mutter this time?" Aggie said to Lisa about her own daughter.

CHAPTER 40

It wasn't a dark and stormy night. Should have been, though. The bright, sunny, late afternoon insulted Aggie's mood. Their work completed, Clara had left. Aggie was too tired to read, text somebody, or talk on the phone.

She couldn't decide whether she was pleased, puzzled, or both, at the absence of threatening missives. Upon returning from their travels, with great trepidation Agatha had invited the Schwartzkopfs in for a cuppa. Perhaps sensing her fears, Peter checked every nook and niche, and Lisa went through the mail. Aggie, meanwhile, verified that no ominous threats awaited her via e-mail, fax, text, answering machine, or her own cell phone's voice mail.

Nothing. Why not?

Agatha stared across her bright yellow kitchen at her sun-yellow phone. She almost shook a finger at the offensive instrument, like reprimanding a misbehaving child. As if a scowl, a tch-tch, would frighten it into keeping silent forever more.

The phone pealed anyhow, as if in defiance of her edict. Nerves rattling, Agatha jerked, as if making ready to leap from her chair. Could be anybody—family checking on tomorrow's dinner arrangements, friends, business people, neighbors, church or committee members. Or it could be the whisperer, commencing anew, now that word of her return must have got about. Aggie should have switched on the answering machine, as Joan recommended, use it as her electronic receptionist, a screening device. If nothing else, inhibit the telemarketers and wrong numbers from reaching her in person. Although of course she had alerted the marketing hotline to block telemarketers, they still occasionally got through on her computer with their pesky spam.

Like a robot, one blue-veined hand ran over her bald pate, still with no more than a stubble. She missed her own salt-and-pepper hair, once typically styled in the manner of former vice-presidential candidate, Geraldine Ferarra. Shaking as if with palsy, Aggie's other hand picked up the receiver. No need, of course, since the ID readout brightly alerted her to Steve Norman's number.

"Hi Aggie, how you doing?"

The familiar husky bass of her rancher friend, her granddaughter's fiancé, sent tremors of relief tingling down Aggie's body. She could hear background noises from some tavern. "Where are you, Steve? Airport bar, or downtown?"

"Airport. You didn't answer my question, lady. You okay?"

"Never better," Aggie lied. What did the young man expect, her husband dead these few months, her week spent cleaning, cooking and baking, and—worst of all—remembering last Thanksgiving when Randy was at her side. Randolph Morrisey would have to go and die just three days before their forty-first wedding anniversary. She missed him terribly.

Aggie lifted the phone from the ledge that separated kitchen from breakfast table, and walked around it to reach for a chair. That made her want to cry, too. She and Randy together had discovered the discarded antiques. They loved this furniture, polishing them, and chatting from the chairs as they gazed across the table over sipping their morning and afternoon tea.

A giant in body and soul, Steve was tall, broad of shoulder, strong, casual, and invariably smiling. Steve Norman had so much savoir faire, also savoir vivre, then, too, he was a nurturer. An interesting mix of characteristics out in this land that comprised the still rugged West. Aggie could see Steve in her mind's eye. She would have preferred the eye of her web-cam, talking to him over Skype.

Pulling close the flowered teapot—flowered in roses, roses like her great-great-grandmother Rose and all those other Roses—Aggie poured herself a spot of apple-cinnamon tea. She continued to picture Steve at the popular bar.

In the middle of Cheyenne sits the municipal airport—a Bob Feller throw from the capitol and other state buildings. An airport made momentarily famous by the crash of Jessica Dubroff, the seven-year-old who had attempted to make a cross-country flight. She had taken off from her first layover, in Cheyenne, with too heavy a load in too rough a storm: updrafts, downdrafts, freezing rain, hail.

In the heart of the airport is the airport bar, the Cloud Nine Lounge, not famous for anything, particularly, but a natural watering hole of the governor and cronies. Government officials, wealthy ranchers and their sidekicks, lawyers, business people, sales reps, tourists and other one-time visitors, all stop by. A rich mixture of classes and genders drop in occasionally or hang out regularly at the airport bar. Aggie knew the scene well and so did everyone else in her extended family, perhaps in the whole of Wyoming.

Steve would have bought a round before placing his call to her. Which meant, Aggie thought, that her granddaughter had yet to arrive. Nicole wouldn't have made a definite appointment. Raised in casual cowboy style, cared for as much by her father and his father as by her mother's people—and despite her mother, Joan's, campus formality—Nicole would show up, or not, when or if the idea occurred.

Meanwhile, Steve would be center stage, knocking back his liquor straight, talking about whatever ranchers were debating these days: bitching over the price of beef, giving Wyoming politicians an earful of advice about how to run the state, exchanging opinions on federal and international topics including their fretting over action in the stockmarkets from New York to Hong Kong and London.

"You must be exhausted," Steve said in Aggie's ear. "Getting ready for Thanksgiving on top of your long trip?"

"I appreciate your thoughtfulness. Having you as a grandson will be wonderful. How're your girls?"

Aggie didn't ask after Norma Norman. Steve's ex-wife, the pseudo-intellectual, sophisticated Boston woman had not warmed to her husband's friends. A golf foursome with dinner afterward was enough for Randy. "Let's avoid any more social commitments with that cold lady," he'd said afterwards.

Agatha knew that Steve called his little girls every day, although half the time, apparently, he found himself battling with the children's mother or their au pair, who was probably instructed to make Norma's excuses. Steve flew back every month or so, besides, but his pain at parting with his daughters, on top of losing his father and brother, must have been horrible, for she often perceived a film of sadness beneath the perpetually smiling and congenial curves of his face, already lined by frequent exposure to sun, wind, and Wyoming weather off the back of his horse.

"Cindy and Sissy are okay, I hope. I wanted to bring them home with me through Christmas, until after the wedding. Norma said No. Can't prove much over the telephone. Reminds me of you, Aggie."

"What's that mean?"

"You think Nicole hasn't told me what's been happening? The threatening notes, letters, phone calls, and faxes you've been getting?"

"Oh, that Nicole! It was supposed to be a secret." Aggie's shaking hand broke a wee cracker into bits.

"Some secret. You make it sound like Christmas for kiddies." Ignoring her feeble protests as she tried to interrupt, he barged ahead. "Nicole says these threats refer to the family history you and Lisa are researching. Why do you think somebody wants you to quit the project? Have you unearthed a family scandal as yet? Or perhaps you could, any minute, I suppose."

"Not yet. Even if we did, so what? It was never intended as an expose The document isn't a tabloid reporting malicious gossip. Let the scandals, if there are any, die with our generation. That's what Nasty One says. Besides, yesterday's bad news stories are today's ho-hums."

"Eh? Such as?"

"Babies out of wedlock, things like that," she said vaguely. Agatha nibbled on her cracker.

The clamor of bar and patron noise grew louder. "Nicole mentioned embezzlement, a prison sentence."

"How does soap-opera news make our family different from any other American family?" Aggie broke another cracker and stuffed half in her mouth.

Beats me," Steve said. "Somebody must think it does. Otherwise, why the intimidation?"

"You're taking this seriously, Steve? I didn't want to tell people about it. Including you. Thought you'd laugh."

"Me? Never. Not spilling the beans to your family, except for a selected few—Nicole, Lisa and Peter—is a smart idea. Must be somebody in the family, or close to it, who wants you hushed. Nicole says that if the news has got around to Nasty Two, then everybody knows already."

Choking on crackers, Aggie rattled the teacup. "Steve, I was afraid the family—my daughter, Joan, especially—would think I'm a scaredy cat. A lonely old widow lady looking for attention. Joan analyzes everybody. Your turn will come, Steve, as Nickee's new husband. Your mother-in-law will analyze you to pieces."

"I don't care, let her try." Steve had also picked up on her self-definition as *the old widow lady.* Meanwhile, mid-fifties is hardly old. Aggie, my advice to you is call the police. And be careful."

She remembered to turn on the answering machine. She wasn't going to be surprised by any more odd or hateful calls, and she wasn't up to voice mail messages lurking in the woodwork, as it were. Or seemed to be.

Joan would criticize as usual if she could see her mother now, Aggie decided as she hurried upstairs to the third-floor suite, rearranged as her own, with bath and dressing room, bedrooms and long living room ending in the tiny kitchenette. The long room, with windows facing east on one end and west on the other, was now her office. She had left Randy's den downstairs almost the way it was, save for plowing through his financial records on both paper and computer. In Aggie's private space up here were desk, work tables, a new computer station, a television set with DVD player, and Randy's old recliner.

She gazed longingly at her hubby's favorite chair. It reclined to full, flat position. It practically screamed for reupholstering, but she padded it with old quilts and robes to tuck over her for the occasional afternoon snooze.

Wondering whether Lisa would call or drop by for tea, Aggie fluffed her wigs sitting on their Styrofoam heads in her dressing room. One wig Randy had particularly liked because it was so much like her own real hair. She preferred the short, wavy red one or the fluffy platinum one. Yearning for her lost love, Aggie felt the tears sprout. This holiday season wasn't going to be easy.

Quickly she grabbed a plastic sack, into which she dumped the rubbish from a box. Was there such a thing as a rubbish fetish? She liked clean trash receptacles, but now she wouldn't even drop a tissue in one of dozens of buckets and baskets and cans of all styles and colors. All over the house were her pretty trash cans, they were made of leather, wicker, vinyl, plastic, fabric, even glass and china. Agatha kept them tidy by leaving them empty, putting her rubbish into boxes. Only now the boxes seemed like trash cans so she had to rush about emptying the dumb boxes into plastic sacks. Stupid.

Ahh, there was the doorbell. Must be Lisa or Nickee.

Nicole, like her mother, had her own key and was standing in the bright airy kitchen by the time Aggie descended from the third floor by the back staircase. Nickee was wearing her orange dress. She said she'd just come from doing a charity auction for Soroptimists, a women's international organization.

"Didn't make any money," Nicole said ruefully. "To get known as an auctioneer, though, one must do this kind of thing." The girl admitted she was proud that the auction had rendered well over ten thousand dollars. "Got some good referrals, too, I believe."

Nicole said she was going downtown to meet Steve. "Stevie's out in the pickup. I'm driving one of dad's old things. My car's a wreck, you know. I'm running late. Oh well."

Nicole hugged her grandmother before pulling back to stare fiercely into Aggie's big round dark eyes. "I knew you and Clara would have finished baking and she'd have gone and left you. I hate to see you alone, gam. After dinner tomorrow, you must consider moving in with Lisa and Peter."

Perky again, from Nickee's company, Aggie resisted the very notion.

"Just because you haven't received any more warnings, doesn't mean you won't. Promise me, gam. One more nasty notice and you'll call the police. Really, you should've done it before you and Lisa left town. For all you know, the stalker, or whatever he is, doesn't know you're home yet."

The telephone rang again and, despite the answering machine to record the call, both Aggie and Nicole all but jumped out of their shoes.

CHAPTER 41

At the airport bar Nasturtium Three, in her forties, walked in and ordered a martini—up, very dry. Next came the state superintendent of public instruction, also in her forties, who ordered a Scotch-rocks at the bar to carry across the room to join Nasty on the banquette. Backs to the wall, they could see everyone who was there, and everyone who entered.

These women were two of the state's top five most powerful elected government officials. The governor, attorney general, and treasurer were the others. Just as Nasty Three's family had been influential in getting her elected, Wilma's family had done the same for her. The black family, descended from the frontierswoman, the wealthy Willamena Jackson, was well-respected in the state.

The two women toasted each other—for having survived another day, onlookers might have surmised. Steve Norman thought he knew better. Across the saloon, watching them, he was aware of that day's meeting at the state capitol.

Nasty Three and Wilma Sanford had escaped from a battle, a shouting match representing naturalists on one side and commercial and ranching interests on the other, with the state's public school system caught in the middle.

"It appears that everybody wants to brainwash the children," Wilma said. "To their own opinions and values, naturally."

For Steve's ears, who joined them, the women rehashed the meeting. "Business people claim our kids, especially teens, know little or nothing about economics, namely, effective consumerism—credit, spending versus saving, and so on. Much less what supports the state's economy—the mining and petroleum industries, agriculture, commerce, tourism. With energy uppermost," Wilma said.

"Meanwhile," added Nasty Three, "The naturalists say, in effect, 'Prosperity, hell, where will we all be without our natural herbs and

AGGIE'S DOUBLE DOLLIES

wildflowers. Where will we be when there is no Wyoming, no fresh air, water, and all the animals and insects disappear."

Nicole headed first to the airport coffeeshop to order a bowl of Rice Crispies for Stevie. Long-time friend Hannah the waitress agreed to watch over him. Hannah and Stevie might play spaceman and alien, she said, or astronaut and robot. At this time of evening, when neither arrival nor departure planes were due, and everybody within lassoing distance headed for the Cloud Nine Lounge, Hannah had little to do at the food counter. No customers except Stevie and a straggly-haired homeless fellow who regularly showed up in the cafe for an hour or so of warmth and a cup of coffee, if some charitable person would buy. Steve Norman often bought the old codger a whole meal.

When Nicole rejoined Steve, Nasty Three was saying: "And we're supposed to accurately identify what the public wants so we, as their representatives, can provide it. If we don't please the voters, we don't get elected again. Sometimes I'm not sure I want to serve another term."

"Of course you do," Wilma said matter-of-factly, as if she were Nasty's campaign manager. "The state needs your practical leadership. You know you've got the Indians' vote."

Steve knew what it meant to be PC, politically correct. "Don't you mean 'native Americans'?" he said to Wilma.

"No, I don't, Steve. Native Americans includes Eskimos and Hawaiians."

Nasty patted Steve's hand, while simultaneously plucking at Wilma's arm to pull her forward for a hug. "Another thing about our past, Steve, which you should know if you're going to be marrying Nicole. Wilma's family and our family are all one big clan. Her great-great-grandmother's sister, Willamena Jackson, and our great-great-grandmother, Rose d'Gade, were closer than sisters. For four decades they lived together, worked together. They helped each other produce several fortunes apiece. Other than marriage, you can't get much closer than that."

"Four decades?" said Nicole, astonished. "That's nearly half a century."

While Nickee had height, Nasty Three had width. They both had red hair, though, and some other similar features, like Essie Deighton's nose and Luther Auld's hearing impairment. Neither had a clue about what they might have inherited from either Rose or Etienne d'Gade.

219

Later Steve told Nickee about his chat with her gam. "I wonder if Aggie called the police. Maybe I should have done it for her. What do you think?"

"I think she's so independent, we'd better let her do it."

CHAPTER 42

Lisa dropped by, using her own key as usual. Aggie nearly jumped out of the wig she was wearing when she stepped into the kitchen to find her cousin with a cup of tea in her hand. "You scared me to death, darn it," Agatha said.

"I've got to quit popping in without ringing the doorbell. You could have a heart attack."

Vowing to keep silent did no good, Aggie needed to talk. After pouring a cuppa for herself and sitting at the round oak table, she blurted, "Lisa, I'm going to tell you something that I want kept in the strictest of confidences."

"You can count on me, love."

"I don't believe these threats are about stopping us from producing the family history at all. This is about money! So I have nothing to worry about."

"What in the world are you talking about? Of course you must worry if somebody is trying to get your money away from you. Actually, I'm not the least bit surprised. This is something we should have discussed in detail. Every con artist in the book is likely to come crawling out of the woodwork with some sort of money-grabbing scheme, from Ponzi investments to God knows what."

Agatha waited until Lisa ran down. "I have no money, Lisa. I'm practically broke."

"How could that be? All your and Randy's investments—stocks, bonds, real estate. Plus you've got that half-million dollars in insurance money."

"The money's all gone, Lisa. And the insurance is not mine to use. I'm almost convinced of that."

Slack-jawed, Lisa didn't know what to say.

"I've searched through Randy's computer and paper records. Then I verified my findings with our brokers and bankers. Unfortunately, I'm probably correct. It seems that Randy sold the stocks and bonds, and took out a hefty mortgage on the house. What he did with the money, I haven't the vaguest notion. Which means that if he were really in such terrible financial trouble, he might actually have killed himself. As for his policy, I must turn back the money to the insurance company if that's true. You realize they don't pay off on suicide deaths."

"Agatha, dear, what in the world are you thinking? He couldn't have committed suicide. Randy died in a head-on collision with a truck." Lisa paused to think. "Oh. You think he drove straight into somebody? That's not like your Randy. To risk killing somebody else."

"I know. I've been worried sick about all this. You thought it was all grief? Nosiree Bob."

"Our ancestral home—your home. The Arizona villa. Everything gone? All our trips to exotic places—no more?"

"Looks that way."

"No more beautiful fur coats, jewelry, luxury and fun?"

Aggie tried to smile. She hoped she didn't look the fool.

"What's funny, dear?"

"I've been thinking about Rose and Essie, and how they survived and prospered when they'd started from zero. If they could do it, so can I."

"What? You mean, get a job?" Lisa appeared horrified.

"Why not? Surely I'm not too old."

"You don't know how to do anything."

"I'll learn. If they could do it, why not I?"

Lisa decided to ask Peter's opinions. Her husband always had fresh ideas about everything. She left Aggie's house all in a dither.

In the flush of hearing such terrible news, Lisa had forgotten where they'd started. If the threats did in fact have to do with money, so what? Even if she were still well-endowed financially, how did the perp or perpetrators who were badgering Agatha propose to get their hands on it? Nobody had been kidnapped and held for ransom. Aggie surely didn't have any secrets somebody could use to blackmail her with.

Why, everybody must love Aggie Morissey all to bits.

"Think again," Peter said, when Lisa had told him the bad news and Aggie's suspicions. "Somebody sure has it in for your cousin."

Then his wife clapped a tiny hand to her mouth. "I wasn't supposed to tell. I promised."

#######

The perpetrator gained entrance into Aggie's big house by breaking a window into Randolph's ground floor study. No point in worrying about noise. The little widow couldn't hear very well, and the house was sheltered from neighbors by tall, hundred-year-old pine trees, rows of neatly trimmed hedges, and several hundred feet of sloping lawn on each side of her house.

Quiet footsteps tiptoed up the front staircase and into the master bedroom on the second floor. The lump in the bed never moved.

Raising an ax, the killer paused at the last moment to switch the implement of death to the blunt side. Down crashed the ax onto the sleeping head. Then the killer paused, to wait for sounds of life.

All was silent.

There was plenty of time to destroy the Morriseys' computer. And to gather the files. The guy who'd put out the contract on Aggie would be pleased.

CHAPTER 43

1885-1889

Rose d'Gade didn't trust anybody. She had seen too much, and experienced too many traumas, enough to last her through several lifetimes.

She certainly didn't trust young Rose and Estelle. Any minute they would be bursting into young womanhood. Once puberty struck them full force, she couldn't trust their brains to override their bodies' demand for breeding. They wouldn't know that, of course. No, they would insist it was pure romance and true love. Time would tell whether, in the heat of passion, they gave themselves unwisely to the wrong men at the wrong time.

Oh dear, it was so difficult these days trying to bring young girls to the altar with their virginity intact. It was better in the old days, surely. In Paris the chaperone was common. The French and Italians seemed to know a lot about what love did to the female body, even a century ago.

Willamena Jackson was the single exception. Rose would trust Willie with her life. All those years Rose had longed for Essie, the woman who Rose had thought of as her best, her only, true friend. Had Willie felt jealous? Watching Rose write all those letters to Essie, and then Rose reading Essie's letters. Willie's being forced to listen while Rose talked about the friend she had lost—lost to the horribly demanding circumstances of their life on the frontier.

In truth, Rose and Essie had only been friends in Nauvoo for four years, with another two years together on the trail. Six years total, beginning when she was but a mere lass of sixteen. She probably didn't even know Essie. Essie sure didn't know her. So many things had changed her during their separation. No doubt the same could be said for Essie Deighton. Funny, peculiar, that despite two marriages, Essie ended up with the same surname she had in the beginning.

By contrast, Rose and Willie had been together for over four decades! Didn't seem possible. In their seventies now, they were both still healthy. They probably had time to see and do a lot of things. There was yet time to pile ever higher their financial successes.

Rose and Willamena eventually received some of the money due them from investing in a Centennial gold mine. Herbert Claybourne, gold miner and one of their debtors, won a pot of gold playing poker at the Cheyenne Club. The Club was home to a number of cattle barons who wintered in Europe. Rose and Willie were cattle baronesses, they supposed. They, too, traveled in Europe, but they didn't live at the Club.

Claybourne had cheated Rose and Willie more than a decade earlier, but had not paid one red cent on the money loaned to him. "Not all of our investments have been wise ones," Willie had commiserated with her friend back then. At last Rose had caught him coming out of the Cheyenne Club in company with his raucous gambling buddies.

Standing there on the veranda in her beautiful silk gown with bustle, layers of petticoats, and a big floppy beribboned and beflowered hat, Rose was flanked by Territorial Governor Thomas Moonlight on one side and First Lady Ellen Elizabeth on the other. With haughty chin raised, she held out one daintily clad, lace-gloved hand, and in a firm voice demanded her due. Herbert Claybourne flushed and glanced furtively to each side. In the silence, he must have observed the fault-finding scowls all round, not only from the gamblers but especially on the faces of the governor and his wife.

Thrusting the bag of gold he held into Mrs. d'Gade's hand, Claybourne stammered. "H-here, ma'am, this oughta c-cover my debt to you."

Rose admired this governor, and he respected her. Serving in the Civil War as lieutenant colonel, he'd become a Brigadier General when ordered out West to take command of various posts and stations of the northern plains, making his headquarters in Fort Laramie. Jim Bridger, of Fort Bridger fame, had served Moonlight as a guide. In 1887, President Grover Cleveland had appointed Moonlight to serve as the seventh territorial governor.

In the governor's mansion, Ellen Elizabeth Moonlight, besides birthing nine children, served the territory also. She hosted many Cheyenne social gatherings, for she was well-read in literature. Rose and Willamena were frequent guests, Willie in her element to be exposed once more to Shakespeare, and Rose tolerating the scene for propriety's sake.

About her nine children and the possibility of having more, Ellen said, "It's in the lap of the gods." Which produced among the literary circle a debate over the origin of the statement. "I believe it's from Homer's *Iliad*." This introduced Willie (but not Rose, she wasn't listening) to another among literary giants.

"It was also in the *Iliad*, Book II, that Homer stated: 'His friends around him, prone in dust, shall bite the ground'," said Ellen. Willamena poked Rose in the ribs to suggest attention.

Back at the Inter Ocean Hotel, where Rose, Willie and young Rose and Estelle were staying until their house was ready, Rose dropped the sack of gold on the bed.

Young Rose and Estelle squealed and ran their slender fingers through the pile of pretty stones. "Can I have one?" begged young Rose, she of the dark hair and olive-complected skin, just like her grandmother.

"'May I', child. 'Can I' denotes having the ability. 'May I' asks permission."

"May I, Grandmother?"

"Ask Aunt Willamena. Half of it belongs to her."

"Yes, darling," Willie said. "You and Estelle may have one. Just one."

Young Rose immediately chose the biggest and brightest for herself. Seeing the disappointment on her friend's face, who couldn't find any stone nearly as large, young Rose quickly relented. "Here, Estelle, you take this one. I like that one better anyway. It's a funny shape."

Such was the pattern of their relationship, ever since Estelle had come to live with young Rose and her grandmother. Rose was invariably first and quickest. She could readily identify the best of anything. She also usually deferred to her friend, Estelle, the petite blonde with the uptilted nose. Just like Essie's, grandma Rose often thought.

Grandma Rose got a safety deposit box, where she placed the girls' gold pieces. "You may look at your gold whenever you wish. When you're grown and the price of gold goes up, you'll have some security."

Rose and Willie would never forget their sojourn in the dugout, when their only security was each other, Willie's knife, and then

Walking Mule. One had to be able to count on oneself. Having more than that was a wonderfully fine thing, however. Wealth could ward off the big bad wolf of poverty and despair.

Another fine thing, a more ethereal security, was that in Wyoming Territory, early on, women had the vote. In an effort to attract women to the territory, the first legislature had passed the law in 1869 that gave women the suffrage. The second legislature, still under their first governor, John Campbell, tried to rescind the first vote. It was a tie, until Campbell voted to keep the law.

Who could have guessed that these two young women, like their grandmothers, would remain lifelong friends. Unlike Rose and Essie, however, Young Rose and Estelle agreed they would never be parted. Even harder to imagine was that they would become kin-in-law, when several of Rose's sons would marry several of Estelle's daughters.

But then it was that Essie had died in a train-buggy accident soon after Rose and Essie were reunited in the 1870s' "Gilded Golden Age" of Cheyenne's history. Which meant that Essie did not make time to pass on her knowledge of birth control. Because neither Rose nor Willamena had ever heard of such a thing, wee Rose and tiny Estelle would grow up to birth ten live children apiece—not counting miscarriages and stillbirths. Due to their fertility, they would have plenty of descendants.

Rose d'Gade and Essie Deighton thus unknowingly established a great dynasty. For the offspring of their children would become Wyoming power brokers, wheelers and dealers of financial deals, and movers and shakers in the political arena. Money, along with physical and personality traits, passed on.

Thus it was that neither Rose nor Willie needed to spend their gold, as a means of livelihood. They had plenty of other money, realized from the sale of many businesses, hotels, and land investments in South Pass City, Rock Springs, Rawlins, and Laramie—the latter three of which were strung out along the Union Pacific Railroad line, like knots on the end of a kite. In 1867, gold was discovered near South Pass, and, in 1876, in the Medicine Bow forest west of Laramie. In that one-hundredth anniversary year of the nation's birth, the mine was named Centennial and so was the town, the only town in America so named.

Willie used some of the interest off her investment money to buy land in and around Cheyenne. At last able to locate, through the Pinkerton Agency, a sister, Willamena was reunited with Louise. Although Willie had never married, Louise had. When Louise Beasley arrived in Cheyenne, she brought with her two daughters with the good Bible names of Deborah and Delilah. Debbie with her Italian husband eventually begat Maximillian, and Delilah begat Dorothy, who begat Doris, who would begat Wilma.

Serving in the twenty-first century, Wilma would be elected Wyoming State School Superintendent of Public Instruction. Thus the genes, personalities, and dreams of one generation were passed down the line. Among these were a love of education and literature, ladylike behaviors, visions of security through sound financial planning, and a desire to help and lead children across the treacherous waters of adolescence into adulthood.

The national financial panic of 1887 did not affect the trio of Rose, Willie, and Louise. Their money was in real estate. Rose owned a hundred thousand acres of prime wheat-growing and ranch land, that which had been left to her by dear Essie. Rose would derive a fine income from it. Otherwise, she held the property in trust for Estelle, the granddaughter Essie did not get to see reach maturity.

All the youngsters, both black and white, were raised in the safety of luxury. They wouldn't have had to lift a finger, at manual labor, to maintain their households or at any kind of work to secure a livelihood. Ah, but they all did. Rose, Willie, and Louise saw to that. The girls graduated from the University of Wyoming, established in 1887 under the presidential administration of former governor, Dr. John W. Hoyt. Young Rose, Estelle, Deborah, and Delilah all completed one or more college degrees apiece—in literature and the arts, in economics and finance, in math and the sciences.

These wealthy women traveled, sometimes with each other, often with the girls. Like the early Mormons under Joseph Smith's leadership, education, by all manner of methods, was held in high esteem. At Lake Bomoseen in rural Vermont, Rose with Young Rose and Estelle, stayed in a gracious hotel where the entertainment included rocking on the veranda, and afternoon teas and lawn parties where they could wear their beautiful gowns with the many petticoats and fashionable bustles, and their large variety of huge colorful hats.

What would Rose have thought, had she been able to look in a crystal ball to discover that on those very shores of Lake Bomoseen, several generations later, Aggie Morissey would attend a seminar? Or that Agatha, who looked so much like Rose d'Gade, would capture a serial killer!

Other activities the dignified ladies with their young charges enjoyed included croquet and boating, dancing and swimming.

They all traveled on great ocean liners to western Europe—to the great cities of London, Paris, Amsterdam, Florence, Venice, and Rome. They were at home as world travelers long before it was the vogue among the middle class.

By the late 1880s, Rose's house was finished. She would some day pass on her mansion to Young Rose, for by that time Estelle would have married well, and she and Luther Auld would have their own lovely Cheyenne home.

Willamena and Louise built a fine house too. Besides traveling to Europe, Willie and her sister also wintered in New Orleans and Virginia. For such locales were home to the two black women in their youth. In Cheyenne Debbie and Delilah married well, too. They built a large house together, big enough to accommodate themselves and their own descendants.

They all knew, moreover, that the two families would be equally welcome in the other's clan. Rose and Willie loved each other like sisters, and their descendants loved like cousins, which counted more than blood, color, or origin.

Personal memories of what they had endured and accounts of other settlers' horror stories had made Rose proceed with caution in the construction design of her house. The architect and a single, old, tight-lipped carpenter were the only ones who knew Rose's request. Besides the great curving staircase in the front foyer, and another set of stairs in the back that led from the kitchen to the third floor, Rose wanted a secret staircase, one that would run between walls from the top floor to the basement, with entrances onto each floor hidden behind built-in bookcases. She sought an escape route in times of turmoil.

CHAPTER 44

Thanksgiving dawned clear and bright. No storms were predicted that would spoil the family holiday at Aggie's historic home.

"I'm worried about her, Peter," Lisa said in the Schwartzkopfs' kitchen.

Peter liked to roast the turkey, he'd done it for thirty-five years, at home or abroad. Lisa puttered with potatoes and gravy. "I think there's good cause, Lisa. Too often people think that threats are only that, when they're really preamble to deadly mischief. We'll bring Aggie home with us tonight and call the police."

About Agatha's financial problems, Peter said nothing. Perhaps he hadn't heard his wife, or he thought the grieving had made Aggie fearful.

Ned Fleetfoot packaged his macaroni dish with an aluminum foil cover and got in his car. He hoped his mother could get free of her miserable tag-along husband long enough for him to talk to her. He couldn't stand Harold Morton, and saw no reason why his mom, now Wyoming's secretary of state, should have saddled herself with such a jerk.

Ned was thinking about the reservation—going back up there to live, or at least renew contact with his people. He was still torn between his father's Indian tribe in north-central Wyoming and his mother's clan down in the southeast corner of the state.

Now dead, Ned's father was no longer around to hurt his mother or to embarrass Ned with his mean drunken temper. But Ned had friends and would like to get back to his roots. He had spent most of his life with the Arapahos on the Wind River Reservation up near Yellowstone. Ned liked the ancient chants, songs, and dances as part of religious ritual. He had the Indian's traditional attitude toward work—the tribe came first. To relocate off the reservation in order to find employment was less important than staying close to family.

While they lived among the Arapaho—like Rose, before her, or so Ned had heard—his mom had willingly become acclimated to the culture. She'd beaded her own moccasins for the special ceremonies, the pow-wows; she'd lived by their rules and lifestyle, though never forgetting her own origins or place among the Vicente-Aulds. Nasty Three had left Ned's father several times, always returning to Cheyenne. The last time was after she'd buried her husband. Since then, she'd never mentioned her husband or told Ned why she had run for public office. She certainly hadn't told her son why she had married Harry Morton so soon after winning the election.

Wilma Sanford and her mother, Doris, arranged the centerpiece, as always, for the big table that would be let out with several leaves to accommodate all the adults. Thanksgiving was a formal sit-down dinner. The children would eat in the kitchen and the teenagers, including Wilma's son, Mark, would occupy the sunroom next to Randy's study.

The pair of velvet-skinned women would set the table with sparkling crystal, freshly polished silver, white linens, and century old Bavarian china, which Rose and Willamena had bought before World War One in Germany. Doris would select the wine from the wine cellar in the Morrisey's basement. Wilma's mother had learned from her mother, Dorothy, an experienced sommelier. Both Dorothy and Doris had accompanied Grandmother Willie and "Aunt" Rose d'Gade to Paris and northern Italy several times on just-for-fun trips to the continent by ocean voyage.

While the ladies dressed the formal dining table, Brad Gifford and his father-in-law, Peter, would arrange the kitchen and sunroom tables, and Beth and Lisa would set them with paper napkins and accoutrements.

Like a series of formal dance steps, all these things were ritual. Everybody had done the same things for so long, they knew exactly what to do, how to do it, and how long their assignment would take. There was comfort in tradition, the double cousins insisted, even though the young people sometimes suggested it might be interesting to change things around every which way.

"Isn't all the new technology change enough?" asked Nasty Two, who didn't know a computer from a compass.

While Doris worried over the cornucopia that sat on her lap in the passenger seat and Wilma drove them down the street to Aggie's house, Wilma fretted over her two friends, Nasty Three and Agatha. "They aren't themselves these days, mama. Agatha, I can understand, she's still grieving for Randy. Recently, however, she has become jumpy and absentminded."

"Oh, my dear, Agatha Morissey is always absentminded. 'Jumpy' though, what's that supposed to mean?"

"It's just a vague feeling I have that things aren't going well for her."

Mark reached over the front seat to help his grandmother settle the Thanksgiving centerpiece more steadily in her lap. "I'll carry the cornucopia into the dining room for you, grandma."

"Hush. You've got your guitar to worry about."

Both Wilma and Doris were tall. Both women wore their hair short cropped, and matted tight to their heads. An athlete, Mark was also a musician. First it was the violin and then, in adolescence, he had switched to the guitar. Handsome, with symmetrical features, short hair, and milk-chocolate skin, he was physically fit, well-muscled from working out on the Nautilus equipment his mother had bought him for Christmas. Girls found him attractive and also "nice." Courteous to them, respectful to his elders, and attentive to his teachers, Mark was the ideal son, Wilma had told her mother more than once.

"What about Nasty Three?" Doris asked her daughter, now. "She's not willing to share her secrets with you yet?" Everybody knew the secretary of state and the state superintendent of public instruction—two of five of the most powerful positions in the sate—had been best friends for decades.

"Nope, not a peep out of her." Wilma and Nasty Three were confidantes, like Rose d'Gade and Willie Jackson, a century earlier. "Of course she's busy with affairs of state, all those corporate and economic things she's responsible to and for. The Indians, like a lot of Wyomingites, count on Nasty to protect their interests. Besides money from their casinos, the Indians get royalties from the oil and gas industry along with mining. The more prosperous these businesses are, the better off are the Arapaho and Shoshone, each of whom gets a share or dividend. And then Nasty's got Harold the Hun to contend with."

"I agree. He is someone up with whom I would not put." Doris, like her ancestor, Willamena, appreciated correct language. Paraphrasing Winston Churchill's statement, as an example of avoiding prepositions at the end of one's sentences, was the type of intellectual game that tickled her most. Her and Joan.

Moving silently about their kitchen while making ready for the big day were Hepzibah and Isabelle Vicente. But no Rudolph, he of the bulbous nose. Hepzibah's son (Isabelle's husband) had sent a telegram from upstate New York that he couldn't make it, he was hard on the trail of tracing some obscure church that might want him to preach his special firebrand style of religion.

Isabelle tossed a pile of finished crocheted poncho shawls into the car for the women of the family. She slid gingerly into the driver's seat, while Hepzibah carried the sweet potato pie. Isabelle's arthritis was acting up.

"With Agatha collecting clues for the family history, somebody's likely to ask us something about someone, Isabelle. You keep yer mouth shut, you hear?"

"Yes, mama," said Isabelle. She didn't complain about her aches and pains and she didn't ask Hepzibah how she felt. The two quiet women fell silent.

Brad and Beth Gifford, with Brianna and Brittany, got in their new Oldsmobile with the plush baby blue upholstery. They placed their bowls filled with vegetables and salads in the trunk for safety.

"Oh, Brad, helping Nickee and Steve plan their wedding is going to be so much fun. I do wish they'd waited until mid-summer, though," Beth said wistfully. "By then we'd have such gorgeous flowers in our garden to contribute."

Brad seemed preoccupied. At length he said, "Sweetheart, there's something I've been wanting to tell you."

Oh, oh, with that serious tone, it must be something terrible. He had contracted an incurable disease? He was having an affair and wanted a divorce? He'd lost all their money? What? Beth held her breath and closed her eyes.

She must try to distract her husband, keep him occupied with all sorts of piddly errands before dinner. Beth didn't want Brad to spoil everything, not today. Their life was so perfect: beautiful children, lovely home, good income, family and friends, they had their health and so did the twins. What could it be?

Before she could instigate her strategy, Brad continued as if anxious to spit out a mouthful of soapsuds.

"I want to quit my insurance business. I can get a good price for the agency and all the clientele I've established. I'll use the money to buy a big semi-trailer truck. Honey, I want to be a cross-country trucker."

Oh God, please, no, no, no, not that. "We'll talk about it later," she mumbled, as they pulled up to the Morissey mansion.

Although not double cousins, some plain first cousins were invited. Just for Thanksgiving, though, not for the really special Christmas holiday dinner. Rose and George Washington (G.W. for short) Vicente begat two daughters following their first four sons. These girls were named Opal and Pearl, who begat Betsy Ross and Martha Washington, respectively, who in turn begat Matthew, Mark, Luke and John. Which made two teenage Marks at the dinner.

The boys would be company for Wilma's Mark. He could hardly be expected to eat and socialize with young Stevie and the BB twins.

"Oh, Steve, it's going to be so exciting, introducing you to family members you haven't met yet," Nicole said. "Afterwards, you can tell me who you think we should include in the wedding party and who we should omit."

Steve guessed rightly that Nickee would choose Beth as her matron of honor. "I'd like for Brad to be best man," he said.

Steve knew Nickee's bridesmaids, for the trio were planning to host a shower for the bride. Lauren, Kendal, and Cherri had come over the hill to meet Nickee and Steve at the downtown bar. They were Professor Joan's students and mentees, and Nickee's good friends. Following Cowboy Billy's incarceration at the prison in Rawlins, and Nickee's divorce, she had gone out partying with them.

Three more different women you could hardly expect to find chumming with each other, befriending Nickee, or winding up on the wind-swept high plains of backwater Wyoming. Lauren Lockhart was a slender, wealthy blonde from Los Angeles. Thrice-married, thrice-divorced Kendal Pesci heralded from New York. Cherri Chavez, a part-Cherokee from Oklahoma, was a former nun. A mixed bowl of nuts, Nickee cheerfully called the four of them, herself included.

Hearing the foursome giggle and gossip, Steve reminded himself that his bride was still a young woman, that she had friends and liked to have fun. He prayed that Nickee would be happy with him. Not that he was always taciturn. He could be as social as the next, especially in the senate or with his cronies. Spending days on the ranch without seeing another living soul appealed, too. He didn't dismiss the ranch cook and cowhands, but off on the range, alone on his palomino, he could go for hours, days, without company. That kind of solitude might not agree with his Nickee.

"What about me?" Stevie asked from the back seat of Steve Norman's pickup. "What do I get to do? In the wedding, I mean."

Steve and Nicole smiled warmly at each other. "Ring bearer?" Steve suggested. "Guess we'll need two flower girls so both Brianna and Brittany can be doing the same thing."

"How about four flower girls?" Nickee said. "Cindy and Sissy, too?"

Her suggestion warmed the cockles of his heart. He grinned all over.

When Steve, Stevie, and Nicole entered Aggie's house through the big door into the kitchen busy with people bumping into each other, Nickee asked right away for her gam. "Where is she?"

Everybody stopped, like a bunch of wind-up toys whose batteries had all run out of juice simultaneously. Rewound, several people spoke at once, while others looked puzzled.

"She must be around here, somewhere."

"Haven't seen her."

"Too many people bustling about to notice she was missing."

Just then the Nasties arrived—Nasty Two with a baked ham and Nasty Three with roast beef. No Harold the Half-wit. "He said he wasn't feeling well," Nasty Three said to nobody in particular.

"Thank God," muttered Ned Fleetfoot to Cousin Beth.

"Agatha must have overslept," said Lisa.

"Until noon?" Wilma demanded.

"Nap, then," Lisa suggested lamely. "I'm going upstairs to check on her."

"I'll go with you," said Peter.

"Me, too," said Nicole and Beth.

"We want to go, too," said the Nasties.

"We'll all go," said Brad.

"Not us. Too crowded," said Betsy Ross and Martha Washington.

Hepzibah and Isabelle said nothing.

Neither did Wilma's Mark, or Matthew, Mark, Luke, and John, the just-plain second and third cousins. Or perhaps it was second cousins-once-removed.

The little children weren't curious. They were busy playing.

First to step over the threshold into Agatha's bedroom, Lisa screamed. Bumping into her mother, Beth peeked over Lisa's shoulder, then she turned pale and promptly fainted. Nicole reached down to assist Beth, and Steve, Peter, and Brad pushed their way past the women into the room.

An ax lay atop the rumpled bed clothing, a crumpled head of hair lay on the pillow. Steve jerked away the covers, while Peter turned back to shelter the women from the awful sight.

CHAPTER 45

"Hey, wait." bellowed Brad. "It's okay." He held up a wig, and a familiar Styrofoam head that normally sat on a closet shelf holding a wig. Then he pulled out a blanket that was stuffed beneath the sheet. "It's okay, everybody. Agatha's not here. It's a dummy.

At that moment, rubbing sleepy eyes, Agatha stepped out from behind a built-in bookcase. "What's going on?"

Lisa fainted.

Dinner forgotten by most (but not by all), Peter called the police. Beth and Nicole took Aggie and Lisa to the kitchen, where the young women comforted their elders with cups of strong hot tea.

Steve and Brad did a house search, which was when they discovered the smashed computer and general disarray in Randy's study.

"See?" Aggie whispered to Lisa when they made their own survey. "I told you somebody was after my money. All our notes on the family history are safe on the third floor. In here was where Randy kept his financial records."

Peter overheard enough to interrupt. He proposed that Aggie rest until the police arrived but, bent on discovering for herself what damage the intruder had caused, she refused, merely mumbling excuses when Peter demanded answers.

Everyone wanted to hear how Aggie had escaped her assailant, but Steve shooed them into the great room to await the police. "Somebody in this house right now could be the culprit," he whispered to Nicole. "Got to keep everybody from leaving. Go keep them together, Nickee."

Back upstairs in her bedroom, and greatly embarrassed, Aggie described her version of what must have happened. To the police, when they arrived, she demonstrated how she had effectuated her escape.

Also present were Peter and Lisa, Steve and Nicole. These four insisted on accompanying their beloved but humiliated cousin to the scene of the crime.

"It's so lonely without my husband, you see," Agatha said. "I often put a pillow or rolled blanket on his side of the bed. To make it even more realistic, this time I put my wig on its Styrofoam head and laid it on his pillow.

A snicker from the young, baby-faced, uniformed rookie officer made Aggie stop. She looked accusingly at first Steve and then Peter. She'd told the men that people would laugh at a middle-aged woman's eccentricities. She hadn't dared tell them or Lisa and Nickee that she'd gone this far with her mourning.

Determined to tell her story, Aggie continued. "Last night I couldn't sleep, which is often the case. I used the secret staircase to get up to the third floor to sit in my husband's old recliner. That's when I fell asleep. I didn't hear a thing."

"You didn't hear anything?" the snickerer asked in disbelief.

"She's deaf," Peter said.

"Only partially," Nicole said.

"We all are," said Lisa.

Without bothering to explain or expand on the family's physical impairment inherited from Luther Auld, Aggie commenced describing the threats she'd received, with help in her explanations from Steve and Peter, Lisa and Nicole. "But the threats might not have been actually related to the family history, although that's what the messages said."

"Huh?" said the rookie.

"Could have been about the money . . . ." Lisa finished.

"Shhh," said Aggie. "You promised."

Thoroughly confused, the two police officers got no further help from anybody, since Peter and Steve and Nicole were busy with Aggie. Lisa insisted that her double cousin elaborate with an explanation about her financial problems.

"Oh, all right. I might as well tell the rest of you," Aggie capitulated. "You'll find out sooner or later anyhow. I'm broke. Randy committed suicide."

"You don't know that," said Lisa.

"What?" said Nicole.

"How come?" said Steve.

"Shut up, everybody! Hold your horses. Back up," said the sergeant.

"Yeah," said the rookie.

Aggie insisted they leave the scene of the attempted murder—too dismal. The cops placed yellow police tape over the door to secure the room from the curious. The party of nine left the master bedroom by way of the secret staircase to take seats on couches and chairs in Aggie's third-floor office. She retrieved the threatening notes and tapes received earlier via mail, fax, and answering machine. At last her story unraveled, with numerous interruptions from kin and in-laws to elaborate with their surmises, and halts from the officers to demand that the interviewees put their statements in chronological order.

The young skinny, blond, baby-faced rookie cop, Bobby Gilbert, wanted to send everybody else home. The tall, red-headed, husky, bearded, middle-aged sergeant, Walt Fletcher, wanted to get everybody's statement first. He knew the Morisseys, and Aggie in particular. This wouldn't be the first time she'd gotten in the way of a crime. During the downtown Cheyenne bank robbery, her assistance had saved the day. In this instance, Fletcher wasn't so sure. The little widow seemed to be losing her marbles. Maybe her elevator no longer went to the top floor. Walt thought in cliches.

"Yeah, right," said the rookie. "Get everybody's statement first."

Aggie wanted to serve dinner.

"Before everything gets cold," said Lisa.

"We can use the microwave to reheat," suggested Peter.

"The children will get fussy," protested Nicole.

"Hold it." hollered Walt. He directed Bobby to sit down with Steve to sort everybody out. "Make a list up," Walt said. "Find out where everybody's at."

"Not *up*, not *at*," said Joan the grammar cop, entering quietly from the back stairs that led up from the kitchen. "Please don't end a sentence with a preposition. That infernal practice grinds on my nerves, like scratching a fingernail on the chalkboard. Look, guys, it's like this: dispense with both the 'up and the 'at' These prepositions are unnecessary in this particular instance."

"Good grief, mom," said Nicole.

Joan wanted to know what was happening. Answering her questions sent the family into another gush of explanations. In the meantime, Bobby, with Steve's help, made a list up to identify where everybody was at.

"To determine their places in the family," Steve said, after poking Nickee to request her help with the identifications.

"I saw some colored people downstairs there," Bobby said. "Them people the servants?"

"Good grief, no," said Aggie, for once able to hear. "They're as much kin as anyone else. Closer than some in-laws. Oops, sorry, Peter, uh, you too, Steve. You guys know I didn't mean you two, right? I meant Harry Morton."

Greeting them in the great room the small group discovered a roaring fire in the fireplace, and Mark Stanford's guitar music soothing the crowd. Wilma's son had organized the family in singing some of the old cowboy songs. Now it was *Tumbling along with the tumbling tumble weeds.*

Steve suddenly felt nostalgic and sad. Hearing these old familiar tunes reminded him of his dad and big brother. Next thing you know, somebody would put on a CD playing Chopin, his dad's favorite.

Steve went into Randy's study to call his daughters in Boston, to wish them a happy Thanksgiving. He talked about his wedding to Nicole, and told Cindy and Sissy they were invited to be flower girls, along with the Brianna-Brittany twins.

"Tell them I can't wait to meet them," Nicole said at his side. Steve hugged her. His sweetheart was wearing the dress that made her look like a bottle of orange juice. In honor of the holiday, she said.

Mark, Matthew, Mark, Luke and John retreated to the sunroom, after assuring the police there was nothing they knew or suspected.

Wilma and her mother, Doris, filled plates for the children, re-warming the food in the microwave oven. They settled Stevie and the BBs at the round oak table in the eating end of the big kitchen.

The Nasties put the ham, turkey, roast beef, potatoes, gravy, dressing and sweet potato pie in the big double ovens to re-heat.

"Don't forget my macaroni," said Ned.

"Or our vegetables," said Beth.

"Where's Joan's dish?" asked Isabelle, at last breaking silence.

"Hush," said Hepzibah.

"I can't believe it," said Joan, coming in at that moment and motioning to Hepzibah and Isabelle. "They can speak." The professor carried a long glass casserole containing enchiladas.

"Really, mom," Nicole said. "Mexican food for Thanksgiving?"

"Why not?" said Joan. "Adds variety."

"Can we help?" asked Betsy Ross and Martha Washington, their hands full of mince pies.

"'May we'," said Joan.

"How do you like my new wig?" asked Nasty Three, who had arrived minus her straw hat with the daisies.

"Don't stick it in the oven," said Beth. "You'll melt it."

"Really, Nasty, talking about your wig at a time like this," said Lisa. Then she remembered that the Nasties didn't know what she was talking about, so she explained, all in one breath. "Aggie said she'd stuck her wig—the one that resembled Randy's head of hair—on top of its Styrofoam head and put it on his pillow and then she stuffed a blanket in Randy's place under the covers in their big kingsize bed with the soft pillow-top mattress that probably cost the earth."

It didn't matter to Peter that his Lisa sounded a bit dopey, not much different from Aggie herself. Except that with Cousin Agatha acting so discombobulated lately, the Schwartzkopfs decided between them that they must start thinking for her. And make decisions for Agatha, with or without her consent or presence. Apparently, every last cent left to Aggie was now going to be precious and should be stretched to the limit. "Or she'll simply have to do without," said Peter.

"Like Isabelle and Hepzibah."

"Or Betsy Ross and Martha Washington."

"I thought their preacher son-and-husband was well-off?"

"Rudolph? He, of the bulbous nose? Heaven's no. They barely scrimp by." Lisa rolled her eyes at her husband and Colonel Peter rolled his right back.

Lisa admitted in a whisper that she didn't suppose Agatha would want the Nasties to know about the financial fiasco she faced from Randy's mismanagement. What in the world was Randy Morissey thinking of.

"Do tell us what's happening," entreated Betsy Ross, with Martha Washington tagging along. "Just because we're not double cousins, it doesn't mean you should leave us out."

"Good grief," said Nicole, leaving the room to go look for Steve.

Walt and Bobby were interviewing people one by one in the tiny first-floor room with the wall-to-wall stone fireplace—the room that no current family member had ever been able to figure out a practical use for. With each interviewee, Walt alluded to but didn't explain the threats Aggie had received.

Bobby kept interrupting, demanding to know where everybody was at, the previous night. "Around or shortly after midnight," he said vaguely.

The just-plain first cousins were deeply insulted at the questions the police posed. But nobody else was. The rest of The Clan, including Wilma and Doris, were purely puzzled.

"What's going on?" asked Joan, forgetting to reword her query so as to avoid letting it dangle with a preposition at the end.

"When do we eat?" "We're hungry," said the teenagers, tired of listening to Mark play his guitar.

"Why is the Morrisey computer smashed?" demanded Betsy, a clear indication she had been prowling in rooms not open to guests.

"Who trashed Randy's desk and all his stuff?" asked Martha, another prowler and gossiper.

They directed their questions to Rudolph Vicente's women, which availed them nothing, since Hepzibah and Isabelle had rezipped their lips.

Just then the Morissey's land line rang. Peter picked up, and after an exchange of pleasantries, passed the instrument on to Aggie.

Everybody, including the cops, gathered round when they heard the widow Morissey address Dom by his title.

"How am I? Why, yes indeedy, I'm good, Mr. President." You didn't bother the Most Important Man in the world with tales of threats, stalking, and attempted murder. "I do wish you and Julia and Jerica could be with us on this lovely holiday, Dom."

"My stars." exclaimed Nasty Two, after Agatha set down the phone. "The President must be psychic, to call you right now, in your time of travail."

"Not at all," Aggie replied calmly. "He always calls me on Thanksgiving."

Ultimately, the sergeant and his rookie left, as confused as when they'd met the family, but armed with far more information than they ever wanted to know. In the police car, Bobby flipped through his notepad.

"What's Mr. Morrisey's suicide got to do with anything? And who sabotaged the Normans' Cessna?"

"Beats me," said Walt. "We don't know if Randolph Morrisey killed himself or whether somebody murdered Richard and Charley Norman, the senator's dad and brother. Could be we've already interviewed the perpetrator—one or more—back there in that goofy family and we don't even know it."

"Yeah 'goofy' is right. How could those colored people be related to the rest of Agatha Morissey's family? They marry one of the white men or what?"

"Cripes, Bobby. Not 'colored' people. 'Blacks' or 'African-Americans'. Better bone up on your PC."

"'PC'. What's that?"

"Beats me. Something you're supposed to do. Or not."

CHAPTER 46

Lionel Falstaff was nervous. Lucy, his wife, was excited.

"Well! Somebody must think you're important," she said in her high-pitched squeaky voice that hurt his ears. "Don't screw up, you've only got until Monday to prepare."

Lionel wondered if Lucy anticipated his falling in a faint right in front of the government class. Laramie County Community College, L-Triple-C, or its even shorter nickname, "L-Trip," is located on a hill south of Cheyenne. Outsiders had suggested to Lionel that all the Laramie names were confusing. There was Fort Laramie, in Goshen County; Cheyenne, in Laramie County. The city of Laramie, the Laramie Rivers (including the Little Laramie), and Laramie Peak were all in Albany County. All of these were named for Jacque LaRamie, the French Canadian trapper who was killed, allegedly by Indians, on the bank of the river in 1820. That was the river, with its two branches, both of which now carried the name, Laramie.

This would not be Falstaff's first lecture on Wyoming politics at the college. However, it was the first time since his name had been linked—via a slip from the press—to the Governor's War on Weeds, with Lionel in opposition. He was terribly afraid of the repercussions. He was already getting a cold shoulder in the capitol, with the big man's cronies saying he was disloyal to the Party.

What would happen now, he mused, biting his tongue. Surely he wouldn't lose his job, not with Nasty Three on his side. Whether she was for or against him, he couldn't be sure. He'd damn well put in enough time on behalf of the secretary of state's campaign. She ought ta know she owed him. Big.

# # # # # # #

Aggie sold her stock and cashed in the profits she had made off of Randy's insurance money. In the months since her husband had died, she had lived on the interest. With the fund intact, she returned the full half-million dollars to the insurance company. She was convinced Randy had died on purpose.

However, she refused to move from her ancestral home, despite the second mortgage that the bank could call in at any moment, and the several invitations proffered that she move in with kinfolk. In the meantime, a compromise was proposed. Nicole and Stevie put forward the notion that somebody stay with her at all times. The young lovers took the first shift, taking bedrooms on the second floor next to Nickee's gam. For the sake of appearance, they slept apart.

Steve hauled Nicole's trailer out to his ranch. She wasn't yet willing to part with it, she said. "It'll save my packing, Steve. Everything Stevie and I own is inside. It may not be much, but it's my safe haven, like a cocoon."

What Steve wondered was whether, even subconsciously, the trailer might also be her escape hatch. In case their relationship didn't work?

Nicole's networking resulted in getting another charity auction, up in Cody, in northwestern Wyoming near the entrance to Yellowstone National Park. With the insurance money on his dad's plane, Steve had bought another Cessna, a four-seater 210. To save time, they would fly north.

Stevie stayed with the Giffords, as usual. He and the twins were enrolled in the same private preschool.

"You're going, too, gam. We're not leaving you alone," Nicole said. "You're coming with us and that's that."

No arm twisting necessary. Aggie readily agreed. Having people care about her was wonderful. Rather than frightened out of her wits from the harrowing ordeal of missing death by a hair, she felt relieved. There was no longer the need to worry that in her widowhood she'd become paranoid. Or that people would suspect her of weird eccentricities. The danger to her life was real!

#######

Harry called Dollie from a public phone at the airport. While listening to it ring, he stared admiringly at his reflection in the darkened window of the bar opposite. He puffed out his chest—which hardly made any difference. "Harold the Handsome," he mused, thinking that the Grecian Formula was doing the job advertised, it covered his gray hair. He looked terrific in the new pinstriped charcoal suit, with the lavender pocket handkerchief and matching tie.

"I can't come over no more," he whispered, when Dollie finally answered. "Too risky. I'm sure that blasted Norman saw my car parked outside your trailer." At mention of the rancher, Harry's cheek began to twitch. Then his left eye.

"Who cares?"

"I care! And you'd better. My wife, the secretary of state, heard that me and you were seen together at the bar, so I can't be dropping in there either."

"Who cares?"

"Wait a minute. I thought you cared. About me. About us."

Dollie Domenico cared about the rancher, the senator. For all the good it did her. His engagement to Nicole was due to come out in the Sunday paper—that was the gossip she'd overheard in the bar. Her last chance to get a really good guy had gone up the tubes like smoke up the chimney. Or was it "down the tubes"? Yeah, down the tubes, like pee in the potty. So much for dreams. That's where Harry's schemes should go, too—right down the sewer.

"You talk big, little man. But I don't see you doin' nuthin' lately." She ignored his sputtering on the other end of the line. "Besides, you never did 'splain nuthin'. You're still married to Nasty Three and it don't seem like you're eager to get out of that marriage. So why hang around me, anyway?"

"Patience, baby, patience."

"Don't call me baby."

#######

The big burly man with the bushy eyebrows had arranged to meet his paymaster south of town. The truckstop on Interstate 25 on the way to Denver seemed like a safe distance. Who could know about their liaison? Mostly truckers and tourists stopping off here.

Once the job was done, Burly Boy left town for Denver, a hundred miles to the south. Be good to get away from Wyoming. Ought a be safe and anonymous in the crowded metropolis.

He hadn't picked up a Cheyenne paper either, so he didn't know who had found his victim. He'd merely left the data files in a knot hole in a cottonwood tree, and mailed his client a note about when and where he expected payment. That was close enough to the instructions he'd been given.

In a booth far at the back of the truckstop café, he waited. And waited some more. He drank enough black coffee to fill a bathtub, but was afraid to go take a leak, probably miss connections. He filled two plates from the food bar. Couldn't wait no longer, had to find the men's room. He barely made it.

Upon returning from the restrooms, he spotted the Guy.

Wouldn't you know, the minute he turned his back the Guy shows up. Look at him, standing there in the cafe entrance for all the world to see, scowling, shuffling, peering around suspiciously. Oh yeah, going to leave without paying me. Some excuse.

He caught the Guy by the arm as he was pushing through the swinging exit door. "Hold on, buddy. You'd like that, wouldn't you, excuse to cheat me. The jobs are done. I want my money."

"Stop pawing at me. You're hurting me. Anyway, the job isn't done. You bumblehead jerk. She's alive."

"Whaaaat?"

Besides everything else going wrong, his food got cold.

CHAPTER 47

"With all the action it's getting lately, I'm going to wear out my orange dress," Nicole said. Joking, not complaining.

"No problem, I'll buy you all the dresses you want."

"Actually, I don't want any more dresses, but if I did, you'd have to buy them. These charity auctions aren't making me any money."

The trio checked in at the Holiday Inn, Nicole's room courtesy of Cody's Olive Glen Country Club. Aggie shared the room. For lunch Steve escorted the ladies to Maxwell's restaurant on Sheridan Avenue, one of the town's main business streets.

"I'm sure you'll get some paying assignments soon," Aggie said. "Or do you mind?" She wondered whether this auction business was merely a passing fad, and after the wedding Nicole would settle into ranch life, and housewifery.

As if reading her grandmother's mind, Nicole grinned. "You're wondering what kind of housewife I'll make, is that it, gam?" Aggie shrugged and blushed. "Could be fun for awhile," Nickee replied nonchalantly. "You know me, though, gam. Up and at 'em. Flit here and there. As Beth says, I'm a hummingbird."

Aggie read the look on Steve's face as amusement.

What Steve felt was something else. One minute Nickee talked about choosing a horse from his stock. The next moment she fretted about how to market her auctioning skills—parlay these charity freebees she was getting into the big time. An hour later it was plans that she and Beth might implement to promote their partnered travel agency. In the middle of the next breath she was proposing names for the little girl they were going to birth together. Steve sighed. What was he getting himself into by marrying Nicole?

"Gam wants us to name our little girl Rose," Nicole said abruptly, changing horses, as usual, between her mental Pony Express stations.

Aggie smiled too. Not because she found her granddaughter's conversation difficult to follow, that was normal for Nickee. Rather, because the girl had actually remembered and taken seriously her gam's plea to get the Rose name back in the family.

Aggie and Steve, more so than Nicole, were well-known throughout the state. All manner of folk stopped by their table, where Steve and Nicole—but not Aggie—were dressed in western suits, complete with matching fringed buckskin jackets. They reminded Agatha of the Jackson-based lawyer, Gerry Spence.

Dressed demurely in a gray wool skirted suit and purple silk blouse, tie at the neckline, with small silver earrings and matching lapel brooch, and sensible low-heeled black leather dress shoes, Aggie could have been running for political office, or sitting at the head of a corporate executive meeting, or chairing a volunteer committee of tree huggers. Of course she didn't want to do any of those things. She simply had her own notions about how a lady should dress.

A grizzled sixtyish man, board member of the Buffalo Bill Historical Center, stopped by to ask Aggie if she would visit the Center. "New exhibits up."

"Wouldn't miss it," she replied, introducing Nicole but not Steve, who rose to shake hands and share a memory about his dad, Richard Norman, with a man the senator apparently knew.

The country club auction, arranged as a fund raiser for the Center, was scheduled that evening to enable Cody's moneyed people to attend and be parted with some hefty cash funds in return for priceless paintings, sculptures, and other *objets d'art*, which had been donated. Like playing musical chairs, the items would pass from one to another owner in rotation while remaining within the community.

Nasty One's sons lived in Cody with their families. Double cousins to Lisa and Aggie, and brothers of Nasty Two, Tom and Jeff (named for their father, Thomas Jefferson Vicente, Nasty One's husband) were among the state's movers and shakers. Like Steve Norman, both men had served in the state legislature. They had also been, in rotation, Cody's mayor, and had served terms as members of the city council, the county commission, and the school board. It was partly through their influence that their niece, Nasty Three, had been elected to her office. Their children grown and gone, both Vicente couples were presently traveling in the Far East, in Japan and China.

Cody was also home to the Simpsons, Alan and Peter, along with their parents (once upon a time), Millard and Lorna Kooi Simpson. Governor from 1955 to 1959, Millard served as a role model. Their son Alan was elected to the United States Senate, retiring in 1996 to direct the Harvard School of Government. Feisty Alan, known for his sharp wit and sharper tongue, had introduced a number of bills in the U.S. Senate, most of which were passed into law. The Normans and the Vicente-Aulds knew the Simpson family well.

The trio spent the afternoon at the Buffalo Bill Historical Center, which houses the Harold McCracken research library, The Cody Firearms Museum, the Indian Museum, and a room devoted to Buffalo Bill Cody, founder of the Wild West show that traveled the United States and Europe during the last two decades of the nineteenth century. Buffalo Bill was also a spokesman on a variety of issues—women's suffrage, among them, along with conservation, and Indian rights. Another room was devoted to the Whitney Gallery of Western Art, with five artists featured, including the works of Charles M. Russell.

Steve, an artist, said he could spend days—hours per painting—studying style, design, technique, detailed brush strokes, color, perception and reality.

Aggie said, "They help make western history seam real, not just fodder for western movies. I'm thinking of the life and times of our Rose and Essie."

The room displaying Indian artifacts, encompassing authentic beaded costumes, reminded the two women that Nasty Three had spent the better part of two decades living among the Arapaho on the Wind River Reservation.

"Nasty says the Indians got a lot of their beads from the Italians," Aggie said. "Wouldn't it be something if grandfather George Washington Vicente's family was involved in acquiring and selling some of those beads way back before statehood? Coincidences like these make my head spin."

Following tea time in the refreshment area, they set off to pursue their collective and individual interests. At length they were back in the front of the large sprawling facility, as everybody was interested in viewing the current display that was changed frequently.

"Oh, look," said Nicole. "The furniture of Wyoming's first Territorial Governor, John Campbell. It's set up like a parlor."

John's laconic diary entry for his wedding day, February 1, 1872, read simply: "Married at 6:00 p.m. Started for Boston."

# # # # # # #

"Didn't you think Nickee was absolutely splendid?" Aggie demanded of Steve following the auction and Nicole's performance. At the post-auction reception they were again surrounded by old friends and acquaintances.

"Of course she was. She's a natural auctioneer," said Steve, his big arm gently encircling the waist of his future bride.

"Aggie, my dear, you really must visit the Buffalo Bill Fur Salon while you're here. A plane load of lovely Russian furs just arrived. To die for." The dowager stood chattering, her body awash in sable.

Nickee smiled and nodded. Steve knew she wasn't into real furs.

"Twins! You two are dressed like twins," exclaimed another middle-aged matron, this one wearing a diamond choker with matching earrings and a mink stole draped around her shoulders. She too wanted to talk about furs. "They've got in some of the latest fashions from Russia. You know they stock simply dozens and dozens, perhaps hundreds, of fine furs, ship them to their wealthy clients around the world. You must get yourself a couple of them. Dear me, Aggie," the dowager said, seemingly without taking a breath. "You're so short, the cocktail length would be full size on you, and then perhaps a cape . . ."

Aggie smiled, a bit ruefully, since those days of buying whatever she fancied were long gone. At least until I regroup, find a niche, she told herself, thinking that perhaps, like Nickee and Beth with their fledgling travel-agency partnership, the "Widow Morissey" might also become some sort of entrepreneur.

Selling what type of product? Providing what sort of service? Those were the big questions.

Hmmm, instead of living on the few thousand that remained in her bank account, she'd best follow the advice learned from Rose's journal, namely: "Buy low, add value, sell high, and never ever spend the principal." She must learn how to parlay her paltry funds into bigger chunks, then plant those chunks like seeds in a garden to grow into lovely flowers, and scatter these larger flowers around among dozens of silver vases. Caught up with the metaphor, Agatha forgot what she was thinking about. Oh, yes, making her money work for her instead of the reverse. She had no idea how to proceed.

"Gathering moss?" Steve asked. "Or trying to decide on a fur coat?"

"Tell you later." Aggie supposed that as usual she'd been standing around looking like some dippy dame.

Pete Simpson and his wife, Lynne, approached Aggie. Before retirement, Alan's brother, Peter, had served the state's only university as vice president in charge of development. His wife at one time directed Laramie's senior center.

"I hear you're working on your family's history," Lynne said. "We thought you might be interested in a grave down at Meeteetse."

Aggie's eyes lit up, while Steve and Nicole looked puzzled. Nickee's gam chatted awhile with the Simpsons.

When they left, Agatha turned to Norman. "Oh, Steve, please make time tomorrow before we fly home for us to drive down there and take a look."

Steve said he was eager to get home, see about the ranch. Also, Nickee liked his saddle store idea. The two of them meant to look for some financial backing in Cheyenne on Monday, he told Agatha. Over the weekend, they wanted to further develop their plans: drive around town looking for an empty or rentable facility, draft store layouts and a name and a logo for the firm, identify the market and calculate estimated sales and expenses.

Seeing the pleading in Aggie's eyes, the fear that he would say no, Steve put aside his and Nickee's desires. It appeared that in this family one must be ready to change at the drop of a boot, he suggested with a loving smile.

Agatha and her granddaughter exchanged knowing winks. Aggie wondered whether Steve would be able to adjust to the many clan members' idiosyncrasies and eccentricities.

"Sure, Aggie. We can do that," Steve said calmly.

#######

In the little village of Meeteetse, between Cody and the Indian reservation to the south, it was easy to locate the cemetery, but difficult to find the gravesite. The Simpsons had provided no names, and no description of the tombstone. Just a vague memory that it had something to do with the Vicente-Auld clan.

No sexton was on duty that Sunday. City Hall was closed, of course, and so was the cafe. They must do a grave-by-grave search, Steve proposed. Drawing packets of Doritos Spicy Cheese crackers from her handbag, Aggie passed them around, suggesting they make do with a light snack until they could return to what she called "civilization."

Nicole ran to the rental car, a Jeep Cherokee in case of bad weather, to get bottled water.

"No problem," said Steve. He confessed he was eager to get his Cessna in the air, so they could return to Cheyenne before dark. But Aggie's quest was important to her, so he said he could adjust. To himself he said he must try exercising patience.

The crackers gone and the bottles of water exhausted, it was Aggie who stumbled, literally, over the round, rose-colored marble stone sitting atop a cement block in the middle of a large cemetery plot with no other graves or grave markers nearby.

"I found it! Oh, oh, at last we've found our Rosie."

Rose's Rosie, once upon a time Mrs. Francois DuBois, was no longer lost.

CHAPTER 48

Nicole and Beth quickly turned the Gifford dining table into a cluttered mess with bridal magazines and catalogs, etiquette books, florists' brochures, and Beth's clipboard with pages of notes scattered all about.

"Who's paying for the wedding?" Beth asked.

"Big Jack and granddad JJ, of course."

Her lap piled with Nickee's mending, and her mending basket sitting on the table beside her, Aggie had offered to help her granddaughter catch up on small chores. Now she was taking in the scene like a voyeur, or a lapdog, eager to lap up every scrap of family gossip and nuance under her nose. Not that Agatha meant to tell everybody. She was no twin of Cousin Nasty Two in the rumor department. No, Aggie would savor the young people's comings and goings. This was a half-happy, happy-anxious time in their lives, after all: Nicole and Steve planning their wedding, with the help of Beth and Brad. And meanwhile, Brad was about to launch his new business, in the face of all his wife's fears. Beth did not appreciate change. She preferred the status quo.

Steve and Brad came in just then with Stevie, Brianna and Brittany in tow.

"Can I help?" Stevie asked, jumping on a chair to promptly send a pile of brochures fluttering like snowflakes.

"'May I'," Beth corrected without thinking.

"We're just passing through," Brad said, herding the little ones ahead of him. In the kitchen he poured apple juice for the kiddies and coffee for the men. The children sat at the table and the men at the bar. From the desk at the Giffords' communication center, Brad selected a number of brochures, all about trucks and the trucking industry, training programs, and truckstops.

"This is what I've been thinking about for months, Steve," Brad said, in a whisper as if he were parting with CIA secrets. "Can't get it out of my mind." He sighed. "Beth's not interested, and I don't know how to sell her on the idea. After all, what's in it for her? Me away on the road most of the time."

Steve looked embarrassed, like he didn't want to be thrust into the middle of a family argument. One could easily guess what people were thinking: give up a lucrative insurance and real estate agency to become a cross-country hauler? Beth more than Brad, Aggie thought, ought to have "the wanderlust," as the clan called the Vicente-Auld clan's propensity for travel.

Unheeding of Steve's silence, Brad fanned the brochures across the kitchen bar top, his voice full of excitement, his eyes bright with the dream. "See, I've been taking a correspondence course, studying downtown at the office. Now I'm ready for the actual hands-on training. Back in Detroit."

"What about the agency? And your family?"

"I took care of all that. Got a buyer for the business already. With the money from the sale I can buy my own truck. I've also made some pretty sound investments lately. I've worked like a sheep dog herding critters day and night for years. There's enough income to keep the family going with our current lifestyle until my trucking business pays off. Beth and the girls won't miss a thing."

"Except you," Steve said dryly. What with Nicole's plans for hopping about here and there and doing this and that, Steve's sympathies were more aligned with Beth than with Brad.

Aggie watched the pair of men through slitted eyes, reading their lips when she couldn't hear their words. In the meantime, she pretended to concentrate on Nickee's mending. Aggie didn't have to be told, she suspected she knew what Steve Norman was thinking—two spouses left behind at home.

"What are you guys doing?" Nicole asked, coming up behind them to plant a kiss on the back of Steve's weather-worn neck before checking on the kiddos. She lifted the tea cozy to pour second cups of tea for herself and Beth.

Unaware of Beth's pout, Brad briefly outlined his proposal to Nickee.

"Oh, fun! You'll love it, Brad, traveling from coast to coast and border to border, seeing the country—new places, new faces, eating at all those truckstops."

"Getting sick, lonesome, far from his family and his home," Beth said, joining the discussion from across the dining room table.

"You could come with me, sometimes," Brad said wistfully, pleading with his eyes and the plaintive tone of his voice. But Beth dropped her head, refusing to look at him so he could catch her eyes, make her melt with his loving looks.

"Sure, Beth," Nicole quickly responded. "You can travel with him sometimes. The girls can stay with us. It's about time I took my turn at helping you guys, for a change."

Disgusted, Beth whirled around. She said she thought they were planning a wedding.

"I'm tired of all this, Beth. Besides, we shouldn't do any more until your mom gets here." Nicole hugged Steve. "We'll ask what the groom wants, too."

"Sure, baby," he said, glad for the interruption and a chance to change the subject. "Nickee and I are thinking about opening a store here in Cheyenne," he said to Agatha and the Giffords.

Not to be detoured, Nicole continued heading down the lane from whence she'd started. "See, Beth, we'd be right here in town to look after the girls while you're on the road with Brad."

Beth groaned. Brad hopped off the bar stool to pluck at his wife's arm, hold her close, and whisper, "I love you, sweetheart. That's never going to change. Just let me pursue my dreams, too."

"Do you really hate selling insurance and houses that badly?"

"Yes, I do. Always have. Working with people is fine, but not trying to sell them something that's all about the disasters that might befall them. It's depressing. Besides, I'm not a salesman."

Aggie was glad Brad hadn't asked her opinion. She'd rather wait and see how things developed. She hoped to get ideas about how to make a living herself. Perhaps she could study to pass her real estate license and pick up some of Brad's business along that arm of the firm. Before the Gifford debate could switch into a high gear, full-fledged marital battle, Lisa arrived. Brad got out more cups and Beth poured tea.

"Don't let me interrupt," Lisa said. "What're you talking about?"

Lest the trucking topic produce Beth's tears, with everybody taking sides, Aggie quickly interrupted to invite Steve to describe his western store project.

"Oh, Steve, would there be a job at your store for Aggie?" Lisa leapt on the proposal, as if swinging aboard Norman's prize palomino.

Nicole followed suit immediately. "Why, I bet Gam could manage it."

What a family! Aggie loved them all to bits, their thinking of her welfare and meanwhile protecting Brad's dream. Steve hadn't even lined up the money to open his store yet, and here were the women grasping the reins away from him.

"Hey, hold the buggy." Aggie said, lapsing into ole-timey talk. "We haven't heard Steve's opinion yet. It's his store."

"His and mine," Nicole said quickly but firmly.

"Never mind," Aggie countered, shifting away from another potentially iffy topic. "I'm not at all sure that store management is what I'd want to do. Even if I could. I know nothing about the retail business."

"Silly. You could learn," said Lisa. "Besides, you love prowling houses."

#######

Morton the Manager, as Harry thought of himself, was a member of the management committee at L-Triple-C. Harry didn't know it, but when the chairman of the business administration department at the college had asked the bank vice president for the name of someone who would serve on an advisory board to go over curriculum, nobody at the bank wanted to do it.

Harry's next-desk colleague had suggested Morton. "He doesn't do much around here, anyway. Doesn't drum up any banking business, puts off the clients he does get. Name Harry to the committee."

His brow furrowed, his finger to his face like the Thinker, Morton the Mouse harumphed and pontificated. Or meant to. His high squeaky little voice made him sound ridiculous. The younger more innocent college faculty on the committee leaned forward to catch every word Harry muttered. The older more experienced faculty leaned back in their chairs and fiddled with their pens and pencils. The chairman doodled on his yellow lined pad. The lone woman instructor wished she were in class. Or her office advising freshmen. Or in the Cloud Nine Lounge. Anywhere but here in this boring meeting.

When the session finally concluded, Harold the Hussen, pretending he belonged, strode manfully (he thought) along the lengths of corridors that connected one building to another—to protect students and faculty from bad weather. In the library he perused business journals. In the faculty dining room he sipped black coffee. He poked his head into the auditorium, darkened for a video assignment, and got a "Shhh" when he asked, "What's happenin, man?"

Back in the business department, Harry used the copy machine under the disapproving glances of the secretary in charge. Then he left the L-Triple-C campus to drive around town before returning to work. He felt so important.

# # # # # # #

Out at the airport coffeeshop, Hannah had just served *The Guy* a cup of coffee, when he jumped up, spilling the burning liquid down the front of his pants. That made him look like he'd wet himself.

Directly in front of the guy's vision was Burly Boy, carrying a duffel bag to check through airport security. With no thought of who might spot him, the guy rushed out of the coffee shop without paying. Stumbling down the steps and, pulling at his soaked pants, he lurched forward, with Hannah yelling after him, "You forgot to pay."

"You can't leave town yet," he gasped in a harsh stage whisper. "Give me back my money for the robbery, or else try again until you get it right."

"Huh? What you talkin' bout?"

The guy seized the duffel bag and pulled Bushy Eyebrows out of line. "You got the wrong files! You owe me."

CHAPTER 49

In San Miguel de Allende, Nasty One sat on a park bench in the plaza nibbling on a bit of *bunuelos,* a desert comprised of a fried tortilla wedge topped with dabs of strawberries and whipped cream, or, in the late autumn and in this place she might be eating frozen fruit and artificial cream. Before that she had also eaten a meatless chili relleno dish. She loved this town. At something over six-thousand feet in altitude, San Miguel reminded Nasturtium the First of Flagstaff in Arizona, and Santa Fe, and Silver City in New Mexico.

She liked Mexicans with their beautiful language, colorful clothes, and gentle manners. And their music, that ranged from bright and bouncy to plaintive and sad. She liked Mexico: the eastern coastal cities of Veracruz and Tampico, the raucous border cities of Tijuana and Ciudad Juarez, but most of all the smaller places like here and Puerta Penasco near the Mexico-American border. And Durango, in the mountains. Oh yes, and Mazatlan, on the coast with its wonderful beaches. She loved swimming in the Pacific, even if her withered thighs did appear lined with old-age wrinkles. So what, she liked having fun.

Nasty and her husband, before his early death (bless his heart), had visited the country together many times. In Mazatlan they preferred eating seafood at Marinaro's, on the waterfront—drinking fresh-lime daiquiris, eating the range of fresh sea food, and listening to the strolling violinists playing their romantic music. Ahh, those were the days, when love was in the air and in their hearts. The eldest Vicente-Auld clan member still missed him, her one and only husband, her one true love. Of course Hepzibah was older than Nasturtium, the Original, but she didn't count. She was an in-law, not even a just-plain-first cousin.

Maybe Nasty was getting too old. Her great-grandma, Rose d'Gade, had lived to be a hundred and eight or nine, but already, at only ninety-two, Nasty One was slowing down. It was difficult these days to keep up with the memorization assignments in the Spanish class she was taking. Her hands shook with arthritis in the drawing class. She was spending more time with the Americans in their colony and in their local bar than with the Mexicans. She longed for her home in Cheyenne and her family. She couldn't imagine what they could be up to by now.

Few people were left sitting in the plaza, too cold at this altitude, at this time of year. Just then, plop went pigeon poop on her shoulder. Disgusted, Nasty arose to wander slowly back to her room in the hotel next to the convent.

En route on the dusty path, she followed an old crippled man in ragged clothes with a donkey and cans of milk tied on each side of the poor animal's sagging back. Bringing the milk to market, where it would be sold in the same condition at open markets to consumers and restaurants. She, like the other tourists, would be expected to drink the unrefrigerated, unpasteurized milk and pour it over their cereal. Instead, she ate boiled eggs and drank boiled tea. Still, she got Montezuma's Revenge, diarrhea. She got it every single time she traveled in Mexico, until her immune system could adapt. This time it had been worse, and moreover, it had lasted longer. Perhaps it was time to pack it in.

In London her home would be called a bed-sitter, in America, an efficiency apartment. Here, it was just a room. In the traditional Mexican style, the patio and garden were hidden away in the center of the hotel property. Here was where the tangled, untrimmed vines of ivy twisted themselves haphazardly among and between the tired bougainvillea with its large, showy red and purple bracts pleading for attention.

Also on this patio were two brightly colored parrots, squawking loudly. Named Olive and Stan, their wings had been clipped. The couple passed the same messages back and forth, over and over, all day long. Stan said to Olive, "May I hold your Palm-olive?" She replied, "Not on your Life-buoy." Funny at first, Nasty's ears ached from it now. She must drop her classes, forget it all.

That night Nasty One called Nasty Two. "Daughter, I'm coming home. What's happening?"

Nasty Two told Nasty One all about everything.

# # # # # # #

Out at the Cheyenne airport while awaiting her mom's arrival, Nasty Two cornered Sergeant Walt Fletcher with his sidekick, Bobby

Gilbert—the same two officers sent to investigate Aggie's bedroom disaster on Thanksgiving morning. Motioning to Hannah behind the counter at the coffee shop for refills all round, Nasty Two regaled her captives with more than one gossipy story, each intermingled and mangled.

Fletcher and Gilbert couldn't keep up or keep track, although baby-faced Bobby tried real hard to jot notes in his book. "Wait a minute, back up," he said. "Repeat that."

"Which part?" Nasty Two asked, reaching for the sugar and knocking over the cream pitcher. "Oops, sorry."

"No problem," said Walt. "Yeah, repeat this business about the secretary of state. I don't get it."

"She's my daughter," said Nasty Two. "Married to a complete idiot—only God knows why and He's not talkin'. Before that she was married to an Arapaho, lived off and on up on the Wind River Reservation, kept comin home, with or without her son, Ned, leaving her husband, returning, then he dies in what seemed like suspicious circumstances. So then she runs for office and as you know gets elected—her job entails looking after corporate and business rulings, compliances, notaries and elections, trademarks and trade names, securities and brokerages, agricultural and mineral products, all that sorta thing. And before you can say Jack Sprat, Nasty Three ups and marries Harold the Hun Morton the banker who's own first wife died pretty suspiciously too if you ask me. And then my double cousin Aggie, well, her husband gets killed, could be suicide. Now Steve Norman's marryin' into the family and look what happened to his brother and pa, they were killed too. So now Aggie's attacked with an ax, right in her very own bed? You guys got work to do."

Later, Bobby the rookie said to Walt the veteran cop that he couldn't keep up with all that and wondered if they should get the police chief to put a whole team to work on all these murders and suicides or whatever they were.

"Nah, probably just accidents. Old woman's day-dreaming, wants attention. Or losing her marbles. Mind's confused."

#######

With Aggie's ankle still weak, the double cousins had not as yet resumed their power walking regime during the seniors' preopening session at Frontier Mall. But they did return to their AquaRobics class at six o'clock in the morning three times a week. "We aren't seniors yet, anyhow," said Lisa, fussing at her double cousin to quit complaining and come up with some easy exercise program.

Aggie and Lisa were determined to settle down and organize their notes—the project they had promised themselves to do after Thanksgiving. "Should have started right afterwards, while Joan was off duty," said Agatha. "I hate to proceed without her. I'm not at all sure we know what we're doing." She stared morosely at the array of working materials scattered about her round oak table.

"Oh, posh, Aggie. We're just writing notes on note cards and sticking them on the walls. We can't work on the wedding. Beth's too upset with Brad."

"And Nickee said they'd already done enough for awhile. You know she can't stay put or stick with anything for long."

"How are she and Steve going to adjust to each other? He seems steady and stable as an iceberg in a hurricane. And Nickee's the big storm."

Ignoring her double cousin, Aggie suggested they get busy. "Let's finish the family history before Christmas," she blurted. "I'm sick of it, or at any rate of the animosity our pursuit is generating from somebody. I want to know who."

"And why, for heaven's sake."

It was not enough that Nicole and Stevie were sleeping in the bedrooms next to Aggie's. They were seldom around in the daytime. Since nobody wanted Agatha to be alone, it was agreed that Lisa and Peter, or Beth and the twins, would stay with her during work-week days. Or they would make sure she was with one of them, always.

The Nasties were too busy, Nasty Three not only with state business, but also with Harry the Hostile. Nasty One had only just returned from Mexico, she must be plumb worn out. Nobody could think what good Nasty Two would be to Aggie. On the other hand, Lisa chortled, their other female double cousin would probably talk an attacker to death.

In her third-floor office, Aggie turned on the computer to check that their documents were safe. "Won't take a minute, Lisa."

"Doesn't matter, dear. You've got back-up, right?"

"Naturally. With the first threat, I duplicated everything. Joan has a copy, and the original data is on a memory stick, which is in my safe deposit box."

Lisa suddenly had a terrible thought. "At Harry's bank?"

"Oh, no! You don't suspect Harry the Horrible, do you? If so, could he get access to people's private boxes without their permission or knowledge?"

"Who knows how banks work? Meanwhile, me suspect Harry? I'd suspect Morton the Mournful of anything. He slinks around too much, acts like a weasel, a mole, a mutterer."

"Morton the Mischief Maker."

"Morton the Miserable."

"Why do we do this, Lisa, make fun of him all the time? We're not nice."

"Nice! Why should we be nice to him? When was he ever nice to any of us? Ah, you're the one who's too nice. Forget it. Let's get to work."

Over the long afternoon the three-by-five inch cards they had talked about while on their trip began proliferating, like baby rabbits from a promiscuous mother. Peter, when called, came to their rescue with a trip to Walmart, where he bought thumbtacks and huge cork bulletin boards, which he mounted on every available wall surface around Aggie's third-floor office. Of course they could have done all this on the computer, but that was more Nickee and Beth's mode of operation. The middle-aged women preferred paper and pens, things you could see and handle, with cards or sticky notes they could stick up anywhere, or move somewhere else as their moods dictated.

Dressed in comfortable, colorful warm sweatsuits and walking sneakers, the cousins created card after card: white cards for general data, pink cards for females and blue for males (they were traditionalists), and green for questions—the answers to which they should pursue later. Sticky notes formed theme titles.

Down one line they tracked the descendants of Rose and Etienne d'Gade and down another the offspring of Essie and Darwin Deighton. Some of the progenitors merged with the twentieth century marriages: some of young Rose's sons, named after U.S. Presidents, had married some of Estelle's daughters, who were, in turn, named for pretty flowers, with numerous kinfolk left over.

Estelle and Luther Auld had birthed twin sons first—Ezekial and Ebekenezer. Ezekial was killed in action in World War One, Ebekenezer died of the cholera. For some unknown reason (green card?), Estelle did not get pregnant again for several years. Then she had seven (or was it eight?) girls (pink cards) in rapid succession: Nasty One, Lilac, Violet, another set of twins—Pansy and Petunia (green card for each of the latter? Plus their pink cards?), Camellia and Daisy. Wasn't there another Auld girl? (definitely a green Question Card here).

Rose and George Washington Vicente had also started their family in the early 1930s and 1940s, but they had kept right on going, making each of the Vicente children nearly a half-decade older than each of their successive counterparts among the Auld girls. Here was the Vicente line-up: Thomas Jefferson, Abraham Lincoln, Grover Cleveland, James Madison, then the twin girls, Opal and Pearl, then two more boys, Ulysses S. Grant and Teddy Roosevelt, followed by another gem, Ruby, and, bringing up the end, Woodrow Wilson.

"I wonder if the clue to the family mystery might lie perhaps with the missing Auld girl. If there was one. I wish we knew how to find out."

"I do wish Nasty One would return," countered Aggie. "Bet she knows."

#######

Flying home at thirty-six thousand feet above the planet, and wearing two of Isabelle Vicente's poncho shawls, the sun-yellow one atop the black-mourning one, making her look like a short fat toad in a white-haired topknot (nearly bald at the crown), with wire-rimmed glasses sliding down her nose, Nasty One dreamed some of the old dreams. She tried to imagine what her mother-in-law Rose had done with the gold nuggets she'd been given by the debtor, Herbert Claybourne. Nasturtium the First wished she'd asked her gramma about that.

CHAPTER 50

1860-1930

Rose d'Gade lived to be a hundred and nine years old, with most of her faculties—except hearing, of course. In her lifetime she saw the settling and civilizing of the West. She saw territorial governors replaced with state governors, as Wyoming gained statehood in 1890. By then women had been voting a long time in Wyoming.

In the Cheyenne literary society, Rose and Willie had discussed with the other ladies such works as Charles Dickens' *Great Expectations*, Lewis Carroll's *Alice's Adventures in Wonderland*, Mark Twain's *Tom Sawyer*, and Charles Darwin's very controversial *Origin of the Species*.

With Thomas Edison's invention of the phonograph in 1878, Rose and Willie bought one, and then they could listen to music at home, such favorites as Verdi's *La Traviata* and Johann Strauss' *Blue Danube* waltz.

Wonder upon wonders! They were among the first in the city to get electricity, indoor plumbing, and the telephone, all of which were invented and patented in the last quarter of the nineteenth century. Some people claimed the privy should be left out back of the house, not brought inside: oooh, filthy! Rose had not one but three bathrooms installed, one on each floor: oooh, ostentatious! Rose tossed her head, and told Willie, "Oh well."

George Eastman marketed the first Kodak camera, so of course they got one of those, too. They took and kept photos of everything and everybody that mattered, which went into albums. (Later, Estelle would rip out Iris' photo, forgetting that her lost daughter appeared in another group picture.)

About Joseph Glidden's 1874 patent for barbed wire, they weren't so sure. The cattle barons, including Rose d'Gade and Willamena Jackson, were accustomed to grazing their cattle on unfenced open range—their own, their neighbors, and also on federal land. Fencing? Unheard of!

Their ten-thousand cattle ranged over three-hundred-thousand or so acres.

President Garfield was assassinated in 1881 and President McKinley in 1901. "Pay attention to national and international news," Rose told her girls. "See that you learn and care about politics and government and what the president is doing. Private citizens <u>can</u> make a difference."

Another time Rose told young Rose and Estelle: "Plant pretty flowers, nurture them, watch them grow. Take care of the land."

Little wonder these girls named their sons and daughters after presidents, flowers, and gems. Rose's gold nuggets still sat in the bank box, her safety net for an uncertain future. In 1893 there was a financial panic with a severe national depression. Rose and Willie and their girls were safe, though. Their capital was in real estate and ranching. And also in gold.

The nation's first commercial oil well was drilled in Pennsylvania in 1859 (a year after the first stagecoach service traveled between St. Louis and San Francisco), but it wasn't until 1901 that oil was discovered in Texas. Wyoming beat Texas, though, by drilling for oil in 1883. By 1894 a crude oil refinery was built in Casper. Meanwhile, the city's name got changed from Caspar to Casper when a telegrapher made a spelling error. "See?" Willie admonished the girls. "Pay attention to spelling, grammar, and word choice." (Little wonder Joan went into communications and became the family's Grammar Cop.)

After the first oil gusher came in, much litigation resulted from conflicting, overlapping claims filed under the mining laws of 1872 and 1897. Unless one camped on his claim with a force of armed men, a band of rowdies was likely to move in or destroy the stakes and take possession. It was no place for a man (much less a woman) without oil experience, capital and gall. Rose and Willie were not as yet tempted to invest in the fledgling oil industry.

Coal mining was far more important to the state, and would be for a long time to come. Under the 1864 Pacific Railway Act, the Union Pacific received mineral rights, along with its land grant, which totaled four-and-half million acres—assigned in odd-numbered sections of a strip forty miles wide, or twenty miles along each side of the Union Pacific Railroad. UPRR fueled its locomotives with its own coal, which was also its chief hauling commodity. The company hired more Chinese than white men to mine the coal in its own mines.

The Chinese were not settlers, they generally left their families at home in China, for they planned to return some day. They were willing to work for lower wages, which the whites resented. White miners would strike, Chinese miners wouldn't. Resentment between the races erupted in the 1885 Rock Springs Massacre, in which twenty-eight Chinese were killed, fifteen wounded, and several hundred driven out of town.

Governor Francis E. Warren took the train west to check on the disaster, then he wired President Grover Cleveland for federal troops to protect the mails and arrest criminals, since the territory had no militia. One week later the Chinese were escorted back to town and the troops stayed for thirteen years to provide them with protection.

Rose and Willie thought their hearts would break. Rock Springs was, after all, one of their early homes, and the ladies had employed many Chinese in many of their businesses. To think that such murderous men could live in and about the region, or that ordinary men could be whipped into a mob to commit mass murder! In Cheyenne, the ladies promptly took their laundry to one of the new Chinese services—their way of making a statement, which was but one more of their many charitable acts on behalf of people beyond the family.

Speaking (or "making unspoken statements") on behalf of nonwhite people was nothing new for the ladies. Rose had been defending Negro people since long before she'd met Willie—back in her and Essie's Nauvoo days, when the saints under Joseph Smith's leadership had refused to go along with southern Illinois and Missouri in their attempts at recruiting slavery advocates. Both Willie and Rose, and others, such as William F. "Buffalo Bill" Cody, had been addressing Indian rights since they'd survived under Walking Mule's experienced and brotherly care.

In their leisure years, Rose and Willie provided many services as volunteers and contributed many dollars to charities and to other worthwhile social efforts. Now they were called philanthropists.

Willamena and Rose saw and rode on horses and mules, covered wagons, stagecoaches, trains and cars, even airplanes (for Orville and Wilbur Wright's first successful manned flight was in 1903), and on great ocean liners. They booked passage in 1912 when the Titanic made its maiden voyage. Traveling first class, they were among the first to board a life raft and suffered the agony of observing and mourning their fellow passengers, many of whom drowned or froze to death in the icy waters.

"We survived blizzards in a dugout with Rosie and Walking Mule, we'll live through this," Willie whispered as they bounced and swayed in the life raft awaiting rescue.

The pair buried loved ones. They stood by helplessly while some of their descendants made poor, even dreadful, life decisions. They got sick and nursed each other and a lot more people in the family back to health. They listened and sympathized. Mostly robust in health themselves, it was difficult to emphasize.

"They'll make it, somehow they'll resurface and pick up the shreds of their lives," Rose said, of her descendants who made bad choices, especially in romance, but also in business. The ladies prayed plenty.

The two women who had lived in freezing hovels and worked from dawn to dark, had personally lived through, seen or heard about so many things, from inventions of new technologies to literary and musical works. Yet it seemed that the invention of the automobile changed everything and everybody. Autos needed petroleum products and autos needed roads and eventually highways.

Thus dawned the revolution of an entirely new way of living. Communications was no longer tied to transportation. Willie and Rose talked about how it used to be. Once upon a time, to get news and mail anywhere, these items had to be physically transported—by stage coach and Pony Express and ship. "Also by word of mouth and carrier pigeon," Rose recalled.

Now there was not only telegraph but the telephone. The transporting of people and products changed too. Railroads once predominated in the business of shipping goods and people, but they were restricted to railroad tracks and corporate schedules. Automobiles and the resulting trucks could go almost anywhere and at any time their individual owners desired. Ahh, Freedom.

Rose's family was not exempt—everybody wanted a car. For the Vicentes and Aulds, though, automobiles would become their very lives and livelihoods, the source of their own fortunes and the cause of both celebrations and betrayals.

Rose, Willie, and Willie's sister, Louise Beasley, were among the first to make the plunge, with three separate Model-Ts by Henry Ford. Now Rose and Willie (but not Louise, she stayed home in Cheyenne) and various among Rose's great-grandchildren chugged along the deep ruts of dirt, gravel and muddy roads to explore the state the old ladies thought they knew. They visited Yellowstone National Park, Jackson, Cody, and Thermopolis with the hot springs the Indians had ceded to the whites in the late 1800s, the Big Horn Mountains and the site of Custer's last stand, Sheridan and Buffalo, the Wind River Reservation—home of the Arapaho and Shoshoni (bitter enemies until forced onto the same land, with Arapaho to the north and Shoshoni to the south). They visited Casper, the home of Fort Caspar, near where they'd once struggled for survival in their dugout with Walking Mule, and they saw Sundance and Devil's Tower in the northeastern corner of the state.

Rose would not live long enough to see her great-great-grandsons move to any of these Wyoming locales. It was Casper and Cody and Jackson where they would gain prestige and political power, and from which bases they would exert influence over and serve others, where they would call in their markers to see that their niece (or double cousin, cousin, or second cousin once removed) got elected to the state's second most powerful position.

Meeteetse, a stop-over between Thermopolis and Cody, was merely a unique mountain village, a place to get a cup of coffee and make a potty stop. It did not occur to Rose and Willie in that decade of the World War (the first one) that there was anything special about Meeteetse, or that they should visit the cemetery. Hence another two generations would pass before Rose's Rosie's grave site would be discovered; by Agatha and her granddaughter, Nicole.

Meanwhile, young Rose, Rosie's daughter, met and fell head over heels in love with an Italian from Rock Springs, George Washington Vicente whose father Mario had immigrated from Sicily to find work in coal mining. In management by then, G.W., following their wedding, switched to lobbying. In that first decade of the twentieth century, the young couple settled in Cheyenne during the legislative sessions. Because young Rose didn't want to leave either the capital city or her dear grandmother Rose, G.W. went into government service to continue seeking support for the mining industry. From that position, he changed careers again to manage his mother-in-law's financial empire. They made Cheyenne their permanent home.

At last Rose decided she'd found someone she could trust.

Neither Rose nor young Rose had the slightest idea about how to prevent conception—Essie and Estelle having died before they could pass on this precious knowledge. Young Rose glowed with each pregnancy and birthing was relatively easy for her. The image of her mother and grandmother, young Rose was small, dark, petite, and very pretty. She and G.W. adored each other all of their married days, so young Rose wasn't about to give up loving—one of the standard birth-control methods of the times when, after a few births, many women simply closed their legs and their bedroom doors, having moved their husbands elsewhere. Thus it was that Rose and G.W. begat ten living children.

Estelle, daughter of Estelle and granddaughter of Essie and Darwin Deighton, met and married Luther Auld, also in the early 1900s. He could trace his forebears back to Ireland where David Auld was born in 1742. David lived to be one hundred and four. His seventh son William begat a seventh son William, who begat a seventh son, Luther. Because each of these men lived long lives, married late, and birthed their sons (upline from Luther) late, there were fewer generations, just four, in this Irish line, between David Auld of Ulster, Ireland, and Luther Auld, husband of Estelle.

The Aulds, of which Luther belonged, settled in western Pennsylvania before migrating by covered wagon to Wyoming. In this wild new territory, they raised, trained, and sold horses near Centennial during the great gold-mining days of the 1870s and '80s.

Although Estelle's eyes were clouded by dreams of romance when she married Luther, she did not stay as enamoured of him, as Rose did of G.W. Nevertheless, just as many live babies came to Estelle and Luther as had come to the other couple.

Estelle birthed twin boys within nine months of her wedding. She lost the next four babies: one son to crib death, the next to still-birth, and the last two boys to miscarriage. With the last one of these, she had fallen down the cellar steps to collapse in a puddle of blood. Estelle passed out and stayed put until Luther came in from the stables.

Her husband didn't believe that his wife had miscarried naturally. He accused her of throwing herself down the stairs as a means of instigating miscarriage.

"Aborted yourself! That's what you've done. What was it?"

"A boy, just like all the others we lost."

Luther didn't offer to pick her up or clean her up. Instead, he shook an accusing finger at his wife. "You killed my sons."

Luther no longer trusted his wife. He brought his old-maid aunt to live with them, whose only job in return for her board and room, Luther said, was to keep an eye on Estelle, ensure that she no longer resorted to murder.

Estelle finally quit trying to convince him otherwise. Maude was good company. No substitute for Rose, of course. But now Estelle had an excuse to stay mostly in her room, often in bed. As for Luther's accusations, Estelle kept them to herself. She had a horrible thought. What if Grandma Rose or Estelle's best friend young Rose believed Luther? Estelle would rather die than lose their trust. Bad enough she'd lost Luther's and through no fault of her own. It wasn't fair! She too mourned the loss of those four little boys.

Estelle left Luther after birthing her tenth child, nothing but daughters following her twin boys, and after losing all those other boy babies. Estelle Auld spent the rest of her days in Cheyenne, except for six months when she returned to the horse ranch to care for Luther who went blind. (He had gone bald in his early thirties, too, which was where the Nasties got their bald-going crowns, and, of course, Luther was also nearly deaf, another impairment that got passed down to members of succeeding generations.)

Both Rose and Estelle lived many years and saw amazing changes and technological innovations. The romantic liaisons were the most astounding.

In Cheyenne Rose and Estelle with their Grandma Rose watched in amazement as five of Rose and G.W.'s president-named sons fell madly in love with four of Estelle and Luther's flower-named daughters.

The four women, Rose and Willie, Estelle and young Rose (as she was called until the day she died, following World War II), sat on Grandma Rose's screened wrap-around porch for tea. It was 1928, the economy was booming, everybody was making money, in the nation and in Wyoming. George Washington and Rose Vicente's boys were raking it in.

To describe the latest fashion, their young-adult children called it "the cat's meow." They got gasoline at the filling station, bought sewing materials at the dry-goods store, sifted their flour for making cakes, and spoke with disdain of "ragamuffins"—people of the lower classes.

"Who would have believed such a legacy?" Grandma Rose said. "I wish your grandmother Essie could have lived to see it."

"A dynasty," Willie confirmed, "That's what you've got here, Rose. And you are the prima dona, the head of it all."

"Oh, I wouldn't go that far," Rose said modestly.

Young Rose and Estelle laughed, holding aloft their delicate Wedgwood china teacups. "A toast to us," Estelle proposed.

Dark-complected and brunette, young Rose said wistfully that she wished Estelle hadn't lost her only two sons in the War. Petite, blond Estelle dropped her glance to fumble with the teapot. Willamena Jackson, who'd had her own suspicions back in the early 1900s, coughed and harumphed. Grandma Rose spilled her cup of tea, cracking the thin cup from rim to bottom.

"Oh, Grandma, how awful," said young Rose, jumping to the rescue and thus failing to notice everybody else's discomfort over the taboo topic, taboo to three but not to all four of them, for young Rose never did suspect that Luther blamed Estelle for the loss of his sons.

With the tea and teacup mess cleared away, Estelle said demurely. "But I do have all these wonderful sons-in-law, your very own sons, Rose." Estelle turned to Grandma Rose, continuing the liturgy: "Your great-grandsons, Grandma. Rose's Thomas Jefferson married to my Nasturtium, Abraham Lincoln married to my Lilac, Grover Cleveland married to my Violet."

Estelle stopped, grew pensive. "I do wish Pansy had married your Teddy Roosevelt, though, Rose. Instead of getting herself pregnant by your James Madison."

"Like I always say," said Willie. "You can tell 'em and tell 'em, but you can't tell 'em much'."

"Careful, Willie," said Grandma Rose. "Don't be a stool pigeon." Then Rose d'Gade bit her lip. What if young Rose had noticed that Grandma and Aunt Willie were hiding Estelle's secret?

Willamena quickly covered Rose's slip of the lip. "Aha, at last I've got you quoting Shakespeare."

"Whatever are you talking about?"

"'Stool pigeon', that's from *The Tempest*. Gotcha."

Grandma Rose rolled her eyes. Estelle smiled knowingly. Only young Rose looked puzzled, but then she forgot the strange conversation. She dismissed it as simply the garbled muttering of old women. Estelle's secret was safe.

"Whatever is Iris up to, Estelle?"

Everybody got busy with something again—the trio of white women replacing their cups on dainty saucers. Estelle blushed, pursed her lips, and fussed with her hair in its huge perfectly coifed topknot. Young Rose excused herself to see about something indoors.

Grandma Rose puttered with the silver tea tray accoutrements, her old blue-veined shaking hands setting the teacups to rattling. The tray tipped over, fell to the floor, and all four cups crashed into tiny bits.

"Oh, Rose." Willamena exclaimed. "That's the last of your precious cups, left over from Rock Springs, our first real home."

"Mmm, yes."

Young Rose returned in time to see the new mess. She sighed.

"Guess I should learn to keep my mouth shut," Willie said, the closest she could bring herself to apologize.

Estelle said sternly. "That's something we don't talk about in this family, Aunt Willie. Iris is a closed book. She may be my daughter, but I don't want her name mentioned ever again."

CHAPTER 51

Since meeting Steve, Nicole had been to the Missouri Auction School, and to a couple of UW-Cowboy football games, she had seen her Jacquot men in Douglas, and auctioned at their sale barn. Then she had performed two more auctions, the no-income charity type of affairs. And, she had also been to the Norman ranch twice.

There was the traumatic Thanksgiving day at her gam's, and suffering through what might have happened to Aggie. That was the worst event of all.

It surprised both Nicole and Steve that she had not as yet seen his Cheyenne home. "'Our home', I should have said," he said.

Nicole didn't get carried away by touring houses like Beth and Lisa did. Houses made her nervous, anyhow. To her they represented a lot of work and responsibility. She and her mom had never had one.

Joan said, "Possessions own you, you don't own them." Which was why, while Nickee was growing up, she and her mom had invariably chosen to live in efficiency apartments, single rooms, trailer houses, or with family members.

Steve stopped his pickup truck in the circle drive in front of his Cheyenne home. Glancing at Nickee, he appeared eager to see her reaction. Two-story white pillars flanked the huge polished oak double front doors with the big brass knocker. Southern-plantation style, the front of the house was symmetrical, with matching windows on both sides of the door and on both floors.

Would Nickee be like his mother and, a generation later, his wife Norma? He supposed that Nicole, like her predecessors, would immediately set out to remodel, redecorate, and rearrange everything.

Steve liked this house, nearly as much as he did the ranch. He grew up here after all, before his mother took them both to live in Boston with her family.

How would they manage their lives? Would they be living here mostly, with Stevie and perhaps Cindy and Sissy enrolled in the Cheyenne schools and then spend summers on the ranch? He could commute to manage the Norman spread. Or would they forget this place and live full-time in Albany County, sending the boy—or all three of the children—on the bus into Laramie? Steve was impatient, he wanted all these details of everyday living worked out now.

To his disappointment, Nickee didn't say a word. Wearing scruffy old jeans and boots, her auburn hair caught up in a loose, messy pony tail, she stepped out of the truck on the passenger side and stood silent, staring at his beautiful city home. Steve got out of the truck and walked around to stand beside his sweetheart. He was all spiffed out in a three-piece business suit, having come from an interim-session of a legislative sub-committee meeting.

Just then both front doors flew open and down the steps tumbled his own little twin girls, straight into his outstretched arms.

Nicole gasped. Busy with the twins, Steve didn't notice at first. But there in front of them, framed by the white pillars, and dressed in a finely tailored navy blue wool suit with full-length mink coat, stood Norma Norman.

True to her promise, Steve's wife had come West with their daughters. He was happy as a blubbering idiot let out of an institution for the mentally insane.

With Cindy and Sissy clinging to him, Steve blushed and fumbled with the introductions. "Nicole, I'd like you to meet my wife, Norma."

Nicole turned slowly and stared at Steve. She couldn't stop staring, until he wondered if he'd grown two heads. Without a word, Nickee pulled off her engagement ring and threw it on the ground. Then she ran around the pickup and jumped in the driver's seat. Steve had left the key in the ignition. With Norman gaping and Norma smirking, Nicole gunned the motor and drove away.

"Daddy, Daddy," Cindy squealed, "Why did that woman steal your truck?"

"Steal your truck, steal your truck," echoed Sissy.

#######

Wilma Sanford cornered Nasty Three outside the latter's office in the capitol. "Coffee?" Wilma suggested.

"I need something stronger."

At the downtown saloon with the long, long bar encrusted with silver dollars in its glassed top, Wilma ordered a Scotch-rocks and Nasty a martini. "Up, very dry," the secretary of state told Dollie Domenico, who waited on them in their dark corner that quiet mid-week afternoon.

Dollie was feeling very nervous. Did the woman who might be the next governor know that Dollie was still Harold's honey, though married to Nasty?

Did Nasturium the Third know how hard her husband was working to get her elected governor, or that, even before she willingly threw her hat in the race, he was mapping out her whole political campaign? Dollie wished the women were sitting at the bar. She wanted so badly to eavesdrop.

Dollie saw the women talking fast and serious, using many gestures, and she felt certain they were talking about her and Harry. Any minute now the pair would rise from their chairs to confront their bartender. Thank goodness the bar stood between them to protect her.

Wilma and Nasty Three were talking government and education. By the time she was half-through her drink, the state superintendent of schools was tired of talking politics and curricula. She changed the subject. "Don't make it obvious, Nasturtium, but look at the bartender. She can't take her eyes off of you. Have you and Harry been coming in here recently?"

Nasty Three leaned forward conspiratorially. In a quiet voice, she muttered, "She has good reason, Wilma. I don't know why we came in here, I'd forgotten she works here."

"You wanted to avoid her? Why? Who is she?"

"Harry's second wife."

"Oh no! I'm sorry. I should have suggested somewhere else."

"No matter. I know who she is, and she knows who I am. What's more, she knows I know who she is."

Dressed in a black wool dress with short jacket and a gold and beige scarf tied around her neck, Wilma tugged at a gold earring, and pushed a dainty gold-link bracelet up and down on her wrist. "Shall we leave?"

"No, this should be fun. Watch, I'm going to beckon her over here."

Dollie approached, with mouth dry and bowlegged knees shaking.

"What have you and Harry been up to, lately?" Nasty asked. Wearing a brown wool suit with pearls and her daisy-trimmed straw hat, the diminutive older woman was intimidating sitting there. Not smiling.

Dollie found the secretary of state stern and unbending. She wondered what Harry saw in this woman. What did Nasty Three have that Dollie didn't? Dollie was younger, thinner and, she bet, a whole lot sexier. She supposed that wasn't enough, not when Dollie was competing with money, position, and power.

"Uh, ma'am, he just comes in here now and then. Like, you know, when he takes a break from the bank," Dollie mumbled, around the big wad of bubble gum she popped and chewed furiously. "Harold's all excited about your governor campaign, ma'am. Sounds to me like you might have a good chance."

"'Gubernatorial'," Wilma corrected, before thinking. Turning in her chair, Wilma accused her friend and government colleague, "Nasty! You're going to run for governor? Why didn't you say so? You'd be great, of course, but why haven't you told me before now?"

Nasty was so stunned she just sat there, half-paralyzed. News to Wilma? News to Nasty! What was happening?

"Oh, yes, ma'am," Dollie said again, tickled that poor little Dollie Domenico knew something she could tell the tall distinguished black woman.

To her competition—the woman Dollie hated most in all the world (next to Nicole)—the bartender said. "Harold says that you can't wait around for the governor to die in office so you and Harry can take over the reins of government. He says he's gotta strike while the iron is hot. Uh, pardon me, ma'am. I mean you gotta go after the governor's chair. Soon as possible."

Nasty Three was too stunned to think. She told Wilma she had no inkling that Harry wanted her to be governor. So naturally she hadn't told Wilma, or anybody else. How could she? The very idea had never occurred to her. "I don't think I even want to try for another term as secretary of state. Why borrow trouble?"

"So, why does Harry want you to be governor? So he can be First Man? Or whatever you'd call it. First Gentleman?"

"Hardly."

# # # # # # #

Nasty Three left the saloon with her head in a tizzy. Stupidest thing she'd ever heard. And why tell Dollie all about his so-called gubernatorial campaign for his wife, anyhow? If Nasty were to run for the highest office in the state, she surely wouldn't ask for Harry the Haberdasher to manage anything for her, much less to spearhead the group who would work with her in developing and promoting her political platform. Oh sure, Harry was on the team when she was running for secretary of state, making calls, stuffing envelopes, no big role. What in the world could possibly make him think she would invite him to run things?

If she were to run, she would rein in the support and advice of her uncles, and the second and third cousins, from all over the state. They were among the most significant power brokers who had helped to get her elected to this office.

As she drove to her son's Laundromat in south Cheyenne, Nasty's mind went into overdrive. As governor she could help Wilma promote the use of some terrific learning materials. She could try to get the naturalists, herbalists, environmentalists and animal-rights people to see things from the viewpoint of livestock growers and corporations, and vice versa. Get people to cooperating, and compromising, instead of competing all the time. Nasty knew it was a delicate balancing act, but she might like to try. There were only so many resources and so much capital in this state, there had to be a variety of methods she could employ, as governor, to make them go around.

"Please all the people some of the time and some of the people all the time," she thought, inadvertently paraphrasing Abraham Lincoln—the President, not her great-uncle Vicente.

At the Laundromat Ned was "counseling" a dirty, disheveled young man. That's what Ned's mother called it—"counseling." Mostly her son lent a listening ear with the occasional, very occasional, word of advice. Ned pitied the poor drifters and unkempt souls who frequently hung around his establishment. Nasty suspected that all they wanted was a handout, money for another fix.

But of course that was a stereotype, the secretary of state chided herself. Some of the hangers-on were genuinely hungry, perhaps homeless, she supposed. As governor, she ought to do something about that, too. And them. She would ask Ned's advice, and listen to people who knew the score, not just the white-collar social workers. Well, of course the governor should hear them, too. Listen to everybody about everything. She sure would listen to the Arapaho and Shoshoni. She understood many of their needs already, but of course not all. And she would organize groups of African-Americans, Latinos, and Asians to advise her. Then, as governor, there would be all those boards to serve on, all those ceremonies to attend, the media to answer to in her press conferences.

What was she thinking? She didn't want to be governor! Or did she?

When free, Ned turned away from the sorry soul, and from the repair of a dryer to give his mother the second of her daily share of shocks. "I'm thinking about heading up north to the Wind River Indian Reservation," Ned said, dropping his eyes to the floor. "It's been a good long while since either of us were there."

"What? To live? Ned, dear, you can't. You can't even visit. Don't you remember? Ned, darling, you can never return. Surely you know that."

"Why not? You mean because of what happened to dad? But he died down here in Cheyenne, not up on the reservation."

CHAPTER 52

Aggie, Lisa, and Joan sat in the Schwartzkopfs' hearth room with old journals and new green query cards scattered about. Peter greeted the ladies before excusing himself to go upstairs to the sports room, where he planned to watch reruns of golf tournaments on the DVD and the sixty-inch television set.

Joan set her micro-recorder on the coffee table in front of Nasty One. "Don't worry, it'll pick up your voice," she said, returning to sit yoga style on the floor in front of the fireplace, where she could add logs and stir the hot coals.

Nasturtium the First was responding to the cousins' plea to share her version of the family history. She would serve as the link between Rose and Essie's journals and diaries, and her own real live oral account, she said. Aggie recommended that Nasty dictate her knowledge in the form of video recordings. Nasty balked at the camera, so Joan brought the recorder. Sound, but no visuals.

Aggie and Lisa thought they knew most of their own nuclear families' backgrounds. Although they were baby boomers, they had listened to their parents' accounts of the twenties, thirties, and forties.

Thomas Jefferson with Nasturtium had opened an auto agency in Cheyenne. Many people were buying cars back then, and Tom was moving them out at the rate of a half-dozen sales a day. He soon prevailed upon two of his brothers to open branches. Thus Abe with Lilac, Lisa's parents, moved to Rawlins, while Grover with Violet, Aggie's folks, moved to Laramie.

Wall Street crashed and, in the early thirties, the banks closed. And the clan's company went bankrupt. The thirties were pretty dismal, thus two of the three couples somehow managed to wait until the forties to birth babies. Aggie wondered, somewhat irrelevantly, whether the wives had merely shut their legs and shut their hubbies out of their bedrooms. She'd heard of that method of birth control before. Still, it sounded like cutting off your nose to spite your own face.

Lisa interrupted now, to pour tea, suggesting that Nasturtium might need a break. The ladies wore their usual daytime sweatsuits and sneakers, including Nasty whose favorite color was blue. Scratching her bald spot, adjusting the wire-rimmed glasses, and clearing her throat, Nasty One prepared to fill the gaps left by Rose and Essie's journals and to move on from where their records ended.

"We three oldest Auld girls—me, Lilac, and Violet—were the three musketeers. We did everything together, getting into trouble on our own or while following the boys all over the place. We idealized them—our own Ezekial and Ebekenezer, and G.W. and Rose's three eldest—Thomas Jefferson, Abraham Lincoln, and Grover Cleveland."

Surely you didn't call them by such long names," Joan said

"Of course not. Our brothers were Zeke and Eb, and the Vicente boys went by Tom, Abe, and Grover. Zeke and Eb were handicapped by all the little Auld girls, though, including Pansy and Petunia. On the nanny's day off the boys were in charge. That's when the Vicente boys came to our house to play games.

"Mama stayed in her room most of the time. That's about all we remember of her in those early days. Her personal maid looked after her, I suppose. Oh yes, and Aunt Maude, who never seemed to leave mama's side. Tacitern Aunt Maude didn't even look after us when the nanny and later the governess were away.

"When we—the three musketeers—were older, Mama Estelle would come downstairs about once a week to give us instructions. We had to know how to clean so we could direct the maids. We had to know how to cook so we could manage Cook's menus and marketing. We were taught how to manage accounts and do the banking so none of the household staff or the bank would cheat us.

"Our dad, your Grandfather Auld, had a very prosperous business—buying, training, and selling horses. Also, the cost of domestic labor was low in those days. The servants lived on the third floor, their job benefits included room and board. They probably earned no more than a pittance in wages. The staff had to live with us, they didn't have transportation. By then the Aulds had moved from Centennial to a ranch north of Cheyenne.

"Oh, never mind all the minor details, let's move on to the War. World War I—it wasn't called that until WW-Two, of course. Anyway, that blasted world war took our beloved Zeke and Eb. Cry? We three musketeers sobbed our hearts out. Dad didn't, not that we noticed. In our memory, he always was cold to mama and she seldom spoke to him. At the dinner table she'd say things like 'Pass your Father the salt and pepper', or 'Ask your Father if he wants dessert'. Of course when Rose d'Gade and Aunt Willamena Jackson came over—those two dear old ladies were invariably together—then mama pretended that everything was fine between her and father. I don't think Rose was ever fooled. Willie, maybe, not Rose. She was one sharp lady, very observant of her loved ones."

"Sounds like a pretty loveless household," Aggie said sadly.

"Not really. With so many children, it was pretty rambunctious. Besides Rose and Willie, young Rose always was in and out. She and mama had great gossipy times together. Young Rose and G.W. Vicente had a lot of kids too, remember, and together the Vicentes and we Aulds had plenty to do: fishing, wading, hunting, while the little girls—those younger than us—played dolls and other girlie games indoors."

Nasty's voice trailed off, her eyes glazed over, memories of happy days apparently returning. The "girls" (Lisa and Aggie in their fifties and Joan in her late thirties) sat quietly, out of respect, despite their eagerness for their elder to continue.

"Things we could all do together, I recall those happy times best: hide-and-go seek, baseball, horseback riding, ante-ante-over, and, oh, the games we'd contrive at the creek or up the mountain. See, we tied a great long knotted rope to a tree limb and we would cling to it to swing across the creek—which, in spring time with the snow melt run-off was turbulent and pretty dangerous. Actually, we Auld girls and the younger Vicente boys and girls were all forbidden to play there, but the three musketeers? We ignored our parents' admonitions and went anyway. We'd play Tarzan, yelling 'Aieeee!' When one of us fell in the creek, the big boys would jump in and help save us. They taught us how to swim, too. On the mountain we had other games—cowboys and Indians was popular, then, also pirates."

"Little wonder you all married each other," Joan said.

Nasty One grew pensive.

Joan added another log to the fire. Lisa replenished the tea and Aggie excused herself for a call of nature.

"The three musketeers broke our parents' hearts, I guess," Nasty One continued when they had reconvened. "We three girls didn't want a college degree. However, young Camellia and Daisy both took degrees. Teddy Roosevelt and Woodrow Wilson Vicente did too. Thomas Jefferson left for Omaha to enroll in Automotive School, where he learned mechanicking, plus sales, and management. That was after the War, following our brothers' deaths.

"Tom returned home a few months later and taught Abe and Grover how to sell and manage. They didn't want to be mechanics. James Madison, the next-in-line Vicente boy, got left out all 'round.

"See, the twin Vicente girls, Opal and Pearl, had come along. They pretty much 'adopted' our little twin sisters, Pansy and Petunia. After that, in the Vicente family, there came Ulyssis S. Grant, Ruby, Teddy Roosevelt, and finally Woodrow Wilson. These Vicente children, like the last two Auld girls—Camellia and Daisy—were looked after by nannies and governesses. To tell the truth, we three musketeers on the Auld side and the older three Vicente boys didn't pay much attention to all those little kids."

"Must have caused a lot of resentment among the Aulds and Vicentes at the tail end of the lines," Joan said, while putting a new disc into the recorder.

"Well, yes, it did. James Madison Vicente got the worst of it. Teddy Roosevelt Vicente, too. I guess both of them were in love with Pansy."

"What about the Auld girls?" Joan asked, as if forgetting she referred to her own grand aunts.

"And Ulysses S. Grant Vicente? You forgot our Uncle Grant," said Lisa.

"No, I didn't. He went off to Chicago. Fell in love with a girl who moved there. Didn't do Grant any good, she never did care for him like he cared for her. He stayed, though. Joined the Chicago Police Department—CPD. Married several times, I believe, had only one son that the family ever heard of, John Francis Hancock, who followed in his dad's footsteps. 'Franc', as we called him, joined the police force and later, I believe, became a private eye."

Aggie and Lisa exchanged glances. So, their knowing look said, somebody in the family had already worked as a private investigator. Their yearning to take out their own PI licenses had its genes in family history.

"You started to tell us how the younger Auld girls resented the closeness you older kids experienced," Joan reminded Nasty.

"Right. For one thing, Iris, Camellia and Daisy never did learn how to cook, clean, or manage a household and staff."

Again Aggie and Lisa exchanged meaningful looks. They had caught Nasty in mentioning the name, "Iris," Ahah! The mysterious missing Auld girl! If the cousins kept still and showed no emotion, maybe Nasty might tell more. Half the story of Iris might slip out right between Nasty's lips. What a coup!

"Pansy and Petunia, the twins, were coddled and spoiled by everybody. Nobody taught them anything, either. Old Rose or Willamena might have, but by then they were far too old, in their late nineties. Uh, my word, I'm practically that old myself! Well, anyway, that was partly the fault of the three musketeers. We were told to teach all the younguns, we just never got around to it. Petunia was sickly and died at age five, so that tore up the family some more, coming on the heels of Zeke's and Eb's deaths a year or so earlier."

Aggie's eyes teared. Peter came through and winked at his wife. Lisa so engrossed in Nasty's tales of yesteryear she didn't notice. ("Tell us about Iris Auld," Lisa longed to plead.)

"Let me skip ahead before I get too tired," Nasty said, breaking the spell. "The three oldest Vicente boys, Tom, Abe, and Grover Vicente—with their parents' financial backing—opened a car agency in the late twenties. They were very successful—everybody on earth it seemed was in the market for a car. Rather like you younguns are now for laptops and smart phones. Remember, the whole idea of cars instead of horses and buggies was brand new and utterly fascinating. Crank the engine out front—that was before the automatic ignition—run around and jump behind the driving wheel and take off—wheeee!

"A few years later Lilac and Violet and I all quit high school. We sent away to South-Western Publishing Company in Cincinnati for a correspondence course in bookkeeping. We wanted to be included in the daily operations of the auto business, too. When the Vicente boys opened branches in Laramie and Rawlins, we were ready for them. I became Tom's bookkeeper here in Cheyenne, Lilac worked for Abe in Rawlins, and . . ."

"And my mother, Violet, moved to Laramie to work for Grover," Aggie finished the litany.

"And they all 'fell in love, got married and lived happily ever after'," Joan said gaily.

"Hardly," Nasty said. "Here in Cheyenne, Tom hired James Madison and Teddy Roosevelt as mechanics. That was a big mistake. But you're right about Tom and I. We were happy."

"And Pansy and Teddy fell in love," Aggie said.

"We all thought so. See, our mama, Estelle, and the boys' mama, Rose, were ecstatic over all this love business between their kids."

"What about the daddies?" Lisa asked. "Weren't our granddads happy?"

"Probably, but as I said, my dad Luther and mama Estelle were barely speaking. She'd left him and the ranch, right after our brothers died, and moved to town."

"Poor Granddad Auld," softhearted Aggie said.

"Don't forget," reminded Lisa. "Grandma Auld returned to care for him after he went blind until he died."

"Yes, both my father and father-in-law died young. In the thirties," Nasty said. "Now I say 'good,' because they didn't live to see the horrible things that came later."

"Good heavens," Lisa said. "Tell us more."

"Ruby Vicente went insane and Pansy's husband went to prison."

CHAPTER 53

"What?" Aggie almost screamed at her granddaughter. "What do you mean, the wedding is off? You actually returned your engagement ring?"

Nicole had Stevie with her. She had picked him up from preschool on her way back to Aggie's to spend the night.

"His **wife**, gam! Steve introduced Norma Norman to me as his wife! Not his ex-wife, mind you. Present tense. He's not free of Norma Norman yet. It's too soon since she left him. Freudian slip, no doubt. He wants her and his girls back, and now that she's here, he's got his chance to start over with them."

"Posh, darling. Must have been just a slip of the tongue, mere habit. Of course it's soon, the divorce was only final a month or so ago. Wasn't it?"

"Who knows? Maybe they're still married and she has no intention of divorcing him. Maybe she heard about me . . . well, of course she would have, from Cindy and Sissy. I talked to them on the phone from right here at your house, on Thanksgiving Day. Naturally those little girls would have told their mother. So what's Norma do? Promptly high-tails it for Wyoming and 'her' home. It's a beautiful house, gam, although how would I know, I haven't so much as been inside yet."

"Does seem odd. The timing, I mean."

"You bet it does. Norma didn't want Steve until she discovered somebody else did." Nickee paused to gulp, a sob slipping from her tight throat.

"Pretty classic."

"You bet it is. Talk about competition, how can I compete with that? Norma—mother of his kids, beautiful, sophisticated, educated, intelligent . . ."

"Come, now, child. You've got a lot going for you, too."

"Such as?"

"Beauty, intelligence, youth, sophistication when you choose to use it. I sometimes wonder, though, if you aren't too quick to jump to conclusions. Remember, you were ready to break up with Steve over the bartender. Tempest in a teakettle . . ."

"'Teapot,' gam. What's your name, 'Mrs. Buchwald'? Confusing things, like Stevie does."

"Don't evade the issue, Nicole."

Oh, oh, "Nicole" instead of "Nickee"? She was in for it, now—"The lecture, huh? I might as well move in with my mom in Laramie. Joan is the master lecturer, but maybe she got the tendency to fuss and fret from you?"

"Think about it, dear. Bill Taylor must have conditioned you to be suspicious of men."

That night, alone in her room after reading stories to Stevie and tucking him in, Nicole had a lot to ponder. Steve's intentions, her marriage to Cowboy Billy. Steve, Bill, the only two men in her romantic life. No, she had wonderful role models—Big Jack and Granddad JJ. (Unconsciously, she did not include grandfather Morissey.) The Jacquots were strong, stable, true-blue men. You couldn't get much more integrity than that.

Why couldn't her mom have stayed with Jack? Why leave such a great guy—the Jacquots' prosperous and wonderful ranch, their fine home, friends, respect from the community, Joan's own extended family. What was wrong with her mom? More to the point, what was wrong with herself? Tears leaked down Nickee's face. She couldn't bear to lose Steve. Yet, did she dare fight for him?

From her gam, Nickee knew that the Vicente-d-Gades and the Auld-Deightens had a ken for travel, that they were eager to discover, like cattle, whether the grass on the other side of the fence might be better than home ground. Or, maybe not, maybe they just liked exploring.

Beth and Ned were the stay-at-home kinfolk. Nosiree-Bob, the stay-put lifestyle was not for Nickee. She was no stick in the mud. Nor was she anxious to settle down in a small apartment or cottage with cooking and cleaning facing her. The tears dried up. Maybe breaking up with Steve was for the best, after all. He'd probably expect her to live with him in just two places—out on the ranch, and then in Cheyenne during the legislative sessions. Well, what was wrong with that? Nicole vacillated, back and forth, forth and back. Stay-go-fight-flee.

She decided to backtrack, do a quick personal history of her emotions.

How had she felt as a very young wife with a baby? Did she and Bill even once think of Baby Stevie as an anchor to tie them down? No problem. She and Billy figured a baby didn't need much space or anything else beyond food, warmth, a few baby things, and lots of love. With their baby and their two trailers (one for Billy's horse), the young couple had traveled all over the West. Had he been a winner, brought home some winnings, perhaps he wouldn't have turned sour on her. Coming in last, coming home morose. Bill began drinking too much after coming in a loser time after time. Which was when he started beating on her if she so much as reminded him to stop off to buy disposable diapers. After that, he'd hooked up with thugs. Might have killed somebody, had he not been caught.

Nicole tossed in her bed, unable to sleep. What was to happen to her? Of course she had several options. Mom would be ecstatic if Nickee enrolled at the U and moved to Laramie. Big Jack and JJ wanted her to join them in Douglas. Her gam would open her arms, her heart, and her home to her only grandchild. Nickee didn't want to settle down, that was for sure. She was young, yet, barely twenty-one. She wanted to have fun. And a man to cuddle with and make love to her. Oh, life was so hard, so many decisions to make. Nickee felt like the wind was blowing her this way and that. Sometimes she longed for peace, time out in the quiet eye of the storm. At other times she was scared to death of being stranded in the middle of nothing.

Nickee thought of all those adventurers she'd read about: Magellan, Columbus, Daniel Boone, Admiral Byrd, Amelia Earhart, modern-day astronauts, mercenaries, women in Congress and heading corporations and studying gorillas in Africa or South America. Nickee was unaware at the moment of her own clan, particularly Rose and Essie's amazing biographies.

Did all those adventuring people leave their mates and children behind? If not, how did they cope without a love partner? If so, how did they coax their stay-at-home family into accepting that the wanderers' distant adventures were worthwhile? Or, what if they weren't worthy? just appealing. How could all those contented, stay-at-home folk, like

Beth and Ned, appreciate that the call of the wild, the distant rising sun, could be at the center of one's very soul—compelling, irresistible?

Fighting the rumpled covers, Nicole suddenly wanted her mother. The great philosopher, analyzer, might have some answers. However, Nicole only needed personal advice—what to do about Steve Norman, let him go or fight for him. She didn't want to hear about the human race in general. After all, Joan had never remarried, maybe she didn't have the answers either.

# # # # # # #

Burly Boy was still in town. He was determined to complete his assignment—the dual jobs of murder and stealing the widow's records. He wanted his money, dammit.

"It'll be easier to go after her on the road. She's leaving town again."

"How do you know that?" the Guy demanded.

"Keepin' my ear to the ground, listenin' to gossip, man."

"Where? Downtown at that old saloon? or out at the airport at the Cloud Nine Lounge?" Nervous, biting his lip, the Guy wondered whether he'd said too much. There were a lot of other places where the hit man could have eavesdropped. The Guy was afraid he'd given himself away by mentioning these specific popular drinking establishments.

"Something like that," Burly Boy said smugly. "I'll leave town right behind the ladies. You watch. In a few days you'll be rid of the Agatha woman."

"Careful."

"Yup."

"What about the records and files I want? You don't expect Mrs. Morrisey to take that stuff with her, do you?"

"She might. She's bound to be pretty nervous these days. Otherwise I'll beat it back to town, collect the data and turn it over to you without nobody knowin nuthin."

CHAPTER 54

That particular semester Professor Vicente had scheduled her two undergraduate classes on Monday and Tuesday and her one graduate seminar on Monday night. By Wednesday morning, with the sky still clear and no blizzards forecast, Joan was ready to accompany her mother and daughter on their trip to the northwest corner of the state.

Joan wore a navy blue wool turtleneck sweater with a blue wool blazer, and jeans tucked into high-top mountain boots. A heavy sheepskin-lined car coat to toss in the back of her mother's van along with leather gloves and wool scarf should protect her should the weather turn worse. Six inches taller than her mother and seven inches shorter than her daughter, Joan thought of herself as the "in-between," in more than one way. She was also half-way between their ages. Her short-cropped auburn hair was the color of Nicole's, but styled like Aggie's—her mom's own hair, before the Vermont fire burned it to the scalp.

With Stevie at the Giffords, where Beth or Brad would take the boy along with their twins to preschool, the trio of women loaded the Morrisey van and left town. The three ladies would take turn about in driving. Aggie was dressed much like her daughter, only in burgundy instead of blue. Nickee wore her usual western outfit. Blankets, food and water, chains and shovel, and cellular phones, digital cameras, and laptop computers completed their packing list of necessities.

Steve had been leaving so many messages for Nickee on Aggie's answering machine, it seemed he would have lost his voice by now. Once more Nicole ignored them.

"Let him stew awhile," she said. "He apparently needs his space, to decide between Norma and me. And I know I sure need to think."

In Casper they stopped to visit Lisa's brothers, Abe and Lincoln and their wives. Their children were grown and gone. Upon leaving town Aggie said she wondered whether somebody was following them. The same dark green car had been behind them in Casper, both before and after stopping to visit their kinfolk.

"Oh mom, you're just paranoid," protested Joan.

Nicole wasn't listening. Her head was foggy with fancies.

In Meeteetse, the tiny village north of the Wind River Reservation and south of Cody, Joan helped her mom locate the cemetery sexton, whose records revealed that Francois DuBois, of Paris, had bought six grave plots in 1868.

"Nobody ever come by to bury nobody else here in a century and nearly half of another," said the sexton. "I been here fifty-one years myself and in all those decades, nobody ever brung flowers for Miss Rosie's grave."

"'Mrs.'" Joan corrected him. "Rosie was a married woman."

On Joan's advice, the women sought more information from City Hall.

The clerk referred to the sexton's affidavit. "All you have to do," the kindly clerk said. "Is fill out a form claiming that you want the deed to these six plots—five of which are empty. I'll then transfer title to them to your name. Obviously, Francois DuBois is long dead. With no other requests in over a century, the plots are yours."

"That simple?" Aggie couldn't believe it. "I don't have to buy them, pay back taxes? I can bury anybody here who wants to be buried here?"

To Joan and Nickee, Agatha said: "This is where I want to be buried."

Her daughter and granddaughter stared at her and then at each other.

"I want to be buried right beside Rosie. Perhaps we should have Rose D'Gade's coffin placed here, too."

"But mom, what about the family plot in Cheyenne?"

"I know," Nicole said brightly. "Put a marker in the Cheyenne plot referring people to this cemetery in Meeteetse."

"Really, Nicole. Like a cross-reference file system. Very peculiar," Joan muttered.

Aggie read a scripture from Second Nephi, *Book of Mormon*: "Adam fell, that men might be. Men are that they might have joy." She looked up and smiled. "I love that concept, that worship and life should be joyful, not all solemn and serious and deadly. Cousin Rudolph should read this."

"Cousin Rudolph, he of the bulbous red nose, is a nut," Lisa said.

In the cold blustery afternoon under an overcast sky, the women sang *Blest be the Tie that Binds*, and *When we meet in that sweet bye and bye*, their tears flowing freely for a long lost great-grandmother they couldn't possibly have ever had a chance to meet. It was the idea, the sentiment, Aggie said. Joan and Nickee, too, were touched, for Aggie had read scraps of Rose's diaries to them on the long drive north.

As they turned away, the dark cloud passed over and a shaft of sunlight shot from the sky like a beacon to stream down and encircle the grave.

"It's an omen." Aggie said.

"For what purpose?" said the more practical Lisa.

"Who cares? We should be on the lookout, however, for dire consequences."

"You ask me, gam, I think it was a good omen. That was sunshine, not hail and lightning that burst from the clouds to bathe grandmother's grave."

Aggie looked pensive. She said she wasn't at all sure about good news. "Most likely we're in for another big disaster in this family. Stands to reason, doesn't it? Nasty One didn't finish her oral history. There's more to come, and will be, if we can catch her when she isn't too tired."

Joan appeared utterly disgusted. "Oh, mom, really. I've never known you to be so suspicious. Let's get out of here, we're all freezing half to pieces."

None of the women noticed the lone man bundled like a homeless person with all his worldly goods on his back. Burly Boy hid behind a tree. He had no idea what the widow was up to, but out of respect for the dead, he decided to hold off doing the dirty deed. He would bide his time. This was, after all, the woman who had saved him when he'd skidded off the highway in the Nebraska blizzard and turned himself upside down.

Back in the car, the women decided to stop in Thermopolis for the night. They checked in at a Best Western, and beat it for the lounge, where the owner, formerly of Chicago, had built a glass-fronted addition to display the one-hundred-forty-three wild game he'd shot around the globe and had stuffed and mounted. They ordered juice-and-rum drinks and sat silently around the small bar table. It might take awhile for Aggie to re-enter the twenty-first century.

Nicole wondered when would be a good time to ask for advice from her mom. Joan was usually so preoccupied, dashing about with her obscure consulting, research, or writing and lecturing assignments. Before Nicole could break silence, Joan beat her daughter to it.

"Mom," Joan blurted at length, staring at Aggie. "I want to confess something to you."

"What's that, darling?"

"I always resented that you and dad didn't help me financially with any of my college expenses."

"That wasn't me, that was your father," Aggie said, before thinking. "Oops, mustn't speak ill of the dead."

"What? Why?"

"You know he wanted you to stay in Wyoming. He would have preferred that you returned to your husband in Douglas. If you'd wanted a college degree—and never did he imagine you'd want several!—then he thought you should go to UW. He'd have paid your way for that."

Nicole decided to wait until the morrow to introduce her own personal trauma topic. Plenty of time on the ride home.

At the bar with his back turned, Bushy Eyebrows, wearing a heavy winter coat and wool scarf, sniggered behind his frosty mug of Coors. Into Aggie's drink, and while the bartender's back was turned, he had slipped a tincture from the nux vomica plant with the genus *Strvchnos*—a colorless, crystalline alkaloid, and highly poisonous.

Wouldn't be long now. He left to check Mrs. Morrisey's room, luggage, and van for the missing family history records.

Her mind on Nickee's shattered engagement, Aggie asked her granddaughter what she was going to do—fight for her man or forget him.

Joan suggested that Nicole complete the university's preregistration forms and move to Laramie for the spring semester, commencing in January. "You and Stevie can live with me. All expenses paid."

"I'll think about it," Nicole said.

Aggie said she didn't think that was the thing to do. "Sounds like a cop-out, running back to college." Absentmindedly, she stirred her drink. Several times she lifted the glass to her lips, but didn't quite get around to sipping it. She wasn't much of a drinker.

Before, finally, reaching over to sample it, Aggie knocked over the glass with an elbow. "No problem," she said, and ordered a fresh one.

Back in their room, a triple, they discovered everything trashed.

"What on earth?" exclaimed Joan.

Shaking as if with the palsy, Aggie fumbled with the phone until Nicole took the instrument from her gam to call the front desk. "We're checking out," Nickee said. "Please send the manager up here first, though. We want to report a terrible act of vandalism."

Joan got her mother settled in a chair with a glass of water and a cold cloth on her brow, afterwards joining Nickee to survey the room and its contents.

"I can't tell whether or not anything's missing," Nicole said.

"You needn't add the phrase 'or not', Nicole. It's built into the concept when you use the word 'whether'."

"Cut it out, mom. Not now."

To the hotel manager, Joan and Nicole explained that their suite had been tossed in their absence. Joan did not elucidate further, as she didn't think he needed to know their private business. Aggie, but not necessarily Joan, had concluded that somebody was after her again.

"Which means I was right. We were being followed."

With their Cody kinfolk in Europe, Aggie insisted they call their Casper relatives. Lisa's brother, Abraham Vicente, said he'd leave immediately to escort the ladies back to Casper.

It was dark by the time Abe arrived. The mid-height, mid-sixties man of Italian-French-Irish-Welsh heritage was double cousin to Aggie, thus first double cousin once removed to Joan and first double cousin twice removed to Nicole.

Over a late, light supper at the country club in Thermopolis, the trio of women shared the long and confusing tale about the stalker's threats—the demands that Aggie should quit the family history, Or else!

"Maybe you gals better just forget it," Abe said.

"What? After all our work?" said Joan, claiming credit for her share of contributions.

"No way," protested Aggie. "We're almost finished. Any day now we should have all the answers. It's like an Agatha Christie who-dun-it, Abe. Lots of family members . . ."

"And in-laws," said Nicole. "Could be one of them."

The women looked sharply at one another, as if that afternoon's sunbeam had suddenly struck all three simultaneously.

"Okay," Abe said resignedly. "You won't quit. But I have another question. Why just Aggie? Why not Lisa and Joan, here, too? You said all three of you have been diligently pursuing the research. Why is Aggie the only one who's been threatened?"

Again the trio was struck, as if by lightening. At last Aggie recalled that she had had that same question in the beginning. She'd forgotten to pursue the idea in the ensuing hubbub. Joan suggested that her mom, with Lisa and perhaps Peter's input, give that some thought. Or check with Sergeant Walt Fletcher.

Abe was driving a new but cluttered pickup truck, so the women followed in the Morrisey van. In Casper they would spend the rest of the night with Lisa's brother and family. Then return to Cheyenne on the morrow, and what they agreed should be an accelerated thrust to complete the family history.

Traveling the sixty-six miles south to Shoshone, and the ninety-nine miles east to Casper, the three women alternated between silence and talk.

"I don't see how you could leave my dad," was how Nicole raised her personal issue. "You ran all over the country, giving me a very unstable home."

"Just as my parents did to me, Nickee."

"Yes, but at least they were together. They didn't break up your family."

"Now, now, child. Don't confuse apples with applesauce," said Aggie.

"There you go again, gam, mixing metaphors." Nickee glanced at her mom for confirmation. "Or do I mean similes?"

Joan looked surprised. "Nicole dear, you are more aware of language, and less vacuous, than I might have supposed. That, or you're growing up."

"Ahah! Mom, you ended that sentence with an 'up'."

Continuing as if she hadn't heard the interruptions, Aggie said, "Your grandfather's work took us around the world. And we both enjoyed traveling."

Constrained by the safety belt, Joan only half-way turned round to stare at Nicole in the back seat. "Is that where you're heading with this confrontation? Why attack me and your grandmother, when it's yourself you want to talk about? You don't know whether you can be happy staying in one place or whether Steve's nature can tolerate your popping about. Is that the issue?"

Nicole gulped. Then she began to cry. Great heaving sobs and wails poured from Nickee, like her very soul was wracked with grief. Joan muttered that the girl needed to get it out of her system. Aggie and Joan let Nicole cry, without interrupting to comfort. Sometimes it was better, their silent exchange suggested, to cry it out.

"I don't know what's wrong with me," Nickee said at last. "Maybe I'm just using Norma as an excuse to break up with Steve. It's so weird, so confusing. When I think about losing him to her, it makes me jealous and I want him so badly. But when I've got him, then I get to thinking I don't want him after all. That another marriage this soon is a bad idea, that he'll try to control me and I'll be right back where I was while under Billy's thumb. I d-don't know what to d-do, mom, gam," Nicole stammered. "I love him so much. Everything is just right, except for . . . for me. If I do what he wants, I'll be miserable, I know it. If I do what I want, he'll die of misery."

"Tch, tch," Aggie said. "Talk to him. Tell him how you feel. Give him a chance. You might be surprised."

"What about Norma Norman?" Joan posed dryly. "I thought you broke up with Steve over his first wife. Now you act like there's this other reason behind the whole thing, that it's yourself you're not sure of. Meanwhile, what are you going to do about her?"

"Fight fire with a fire hose?"

"Now who's mixing metaphors.

CHAPTER 55

Back in Cheyenne the next day, Joan said she had to get back to campus. Nicole, still needing *to think*, she said, drove her dad's old pickup up north to Douglas. She left Stevie with her gam.

Nasty Two agreed to stay with her double cousin, since Aggie wasn't willing to move in with the Schwartzkopfs under Peter's protection. The Morrisey house was in proper order, nobody had trashed these premises.

Aggie didn't think to check the computer, though.

She called Steve. "We're home, and I need to talk to you."

"About time somebody's willing to," the young rancher growled.

A half-hour later Steve arrived at Aggie's with his four-year-old twin daughters. He said that Norma was staying at the Little America Inn.

"Oh, boy, more playmates," Stevie cried gleefully, leading Cindy and Sissy to the basement with all its small niches.

Aggie trailed along to do laundry. And eavesdrop on the children.

"Let's play hide and seek," Cindy proposed. "Me, too," echoed Sissy. Neither girl fussed for mommy. Being with daddy was great, Cindy said.

"Okay," Stevie agreed reluctantly, afraid perhaps of losing control. "But then we'll pretend something else. "You hide in that big empty box. It's a dugout, and I'll be Walking Mule, an Indian come to rescue you from starvation and, uh, and, uh, from wild animals and bad guys."

"What's a dugout?" Sissy demanded.

"A cave," Stevie replied scornfully. He'd heard many times from his mother and gamsy the stories of Rose and Willie. Playing the role of Mule was one of his favorite pretend games.

Agatha smiled. Left to themselves, the kids were getting along fine.

Aggie didn't plan to betray her granddaughter's confidences, but sharing with Steve some of Nickee's wanderlust heritage might help him to understand his fiancee's hesitation at making a lifetime commitment.

"She could be afraid she won't be able to fulfill your idea of what you think a wife should be," Agatha told Steve, while pouring him a mug of coffee.

"She's got no clue to what I want in a wife." Steve said angrily. "I just want her to love me. And I want the chance to love and protect and care for her."

About their Thermopolis motel room getting tossed, he wondered if it might be coincidence.

"And also my van? I'm sure somebody went through that, too. What could they be looking for?"

"Your family history, I would imagine, if you were in fact meant to be the specific target and it wasn't just happenstance. Did you call the police in Thermopolis?"

"Yes, but you can guess what happened. It was while we were waiting for Lisa's brother, my double cousin, Abe, to drive from Casper to escort us back that far. The police took our statements, completed forms, and suggested the motel management move us to another room. Which we didn't want, because we were leaving. In the middle of the night and following Abe."

"Call Sergeant Fletcher. See if he's done anything on the case here in Cheyenne. Give him all the details. If you're right, then there could be a connection."

# # # # # # #

Harold's position gave him access to the bank vault during working hours when it was unlocked and standing open, but not to individual safety deposit boxes. He was determined to get a look into Agatha's box.

Harry had overheard his wife and her mother talking—Nasty Three and Nasty Two mumbling something about the contents of the Morriseys' safety deposit box being valuable. Yeah, Harry bet it was. He figured he knew what the box contained. Exactly what he needed.

Only, how was he to get at it?

At his desk, Harold the Hateful took out the laser pointer to resume playing his bright-light-in-the-eyes game with pedestrians. Could he somehow steal Agatha's safety deposit box key? Then what? The bank clerk in charge guarded her set of bank keys religiously. Or did he mean assiduously?

Where was I? the man with the short attention span wondered, as he flash-flashed passers-by in the eyes. Oh yeah, getting into Agatha Morissey's box.

Keep it simple, he concluded. Blow up the bank.

# # # # # # #

Police investigators Walt Fletcher and Bobby Gilbert arrived at Aggie's, while Nasty Two (who'd been banished from the small side room with the floor-to-ceiling and wall-to-wall stone fireplace) listened avidly with her ear pressed to the closed door. For all the good that did. Perhaps pressing an empty glass to the door would enhance her poor hearing.

The baby-faced rookie cop assigned to Fletcher harumphed and flipped through his soiled notebook with the pencil-smudged pages. It looked like an act, straight out of a movie. Aggie wondered who he was trying to impress. Listening, or trying to, from the other side of the wall, Nasty Two didn't glean a blessed new thing.

"Let's see, you say you were attacked in Thermopolis this time? What kinda weapon? What sorta method—gun, knife, poison, pillow over your face smothering you, rope strangulating you, what?"

"Stop that, Bobby," Walt commanded quietly. "You don't have to be so graphic with the violent suggestions."

"Huh? Okay, I guess not. Okay, ma'am, you tell it. In your own words."

In the warm room, with Nasty Two behind the door, and in the presence of these stalwart officials, Aggie felt ridiculous. She may once have thought of the detective sergeant as a friend, and she supposed, in return, that Walt had respected her. But now she must appear plumb silly. Joan was probably right. Getting their motel room trashed could be merely an act of random vandalism. Probably. Or perhaps not. Agatha hemmed and hawed, hedged and dodged.

She couldn't understand herself lately, all this vacillating. First she was frightened and took the threats seriously. Next, she thought it was a prankster. In New Orleans, she'd been followed and then pushed into traffic, or so she'd thought. Oops, she remembered something else. Before that trip and the more recent events, she and Lisa had traveled to the British Isles and then to the Continent. She'd thought somebody was following her all over the place over there, too. But nothing had come of that frightening experience, which was one more reason for suspecting her grief had made her paranoid. After a lifetime of having Randy there to protect her, or at any rate believing he could have saved her from unspeakable horrors all over the world, she wasn't accustomed to thinking of herself as a single person, all alone to take care of herself. Surely that series of harrowing episodes in the British Isles was nothing but her imagination. All of which meant, what? That along with her grief, she was suffering from paranoia?

How could she expect her family to take her seriously? When she complained and they came up with a solution, Agatha backed off, she, herself, even ridiculing the idea of a stalker. She wouldn't move to the Schwartzkopfs, she hadn't wanted to bring in the police. She was simply a vacillating mess.

Wait a minute. Wasn't Nicole experiencing some of these same feelings? Losing a husband to divorce, especially when he was sent to prison, must be very devastating, too. Nickee was in love with Billy, at least much of the time. Divorce, death—both ended in the loss of a loved one, both produced grief, and that sense of utter aloneness. She and her granddaughter were both falling apart. Finding it tough to make decisions, couldn't sleep, which fogged the brain further and exaggerated everything else. Okay, so if grief over loss was the problem, what was the solution? People told you to get busy, get involved, help others. Aggie consistently resisted. Instead, she'd wanted to crawl in a hole, preferably her nice warm safe bed, and pull the covers over her head.

She didn't even notice the two officers walk out the door.

"Whadda ya think of that?" Bobby asked Walt back in the patrol car.

"Not much. Obviously, we can't put a twenty-four hour surveillance on Mrs. Morissey, not when there's been no real crime committed yet. Well, her husband's computer stuff constitutes a B&E, of course."

"B&E? Oh, yeah, breaking and entering."

"You check the files, any other B&E's recently?"

"Oops, I forgot. Get right on that, chief."

"Don't call me chief."

# # # # # # #

Several visits to the Morrisey family doctor over the past few weeks had revealed nothing. In desperation, Aggie eventually started checking with every doctor throughout the region, encompassing Fort Collins, Colorado, to the south, and extending north to Billings, Montana.

Routine question: had her husband been a patient? They couldn't or wouldn't say. Like, how'd they know she was his wife or had authorization?

At last a cancer specialist up in Billings agreed to instruct his staff to check their records. Eventually, the doctor returned Aggie's call with the bad news. But only after she told him that Randy had died months earlier. "Oh, of colon cancer?"

Randolph Morrisey's cancer was discovered too late, it was inoperable, the harried doctor said. "I told him then he had six or fewer weeks to live. Guess my forecast was about right, eh."

Forecast? Like a meteorologist predicting an upcoming tidal wave? Aggie supposed a doctor specializing in cancer saw so many cases, that her Randy's was merely one more file, among many. Now that file was closed.

Agatha left immediately to go meet with several bankers. She needed an extension on the mortgages Randy had taken on the house. Her precious home, that had been in her family and—obviously—paid for, for well over a century.

Aggie had yet to offer her furs for sale, as a means of raising revenue. She didn't know quite how to go about doing that without attracting attention.

At Harry's bank, Agatha didn't notice Morton sneering and smirking at her from behind a manila file folder. She was too busy thinking, on so many issues it felt like her head was coming unscrewed from twisting it in so many directions. Right now, about her vision. Upon approaching the front door from the sidewalk, she'd caught a very bright light in her eyes, blinding, really. She squinted her eyes tight and wondered what in the world.

Bank President Carl Vladimer had more bad news. "Since you were here last time, Mrs. Morrisey, we've discovered that a group of scam artists was operating in town awhile back. This information only came to light, however, when some of our debtors couldn't make their loan payments and finally admitted they'd made some rather terrible investments. You'll be reading about their con games in tomorrow's paper, probably."

"Call me Aggie, Carl."

"Of course. Randolph was my friend and the occasional golf partner. Everybody respected him. However he managed to get taken, I find it difficult to believe. I would never have thought he could be so gullible . . ."

"The point, Carl? What's the conclusion?"

"Yes, yes, of course. The point being that several months ago somebody or perhaps a team showed up in town. Apparently the police now believe they may have been some slick operators from the West Coast who'd offered stock in their company. S'posed to be in diamonds. A diamond mine down in Colorado, well, uhm, just across the state line . . ."

"You mean Diamond Peak, two or three miles south of the Norman Ranch over in Albany County?"

"Uhm, maybe. I'm not quite sure."

"Cut to the bottom line, Carl. Randolph invested a fortune in this scheme, is that what you're saying? My Randy? the experienced petroleum geologist?"

"Diamonds are different, though."

Aggie recalled what the stockbroker had said. That Randy had lost a bundle on some damn speculative stocks.

Had Randy discovered by then the doctor's verdict? Was that what made him so incautious? She reached into her handbag for bottled water. Opening it slowly, she sipped and pondered.

Ah, of course. It made sense that Randy would want to leave her a fortune. Instead, poor baby, he had lost not only his own money, but her whole inheritance as well.

"Have they caught the con men?" she asked.

"One of them, I guess. Out on the Coast. Hasn't as yet named their local contact. It'll be in the papers, I said." The banker rose, eager to get free of her, she supposed. She remembered now, he liked smooth sailing, couldn't stand setbacks. Vladimer wouldn't appreciate having to deliver bad news like this.

Aggie couldn't wait. From the bank lobby, she called Joan in Laramie. "Your daddy was dying of cancer, dear. So he invested our last red cent in a get-rich-quick scheme to make a bundle."

"And instead, he lost it all?"

"Right." Aggie recounted the banker's tale of woe about the scheme to invest money in a nonexistent or at any rate undeveloped diamond mine. "How can I find out what your father might have discovered months ago, Joan?"

"Try the morgue. Newspapers, that is. Of course you can go online."

Aggie wanted to get her hands on what Banker Vladimer had referred to as "a local operator." Wring his neck! Fleecing her Randy—and thus costing her her fortune. But at the moment she thought less of her own financial predicament than of her husband's desperate effort to provide for her, to leave her something concrete that would cause her to remember him with great admiration. Yes, that was the macho way, the way Randy would think. Oh, her poor darling, how utterly devastated he must have been when he lost it all!

Stunned, Aggie returned to the sidewalk. Again she was struck with that infernal light in her eyes. What was that?

CHAPTER 56

Aggie sat at the antique round oak table in her sun-yellow kitchen staring at the bills. The credit card statement for the Mississippi riverboat cruise was the largest, at over seven thousand dollars. Two mortgage payments were due, utilities were past-due, the gifts she'd charged—the list seemed endless. So this was what it was like to be burdened with credit-card debt and a pile of other due-now bills.

Agatha was still refusing to accept help from the Schwartzkopfs. She must figure out something. Carl Vladimer at Harry's bank—as she now thought of it—had agreed to reduce her mortgage payments for the next ninety days. Reduce, not postpone. She must wait no longer. It was time to start selling things. Her two fur coats and several priceless *objects t'art* that had been Randy's treasures were a couple of logical places to begin.

# # # # # # #

On the Sunday before Christmas, the majority of family members attended the Lutheran Church on Yellowstone Avenue in northwest Cheyenne, parking their cars in the block surrounding the building. Several clan members met on the church steps so they could file in together to their pews. The men wore suits and ties, the women dressed in their Sunday and Christmas finery, sporting corsages made of miniature pine cones, holly, and silk or satin ribbons.

The church was decorated, too. Aggie and Lisa smiled at each other, acknowledging a shared thought. What a beautiful setting for Nicole and Steve's wedding. Surely they would make up in time for the ceremony as planned.

The Christmas service was beautiful, so special, with the choir and the candles and the inspiring sermon. Some of the family took heart, while others used the worshipful opportunity for self-examination.

Lisa prayed that Aggie would capitulate and let the Schartzkopfs help her. Beth prayed that God would make Brad forget his dream of becoming a trucker. Brad vowed to sweet-talk his wife into accepting his decision. Peter nodded, nearly falling asleep.

Willie prayed that she could influence teachers to revise their curriculum: forget some of the animals some of the time in some of the elementary school subjects so they could make room for basic economic and business principles.

Opal's and Pearl's daughters, Betsy Ross and Martha Washington, prayed that the double cousins would take them into the family's inner circle. Their sons, Matthew, Mark, Luke, and John, and Wilma's Mark all wished for snow so they could go skiing.

Nicole prayed for Divine guidance to help her plan her life and decide what to do about Steve Norman.

Aggie vowed to be nicer to everybody, even if it took grinding her teeth to make herself smile at Nasty Three's husband, Harold the, uh, the Banker.

Nasty Three, with Harry beside her, dropped her head in contrition. Protecting her son was a mother's prerogative, perhaps, but a cover-up was unsavory for a state government official sworn to uphold the law. She must pay for what she'd done. But how could she take the official action necessary when to do so would send Ned to prison? At the very least, the secretary of state must resign. Forget her very temporary and very tentative dreams about what she would do if elected governor.

Ned Fleetfoot wasn't there. Against his mother's admonition, he'd left town for the Wind River Indian Reservation.

Harry the Huffy didn't vow or pray anything. He simpered behind his hymn book.

#######

Norma showed up early that Sunday morning at Steve's house. Together, the young parents took Cindy and Sissy to the Methodist Church for Sunday school, before leaving to head for the quiet Wrangler Hotel dining room for a serious talk over coffee.

Yes, the girls could stay with their daddy until the wedding—if there was one. No, Steve couldn't have them again until summer. If he wanted to see them in the meantime, he'd have to come to Boston.

Norma hated this backwoods state and didn't want Cindy and Sissy to see any more of it than absolutely necessary.

#######

Lionel and Lucy Falstaff emerged from the Baptist Church to walk down the street where they had left their car. They mingled with the Lutherans, who were also leaving their service. Lucy bumped into Nasty Three.

Lucy wore a black cloth coat over a black polyester pantsuit, with black felt hat and veil. She looked like a mourning widow, Lionel thought with disgust. Why didn't she know how to dress? Glancing at her face, scoured from adolescent pimples and her narrow squinty eyes, Falstaff couldn't imagine her standing at his side to take oath in the inauguration that would make him Wyoming's new governor.

"Oops, pardon me," Nasty Three said, while Harry tugged at her elbow and whispered to her to come along and ignore the Falstaffs.

Lucy blocked their path. When the Mortons moved to one side, so did Mrs. Falstaff. When the secretary of state stepped in the other direction, Lucy did a quick dance step that took her in the same direction.

Standing with legs spread and arms akimbo, tall Lucy bent over to stare in the eyes of short wide Nasty. "All right, Miz High and Mighty! What I want to know is why you and your capitol cronies insist on ignoring Wyoming's Lieutenant Governor. My husband is every bit as important as the rest of you."

"Wha-who?" Nasty stammered. "What are you talking about? This state has no such position as lieutenant governor."

With that, the Mortons made their get-away. Lucy was left staring open-mouthed at her husband. "Did you hear that? Either that was a bald-faced lie or, Lionel Falstaff, you've got some explaining to do. What do you have to say for yourself?"

#######

Hepzibah and Isabelle Vicente didn't go to church. They got enough preaching when Rudolph was home. If they believed anything, the dogma they would have sworn by would have come from the Latter Day Saints.

Hepzibah, one-hundred-four-year-old widow of Teddy Roosevelt Vicente, had always known she was second choice. Teddy never had got over Pansy Auld. The last night of Teddy's life, it was Pansy's name, not Hepzibah's—his wife of half a century—that he'd uttered in love and remembrance.

On that Christmas Sunday, the old women did pray, however. Hepzibah and Isabelle both had the same prayer: that Aggie and Lisa could find the answers to their quest, so Rudolph Vicente's mother and wife could continue to keep their lips zipped.

#######

Out on his Albany County ranch that nestled up against Sheep Mountain, Tom Rotter cuddled his old family Bible to his chest. Under his mother's afghan, the cantankerous codger closed his eyes in eternal sleep.

#######

In south Cheyenne, Dollie Domenico emerged from the Pentecostal Church with grim determination. It wasn't enough that God had forgiven her sins or that she'd promised to "Go and sin no more." She must save Harry, too.

Dollie couldn't imagine what Harry was up to now. Something bad and something strange, she was sure. Knowing Harry.

His latest assignment for Dollie was to demand that she go to the rental store and pick up one of those "dolly things," he called it. Because, he said, he wanted to move something heavy.

CHAPTER 57

The ladies again convened at Agatha's house over teapot and dainty china cups, Nasty One dictating family tales, and Peter upstairs watching football. This time he was joined by Brad and Steve, each of whom wanted the retired colonel's attention and advice—Brad about how to convince Beth that he should become a truck driver and Steve about how to convince Nickee of his unwavering love.

With the family's help, Aggie's house glistened in readiness for Christmas. A tall blue spruce graced a corner of the living room. It was decorated with many old baubles and doodads. Long ago Rose and young Rose had made it a practice to buy one very expensive and unique ornament for each Christmas.

"Where was I?" said Nasty One. "Oh, yes, well, we lost Willamena Jackson, and the very next day, dear grandma Rose died. Everybody called Rose 'grandma,' although she was my great-grandmother. Both of the ladies died quietly in their sleep. Everybody in town turned out for the double funeral. Standing room only at the Lutheran Church, people milling about outside. At the viewing the night before, the line of mourners was four blocks long, over three thousand people—they all signed the guest books. Flowers, my land, we contributed flowers to hospital patients and shut-ins. It was a sight to see, with enough tears to float the Titanic.

"It was the end of an era. Both young Rose and Estelle were devastated. You'da thought those two old women, Gramma Rose and Aunt Willie, were s'posed to live forever."

Aggie and Lisa turned the pages in the old photo albums and passed them around. Beth and Nicole were new to this session of the family's oral history, having joined Joan, Gam, Lisa, and cousins Nasty One and Two. Faint sounds of cheering from the televised football game drifted down from upstairs. The fire crackled, the tea grew cool. The women were oblivious to all but Nasty's account of the family during the decades of the twenties and thirties.

"Next, I gotta tell you about the troubles the Vicente Motor Car Company got into. I told you the other day that Thomas Jefferson and I operated the Cheyenne agency, Abe Lincoln and Lilac the Rawlins agency, and Grover Cleveland and Violet the Laramie agency. See, it was one corporation, with everybody owning stock, including the women whose shares were equal to the men's, so we had as much say and equal votes as the men.

"James Madison and Teddy Roosevelt Vicente didn't. They weren't owners or corporation stockholders, they were just employees—mechanics. Pansy, one of the Auld twins—remember, Pansy's twin Petunia had died at age five—didn't at all care for the arrangement. She and Teddy Vicente were in love, but she wanted a voice in the business. Teddy didn't care. He was kinda laid back, cool, I guess you'd call his type nowadays.

"Which could be why Pansy hooked up with James Madison. He was desperate to get inside the inner circle, and so was Pansy.

"Iris, Camellia, and Daisy Auld didn't count. I mean in the corporation squabble. They were all off doing something else, going to beauty school—that was Iris, lolling about the country club—that was Camellia and Daisy. Despite their university degrees, which, far as I know, they never did much with. They liked wasting their time and their allowance—from the trust funds left to them by Grandma Estelle. The rest of us invested our money in the business—also in the mining and petroleum industries. By this time both ranches had changed hands—the one belonging to great-grandma Rose was sold, and the other one, the one belonging to great-grandma Essie, got passed down to my mother Estelle.

"About Ulysses S. Grant Vicente, remember I said he'd gone off to Chicago to become a cop. Woodrow Wilson Vicente headed in the other direction, to San Francisco. We only rarely heard from either of them right up to the time of their deaths a few years back, and we hardly ever got to see either of them anyhow. So you might say it was practically a closed book on both. They might as well have been strangers, for all the blood-kin connection.

"You know that Opal and Pearl Vicente stayed in Cheyenne, also their daughters—Betsy Ross and Martha Washington. None of these people were gadabouts. Not like the rest of us wanderlusts."

Nicole lifted her glance to stare into the eyes of her mother and gam. Apparently not everyone in the family had the itch to travel.

Beth and Lisa also exchanged looks. Lisa knew that stay-at-home Beth dreaded the idea of Brad traveling in a truck all over the continent.

"What about Ruby Vicente?" Beth asked Nasty.

"She went mad. See, in those days, without birth-control knowledge, people were trying all sorts of weird remedies. Women poked things up their vaginas, devices to block the sperm from getting into the uterus. Or they gave themselves douches comprised of strong chemicals to try and kill the sperm. Men were giving women oral doses of stuff that must have been pretty dangerous some times. I don't know what combinations Ruby used, but she lost her mind as a result and had to be put away. Died in that home off in Lander."

"How awful," said Beth.

"So different from nowadays," said Nicole. "Seems like everybody's trying to get pregnant these days. Why are things so different?"

"Because you young women have a choice! We didn't. Before women got the vote—in the nation, not just Wyoming—the dispensing of birth control information, much less devices and products, was illegal. You young people with The Pill can't imagine what marriage was like. Never knowing when or how often you'd get pregnant, or how many babies you'd have, maybe a dozen or more per woman, before you died in childbirth or of other 'female' problems, long ahead of old age. Why, in 1915, Margaret Sanger was jailed for advocating birth control."

"Why? I don't understand," Beth said. "We learned in school that farmers had lots of kids on purpose in order to help work the farms."

"Silly notion," Nasty One hooted. "That's all backwards. People lived on farms because they didn't know what else to do to make a living, because their parents were farmers, and to have a place to grow crops and produce and raise animals to butcher, and milk to sell. All so they'd have food with which to feed all those mobs of youngins.

"Anyway, the common belief was that babies arrived according to God's will and their appearance, or not, should be left to God and not tinkered with. I don't know whether this idea came out of the churches or the legislatures. Don't matter, do it?"

Nasty One smirked at Joan. They all knew the old lady was educated and could use the language correctly when she chose. She did get a kick out of taunting the Grammar Cop, though.

"Either way, it was men who were in charge, making the decisions about women—their bodies and their lives.

"Where was I? Well, that was my parents' generation and all the generations earlier. My sisters—your mothers—and I collected the gossip whispered among women. Our generation did some strange things to avoid pregnancy. Aggie, your mother Violet would only have intercourse in the mornings so she could walk around upright all day, hoping that Grover's semen wouldn't run uphill."

Aggie and Lisa burst out laughing.

"No funny matter, me girlees," Nasty contradicted. "Tom and me, well, I don't know what happened. We had Abe and Lincoln and then Nasty Two and that was it. Tom, he had the mumps after Nasturtium was born and, I guess, that can make a man infertile." That thought sent her off on another tangent.

"That was another thing. Listen, me fine girlies, to the thinking of the times: if a woman didn't get pregnant, **she** was barren, it was her fault, not his. When she did get pregnant, it was <u>his</u> child, not hers or theirs. When she had girls and not boys, it was also a fault-—hers, the man apparently not having anything to do with the gender."

"Whew, times sure have changed," Beth said.

Eventually Nasty One had birthed three children, and so did Lilac and Violet. Doctors wouldn't agree to "tie or cut tubes" on a woman until she was past forty or had had a dozen children, because, they said (Nasty One said): "All your children could die and you'd want more. Even if you'd started with thirteen."

Nasty didn't say how Lilac and Violet had stopped having children, and her audience of females somehow sensed it was better not to ask. "Camellia and Daisy, at the end of the line of Auld flower girls, sure had plenty."

"Tell us more about Pansy and Teddy," said Aggie.

"And please don't skip over Iris," said Lisa.

"Nobody knew exactly what happened with Pansy and Teddy. One minute they're planning their wedding (here Nasty paused briefly to look meaningfully at Nicole), and the next she runs off and elopes with James Madison. Heavens to Betsy, her wedding invitations to Teddy had already been mailed, and the announcement was in the paper."

"Just like Nickee," Joan said, who'd missed the visual exchanges between the other women while she was busy poking the fire.

"James quit working for the Cheyenne auto agency. He and Pansy opened their own mechanic shop in Laramie. James was one good mechanic, the best. So that part of the business was in competition with the Vicente Motor Company operated by Abe and Violet—your parents, Aggie. That pair, James and Pansy, had no kids, none at all.

"Well, wait up a moment, I'm not really so sure about that. See, we all figured she'd got herself pregnant by James Madison, which was why she'd married him so fast. She was putting on weight, too, and looking pale and sickly. She'd run off to the bathroom . . . . Well, we girls figured to vomit. Naturally we expected that a bundle from heaven would arrive within a few weeks after they'd returned from their wedding trip. They went away on an extended honeymoon and when they got back, no more tummy bulge. We three musketeers figured James had aborted Pansy. Because he always said he didn't like kids.

"Pretty soon, for no earthly reason that anybody could see, Pansy up and runs off. Where to, nobody ever knew. We never saw her again. Kaput, off she goes, disappears into thin air."

This time it was Aggie and Joan, and Joan and Nickee, who exchanged silent glances. This trio felt closer now, for all their verbal haranguing and their blaming of each other in the Morrisey van en route from Meeteetse to Cheyenne. Along with their harrowing hotel experience, which may also have served to bring them closer together, the three-generational trio could feel more bonding between them than they had in a long time.

After her last couple of visits to Douglas, Nickee also felt closer to the Jacquot men. Which gave her two more reasons—beyond her own trauma of self-examination and distrust of Steve's motives—to feel pulled in several directions. She still wasn't talking to Steve, who was getting so frantic he'd taken to sending flowers and leaving love notes. The night before, while Nicolle was still on the Jacquot ranch, he'd begun singing love songs beneath her window.

Following a break to run to the powder rooms and replenish their food plates, Nasty One offered to answer questions. Agatha located one of Isabelle's crocheted poncho shawls for Nasty, and tucked it around the old lady's shoulders.

"Meanwhile," said Nasturtium, "Teddy Roosevelt Vicente married Hepzibah, and you all know Hepzibah and their son, Rudolph—he of the ridiculously devout fanaticism. You ask me, Hepzibah and Isabelle are a pair of peculiar women.

"All right, to continue: by the early thirties, James had opened mechanic shops in Cheyenne and Rawlins, just like the family corporation. That was while Pansy was still with him. James also hired salesmen, so he could get into new and used car sales, just like his older brothers. Except that James began double and triple-dealing. He financed all his cars with two and three banks apiece. By this time it was 1931, Pansy had disappeared, and the President declared a bank holiday. Plenty of people lost all their money. They couldn't make their car payments, so they just drove 'em up and left 'em at the auto agencies. The three-musketeer couples lost plenty, too, but not everything, because we'd been carrying the financing ourselves on the cars we'd been selling ourselves. Plus we had also invested funds in land, oil, and mining.

"James got a job in the court house, where he embezzled funds. They caught him and sent him to prison."

"Good heavens," said Beth.

"Good grief," said Nicole.

Nasty Two looked smug. She knew all this.

Lisa and Aggie and Joan didn't say anything, either. They too knew this story, since they were descended from the other two of the musketeer couples.

"I need a nap," Nasty One said abruptly, reaching for the cane she had purchased before returning home from Mexico.

Thus terminated another of the ladies' oral history sessions. Except their elder, Nasty One had another big bombshell to dump on them.

Nasturtium reached into her handbag to retrieve a musty old book. "I saved back this journal, girls. I never showed it to you, or let you read it, before," Nasty said with a smirk. "It was Essie's. I think you're ready for it now." Without waiting for a reaction, she promptly left to go catch a snooze in the sunroom under a fluffy comforter on the colorful daybed.

Aggie and Lisa were too excited to wait. Together they poured over the pages, reading aloud. Soon they discovered Essie's account of her hog ranch, or "whorehouse," which was how she'd come up with her first stake.

"Good heavens." said Aggie.

"Can you believe this?" said Lisa. She passed Essie's journal to Joan.

"Sure, why not," said the professor. "Look, Essie wrote that the prostitutes she met who were en route to Oregon Territory told her to 'sell it or sit on it'.

Oh, my goodness." Joan continued scanning the rest of the secret pages.

"What? what?" Nicole and Beth shouted together.

"Essie also learned birth control from those hookers. No wonder she had no more children after Estelle, even while 'practicing her trade'."

"Too bad she didn't get a chance to pass on this knowledge before she was killed in that train-buggy accident."

"Oh yeah?" said Beth. "Then our grandmother Estelle would have stopped birthing babies after her first two sons. None of us would exist."

"All on the turn of fate."

"Changing the subject," Aggie said. "Let's have another look at the photo albums from the 1920s. I had a question earlier but didn't want to interrupt."

She found the photos she was looking for, several group pictures of the youngest three Auld girls taken after they'd reached adulthood. "Look at Iris, everybody. What do you see?"

Silence reined while the ladies crowded around. Lisa clutched the magnifying glass that Nasty One had used to enhance her failing vision.

"Well, what do you see?" Aggie demanded.

"Some old-fashioned clothes," Beth suggested, ever conscious of style and fashion. "What else are we looking for?"

"She's not smiling," said Nicole, aware of her own look when feeling sad.

"She looks familiar." Lisa said excitedly. "Who do we know who resembles Iris Auld?"

"I can't imagine," said Joan, who was impatient to leave. She replaced Essie's diary in her case, to nestle with Rose's journals and the old photo albums. Since the horror of Thanksgiving, Joan had agreed to keep them safe.

None of the ladies present knew that Burly Boy was driving himself nuts trying to think where these self-same documents could have disappeared to. He wouldn't get paid if he couldn't find them. Time was running out. The Guy was impatient.

CHAPTER 58

Torn between getting rid of his ex-wife, which would mean giving up his little girls, and losing Nicole, Steve didn't know what to do. He could send his children away, and still not win back Nickee's love. He wanted to keep his cake and frosting both.

He didn't care whether Nickee flew or drove away every other week, so long as she would agree to be his wife. He loved her like he loved his own life—better than the ranch, better than his horses and houses. He'd sell everything and travel with her, if that's what she wanted.

Steve didn't share his feelings with Peter and Brad, and he hadn't told Aggie or anybody else, either. If only Nickee would come round, he'd tell her.

He didn't realize that Nicole was downstairs, and she didn't know Steve was upstairs in the same house. Everybody had kept mum.

All that family history—the scandals over love affairs and pregnancies, the problems with business and financing and the law—all those dreadful things Nickee had heard about her forebears made her own problems seem petty. She ached for Steve's arms around her, she hurt so badly she thought she'd throw up.

The women's session was breaking up just as Steve appeared mid-way down the curved front staircase. Without thinking one more troubling thought, Nicole rushed into his arms. He clutched her and held on like he'd never ever let her go, not in a whole lifetime. He wanted to tell Nickee that Norma had returned to Boston, leaving the girls with him until after the wedding. But he bit back the words. Just because she hugged him didn't mean she'd marry him.

Peter and Brad arrived from upstairs, Brad still in a quandary about whether his wife would go along with his trucking business. He stood silently on the steps, looking over the heads of the group into his wife's eyes. She smiled. He breathed a sigh of relief. Whatever her smile was supposed to mean, at least she no longer appeared to be mad at him.

Beth made a circle of thumb and index finger and held it up to her husband. When he raised his eyebrows, running one hand through the air like a truck and saying "Vroom, vroom?" she caught his question and nodded her approval.

Rose and Essie and Willie and all those other ancestors had done just about everything they'd ever dreamed of, without or in spite of fear, so of course Beth could too. She imagined she'd be busy getting her travel agency off the ground, perhaps she wouldn't even notice Brad's periodic absences. Yeah, in a pig's eye.

While Brad and Beth were communicating in that nonverbal language that loving married couples long familiar with each other often do, Steve was whispering in Nickee's ear the many concessions he was ready and willing to make.

"Silly boy. I don't want to travel every minute. I love the ranch, you know, the horses and dogs and cattle and everything that goes on there, and of course your family home. Getting the occasional auction job should be sufficient. We'll go to Boston to visit Cindy and Sissy. Besides, I'm going into partnership with Beth on the travel agency, which means that you and I together can take advantage of some travel perks."

Their solemnity sugared with the joyful grins and loving glances of their reunion, Steve placed Nicole's engagement ring back on her finger. To seal their commitment, they kissed, long and lovingly.

"I guess it's too late for a big Christmas wedding," he said sadly.

Around them, everybody, including Peter and Brad and Nasty One, who'd awakened from her brief nap, gathered to wish them well, and to squeal their congratulations.

"I knew it, I knew you belonged together." exclaimed Beth.

Everybody, including Joan, let Aggie take center stage. She was the first to reveal the big secret they could hardly bear keeping all these long days.

Unknown to either Steve or Nicole, the rest of the women in the family had been busily pursuing fruition of their dream—without the young couple's consent, knowledge, or participation. The wedding invitations were in the mail, the church and minister and musicians reserved, the cake and flowers ordered, the reception arranged.

"Everything's ready." Lisa said. "Your wedding dress awaits you upstairs on the third floor. Beth's matron-of-honor dress is at my house."

"Your three bridesmaids are ready, too," said Nicole's mom.

It was appropriate that Joan should make this announcement, since Lauren, Kendal, and Cherri were her students. "My *chickadees*," she called them. The previous fall semester, after Nicole had filed for divorce from Cowboy Billy but before she'd met Steve, she and the trio of university coeds had enjoyed partying and gossiping together. Though Joan would have preferred to see her daughter enrolled at the U, she was pleased that her mentees and Nickee got along well.

"You won't have to do a thing." Aggie said. "Except be there."

"I don't know whether to be grateful or angry that you didn't wait for us to make a decision," Nicole said.

Joan, of course, had mixed feelings. She was happy for her daughter and Steve. At least this husband was sensible, smart, courteous and caring, and educated. Ahah, she had another thought. With Nickee living at least part of the time on Norman's Albany County ranch, she'd only be twenty or thirty miles south of Laramie. There was plenty of time for Joan to work on her daughter. Between auction jobs and traveling, before or after more babies arrived, Nickee could become a bona fide college student. Perhaps the couple would postpone any future babies until Nicole matriculated, got that all-important college degree.

Joan was currently off campus for the university's month long, mid-winter break. She would need to return home to pack some things, if she were going to stay with her mother until after Nickee's wedding. The professor also decided to postpone her trip to Italy until after Christmas. She would work on her mom to accompany her. A trip to the Continent would be good for Agatha.

"Yes, mom, I insist on staying with you," Joan told Aggie, after everyone else had left. "Nasty Two probably wants to return home. With Nickee and Stevie here, we'll have four generations under one roof. Isn't that wonderful?"

Aggie agreed, of course. There were plenty of rooms, despite the rust in the third-floor bathtub and the pokey flow of the water up there.

She further suggested that Joan return all the documents she'd confiscated for safety on Thanksgiving Day. "I want to study them some more."

"Nosiree-Bob," Joan said, laughing at her mom's surprise. The expression was one of Big Jack's favorite expletives. "You've already said that everything's been wiped off your computer. I'll admit, I found it difficult to believe in Casper that we were being followed. With the discovery that our motel room was vandalized, and now that your computer's also been broken into, I'm no longer skeptical. Besides the need to finalize the wedding plans, I do believe, mom, that you can use all the protection you can get."

Aggie had finally succumbed and called the police to report the computer robbery, but she had specifically asked for Walt Fletcher. The detective sergeant, she was told, was off for the holiday.

"Walt was nice enough to return my call, though," Aggie said now. "He left a message on my answering machine to say he'd get back to me after Christmas."

"All the more reason I'm staying with you, mom. First, though, I have an errand in Albany County." Joan said she was going out to Tom Rotter's ranch to see if he'd be willing to share his family Bible with her. "Or at least let me look through it."

#######

Wilma invited Aggie to lunch at Applebee's. Wearing a dress of winter white with gold jewelry and carrying a black leather attaché case, the state school superintendent looked ready for a business meeting. Aggie wore a black wool pantsuit with crimson silk blouse, and her coat.

It was her last chance to wear the Christmas gift Randy had given her a year ago. Aggie was on her way to sell it. She had a buyer! Looked like word-of-mouth advertising still worked. She was convinced, however, that her caller had been put on the scent by one or the other of the Schwartzkopfs.

Following salads and idle female chatter that addressed each of their families, Wilma grew serious. "I'm worried about Nasty Three. She's not herself any more."

Aggie wasn't surprised at Wilma's concern. Their African-American friend must see the secretary of state nearly every day. About Aggie's own troubles, she could only be thankful that Nasty didn't tell tales out of school about the rest of the family. Nasty Two, yes, Nasty Three, no. The secretary of state was so tight-lipped they might have been permanently cemented against the telling of stories.

When Wilma invited Aggie to talk about herself, she said that Fletcher and Gilbert were looking into the B&E case. Wilma reminded Aggie that she was present at the Thanksgiving dinner when Randy's study was ransacked, so Wilma was eager to hear the news.

"You see Nasty a lot more than the rest of us, Wilma—well, except for Harry and the other Nasties. What do you mean, she's been acting strangely?"

"Quiet, more composed, even sad. Absentminded, actually."

"She always was reticent, as opposed to her gossipy mother."

"Yes, but that's not it. She's avoiding me. For awhile, after Thanksgiving, she was excited about what she'd do if she were elected governor. I thought perhaps we could convince her to run. But no more. She's clammed up. Worried about something, I believe."

"Mmmm, I'll think about it, Wilma. And I'll talk to her mother and Lisa. See what they think."

Their waiter looked familiar. He'd introduced himself in the beginning as Benji, short for Benjamin. When he returned to take dessert orders, they refused, settled for coffee. Aggie asked him how long he'd worked there, where he'd been before. The young, gangly chap bent low over the table, said he'd been downtown, working with Dollie Domenico.

Invariably interested in education, Wilma asked Benji if he were a college student. Yes, he was at L-Triple-C, majoring in computer education, he said. His roommate had married and moved out and Benji couldn't afford their apartment alone.

Aggie's eyes sparkled with an idea. "How about a room? Uh, and share a kitchenette, living room and bath. Not too expensive." She had no idea what rent was appropriate.

"That'd be great! You know where an efficiency like that is available?"

"Yes, I do. At my house."

As Wilma looked on with amazement, Aggie and Benji negotiated a deal. Sight unseen.

That afternoon Aggie sold her fur coat and called a plumber. High time she got that third-floor bathtub working. Peter and Brad and maybe Steve could help her move her office equipment and materials back down to Randy's study. Benji said he would post room-rental notices for her on the LCCC housing bulletin boards. Because Aggie had suddenly decided to take in roomers, preferably students. It wouldn't be the first time. Way back when, that's how she had met Dominic Alexander Davidson, and look what had happened to that friendship? Astonishing, how one's life could turn on a dime.

#######

Falstaff was disgusted. Lucy was no longer speaking to him. There was no justification for his lies, she said. "You made me look like an idiot," was the last thing she'd said, before shutting tight both her mouth and her legs.

She _was_ an idiot, never reading or listening to the news. He'd been able to claim his title of Lieutenant Governor with her, if nobody else, for a whole year. How could he convince Lucy that he was Somebody, eligible for the governorship, now that she knew her husband was no more than an administrative assistant in the governor's office?

Of course there were a lot of other people he would like to convince of his position. Falstaff knew who he was. He knew how to persuade the entire world, too. He just didn't want them to know the whole story.

#######

Over the past couple of weeks, Beth had had a good excuse for avoiding Brad. She'd kept busy working on her proposed travel agency. Except for Nicole's absence to travel to Meeteetse with her mother and gam, and then back north to return her dad's pickup, Nicole had been at Beth's side most of the time.

Beth got her financial backing from Brad, and also from her Estelle Auld trust fund. Beth and Nickee selected and rented a facility downtown in the Wrangler Hotel, corner position, with plate-glass window fronting on West Lincoln Way, with parking places available along the busy street and in a couple of nearby parking lots. It was an ideal location to attract both pedestrian and vehicular traffic. The young women bought plants, lamps, and chairs for the lobby arrangement, plus desks, computers, copy and fax machines, and file cabinets, for their office operations. Travel posters and brochures from airlines, hotels and resorts, car rental agencies, and chambers of commerce from around the world would arrive sometime after New Year's Day. A good, cheap way to both decorate and advertise their services.

Let Brad travel the earth, Beth told Nicole. She would run her travel agency, with Nickee's sometime help and advice. Beth wouldn't even miss her darling Brad. Hah, in a pig's eye.

# # # # # # #

Steve and Nicole put his store plans on hold. Together and individually they had too much on their plates already.

"After the wedding and our honeymoon in Hawaii, we can see how things look," Steve said.

Nicole agreed.

Morton the Malevolent would have been tickled pink, to see rancher Norman leave town. He might even have stopped twitching.

# # # # # # #

Nasty Three worded and reworded her letter of resignation. Tears of sorrow rolled down her cheeks. Not for herself, but for her son, Ned Fleetfoot.

Harry the Husband came into his wife's home office to ask her what she was doing.

"None of your business, Harry."

"Don't call me Harry."

"I'll call you anything I choose. Pretty soon, it'll be Ex-husband, Harry. I'm filing for divorce right after Christmas. Meanwhile, I want you out of here. You don't have anything to blackmail me with any longer. I'm confessing."

CHAPTER 59

First Bank blew up. Not all of it, just the vault containing the safety deposit boxes.

Bank president Carl Vladimer instructed his staff to get the list of box renters and call them to come to the bank. Most of the box contents were salvageable. Not all, though.

Harold the Horrible came to work early for once. Now was his chance. He volunteered to sort out the mess after the firefighters and the police permitted entry. Let somebody else make the calls. Harry needed to find Aggie Morrisey's box and pry into it, if he could, without anybody noticing.

Aggie replaced the receiver, immediately calling Lisa and the Nasties.

Nasty One said the Nasties too should go to the bank "Grandma Rose's box came to me by inheritance, as the wife of the eldest Vicente son. Thomas Jefferson was already dead. Can you believe I never once thought to check it? The rental fee was deducted from my bank account year after year."

"What?" exclaimed Nasty Two. "Weren't you curious? I cannot believe the most famous gossiper in the state, before I took over, wouldn't have rushed to the bank years ago. I know I would have."

"Tch, tch, child. What do you expect to find? Old letters, probably. After all, the Auld girls had already received from Grandma Estelle the deeds to our properties and all the stock certificates, bond coupons, all that. So had Rose's descendants. Wait a minute. Let me clarify that. Only the three musketeer couples inherited: Tom and me, Abe and Lilac, Grover and Violet. None of the Vicentes or Aulds who followed—those who didn't produce double cousins—got one red cent. At any rate, there's nothing left to distribute. We already have all the old ladies' diaries and journals. Don't count on secrets, just old papers."

Converging on the bank were the Schwartzkopfs, with Beth and Brad Gifford, Aggie, Joan, and Nicole with Steve Norman, two of the three Nasties, and Opal and Pearl Vicentes' daughters, Betsy Ross and Martha Washington.

Lionel Falstaff rushed in, too, holding his breath. He was about to have apoplexy! Nobody knew that. They didn't even notice the twitchy little man.

Missing were Hepzibah and Isabelle Vicente, who hadn't heard about the bank explosion. Ned Fleetfoot and Nasty Three didn't come. Harry, the soon-to-be ex-husband, had already been and gone. Betsy's and Martha's two sons apiece, who were at the high school taking winter exams, didn't show. The contents of these examinations they planned to promptly forget—in favor of filling their brains with sports scores and the lyrics to the latest hit tunes.

Absent too were the five tots, including Steve's twins, Cindy and Sissy, who were enrolled with the BB twins and Stevie. The children happily munched Santa-shaped sugar cookies on that last day of preschool before the holiday.

Disgusted at having his Christmas Eve day interrupted, Officer Bobby Gilbert arrived at the bank to assist with combing the premises for clues to the perpetrator, and to the method of bombing the bank. Walt Fletcher supervised the removal of the safety deposit boxes from their niches so customers could gain access to them. Later Walt would insist that yellow police tape cordon the vault from the curious, including the bank employees. He didn't want any possible evidence compromised. The sergeant then gave banker Vladimer permission to let the customers open their boxes to look for damage or thefts.

Out in his car, Harry gunned the motor to head for Dollie's trailer, to which he had a key. He could hardly wait to discover what he'd grabbed from the rubble.

Dollie tended bar, eavesdropping in awe at the talk of the explosion. Then she got suspicious. First Bank was Harry's bank!

Aggie, Joan, Nicole, and Lisa, with Peter and Steve's help, searched frantically for the Morrisey box among the collection piled in disarray, but they couldn't find it. The Nasties, with Betsy and Martha crowding close, had better luck. Grandma Rose's box was intact.

In Rose d'Gade's box, Nasties One and Two stared at two items: a huge nugget of gold, and another smaller, funny-shaped lump, both wrapped in buffalo hide, with a note attached. Scrunching together they read the fading handwriting.

"These pieces of gold were given to me as payment on an old debt from Mr. Claymore, who won it in a poker game," Rose had written all those years ago. "It comes from the old Centennial Mine."

Standing apart from the crowd, clearly disappointed, were Aggie and her entourage. "Now, what?" Lisa moaned.

"Look, look." Nasty Two said, having carried the heavy box across the room between and among all the other bank customers to her double cousins. "You wouldn't believe what we found."

Oohing and aahing, the double cousins easily edged aside the just-plain-cousins, Betsy and Martha. Betsy stealthily reached through the bodies blocking her to confiscate old Rose's note.

Betsy and Martha were the first to read the remainder of Rose's legacy. Their faces crushed, they dropped the flimsy sheet of blue paper on the floor. Cut out again. Forgotten, tossed aside like old rubbish.

Betsy and Martha left the bank to go home, to decorate their own tree at Betsy's house, to bake and cook their own Christmas dinner. Wilma Sanford and her son Mark were invited to Lisa's for Christmas, but not Matthew, Mark, Luke and John, or their mothers.

Nasty Two remembered the letter of instruction from Rose. "Wait, we didn't read the whole thing."

Another frantic search. Under Nasty One's cane they found it.

Lisa read: "This gold nugget I will to the kinfolk person or persons who is living in my home at the time the gold and this letter are first discovered. If the house has passed out of the family, the gold should be sold and the money donated to the University of Wyoming for student scholarships. If one or more of my progeny, no matter how distant or how far down the line, does in fact live in my home, this person(s) is now the sole owner of my gold nugget.

"Invest it wisely. Remember just two things: buy low, add value, sell high. And second, live frugally so you never ever touch the principal. When you've done that, you must use some of the interest, dividends or profits from your investments to help others. Your loving Grandma Rose."

All eyes turned to Agatha Vicente Morissey. And then the vault room rang with applause, and dusty musty arms hugged and hugged the widow lady.

#######

Lionel Falstaff waited to peer into his safety deposit box until he'd reached the privacy of his car. He drove around the block, past the saloon with the long long bar, past the Wrangler Hotel and the site of Beth's new travel agency, to one of two small parking lots. Selecting a space far from the busy street, he parked, locked all the doors, and looked around furtively. Nobody near. Time to check.

His box was located in the section most badly burned, the area of the bank where the largest containers were stored. Charred black, the lid popped open.

"No, no, no." Lionel screamed aloud.

Everything was burned to a crisp. Hundreds of thousands of dollars. Gone on the breeze.

#######

Everybody in the family left the bank for the wedding rehearsal at the Lutheran Church, the Giffords and Steve stopping by the daycare center to retrieve their five children. The kids must practice, too, if only for a little while. Excited from their Christmas party, they would already be tired.

Brianna and Brittney Gifford could hardly wait to show Steve's twins, Cindy and Sissy, what they were supposed to do as flower girls. Cindy didn't want to be led by the hand, she wanted to lead.

Stevie thought carrying a pink satin pillow with wedding ring tied to the top with a bow was a sissy thing to do but Norman explained to Nicole's son that carrying the ring was a very responsible task. The girls, after all, had only to strew pink rose petals down the aisle along the white floor runner. Stevie must look after the ring that Steve would place on Stevie's mommy's finger to wear for the rest of her life. "It says, 'I will love you forever'."

"Phooey, sissy stuff." Stevie wasn't likely to agree. But his revised expression suggested that he now felt proud and would do a good job.

For the practice run, Lisa and Peter substituted for the bride and groom, Lisa walking down the aisle for Nicole, and Peter stepping into Steve's place at the altar. The Giffords played their own roles, Brad as best man and Beth as the matron of honor. The bridesmaids were ecstatic—blond Lauren Lockhart, from Los Angeles, black-haired Cherri Chavez from New Mexico, and brunette Kendal Pretzi, from New York. With a red-headed bride, the color scheme in heads alone played like a rainbow. Big Jack would give the bride away, but he wouldn't arrive until Christmas Day, in plenty of time for the wedding. He knew what to do, he said.

Mark Sanford would play a medley of romantic music on his guitar.

Matthew, Mark, Luke, and John were supposed to serve as ushers, but they didn't appear, and when Nasty Two called Betsy Ross and Martha Washington to see what had happened, Betsy replied that they would not be able to make it.

"For neither the rehearsal nor the wedding," Betsy said.

"Oh come, now, what's got you ladies all in a dither this time?" The double cousins were used to their just-plain-first cousins getting their feelings hurt. One never knew what set them off, and this time was no exception.

On the other end of the line, Martha snatched the phone from her cousin to squawk at Nasty. "Grandma Rose didn't even mention us in her personal will on that blue paper and **we're born from Vicentes**, not all you Auld girls."

"For pity sakes, Martha, Rose was great-great-grandma to us all, our grandfathers were all Vicentes." Exasperated, Nasty Two took a deep breath before continuing. "Besides, that's irrelevant. Grandma Rose didn't mention anybody by name, merely referred to the present owner of her home."

Betsy was listening from another phone. "Oh, uh, well, I guess you're right. Okay, we'll come. I mean, if you're sure you want our boys in the wedding and us to serve at the reception."

"Of course we do, don't be ridiculous."

The boys appeared, but too late to practice with the group. Brad and Beth said they would volunteer to walk the boys through their roles as ushers and candle-lighters, but they were hosting a family supper. Peter and Lisa gladly stepped in to substitute for the Giffords.

Instead of a dinner for the wedding party following the rehearsal, Steve Norman distributed lavish gifts. Traditionally this meal is the groom's expression of gratitude but Steve hadn't known he'd be a groom until the very last minute. No time to plan.

Everybody—except Betsy's and Martha's boys—headed for the Gifford home, where they would open Christmas gifts to each other. They usually drew names, meaning there was one gift to buy and one gift to receive, per person. Clara, Aggie's former, full-time housekeeper, served the children soup and put them to bed. She said she hoped they wouldn't throw up from the day's heavy dish of excitement.

Clara all but demanded that Aggie keep her on as housekeeper. She adored this family. She wasn't stupid, she whispered to Beth, for Clara knew that Aggie could not afford it. Had something to do with Randy's death, and Agatha's returning the insurance fund.

The housekeeper would soon be surprised. Clara wasn't yet privy to the contents of Rose's "will," and its reference to the huge gold nugget left in the safety deposit box.

Beth, Brad, Lisa and Peter had prepared a light supper of ham and bean soup with tossed salad and cornbread. The adults were going to the midnight service at the Lutheran Church. It would be a time of celebration—with the dual or triple exceptions of Nasty Three's sadness, for some mysterious reason, the Morriseys' missing safety deposit box, and a few other imponderables. Time to set all that aside, including their differences with the just-plain-first cousins. Aggie vowed once more to be nicer.

Steve and Nicole's wedding was scheduled for late Christmas Day. Piles of presents for the happy couple were already arriving at Aggie's.

"What will you do with the gold, mom?" Joan asked, after the small children were bathed and tucked into their beds. "Of course it's too soon to ask, I would imagine."

"Not at all, dear. I know exactly what I'll do with it."

Everybody stopped talking to listen. The hearing-impaired double cousins couldn't hear if there was more than one sound, whether other voices or the background music rendered on television and video and cinema movies.

Peter and Brad said they knew what they'd do with the gold—invest.

Steve proposed that Aggie might buy a round-the-world cruise ticket.

Beth guessed Agatha would take care of her two mortgage payments in default, plus any other back bills. And after that she'd buy back her fur coat.

Joan thought it wasn't too late for her mother to return to campus for another degree.

Nicole and Nasty One knew what they'd do, were it them—they'd travel.

Nasty Two couldn't think straight.

"First I'll pay off the house mortgages and pay the plumber, and probably make some other repairs, perhaps get a new roof. Then I'll invest the remainder. With the house in good shape, I'm going to rent the second and third-floor rooms to L-Triple-C college students. Then I'll turn the ground-floor sunroom into my bedroom and Randy's study into my office. Oh yes," Agatha said, but obviously not as an after thought, for she had turned to her long-time friend. "And of course I'll hire Clara full-time."

Aggie glanced mischievously at her little blond double cousin. "Finally, Lisa and I are going to open a business. Just like Beth and Nicole. We'll use that room with the huge stone fireplace and its own outside door for our clients."

Joan and the Nasties and everybody else, except Lisa and Peter, were flabbergasted.

"What sort of business?" Nasty Two demanded, with eyes wide open in disbelief. "You don't know beans about how to do anything."

"Not much, you're right about that," Aggie admitted, refusing to feel insulted.

"We intend to learn," Lisa added.

"Yes, but what sort of firm?" Joan demanded.

"Private eyes." Aggie and Lisa squealed gleefully, clapping their little hands, and almost but not quite jumping up and down.

"Good grief," said Joan.

"My heavens," said the Nasties together.

"What next?" said Steve, rolling his eyes at Brad and Peter.

"Next," said Joan. "Nasty One is going to interpret what we've found in Tom Rotter's Bible."

"Not tonight, child," Nasty protested. "I'm too tired."

"Tomorrow, then?"

Nasty nodded before nodding off.

Joan turned to her mother. "Mom, I want you to go to Italy with me. Right after Christmas."

"'Mother'. Don't call me Mom, dear. Sounds like a laxative. Milk of Magnesia—MOM, ugh."

"Yes, Mother."

CHAPTER 60

Earlier that day Harry had moved out of Nasty's house to take a room at the Wrangler Hotel. He didn't plan to stay there, the reservation was for the sake of appearances. He was actually moving in with Dollie. Right now he had mixed feelings. Mostly, he was completely devastated over the contents of the safety deposit box he had stolen. Also, his pride needed Band-Aids from his wife's disregard—of his opinions, of his body in her bed, but especially of how her throwing him out would look to everybody important in the whole damn state.

He hadn't decided yet how he was going to pull out of such devastating doldrums. But he still had a few irons in the fire, a few chestnuts to pull out of the fire where he'd set them roasting. In other words, his various optional plans continued to ruminate in his mind, while percolating on the back burner. Harry the Husbander was nothing if not puffed up with his love for himself. Next to his own adorable person, he did love a good cliché.

Dollie's trailer was downright pretty, she decided, glowing with pride. Garlands of red and blue and green and white tinsel chains hung across and drooped down over every window. She'd covered the artificial pink tree with orange and purple baubles from Walmart. A pitcher of eggnog spiked with whiskey, some cheap brand, awaited the arrival of her lover.

Harry the Harried didn't notice all her hard work, or say anything if he did.

"We've gotta move fast," he yelped. "After Christmas, it'll be too late. Did you rent that dolly I told you to? You know, for moving something heavy."

The bartender stared at the banker. She hadn't a clue what he meant.

#######

When you babysit somebody, you usually grow to feel close, like a second mother, Agatha concluded. For many years, Aggie was the babysitter of choice for Nasty Three, who was her little doll. Ten years older, Aggie felt like a big girl the first time, at age twelve, she sat with Nasty. Over the next four decades, Agatha continued to cherish their relationship.

Which was why she felt like she had the right to make demands. She pulled Nasty Three off in a corner to demand an explanation. "Why have you been so different, lately, sweetie? So sad?"

They were interrupted by Nasty's son, Ned, who had arrived at the Giffords in the company of an Arapaho elder. Now, interrupting Aggie's conflab with his mom, Ned asked cousin Beth if he and the older Indian could use the playroom for a private conference. Then he drew his mother and Aggie down to the basement, where nobody could eavesdrop.

Ned Fleetfoot introduced Falcon Fleetfoot, an elder from his father's tribe. Then he asked after Harry the Husband.

When Ned heard that Harry was among the missing, by virtue of his mom's kicking him out, a brief expression of relief flashed across Ned's quiet face. Apparently, Aggie mused, he liked his mother's reply. So, the secretary of state had decided to divorce Harold Morton? Good riddance! Agatha didn't feel a single pang of guilt over her naughty reaction.

Suddenly, Nasty Three began to cry, with great gulping silent sobs. Ned put his arms around her, patted her back, and held her close. "It's going to be all right, Ma. You'll see. I want you to listen to Falcon Fleetfoot. There, there, Ma."

Utterly astounded, Agatha stood there, completely speechless. Nasty's reaction suggested she really had loved Morton the Miserable! Who would have believed it? One thing was sure, there was no telling the peculiarity of people.

"Oh, Aggie dear, you don't know, you just don't know. It's no use. We must confess. Ned and me. I'm so sorry, so very very sorry, Aggie."

Ned stared meaningfully at Agatha, who smiled back, gently but totally befuddled.

Nasty raised her head to mutter, "Ned, I was just about to tell Aggie our tragic story."

He scowled briefly. "Hey, ma, I want you to meet somebody."

In making the introductions, Ned clarified the elder's placement in the tribe. "Falcon Fleetfoot is a distant relative of my father. We've both got something to talk to you about."

Yeah, I'll bet, thought the secretary of state. On the Wind River Reservation, the U.S. government together with the Arapaho and Shoshoni tribal councils worked crime differently than in the states. The tribe handled misdemeanors and felonies committed on the reservation by members of the reservation, but manslaughter and murder were federal offenses. With the first type of crimes, the accused tribe members need not leave the reservation for their trials and sentences. For major crimes, the perpetrator was at the mercy of the federal courts.

"Oh, woe be unto us all," Ned's mother said.

With their meeting completed, the pair of ladies rejoined their family, Aggie's head in a tizzy. Ned departed to return to his own home with Falcon Fleetfoot who would spend the night with Ned in his room behind the Laundromat in south Cheyenne before returning to the reservation.

#######

With the children in bed, nobody but double cousins and their mates (Peter, Brad, and Steve) were left at the Giffords' house to hear the secretary of state's confession. "Which is how it should be," said Nasty Three. "What I'm about to tell you should not leave this room or the inner circle of the family."

Nasty Three stared meaningfully at her mother, the inveterate gossip, before continuing. "Ned's father was a drunken bum, an embarrassment to his tribe and clan, and a horror to Ned and me. I didn't want to give up on him. I kept thinking that all he needed was a good woman who loved him, and he'd straighten out. Didn't work."

Nicole glanced at her gam and mother. The look, Agatha interpreted, suggested that Nickee knew the feeling, as she too had suffered through a marriage with a drunken wife beater.

"You know that several times I left the reservation and returned to Cheyenne, usually with Ned but less frequently as he grew older. The last time I returned to the Arapahos, Ned met me at the door to tell me he'd killed his father."

Gasps and questions all round. Nasty held up a hand to command silence. "The body was gone, Ned was silent. He simply took my arm and said we had to get off the reservation. I couldn't think clearly, just took Ned at his word and let him lead me away. Shock, I guess.

"You know the rest, well, part of it. A quiet rest in the mountains and visits to all the family scattered about Wyoming. Then the boys (she meant grand-uncle Tom's and Nasty One's sons, and Lisa's brothers Abe and Lincoln) convinced me that I should run for office as secretary of state. After that there was the mad whirl of platform design, party caucuses, campaigning, and I won. As for my personal affairs, and Ned's role in ridding us both of his father, I was in a state of denial, like it'd never happened, even my entire marriage to Fleetfoot.

"Working hard as volunteers on my behalf were two very charming guys, much alike in temperament and looks, actually: Harold Morton and Lionel Falstaff. Following the inauguration, Harry continued to hang around. You cannot believe—knowing him since then—how very charming he was. Short, like me—well, like all of the double cousin girls—he didn't seem to mind my girth.

"Charmed the socks off me. He made me feel as though I could do and be anything: corporate executive officer, ambassador to England, run for and win Wyoming's next gubernatorial election. You name it, he said he'd help me achieve my ambitions. Actually, if you want the truth, I don't think I'd really had any ambitions before the uncles and the men cousins pushed me into politics. They said my degrees in business and economics made me a natural, and that the state really needed my expertise and service. If you think my head had been asleep throughout my marriage, you'd be wrong. I'd served on a number of fiscal councils, which Fleetfoot deeply resented. He never really got over his hate for white people, including his own wife.

"Anyway, back to the campaign. There'd been a number of low points throughout the whole campaign experience. The slightest setback could set me back, too, my low self-esteem from all those years with Fleetfoot being what it was. I needed Harry's unwavering devotion, leaning on him more and more.

"Well, when I wasn't leaning on Falstaff. He too was in my corner, expressing his undying devotion in many small ways."

Aggie was well aware of the family's involvement and concern, though she couldn't be sure just who knew which parts of Nasty's story. As for the love angle, if that was what it was between Nasty and Harry, a quick and private wedding following what must have been a whirlwind but short courtship. Nickee and Ned standing up with the couple during Cheyenne Frontier Days. Nasty and Harry showing up for the big rodeo, where the secretary of state had introduced her new husband to the President of these United States.

"Harry must have been in hog heaven—in company with the First Couple," Nasty's mama, Nasty Two, muttered.

"Right, mama," Nasty Three quickly agreed. "The twerp is power mad. I didn't know anything about Harry's private life, didn't realize he already had a wife. I did know that Lionel Falstaff was married. I'd met his awful wife, just once, but Lucy invariably ignored me, despite my lukewarm overtures. Lucy is so uncouth, it's hard to know what to expect from her or how she'll react to one's extension of, if not friendship, at least the normal civilities."

Joan mumbled to Aggie that she wished Nasty Three would get on with it. "She says her son murders her husband and then goes on about marriage to Morton the Monster, as if killing a human being is something you can sweep under the welcome mat."

"Hush, dear, she'll hear you."

"Don't be silly, mom. None of you double cousins can hear beans."

Agatha smiled. Joan was finally beginning to think and talk like the clan.

"Soon after the wedding, though," Nasty Three continued, "Harry turned sour. He was a different man. Said he hated Indians, wetbacks, slant-eyes, black people, all those types. Even Jews. Sneered at my marriage to Fleetfoot, hated Ned and, well, the feeling was mutual, I'm sure. I told Harold that if he didn't straighten up, he could leave." (The couple lived in her house, left to Nasty Three by Grandma Estelle, since the Nasties Two and One didn't want it.)

"You'll all recall that I'd campaigned and won the office under my Vicente birth name, and in this day and age I didn't see any reason to change my name to 'Morton' after the election. All those things made

Harry furious, of course. He wanted more money, too. I countered by asking Carl Vladimer at the bank to promote Harry to a more responsible position. Boy, that was another embarrassing mistake. Harry had no more moxy or worth as a banker than he did as a husband. Or a stepfather. He could barely function as a teller, never could understand the job description of loan officer."

"Why didn't you leave him? or kick him out of your house?" Joan asked.

"First, I didn't want all that fuss while I was in the public eye, wouldn't look good. I'd lose respect and the people's confidence, including the Arapaho and Shoshoni, who, for some reason, really believed in me and seemed to continue caring about me.

"I wanted Harry out, though, wanted nothing more to do with him. It was then that he pitched his blackmail scheme at me. Harold was all too Horrible.

"He said he'd been on the reservation with a group of Kiwanis, up there on a casual tour. Then he claimed to have witnessed Ned killing Fleetfoot. It all made sense. No longer was I in denial, I suddenly recalled with perfect clarity Ned's confession and our late-night escape from the reservation. I'd never returned, and I told Ned that he must never go back, either. Catch him on the reservation, the Arapaho might turn him over to the Feds."

Aggie felt so sorry for her cousin. She held back the tears with great difficulty. Lisa and Peter sat on the couch in the Giffords' great room, holding hands tightly. Nasty's tale was terrible and it had all happened, except for the murder, right under their noses, with nobody in the family the wiser. And then Agatha recalled a real glitch in the get-along. Ned's father wasn't killed on the reservation. He was murdered right here in Cheyenne. Oh no, oh my goodness, that meant that if Ned really was the culprit, then he had killed his father off the reservation, and white people like Walt Fletcher would have the jurisdiction. Aggie was totally confused, and wondered whether Ned as well as his mother weren't both in denial!

With an arm about his fiancée's shoulder, Steve could feel Nickee tremble and could sense her empathetic pain.

Nicole was thinking, "There but for the grace of God, go I." If Cowboy Billy had not been caught, her marriage to him might have come to this—murder.

Suddenly, as if pulling a lever, Nasty Three's sad face broke into smiles, like sunrise over the far mountain. Her son was standing in the doorway, smiling.

"I didn't kill my dad," Ned said. "It's true, I beat him to a fare-thee-well, and I thought he was dead, but it turns out I didn't kill him after all. With help, he traveled to Cheyenne, seeking medical care, maybe, and this was where he was finally killed. Falcon Fleetfoot, my dad's distant cousin, finished the job."

"Ned's innocent." his mother said.

"Mom's free of worrying about me. And free of the worry that she'd participated in a cover-up," Ned added. "She doesn't have to resign as secretary of state. Maybe we can talk her into running for governor one of these days."

Everybody jumped up, even Nasty One with her cane, to gather round Nasty Three and Ned. Hugs and pats, with the men pounding Ned's back. And, from the ladies, squeals, laughter and tears.

All the things, Agatha mused, that serve as the glue to stick families together, whether in fortune or famine, fun or frost.

When the climate finally settled, like dried dandelion fluffs floating to earth, Lisa asked. "You're finally free of Harry? He actually moved out?"

"You bet. Gone and forgotten. Well, not quite."

#######

At Dollie's, Morton was maniacal. Pawing through Aggie's jumble of disorganized papers in the battered box he'd stolen from the bank, he screeched, "It's not here."

"What are you looking for?" Dollie demanded. "And whose box is that?"

"Never you mind. My business."

"Come on, Harry, give."

"No, no, no." Then he thought a moment. "But I know where it is. Come on, hurry. Let's go."

"Where, where? It's snowing outside. It's after midnight. It's Christmas, Harry."

"Don't call me Harry."

#######

Earlier that afternoon the Guy was mad, frustrated, ready to give it up. First, though, he wanted revenge. All the money he'd paid the hit man—who was never supposed to kill Aggie—incapacitate! incapacitate! The Guy still had only a single set of notes from the family history. And that was nothing but a lot of stuff about the Mormons back in the mid-nineteenth century. Who cared about that, or them, way back then?

The Guy picked up the phone and called the police. He had a report to make on a breaking and entering, "B&E," he said smugly, thinking that he knew a lot about police procedure and terminology.

The call was referred to Sergeant Detective Walt Fletcher, who was still on duty over the bank bombing.

By now the police knew it was just a cheap pile of dynamite sticks lit with a short fuse that had blown up First Bank. Meaning the perp had to have left the vault only minutes before it blew up.

The B&E of Aggie's house the night before Thanksgiving was also Walt's case. Besides, he thought of them as friends, the widow Morissey and himself. Walt was very interested in what the caller had to say.

To Sergeant Fletcher, the Guy reported the make and type and color of car that the hit man was driving and then said he had the license number. "He could be carrying drugs," said the Guy, hanging up the phone at the public booth without giving his name and address.

#######

"I don't want to help you, Harry," Dollie protested. "How many times I got to tell you that?"

"Oh, sure, now you're miss Goody-Two-Shoes. What about the murders?"

"Murders? Whose? What in the world are you talking about?"

"The Normans. You punched a hole in the gas tank of their Cessna. They crashed, and both of 'em died. What about that?"

"No way! I couldn't do it. I chickened out, Harry. At the last minute I dropped the ice pick beside their plane and ran. I never went back to the Laramie airport for no more flying lessons. Their crashing the Cessna was an accident, Harry. All this time you thought it was me what did it? No way."

CHAPTER 61

Tom Rotter was dead. Joan discovered the body when she went to borrow his family Bible. She reported it, calling the Albany County Sheriff on her cell phone before she left the Rotter ranch. Then she copped the Bible he clutched in his cold, stiff arms. At the last minute, she turned back and replaced the Bible in the old man's cold hands. She couldn't get his fingers to clutch them, so she just propped him up, his arms leaning on the Bible to hold it in place. Then she backed off and using her multi-use cell phone, she snapped a dozen photos. She would use the flash drive to upload the pictures to her computer.

She wasn't sure why she had gone to all this bother. For one thing, she could send them by e-mail to her mom's computer. If Agatha and Lisa meant to be PIs, they could start with the Rotter case. Perhaps he had not died of natural causes. Wouldn't that be something if the two dainty ultra gracious ladies actually solved a murder case?

Actually, she had disturbed a crime scene, since she meant to take the Bible with her. The photos would prove Rotter had been holding it. If she were ever to get in trouble or be blamed for his death, she had the evidence to prove where the Bible had originated. Of course, the whole scheme could backfire. She might truly be arrested, even convicted, of his murder.

Joan's family didn't mourn Rotter, they didn't know him well. Cousin-in-law Hepzibah had worked as cook on his ranch, but that was many years ago. And she didn't act sorry, either. His death was labeled heart attack, or death due to natural causes, due to age. Nobody seemed to think differently.

At one point Joan overheard Steve's semi-confession to Nickee. "My dad and Charley had it in for Tom Rotter, and vice versa," Steve said. "I never did know why."

Sipping hot cinnamon tea at the wake, Joan strolled away, thinking the Norman men weren't responsible for Rotter's death, no more than she was. She knew she wasn't a killer. As for Steve's dad and brother, the timing was completely off, they were dead weeks before Tom Rotter died.

Joan forgot about the digital photos in her cell phone's memory.

Joan nearly forgot all about the Bible, too, until her mom was heading for bed. Then she turned it over to Aggie, as promised. But Joan didn't mention it belonged in the hands-off death scene.

At home following the midnight service at the Lutheran Church, Aggie said she must retire, which was fine with Joan, who felt like she could sleep for a week. All the commotion in the family, plus the grueling end-of-semester tasks to complete were exhuasting. Joan was limp as Raggedy Ann with fatigue.

Despite the late hour, Aggie had no intention of sleeping. She couldn't wait another minute to read Tom Rotter's notations. They were scattered throughout his old Bible: in the margins, top and bottom, on the flyleaves, and at the back of the book. It would take time to locate, read and decipher the old chap's dim pencil scribblings.

Under the bright light of a desk lamp in Randy's study, Aggie squinted at the barely legible words. She wore a long flannel nightgown with lavender flowers, a purple robe, and warm fluffy lilac colored slippers.

#######

At the Falstaffs, Lucy had been in bed for hours. Across the hall in the room to which Lucy had banished her husband after his confession, Lionel toyed with the old locket on the gold chain. Lionel Falstaff knew who he was and where he came from, because he'd had this locket with the pictures and names of his mother and father since he was a very small boy, possibly since birth.

#######

In Dollie's bathroom, where Harry went in anger and frustration after hearing Dollie's explanation that neither she nor her son were in any way guilty of Fleetfoot's death, Morton the Miserable played with the old locket on the gold chain. It contained photos of people Harry figured might have been his mother and father. But with no names, he couldn't be sure.

The treasure he'd sought by blowing up the bank and getting access to Aggie's safety deposit box included some confirmation of his family, some sound documentation that he was in fact descended from one of those grand old Wyoming families. All his life he'd yearned to belong to somebody special, somebody important, so he himself could be a Real Somebody.

He had owned the locket for years. Not knowing who those people were was killing him. Suffering from the unbearable curiosity ate at him like a cancer. He had to know if they were his parents. He had to discover they were Very Important People. Instead of VIP, he'd got zip. No info from Agatha's box.

Harold had persuaded himself months earlier that he was descended from Grover Cleveland and Violet Auld Vicente, that he was a brother or a nephew of Agatha Auld-Vicente Morrisey. Cozying up to Nasty Three and convincing her by sheer charm—and political dependency—that he was in love with her (and she with him) was a real riot. Because she could very well be his very own double cousin, once (or could it be twice?) removed. All along, Harry had saved the blackmail ploy to use in case the secretary of state was tempted to stray. Clever of him, damn clever ploy.

Oh, you clever boy, Morton told himself.

Yet there was still no clear evidence that his ancestry was actually what he'd dreamed and hoped with all his heart. Egad, suppose he was actually nothing more than a foundling left at the orphanage, before being passed around in that series of awful foster homes.

Never mind all that. Harold had to make his move. And right now.

#######

Suddenly Aggie understood, as though dark clouds had parted and she could see the sunrise. It all came together: the bad news about the diamond mine that had suckered Randy into financial ruin, and—more importantly—had led to identifying the con man, the family history, the old scandals, and, finally, the name of the person who had been responsible for stalking her these past few weeks. Aggie must act and act fast.

Tomorrow could be too late. But damnation, she couldn't find her cell phone. She knew the old trick, call herself, and listen for where the ring was coming from. But her cell didn't ring, it didn't buzz or chirp, it just played a quiet but pretty little tune. She could never hear it from a distance. In fact, she mostly kept it in her apron pocket, or her jeans pocket, or in her pocketbook. Never mind, there still was such a thing in this world as a regular phone that was hooked up by wire and stayed put.

Despite the lateness of the hour, Agatha picked up the land line and, with trembling finger, punched the buttons that would reach into Hepzibah's home and fetch the old lady to the rescue.

"I've been sitting here by the telephone, awaiting your call," the long-silent widow of Teddy Roosevelt Vicente said. "Rocking in my chair and watching it snow. I knew you'd call. I'll tell you only so much, Agatha," Hepzibah said further. "You'll have to guess the rest. If you're right, I'll say so. If you're wrong, I'll tell you that, too. But I ain't tellin' you another thing. So, start talkin'."

Aggie took a deep breath and began. "You were the bunkhouse cook at Tom Rotter's ranch for a lot of years, a decade or more. You saw lots of things, plenty of people come and go. Right?"

"Right."

"Good. Then I'm on the right track."

####### # #

Aggie did not disturb her daughter, granddaughter, great-grandson, or housekeeper. Clara, who had no family of her own, had agreed to spend the night, and would move back in permanently later in the week. She would be needed full-time again, if Aggie was going to rent rooms to college boys.

Jumping up from Randy's bottom-worn leather swivel chair, Aggie ran upstairs to throw on jeans, turtleneck, blazer, boots, and heavy car coat. She looked like an ad for the L. L. Bean catalogue, or for any good wrangler shop in the state of Wyoming. Just before midnight that Christmas Eve, it had begun to snow. Already there was a mushy six inches on the ground and more coming down. She ran to the garage and started her van, pulling the lever to put it in four-wheel drive.

####### # #

At Dollie's, Morton the Maniacal was panicking, he felt like he was going nuts. Maybe he'd missed it. Again pawing desperately through

Aggie's jumble of disorganized papers in the battered box he'd stolen from the bank, he screeched. "I tell you, it's not here."

"What? What are you looking for?" Dollie demanded again, pushing open the bathroom door and insisting that he rejoin her and stop yelling. "You'll wake the dead."

"Wha-, what'd you mean by that?" He looked frightened.

"Just an expression." She saw the burnt safety deposit box in his hands, black streaks coming off on his face where he'd rubbed it. He looked like the chimney sweep in *Mary Poppins*. "Whose box is that?"

"Never you mind. My business."

"Come on, Harry, give."

"No, no, no." He had to locate the information that was his to own.

Then he stopped to think. And think some more. Blowing up the bank was stupid of him. He suddenly realized he'd had access to the information all along and hadn't realized it. At last he knew where to find it—right here at home.

Somewhere among the jumbled litter in his old trunk was an anonymous letter that had come to Harry years ago. Its contents had made no sense then, and now he couldn't remember the gist.

"But I know where the letter is," he told her, as if she were clairvoyant. "Get the dolly, Dollie, and let's go."

"Where? What letter? Where we goin', Harry? It's snowing out, Harry. It's after midnight. It's Christmas, Harry."

"Don't call me Harry."

# # # # # # #

Lionel crept about the Falstaff house in the dark. He grabbed his coat from the front hall closet, but forgot his boots. Peeking one last time at Lucy to be sure she hadn't wakened, he slipped out the side door.

In his little Ford with the slick old tires and no chains, Lionel went slipping and sliding along the icy streets. He arrived at Aggie's in time to see her leave. "What in the name of heaven?" he muttered aloud.

He pulled in behind her van but stayed several car-lengths behind. Theirs were the only two cars out on the icy streets that night. He switched his lights to dim. Mustn't let her spot him. She could panic and run to the cops.

#######

At Nasty Three's darkened house, Harry used his garage-door remote opener to get inside, and then he quickly closed the door behind his car.

"Nasty's pretty deaf, Dollie, so we don't have to be silent, just quiet. Unload the dolly."

"That heavy thing? You do it."

Grumbling and mumbling, Harry hauled the heavy dolly used to move heavy things through the door and into the adjacent kitchen, and on across the living room to the front staircase.

"What in the world are you going to do, Harold?"

"Getting my things," he grunted.

"Can't this wait until tomorrow? It's the middle of the night."

"No, Dollie, it can't. Now you go hide in the front hall closet, and shut up, for once in your life."

Nasty Three was not as deaf as Harry supposed. What with the attempted attacks on cousin Aggie, and Fleetfoot the elder confessing to the murder of her first husband, she couldn't sleep. Awake with nerves jumping, she arose from her warm bed to prowl the second floor.

In one of the spare bedrooms she found the big trunk that Harry had brought with him to their marriage and into her home. She tried to open it. She wanted no part of Harold the Horrible. He'd taken everything else. What on earth was in this thing? She examined it. Locked. Nuts. Well, okay, then, she would just shove it into the mostly unused upstairs closet out of sight.

Nasty got as far as the hall at the top of the stairs, the dim lamp from her bedroom lighting her way.

In that moment she thought she heard scuffling. And whispers. What, now? She switched on the one-hundred-fifty-watt hall light.

At the top of the stairs, dressed in warm pajamas and royal blue velvet robe but barefooted, Nasty looked down on the top of her husband's mostly balding crown. Like hers, she thought irrelevantly, though partially paralyzed with fear and apprehension.

"Harold Morton, what do you think you're doing here?" Nasty demanded.

Surprised in the act of pulling the dolly behind him, Harold almost swallowed his dentures. Yes, he wore false teeth. A necessity, because in college Charley Norman and one of his rich friends had knocked out all Harold's front teeth—uppers and lowers. That was the time they had caught him burning their one and only semester-long chemistry lab notebooks, the night before their due date. Heh hee. The pair of university boys had flunked Chemistry I. Yeah, served 'em right. Harry's dentures were one of his life-time reminders that he would surely, some day, seek revenge on the Normans. At any price.

#######

On Interstate-25, which runs north and south through Cheyenne, Bobby Gilbert and his partner observed a speeding car. It was weaving back and forth across the two south-bound lanes.

"Christmas Eve, and we got drunks out," said Gilbert. He was still on duty. Lack of sleep had made him bleary eyed.

"Step on the gas. We'll pull him over."

Lights flashing, siren wailing, the police car edged up even with the motorist, who neither slowed nor stopped. Instead, the driver mashed the accelerator and charged ahead.

"Hurry up, Bobby. Another five miles and he'll be the state patrol's collar."

Windshield wipers working diligently to push back the heavy snow, visibility near zero with more snow falling, ice crunching beneath their tires, it was all Bobby could do to keep control of the police car. And he was sober. Zooming past a double semi-trailer truck and several passenger cars and pickups, another couple of huge haulers, and Bobby sideswiped the drunk on purpose in an effort to make him stop.

"Now look at what you've gone and done," said Bobby's buddy. "Wrecked our car. Sergeant Fletcher will have a fit."

"Check the license plate on the computer and quick, get out your gun," Bobby said. "This could be a nasty one."

The number matched a B&E alert called in anonymously some time earlier. The officers, with guns drawn, approached the vehicle cautiously. With the license alert, they had legal cause to search the car and trunk.

Weaving about, laughing in their faces, Burly Boy held up his hands to show they were empty. Automatically, without being told, he turned to spreadeagle himself against his car hood. He knew the routine. Been here, done this.

From the car trunk, Gilbert discovered a plastic bag of white stuff. Hidden inside the spare tire beneath the floor mat. "Hah, gotcha." Bobby said, returning to the front of the car and his partner, who by now had handcuffed the resisting hit man behind his back. Bobby held up the see-through sack.

"Huh? How'd you find that?" the perpetrator said. "Look, man, it's not what you think. That's not cocaine."

"Oh no, then what is it?" Bobby demanded. Having opened the bag, and dipped in the tip of his finger, he was about to take a wee taste.

"No, no, don't do that, man! It'll kill you."

"Poison, eh? That's bad news. Come on, you, we're hauling you in."

"I know my rights."

"Yeah, I'll bet you do." Gilbert read aloud from his Miranda card. Oughta memorize this thing, the baby-faced rookie told himself.

"Take me to the station. I've got a statement to make."

#######

Aggie parked her van at the curb and raced to the door of Nasty Three's house. Her boots crunched and she slipped, quickly righting herself.

Meanwhile, Lionel Falstaff edged up to park across the street, where he slid out of the car to follow the Widow Morissey.

She had her own key, as all the double cousins did for each other's houses. She didn't want to startle Nasty by ringing the noisy chimes. It didn't occur to Aggie that appearing out of nowhere in the middle of the night inside the house might be even more scary.

Something was wrong. The stairway light was burning. At this hour? Aggie noticed it just as she stepped through the door, and before she saw the mess at the bottom of the steps.

She lifted her eyes to stare at Nasty, who was standing at the top of the staircase like the salt statue of Lot's wife. Wearing night clothes, with eyes glazed, both hands clasped to her bosom, and pale as a corpse, the secretary of state could have been taken for dead had she not been standing upright. Then Nasty opened her mouth and screamed. She howled, moaned, and screeched.

Dollie Domenico burst out of the hall closet. "What in the world?" Then she spotted her sweetheart, silent at the foot of the stairs. Harry lay crushed beneath his heavy trunk and the dolly she'd rented. Dollie screamed as loud as Nasturtium the Third.

Numb with paralysis, both Nasty Three and Dollie—the two women who had shared Harold's bed—stayed put. They might as well have been planted.

Aggie gulped, before leaning over to gingerly check Harold Morton's pulse. Finding none, she shuddered, gagged, and then caught her breath before lifting herself to stand upright. Things to do. She herded the other two women into the kitchen and slammed the door behind them.

First Aggie pushed Dollie and Nasty into chairs. Next she poured fresh water into a pot and set it to heat. Then she used Nasty's wall phone to dial the police station and asked for Sergeant Fletcher.

#######

Outdoors, Lionel Falstaff returned to his car down the street. He hesitated mere seconds before opening his car trunk to extract a tire tool. Slipping and sliding in his dress shoes with the slick soles, he skidded into the snow, which by now had begun drifting into big piles from the power of the bitter cold wind.

Lionel picked himself up and trudged on toward the house into which Aggie had disappeared. He'd get her yet, or else grab what he came for. Or both.

Finding the front door ajar, Lionel slowly and stealthily pushed it open, the tire tool held aloft ready to strike. Lights blazed, but no sound of human occupancy. No sight of Aggie or the secretary of state. Falstaff crept indoors.

What the . . . . ?

On the floor at the foot of the stairs rested a trunk, and under it lay Harold Morton, Nasty Three's husband. The same guy who had repeatedly kept getting in Falstaff's way whenever he was trying to make an impression on Nasty and the other capitol big shots. For heaven's sake, he wasn't doing anything illegal, merely trying to show what a hard-working political volunteer he was, so they'd understand he was worthy of an outstanding government appointment. Meanwhile, that darned Morton kept sticking his nose in.

Lionel hated Harry—the hackneyed, walking-talking haberdashery. Never mind, he would deal with the bothersome, strutting turkey later. The guy thought he was so smart, spreading his feathers like a peacock. Let him lie there.

Right now Lionel had to get a look at what was in that big container. He shoved the trunk off Harry to look for a nametag before opening it and exploring its insides. The lock was sprung, so it should be easy to get into. Maybe this was where he'd find the papers he so desperately sought.

Hah, clever of Aggie to hide it at Nasty's house. No name tag telling him who owned it, but Lionel had a gut feeling. This was Agatha Morissey's secret cache. In Lionel Falstaff's hands at last.

He pulled the rented dolly used for hauling heavy objects out from under Harry and set the trunk on it. Now to move the container. There, now. Strap it down and he'd be off.

At that moment Harry groaned. The trunk removed from his chest, he could breathe. He caught his breath and sat up. "What's going on?" he croaked.

On his hands and knees Harry crawled over to his trunk, grabbed the handle and pulled himself upright. "Gimme my trunk."

"It's not your trunk, it's mine." Lionel jerked and pulled on one side and Harry on the other. A tug of war.

"No, no, it's mine."

"Mine, mine!

The two grown men fought over the trunk like two little boys bashing each other over a bucket in a sandbox, like animals staking claim to their territory, like war lords battling over disputed territory in a corner of the kingdom.

Morton desperately wanted proof of his parentage.

Lionel knew his heritage, and frantically wanted to destroy the evidence.

Without another thought, his hate suffusing his whole being, his need to protect what he thought was his territory, Falstaff whirled around, and snatched his tire iron from the floor where he'd dropped it. He struck Harry a resounding blow on the head.

Oh, Lordy. Now, what?

Lionel re-opened the trunk, lifted Harry's slight frame and stuffed him inside. He closed the trunk, and strapped it tight to the dolly. Then he took off, trundling the trunk with Harry inside it down the steps, through the drifting snow and freezing night to his car.

Now came the hard part. He couldn't lift the trunk with Morton the Mouse inside. Lionel opened the trunk for the third time, lifted Harry out and threw him in the boot of his car. The old trunk—that was surely Aggie's—he shoved in the back seat of his car.

Home to Lucy. Pretend he'd been sleeping on the couch the whole night.

Visibility was next to zilch. The weather was too bad, and his tires too poor, and he was too cold to do one more thing that night. According to the weather report, the storm should abate by morning. Meanwhile, Lionel had Aggie's secret treasure in his two hot little mitts, right where the cache belonged.

Unloading the trunk into his garage, Lionel made ready to explore before collapsing.

Just then Lucy came stomping into the garage to shout at him. "Come to bed, Lionel, I'm cold without you. I wanna hug and some lovin."

Oh great, just what he needed. She wanted to make up.

# # # # # # #

At the police station, where Bobby got credit for the collar, Burly Boy, or *Bob Brown*, as he called himself, was singing a not very pretty song to Sergeant Walt Fletcher and the rookie. *Brown* told his garbled tale intermittently and disconnectedly, between gulps of strong black coffee. Waving away the Miranda offer of an attorney, he was ready to talk.

If you could call it that. Gilbert raised an eyebrow at Fletcher, his unspoken message that the Vicente-Auld women weren't the only ones who could mess up their statements.

Brown talked non-stop, while Gilbert recorded the confession. The perp spoke of a New Orleans truck fiasco along a cobblestone street, a riverboat cruise on the wrong boat, and a bad cold in St. Louis. He said his car had skidded upside down on the Interstate and he was saved by his victim. He rambled on about an ax he'd used on that self-same woman, which she had survived, which certainly was some sort of miracle, call it Black Magic, maybe, and then he proceeded to talk about the poison he'd put in her drink at the Best Western bar in Thermopolis. He'd gone off to bed, not wanting to be around when she dropped dead. Did she? Hell, no, she turned up as perky as a poodle, even though her glass had been empty when he'd gone back to check.

"The woman's got nine lives, I tell you. That, or she's some kinda witch."

Perhaps *Brown* wouldn't have been so loquacious if he weren't still so drunk.

"Who, who?" Gilbert asked. "Who?"

"Stop hoo-hooing at me," *Brown* said. "You sound like an owl. Mrs. Morrisey, a'course. Who'd you think I was talking about?"

"You did the B&E at the Morrisey's house, too? Twice?"

The drunk claimed he was nothing but a bum hanging around the Laundromat in south Cheyenne when he was approached by a guy claiming he'd pay a bundle for a coupla quick easy deeds. "Like I was s'posed to incapacitate Mrs. Morrisey, and steal her family history records. I ain't no hit man, just a bum lookin' for an easy take. Let me tell you, sonny boy," Burly Boy *Bob Brown* told Bobby. "It warn't no easy job and I ain't got nuthin' to show for all my trouble. 'Expenses, only,' that's what the guy said."

"Who, who? Who paid you? Who?"

"There you go again, Mr. Owl. Yeah, well, I wanna tell you exactly who hired me to do the dirty deeds."

Before *Brown* could name the guy, Fletcher was called to the phone.

"Emergency," said the detective sergeant when he returned. Walt excused himself with a "Hold on," to Brown and a "Come with me," at Gilbert.

The two officers raced away.

Burly Boy passed out on his own crossed arms at the interrogation table. Slumbering the sleep of the drunk, he snored loudly. And fell off the chair.

#######

At Nasty's house, the trio of women stayed in the kitchen awaiting the door chimes that would alert them to Officer Fletcher's arrival. Walt soon showed up, despite the snow storm, with Bobby tagging along.

Aggie attached herself to the sergeant's arm, grabbing and gabbling simultaneously. "Like I told you over the phone, Walt, we've got a dead body here, but it was an accident. Really it was, really and truly."

"Where?" Fletcher asked, looking around with puzzlement. He could see no signs of the mess Mrs. Morrisey had described over the phone.

"Why, right there . . ." Aggie said, lifting a finger and pointing to the floor at the bottom of the staircase.

Then she gasped and shut up. Nasty Three gawked, and Dollie Domenico fell into a swoon.

"Where's the body?" Fletcher asked again.

CHAPTER 62

Five o'clock in the morning on Christmas Day, with nearly everybody in the family present at Aggie's. Not the just-plain cousins, nor Wilma and her son Mark, nor Hepzibah and Isabelle.

A puzzle to most, Dollie Domenico sat silent and stunned in a far corner.

Routed out of bed on Aggie's second floor, Clara put to bed the two sets of twin girls. Within the hour all five children would be bouncing around ready to see what Santa had brought them. In the kitchen Brad made coffee and Peter put a batch of cranberry-apple-walnut muffins from his freezer into the microwave. Beth got butter and cream from the refrigerator and Lisa set up the silver service with big mugs instead of the Wedgwood china cups.

Aggie was in charge of the telling. Quickly the story unraveled, like old Hepzibah's unwound and re-knitted wool scarf that nobody would ever wear.

"Joan got Tom Rotter's Bible when she discovered him dead in his rocker with the book on his lap. She brought this combination family heirloom and diary to me. I deciphered most of Rotter's scribblings and then called Hepzibah to verify my conclusions . . . ."

"After midnight service at the church?" Joan asked. "While I was asleep, right here under your roof?"

"Hush, Mom," Nicole said.

Aggie took a deep breath and a sip of coffee before continuing. People sighed or leaned forward in anticipation. Dollie Domenico sniffled.

"Pansy Auld got pregnant by James Madison, so she dumped Teddy Roosevelt Vicente—who eventually married Hepzibah, who begat Rudolph who begat Teddi . . . Oh dear, never mind all that.

"Pansy surprised the family by suddenly eloping with James. James Madison didn't want kids, though, so after the wedding, when she told her new husband he was going to be a father, he insisted that she get an abortion . . ."

"How perfectly dreadful," said Beth, who wanted to get pregnant again, which might make Brad change his mind about deserting her and the twins for the road as a cross-country trucker.

Aggie continued as if she hadn't noticed the interruption. "In the meantime, James Madison Vicente began having an affair with Iris Auld, Pansy's older sister. Of course Pansy was younger than the three-musketeer Auld girls—the mothers of the double cousins. Anyhow, Iris also got pregnant. And James again insisted on an abortion. Only this time it was the pregnant Iris.

"James then stashed Iris on Tom Rotter's ranch as housekeeper. Hepzibah was already there. She did the cooking for Tom, Iris, and the hired hands. Tom never did marry. Iris knew about Pansy, of course. Pansy was married to James, after all. But Pansy didn't know about her sister Iris until years later.

"Time passed. The Great Depression with the bank closures and business bankruptcies put finis on James' double—and triple-financing deals and he too went broke. He got a government job in Albany County Courthouse, over in Laramie, where he was caught embezzling funds, and he got sent to prison.

"But both Auld women waited for James, while their biological clocks kept on ticking. Pansy returned home to Mama Estelle in Cheyenne while her husband was in prison. But not Iris. Estelle told Iris that getting pregnant by her sister's husband was unforgivable. Estelle said she never wanted to see or hear from Iris again. Among the rest of the family, Estelle wouldn't allow Iris' name to even be spoken. So Iris stayed on at the Rotter ranch.

"With the bombing of Pearl Harbor, President Franklin Delano Roosevelt, on behalf of the United States, declared war on Japan and, in late 1941, America entered World War II. The Vicente brothers were too old to go, but a number of the male descendants—first cousins, that is—joined up."

"Please, mother, not 'up' at the end of your sentence."

"Good grief, mom," Nicole said. Steve poked Nickee.

"James was released from prison during the latter years of the war and Pansy returned to live with him in Laramie—she had not sued for divorce in her husband's absence. Apparently both sisters were waiting patiently—or not so patiently—for the end of the war and the resumption of their love affairs with James Madison Vicente.

"James opened another mechanic shop. No new cars to sell—the country wasn't making any during the war years—jeeps and trucks and planes and battleships, instead. Hanging on to their old cars meant a lot of customers were bringing in their old rattletraps for James to repair. He did a lot of business.

"Still, James managed to again impregnate not just his wife Pansy but both women—all over again. This time they were determined to have their babies. Pansy ran away from James to hide out at Rotter's place. Remember, James Madison was operating his car company in Laramie, not far from the Rotter ranch. And by that time, Pansy must have discovered that her sister Iris was living at Rotter's. If Iris, why not Pansy?"

"I don't understand," Joan interrupted. "What were my grandparents doing all this time?"

"Before the war, Grover Cleveland and Violet Auld Vicente were operating a car agency in Laramie. By the time I was born," Aggie said, "they had closed the business and moved back to Cheyenne."

Lisa wanted to add her two cents. "Another thing that your mom's folks and mine were both doing was destructive—they weren't speaking to James and Pansy. That's what Agatha and I imagine, and can glean from the journals."

"Right," said Aggie. "Estelle Auld had disinherited Iris by then, so apparently my mother, Violet, as one of the three musketeers, had nothing to do with either of her two younger sisters. And my dad Grover couldn't stand his brother James. And neither could Lisa's dad. Guess there was no reason to see James Madison or either of his women, even if both of them were Aulds.

"To continue. Now we've got two pregnant Auld girls living under Tom's roof. Hepzibah swears Tom didn't molest either one, or her either, although he did like having 'pretty skirts around,' as she says he called young females.

"I've got to insert something else here," Aggie said, pausing to sip the coffee that Steve had poured for her. "Remember that Teddy Roosevelt Vicente was in love with Pansy and, he thought, she with him, until she eloped with James Madison. During the Thirties when it was so hard to find work, Teddy applied with Tom Rotter, who hired Teddy

Roosevelt as a cowpoke for not much more than pittance wages, plus room and board. Laid-back Teddy must have found the arrangement amenable. He liked Hepzibah's cooking.

"Eventually, as you know, Teddy and Hepzibah married and produced Rudolph, who married Isabelle, and they begat Teddi.

"So Teddy Roosevelt was in and out, around and about the Rotter ranch during the time that Iris Auld lived there as housekeeper and, eventually, when Pansy showed up."

Nicole pinched her mother in the arm before Joan could object to the "up" at the end of Aggie's sentence.

"Imagine his surprise and the pain in Teddy's heart for the woman he still loved when she showed up. Pansy too came to live with Rotter and entourage. And both women were called *Dollie*."

"What on earth?" demanded Lisa.

"Funny thing about James. Named for President James Madison, whose wife was named Dollie, Madison called every woman he bedded *Dollie* too. James said "It was only fitting that his women go by that name,' Tom wrote in his Bible. So both Pansy and Iris went by *Dollie* in the presence of James and Hepzibah."

"Weird," said Joan.

"Sounds like a nut," said Nicole, about James Madison Vicente.

"He was crazy," said Nasty One, who of course knew her brother-in-law. James was her brother-in-law twice over. For James was brother to Nasty's husband, Thomas Jefferson, and, as her sister Pansy's husband, James was brother-in-law once again. "Nowadays we'd call James a psychopath."

"Wait a minute," said Lisa. "Aggie, you said that both Iris and Pansy got pregnant by James a second time. What happened to those babies? For that matter, did Tom know and therefore record in his Bible what happened to Pansy and Iris?"

"Yes and no. What I mean is, Yes, as for Pansy and Iris, though it took awhile to locate the latter. No, regarding their babies. When we call James a nut or a psychopath, we've hardly scratched the surface of his crimes. He showed up at the Rotter ranch in the middle of the night after Grandmother Estelle, acting as mid-wife, had delivered both post-war babies, within a week of each other. The babies were two and three weeks old, respectively.

"James stole both babies from the nursery that was set aside—by kind-hearted Rotter, with Hepzibah's help. What James Madison did with his and his *double dollies'* baby boys, nobody knew. Iris went insane, though, and James put her away in that home up in Lander . . ."

A round of gasps and moans burst from every mouth present. The family history was growing worse and worse. Little wonder Hepzibah and Nasty One had kept silent all these years.

"Hold on a sec," Nasty Two said. "I thought it was Ruby Vicente, not Iris Auld, who lost her mind."

"James Madison switched identities. It was Iris that James put in the home, not Ruby. Nobody knows what happened to Ruby, actually. So there Iris sat, under Ruby's name, for forty of her eighty years, with none the wiser, until a few years ago when Tom at last unraveled the whole sordid scheme. By then he knew about two descendants of the double dollies, but not what had happened to the third."

"Yes, but," Peter interjected. "How was the switch of identities—Iris Auld for Ruby Vicente—discovered?"

"Tom Rotter was the detective. That's what he wrote in the back of his Bible. He got suspicious, which Hepzibah confirmed to me over the phone."

"Yes?" Nasty Two prompted. "What next?"

"Pansy ran off after her baby disappeared. Joined a circus. Nobody heard anything from her again. Another form of insanity, I guess, or at least denial."

Nasty Three knew what it was to live in a state of denial.

"I don't get it," said Brad. "Didn't anybody call the police, to report the kidnapping of two tiny babies?"

"Guess not," said Aggie. "James Madison left a note, see. Said he'd given the boys away, and if Pansy and Iris—or Tom Rotter or Hepzibah, for that matter—ever raised a fuss, he'd go kill them. The babies, I mean. He wrote that he'd meant what he said and if they didn't believe him, just try him. He hated kids."

"Crazy! Nuts! Whatever happened to James Madison?" asked Steve.

"Died in a car crash a week later, so naturally the trail went stone cold."

"What about the babies? Did Tom or Hepzibah ever find out?"

"Yes, they both did. But not until years and years later. And then they only found one boy, not both. The latter's identity remained a mystery."

Just then five little pajama-clad, four-year-olds burst into the room, rubbing their eyes, and staring in awe at the grown-ups and the bright lights and their Christmas presents beneath the tree.

"Did Santa come?" Stevie asked, determined to be first.

"I want my presents," said Cindy.

"Me, too," echoed Sissy.

"What're you guys doing up?" asked Brianna, bewildered.

"What did Santa leave in my stocking?" asked Brittany.

The adults moved aside so the children could get to the tree. Steve Norman read off the name-tags on each present and distributed the gifts. Peter passed around more muffins, and Lisa refilled the coffee mugs, while everybody watched the children. It was, after all, their day.

Dollie Domenico timidly followed Aggie. All around the house, from living room to formal dining room, from kitchen to Randy's study, to the strange little room with the floor-to-ceiling and wall-to-wall stone fireplace with its side door that might soon welcome clients to Lisa and Aggie's detective agency.

The bartender with the stringy hair was like a puppy dog, trailing Aggie. At the door to the bathroom ("Really, Dollie"), she finally backed off, to put a little distance between them. She blushed at getting reprimanded for shadowing her new role model.

Steve Norman used as an excuse his offer to assist Aggie with putting a pot of water on to heat. He needed a reason to talk to her in private.

"Aggie, did you discover anything about the Normans in Tom Rotter's scribblings? Something to suggest that he finally made good on his life-time threats to get even with my dad for stealing Tom's sweetheart? What I want to know is, did Rotter confess to sabotaging our Cessna by poking a hole in the gas tank with an ice pick?"

At Dollie's gasp and Aggie's look of surprise, Steve explained that the Federal Aviation Agency had found a small puncture, which "looked like it was made with an ice pick."

"It wasn't me! Don't look at me." Dollie sobbed in her own defense. "Honest to God, I didn't do it. Harry told me to, but I just couldn't commit murder. I dropped the ice pick and ran."

"What on earth?" Aggie said at this seemingly irrelevant interruption.

Dollie began to sob, her hands covering her face.

"Hush your bawling and listen to me, Dollie," said Steve. "The FAA concluded that the hole could have occurred at the time of the accident. Something else punctured the tank. Not an ice pick, after all."

Steve put his arms around the pale, sniffling Dollie to hold, pat, and comfort her. "I believe you, Dollie," whispered the man of her recently dashed dreams.

Just then Nickee came through the kitchen door. One look at the couple clutching each other and, without a word, the bride-to-be whirled around and left the kitchen. She slammed the door on her way out.

Steve wasn't buying this pouting scene. He couldn't take it. Not one more tiff with his sweetheart on the very day of their wedding. He abruptly released Dollie and went striding through the door after Nicole.

CHAPTER 63

"Sweetheart," Steve began, as he reached for Nicole to turn her around and face him. "What you saw back there . . ."

"I know, I know. Nothing for me to worry about," Nickee said, lovingly, not sarcastically. "You're compassionate and nurturing, just like Peter and gam. It's one of many things I love about you. Guess I'll have to get used to your bringing home stray dogs, and helping the homeless." She fell into his arms.

Later it would occur to Nicole how terrible mistrust and pride could be. Ruin a relationship, a marriage. Look what had happened to Estelle and Luther Auld. When he'd found his wife in a bloody pool at the foot of the cellar stairs, he had immediately concluded that she'd thrown herself down the cellar steps to purposely abort their son. Luther didn't give Estelle a chance to explain, exactly the stance Nicole had taken with Steve, about first Dollie and then Norma.

Perhaps it was pride that kept Estelle silent for the rest of her life. Or had she tried, but couldn't get through to Luther? It was just like when Steve, gam, and the rest of the family couldn't convince her of Steve's fidelity. Estelle must have still loved Luther. Perhaps she kept hoping he'd come round, for she bore him eight daughters over the next decade. Nicole vowed to keep trust, belief, and sharing alive in her marriage with Steve.

Steve and his Nickee talked about their wedding, now only a few hours away. "Everybody will have time for naps before all the excitement," Nickee said. "Oh, I can't wait, darling! Honeymooning with you in Hawaii will be so wonderful."

"Honeymooning with you anywhere will be grand," he replied.

Following the reception at the country club, Steve and Nicole would spend the night at his home in northwest Cheyenne, a house Nicole had yet to see. The next day, after spending a few hours with Cindy and Sissy, Steve would send his daughters on the plane to Boston, and he and his new wife would commence their life together.

Joan, who was eager to resume her winter travel plans, would accompany Steve's twins (Joan's new granddaughters!) and see them safely home. Then she would be off for Italy. She invited her mother to come along.

"We'll see, dear," Aggie replied, tickled to be included, thrilled to see Joan reaching out. Mother and daughter needed time together, more time, to seal the healing that had begun with their trip to honor Rosie's burial ground up north.

Aggie also needed to forgive Randy. For killing himself, and for losing their money. His suicide seemed truly unforgivable, a sign that he lacked trust in his wife's ability to cope with their disastrous poverty.

Oops, that wasn't quite right. She was forgetting the most important thing. Randy was dying, he had mere days to live. He couldn't take the pain any longer. The doctor had made that clear. Which made all the difference. At least to Aggie.

She couldn't prove it, but Agatha suspected that it was Falstaff who had pulled the con, bilking Randy out of their fortune. She would keep that to herself for now, at least until she could trap Lionel into making a confession.

Alone or with help from the police, she was going after the Morrisey money! Right after Christmas and the wedding. This time she would tell nobody.

If Nasty One could pass from chief gossip to Ms. Lips-Zipped, Aggie too could learn to keep her mouth shut. As a private investigator, she'd have to respect the confidentiality of her clients' secrets. Might as well start right now.

Back in the living room, the family history session resumed.

"Did either or both of James Madison's boys marry and have children?" asked Beth.

Reading from her notes made from Tom's Bible and Hepzibah's confirmation, Aggie replied. "One did. Remember, neither Rotter nor Hepzibah ever found the other child. But the boy they did find also abandoned his own child. Didn't want to be responsible, it seems. Tom reports that one son, born of Iris, by the way, got a girl pregnant and insisted that she get an abortion. She disappeared . . . ."

"'Like father, like son,'" said Nasty One.

"'The sins of the fathers shall be visited upon the sons'," said Nasty Two.

"James Madison reminds me of the *Bad Seed*," said Joan.

"So does his son," said Lisa.

Joan whispered to Nicole, "Look, what if James knew or suspected there was something seriously wrong with him, that he was a psychopath—even if he didn't know the name for it. And that's why he didn't want children. He was afraid of passing down his terrible dysfunction. What do you think?"

Nicole nodded vaguely. What did it matter now?

"Who are we talking about?" said Peter, swimming in confusion.

Before Aggie could answer, Dollie, re-seated in her corner, threw up.

Clara shooed the children ahead of her up the front stairway before they could commence asking embarrassing questions of the adults. The little ones, with their arms full of presents, and their tummies full of cereal, chattered and plotted over which toys to play with first.

Nicole dampened a clean linen napkin from a pitcher of water and rushed to assist the bartender from the downtown saloon. Dollie moaned and clung to Agatha Morissey. "Oh, Mrs. Morissey, please forgive me for all my sins."

"What in the world?" Aggie whispered back.

"What's the matter with her?" Brad asked.

"Who knows?" said Joan. "I don't even know who she is."

"Of course Iris and Pansy knew about each other," Aggie continued when everybody had settled down again. "Not the first half-dozen years, only after they both got pregnant the second time."

Aggie was reviewing, since people had told her they were more confused than when she'd started this tale in the wee hours of the morning. Everybody was tired, comprehension was difficult.

"With Pansy trying to hide a pregnancy from her husband so she could have the child without James making her get another abortion, she ran off to Rotter's house. We can only guess, as Tom and Hepzibah did, that Pansy may have run into Iris somewhere, a grocery or other Laramie store, perhaps, and discovered where big sis Iris had been hiding for years."

"James Madison Vicente, for all his sins, must have been very charming," Nasty Three said, appreciating what it was like to have your socks charmed off.

"Or very frightening," said Nasty Two.

"So there they both were, pregnant by the same man, living together in Tom's house. Hepzibah said they got along all right. Both of them were so scared of James that they may have clung together for comfort and security.

"Madison, the father of the babies they both carried, appeared periodically to storm around threatening everybody, including Rotter and Hepzibah, to keep quiet or else. Then James would turn right around and change his spots—like he thought he still had a chance with both women, romantically speaking, or, a chance of getting them to agree to abortions. At those times, says Hepzibah, he turned into the charming courtier of ladies that had enraptured both women from the beginning of their separate but similar romances.

"At those times he'd call them his *double dollies* and say he was no different from their early Mormon ancestors—meaning Rose d'Gade's husband, Etienne—the great-grandfather of the double cousins. Etienne, with his several wives, like other Mormon men, had often housed his wives under the same roof."

Dollie sat silently behind the family members, who by now sprawled tiredly on couches and comfortable chairs in a semi-circle. Her back to the wall and sitting upright in a straight chair, Dollie moaned again. Once more she began to heave. This time she hit the bowl Nicole quickly held out for the woman who was no competition at all to Nickee for Steve's affections. It was silly of her to ever think Dollie could have been any kind of serious competition.

"Oh, merciful heavens," Nasty Two blurted, pointing a shaking finger at the bartender. "Her name's Dollie."

"Right," said Aggie calmly, before turning to Dollie Domenico.

"And she's pregnant." Nasty Two said.

"What? How do you know?" demanded Joan.

"Naturally, she's pregnant," Nasty One said. "All the double-cousin females and their descendants vomit when we're pregnant."

"What are you talking about?" persisted Joan.

"Oh, no." shrieked Dollie. "I can't be pregnant with my own father's child."

# # # # # # #

Drying out in his jail cell, and forgetting that in his drunken stupor he'd ratted out his paymaster, *Bob Brown* figured that Lionel Falstaff would come up with the bail and then he, *Brown,* could get outta town.

He knew how to evade the bounty hunters. Let the bail-bondsman get stuck for the bail deposit. The burly-muscled, bushy-eyebrowed *Brown* would be long gone by then.

#######

Walt Fletcher and Bobby Gilbert picked up and read the Miranda to Lionel Falstaff, even while handcuffing his wrists behind his back.

Still angry with her husband, Lucy nevertheless sobbed and wailed as she ran after them, down the stairs from the bedrooms and straight out the front door. She was wearing only a flimsy see-through gauze gown that revealed everything from sagging belly to varicose veins.

"Go cover yourself, Lucy," Falstaff muttered, hanging his head in shame. Shame at getting caught and shame over having the officers see his wife, his really ugly, nearly naked wife.

Bobby suggested to Walt that they search the house for weapons. Before arriving they had rousted a judge out of bed in the early morning hours, who had authorized a search warrant with little argument. The officers came prepared, but the judge couldn't understand a thing. Better to sign the warrant so he could get back to sleep. It was Christmas.

Lucy screamed her protests. "Leave my house alone! Can't a lady have her privacy? If you're looking for Mr. Falstaff's secrets, try the garage. He brought home a trunk that doesn't belong to him. In the middle of the night."

In the Falstaff's garage, the police looked in the old trunk, but found no weapons. As for incriminating evidence, they would need time to sort and read all those pages, now jumbled and disorganized from the rough treatment the trunk had taken.

"What's this, though?" Bobby scowled at the spots of blood dribbled over the top layers of papers.

Walt directed Falstaff to sit on the cold cement of the garage floor by pushing down on the top of the prisoner's head. Their suspicions confirmed by dipping a finger into a small pool of the red stuff, Walt stiffened. He turned around and stared down at Falstaff.

"This stuff's blood."

"I, uh, cut myself while examining the papers in there," Lionel explained lamely. "You know, paper cuts."

"Yeah, sure," said Bobby. "And I've got a bridge to sell you. Cheap."

Walt raised a skeptical eyebrow at Falstaff, and then turned to look at Bobby. "Better have a look in the trunk of his car."

# # # # # # #

"But you didn't sleep with your father, dear," Aggie said to Dollie Domenico. "Your father is Lionel Falstaff. His mother—your grandma—was Iris Auld. I noticed from an old family photo in the album the resemblance between you and your grandmother Iris."

"Then wh-who is Harold Morton?" Dollie held out the locket she'd taken from her dead lover's tightly clenched fist.

CHAPTER 64

"Harry Morton the Mumbler was a nothing, a nobody. He was my second husband," said Nasty Three.

"Why are you using the past tense?" said Joan, who would of course notice this small detail of language.

"Because he's dead. I killed him."

The secretary of state didn't throw up, but she felt like it. She wished she could rid herself of the nasty pleasure she'd taken from seeing her nasty husband dead. Didn't that make her guilty?

"No, you didn't, ma'am," Dollie said, jumping up and upsetting the bowl of vomit in the process. "When Harold raced up the stairs toward you, while you were standing up there looking down, he grabbed his trunk out of your hands and shoved it on the dolly I'd rented for him, forgetting to tie it with the straps. I know for sure, because I was peeking through a crack in the half-open closet door. Harold could have caught his foot on the carpet. He killed himself, Miz Secretary of State, crushed by the trunk and his dolly. I figured it out while hiding in the closet. It came to me in a flash. Harold wanted you to run for, and win the governor's election . . ."

"Gubernatorial," Joan corrected.

"Then he planned to kill you, and take over himself as governor."

"Hah, in a pig's eye," said Nasty Three.

"Like Sonny Bono's widow," said Brad.

"Like Nellie Tayloe Ross." said Steve. "Wyoming's first woman governor, who ran for office after her husband died."

"That's the point," said Peter. "Even if Nasty had gotten her name on the ballot and won, Harry would still have had to be elected to stand in for her."

"In a pig's eye," reiterated Nasty, feeling utterly stunned from these revelations, and dazed from the night's horrors. So numb, in fact, she couldn't even feel relief that she had not killed Harry herself. "So Harry is dead," she said.

"Don't call him Harry," said Dollie.

At that moment the doorbell rang. Walt Fletcher and Bobby Gilbert stood on Aggie's front porch. In minutes they explained how they'd turned up the "dead body" Aggie and Nasty Three had expected to find at the bottom of Nasty's staircase.

"Lionel Falstaff killed Harold Morton, ma'am."

A lot of flabbergasted jabber burst from the lips of clan members.

Aggie invited the officers in for coffee and muffins, escorting them straight through the living room, because it was still in a jumble with all the used coffee mugs and discarded Christmas wrappings. "Let's go into the dining room," she said.

Sergeant Fletcher took Aggie aside. "Aggie, when you gave me that clipping from the newspaper morgue, you asked me to get proof that Falstaff was the man who conned Mr. Morrisey into investing in that bogus diamond mine."

"Yes, yes?"

"You were right. We found the evidence."

"Yes, yes?"

"Sorry, ma'am. Falstaff was keeping the money he'd bilked out of Randolph and a lot of other unsuspecting investors in a safety deposit box down at First Bank."

"Oh, no."

"Oh, yes, the bomb explosion took out Falstaff's box. All his money got all burned up."

Aggie gasped again. She couldn't speak. There went her last hope of vindicating Randy, his reputation and his poor judgment—the financial decisions made when he was already terminally ill, too sick any longer to be rational.

She was really and truly on her own. She must learn to cope.

The family crowded around the long oak table, extended now with extra leaves to accommodate everybody. Peter and Brad poured coffee and passed around muffins. Everybody carried in their own cups and Nicole got fresh ones for Fletcher and Gilbert.

"So who was threatening and stalking you?" Nicole asked her gam.

"Lionel Falstaff did the threatening. He paid a guy to do the stalking. A bumbler who, thank God, couldn't manage to murder me."

"Or get the right files when he made off with Randy's records, instead of the family history," added Lisa, suddenly understanding the sequence of threats, attempted murders, and the trashing of Randolph's computer and records. Falstaff was responsible.

Aggie continued: "Lionel was James' bastard son by Iris. He desperately wanted to keep his parentage secret. He might have expected to go insane, like Iris and James, or it could be he was afraid that people would think that. We may never know for certain. Meanwhile, Harold Morton was the son of Pansy and James, but he didn't know it. And he was frantic to uncover his lineage."

Much later, when Nasty Three could think straight, she would recall the bitter battles Harry and Lionel had fought, the mountains they had constructed from petty molehills during her election campaign. Fiercely competitive with each other, both men were seeking Nasty's favors—both romantic and political. Like the Biblical Adam's sons, Cain and Abel, Harry and Lionel hated each other. They were half-brothers, of course, each with a different mother but both with the same father—James Madison. Yes, they had battled over absurd things, for no good reason that Nasty could perceive at the time. Now she thought she understood. Their bent to compete, along with their psychological makeup, could have been passed on to them through the genes—from James Madison Vicente.

For James' two sons—the half-brothers, Harold and Lionel—most of their actions were motivated by a terrible need for recognition and acceptance, for power, authority, and money. They were much alike, in both looks and temperament. Their methods even resembled one another's, for both had worked hard politically.

Nasty Three would ponder all these things and eventually share her thoughts with Aggie, but with nobody else.

At that moment the land line phone rang. Steve took the call, smiled, spoke quietly a few moments, and then disconnected. To his new family, Senator Norman said. "That was President Davidson calling from Air Force One. He and Julia, with First Miss Jerica, have just put down out at Warren Air Force Base. His entourage will put up at Little America Inn. But Dom wanted to know whether the Davidsons—and a few secret service people, I imagine—can bunk here, Aggie."

Agatha and Steve smiled at one another. He was going to fit right into the clan, she thought. Already he could read her mind. "What did you say?"

"I told him, sure. I didn't think I needed to check with you."

Aggie laughed out loud, a quick little puff, releasing tension. "You remembered, Steve. The Davidsons come for Christmas whenever they can."

"Then my father is a murderer?" Dollie wailed, when she got Aggie's attention back. She was still wrinkling her little gray cells over all this new input. "My grandmother Iris went insane? And my grandfather James Madison Vicente was a psychopath? What hope is there for me?"

"Oh, my dear, your life is your own," Aggie said. She moved quickly to sit next to Dollie, and began patting the poor waif on the wrist. "You can make of it what you will."

"We'll help you." exclaimed the Nasties.

"After all," said Lisa. "You're a *Double Cousin.*"

Trembling anew, this time with joy, Dollie unwisely burst out with her confession: "Oh, I do so wish I hadn't helped Harold kill his first wife."

"What?" yelped Bobby.

"How's that, ma'am?" demanded Walt Fletcher.

"Oops, sorry. Well, I didn't actually murder her. But I did know about it. I lied, so Harry would have an alibi. I gave witness at the first Mrs. Morton's inquest that Harold was with me all afternoon, drinking beer. He wasn't. Harold doesn't—uh, excuse me—he didn't ever drink. He also got me to rent a dolly, the first time around, so his name wouldn't be on the rental form. Then he went home to move a freezer. He told his wife to steady the load from the bottom. Then, at the top of the stairs, Harold let go and it crushed her to death. But I didn't know about any of those things ahead of time. Honest! Only afterwards when I guessed.

"You see, now? He had the same notion for doing in Mrs. Nasty Three, there . . . ." Dollie nodded toward the secretary of state. "Before she filed for divorce tomorrow. You see, he never loved her. He just wanted to bask in the reflected glory of her position and power. And, a'course, he wanted to get his hands on her money."

Somber, stern, Walt Fletcher stood to his full height of six feet two inches, and in a stentorian voice announced, "Miss Dollie Domenico, I am arresting you as an accomplice to murder."

"Don't call me 'Miss Domenico.' I just use that name. I'm really Mrs. Harold Morton. We never did get a divorce. Harold just pretended."

Nasty Three couldn't believe it. She was never married to him? Harold the Hardhearted was a bigamist? That was one good thing—she wasn't even married to him. Good thing she'd never used the Morton name. Perhaps people would forget this terrible decision she'd made in marrying the mutt. Bad enough that she'd bedded a cousin.

"Prison? Will Dollie have to go to prison? Oh, no." tenderhearted Beth exclaimed. She'd just found a new double cousin, only to have Dollie torn from the arms of her family.

Peter said, "We'll help you, Dollie. The Clan will put up bail and have you out of jail in hours. You'll be back with your family, this **new** family, in no time."

The poor little waif couldn't believe her good fortune.

Had Tom Rotter still been alive, he wouldn't be going around using that title any longer. He'd thought of her as a *poor little waif* her whole life.

Peter was elated, not about Dollie's misfortune but at last he had found someone who needed the Schwartzkopfs, who might let them help her. Back when Nicole was having so much trouble, marital and financial, she wouldn't let him help her. More recently, Aggie was just as stubborn. Talk about independent women.

Amidst the hubbub, Aggie loudly announced, "Listen up, everybody. I forgot it until now. But Tom Rotter left a Will in his Bible. Everything that belonged to him goes to you, Dollie: the ranch, his animals, the stocks and bonds, vehicles and cars. You're a wealthy woman."

Drat, foiled again, Peter thought. He looked around at the members of his family. Maybe there was somebody else who needed help. Not Aggie, she was on the road to financial recovery. Not Dollie. These independent women today. Even his wife Lisa would go it on her own along with Aggie to become a private detective. Like their uncle, Ulysses S. Grant Vicente, and his son, John Hancock Vicente, who had moved to Chicago to open his private eye office.

And his daughter and Nicole would have their travel agency. Oh well, another day, another trauma.

"Oh Dollie," Beth said. "Before you go on trial, I'll give you a complete make-over. When I'm finished with you, no juror could ever find you guilty. You'll wow 'em in Court."

Dollie no longer felt nauseous. She jumped up from her chair to hug her new-found cousins. Beth, and even Nickee, hugged her back.

*   *   *

AUTHOR BIOGRAPHY

Izzy Auld writes suspense under her mom's name. The first Izzy wrote one novel and that copy blew away in a tornado! This Izzy Auld has been a management consultant, professor, a secretary, and a technical writer for an international chemical firm. Under the Church name she had 24 books published, including the novels A Time of Rebellion and Blast the Castle. IZZY AULD now writes family-saga mysteries and church-crime suspense novels. What's a "church" crime? Stealing flowers and money from the collection plates, confiscating tithes, kidnapping the pastor, or even committing murder. Check out Amazon.com to order IZZY AULD mysteries and suspense novels to download to your Kindle. See Aggie Sees Double, Aggie's Broncs, Aggie's Double Crowns, and Aggie's Double Dollies. The church-crime suspense novels feature Adam Temple in Adam's Zoo, Adam's Yacht, Exhuming Adam's X-Ray, and Adam's Wily Woman.